BOOKS BY STEVEN HARPER

BONE
WAR

The Books of Blood and Iron

STEVEN HARPER

A ROC BOOK

ROC
Published by New American Library,
an imprint of Penguin Random House LLC
375 Hudson Street, New York, New York 10014

This book is an original publication of New American Library.

First Printing, August 2016

For more information about Penguin Random House, visit penguin.com.

ISBN 9780451468482

Printed in the United States of America
10 9 8 7 6 5 4 3 2 1

*To the memory of my grandmother,
Ella B. Karow (1917–2009)*

ACKNOWLEDGMENTS

Thanks go my editor, Anne Sowards, and to my agent, Lucienne Diver, a pair of powerful women, for their help on not only this book but on the entire series.

NOTE ON PRONUNCIATION

The people of Erda tend to sound out all the letters in their names. Aisa's name therefore has three syllables and rhymes with "Theresa." Most vowels have a European flavor, so the *a* in "Danr" is more like the one in "wander" than in "Daniel."

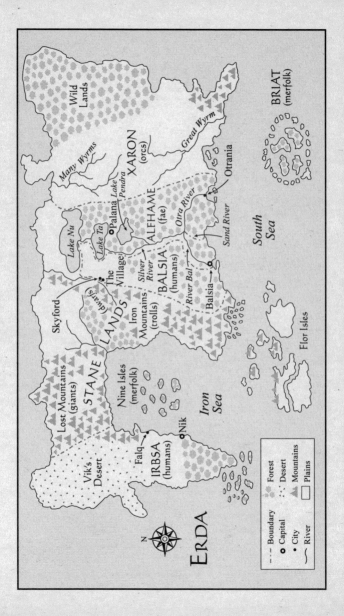

The Story So Far

Welcome back! I know it was cruel of me to leave you with a cliff-hanger last time, folks, but what kind of tale-teller would I be if I gave away everything at once? Besides, from the looks of it, you brought friends. I'm flattered! You know that new people have to put two coins in my assistant's hat, right? Just a joke! But you know the saying: "A coin in the hat keeps the story on the stage."

You've never heard that? Well, now you have.

Yes, I'll get to the story. But for the benefit of the new people, perhaps I should explain where we are and how we got there, yes? It won't take long. For those who already know all this, feel free to pop down to that refreshment wagon over there. It's fully stocked with sausage rolls and beer.

What's that?

What difference does it make if my brother-in-law owns the cart? You won't regret your purchase. Truly!

At any rate, for tonight we're hearing how it all came out—more history of Danr of Balsia, the second hero of Erda; and Aisa the slave, who became the first shape mage; and of Talfi, the boy who forgot to die; and of Ranadar the elven traitor to the Fae; and of Kalessa the warrior princess. It all ends with the War of the Four Queens, a story you should have learned in history class, though I daresay your history teacher's version wasn't quite as riveting as this one.

Rest assured, folks, that this story, called *Bone War*, stands alone all by itself, and you can follow it just fine without hearing *Iron Axe* or *Blood Storm*, the stories I told on previous nights. I will be retelling those later, for anyone who wants to hear them, or hear them again. Meanwhile, that refreshment cart is calling your name.

No, my financial relationship with my brother-in-law has nothing to do with this story. Nothing!

All right—getting you caught up. You already know that thousands of years ago, we were split into the Nine People. The downtrodden Fae (fairies, elves, and sprites) lived under the boot of the Stane (giants, trolls, and dwarfs) while the Kin (merfolk, humans, and orcs) tried to live between the two extremes. Eventually, the Stane decided to exterminate what they saw as Fae vermin, and they created the Iron Axe, a weapon powerful enough to destroy the Fae forever. But the crafty Fae stole the Axe and turned its power against the Stane.

This caused some lively debate among the Stane as to what they should do. In the end, they decided to destroy the Iron Axe, though it would require cooperation between trollwives and humans. They slaughtered a young human named Talfi on a stone table and gathered enough power to crack the Axe into pieces. Unfortunately, the spell broke both the Axe and part of the continent itself. The land dropped straight down, creating the Iron Ocean, with the Nine Isles poking up like dead fingers.

The Sundering drove the tyrannous Stane under the mountains, and the meek, helpful Fae took rule. At first, the Fae were benign dictators, working diligently to restore the shattered world, but over time, they reveled in their power. They enslaved humans and kept the Stane in their underground caverns. They grew in their power and their arrogance and threatened to drain the world dry.

A thousand years after the Sundering, a young man with a trollish father and human mother met a slave woman in Balsia. His name was Danr and hers was Aisa. They were both outcasts, and this bond brought them together. They eventually met Talfi, the human boy who was sacrificed to destroy the Iron Axe. Talfi, it turned out, always came back from being killed, but had few memories of his past. Together with the orcish princess Kalessa and the elven prince Ranadar, they managed to reforge the Iron Axe and stop a second destruction of the world. In the process, they killed Ranadar's father, King Vamath, which greatly angered Ranadar's mother, Queen Gwylph.

Later, they returned to Balsia, where Danr, Aisa, and Talfi were tricked into traveling to the Nine Isles to retrieve the long-lost power of the shape from Grandfather Wyrm. Talfi learned a great deal about his past, while Danr and Aisa learned shape magic. Danr discovered he could take human form and Aisa learned to change into animals.

Yes, just like you, little one! Though changing into a wyrm and roaring in the middle of a story is usually considered somewhat rude, don't you think? The rest of us can't hear, sweetie. If you could just return to your own shape, we'll— Thank you.

Danr and Aisa also learned they could pass the power on to other Kin through their blood, though not all Kin survived the process. Aisa learned this last part the hard way when she accidentally killed a mermaid and angered the mermaid's family, including her mother, Imeld.

Meanwhile, Danr became more and more unhappy about Ashkame, the Great Tree. Nu, Tan, and Pendra, the three Gardeners who plant, weed, and harvest the Garden that grows in the shade of Ashkame, told him that every thousand years, the Tree tips, causing chaos and destruction in the world, especially among the Kin. Danr wanted to find a way to stop it. Nu, Tan, and Pendra, however, had other concerns. The reason the Tree tips is that one of the Gardeners realizes the time has come for her to step away, and she feeds Ashkame her blood until she dies. The surviving two Fates always choose a mortal woman to take her place, and the cycle begins again.

Pendra was slowly bleeding her life away to make the Tree tip, and her sisters Nu and Tan had decided Aisa was the perfect candidate to take her place once she died. Aisa had mixed feelings about this, to say the least.

When Danr and Aisa brought the power of the shape to Balsia, it ignited a civil war between Prince Karsten and the Temple of Bosha, headed by Harbormaster Willem. Willem seized control of a giant golem and nearly destroyed the city, but Aisa and Danr used their newfound power of the shape to stop him. The battle took place during a terrible gale that became known as the Blood Storm.

After the Blood Storm ended, Nu and Tan came to Danr and Aisa to warn them that Pendra had been kidnapped.

Chapter One

The blue arrow thudded into the man-shaped target just above the painted heart and quivered there as if pleased with itself. A tall elf with a whipcord build nocked a second arrow and took aim, his ivy green eyes hard with concentration beneath sunset red hair. He let fly, and the second arrow hit the target just below the heart. Both shafts cast long shadows across the archery range in the late-evening light.

"Well?" the elf said. His name was Ranadar.

The young man next to him made a sound of admiration. He had rich brown hair with a slight curl, eyes bluer than a clear sky, and a head with only a few memories in it. Except for a few snatches of the distant past, the earliest thing he could recall was walking down a road with only one shoe on three years ago. A lot had happened since then. At least he knew his name was Talfi. Somehow that fact always came back to him.

"Wow," Talfi said. "I never knew anyone who could arch like that."

"Arch?"

"If you're an archer, it must mean you arch." He raised a bow and arrow of his own. "Though now that I think of it, I have ten fingers, and I've never seen them fing."

"Just try to hit the target, Talfi," Ranadar said.

Talfi pulled back the arrow and squinted down the shaft. "What do toes do, I wonder?"

"Breathe," Ranadar said quietly. "You, not your toes. Aim a little above your target and open your fingers to release."

Talfi loosed the arrow. It went high and left and skittered into the wall of straw bales stacked behind the targets. Cool spring air wafted over the palisade walls, carrying shouted voices, clanks of wares, and smells of fish, spice, and toasted food from the market on the other side. In some forgotten century, there had been a guard outpost on this spot. In recent years, an enterprising merchant had taken it over and charged a fee to citizens who wanted to keep up their skills with a bow or spar with a sword but who couldn't easily get to the outskirts of town. He did a brisk business. Five other sets of people stood in clumps along the range, aiming at targets of their own. A pair of small boys waited on the sidelines until everyone's quivers were empty, then ran out to fetch the spent arrows and bring them back for quarter-knuckle tips.

"You are jerking the bow upward when you loose," Ranadar said. "A common beginner error."

"Maybe you should show me again." Talfi grinned.

Ranadar gave him a look, then put an arm around Talfi to grasp his bow. Talfi leaned into him for just a moment, inhaling the scent of smoke and wood and . . . Ranadar. His heart sped up a little, and the circle of Ranadar's solid arm felt both safe and exciting. Ranadar was a snatch of distant past he remembered. Long ago, they had met in the city of Palana. Talfi had been a slave, and Ranadar had been—still was—a prince. They had carried on a forbidden affair under the noses of Ranadar's parents, the king and queen of Alfhame, who wouldn't have been happy to hear their royal son was making merry with a human slave. In the end, Ranadar's careless arrogance had exposed their secret and forced them apart. Now they were reunited, had been for nearly two years, but sometimes Talfi still couldn't quite believe it. Most nights he woke up at least once expecting to find himself alone, and it was always a surprise—a thrilling, aching surprise—to find Ranadar, his hair rumpled in sleep, beside him.

Ranadar murmured in Talfi's ear, "Release when you breathe out."

Ignoring the sidelong stares of the other archers at their targets, Ranadar guided Talfi's aim and, gentle as a kiss, disengaged Talfi's fingers from the string. The arrow thumped into the target's stomach.

"Better," Ranadar said in a satin whisper that made Talfi shiver. "I find your shaft quite excellent."

Talfi arched an eyebrow. "Really? Am I getting better?"

"My expert instruction will have you arching in no time," Ranadar said solemnly. His arm was still around Talfi's shoulders.

"I wonder if I could put three arrows into the heart," Talfi mused aloud.

Ranadar withdrew his arm with a short laugh.

"What?" Talfi asked.

"You," Ranadar replied with a shake of his head. "If it's impossible, you have to try it."

"You think I can't do it?" Talfi said. "What happened to confidence in your *Talashka*?"

"Nothing." Ranadar smirked in a way that stirred memories, old memories of harsh words and casual cruelty and hard chains. Talfi stiffened. It wasn't Ranadar's fault that the Fae, his people, had enslaved humans for hundreds of years after the Sundering. Ranadar hadn't even been born when that practice began, and he had been raised to believe that humans and other Kin—orcs and merfolk—were little more than beasts. "But my *Talashka* just asked me twenty minutes ago to teach him archery for the first time. You could not possibly put three arrows into the heart."

Talfi ran his tongue around the inside of his cheek. "Let's make it interesting. If I make it, you owe me a favor for each arrow. No matter what it is."

"And if you fail?" Ranadar said. "Because you will."

"Then I owe you three, my uppity elf."

Ranadar stepped back and sketched a small bow. "I look forward to collecting, my *Talashka*."

Talfi fitted another arrow to the bow. He shot Ranadar a sideways glance. The elf, too damn handsome to be fair, damn it, watched with a confident expression. The smug, lovable bastard. Talfi sighed, breathed out, and sent an arrow down the range. It thunked into the exact center of the heart. With smooth precision, he snatched two more arrows from the quiver at his feet and loosed them. Each pierced the heart between Ranadar's original arrows. Ranadar's mouth actually fell open.

"Fing!" Talfi said.

Ranadar made a small sound, then shut his mouth with an audible clop. He coughed, and his face reddened. "You were holding out on me."

"Guilty." Talfi laughed. "You should see your face. I swear you look like you swallowed a squid testicle."

"Do you often see people who swallow squid testicles?"

Talfi was not to be deterred. "You owe me! Three favors."

"You misled me!" Ranadar protested. "You already knew how to arch."

"Aw." Talfi patted Ranadar on the cheek. "I like that you're already using my words. It shows you're paying attention."

"Hmm." Ranadar took up his bow and flipped the fetching boy a copper knuckle. "So, my *Talashka*, what will you demand of me?"

"I don't know yet," Talfi said airily.

Ranadar slid closer. His eyes, an intense green deeper than any forest ivy, took on a heavy look that made Talfi's knees weaken, just a little. "Do you plan to lord it over me for days?"

"Weeks," he managed.

"And when you do collect?" Ranadar ran the back of a finger down Talfi's cheek. He couldn't help shivering. Even after more than two years, Ranadar could still do that to him, and he was glad.

"As soon as I think of what I want," Talfi said. Archly.

"And will you—"

"Do the both of you intend to put on a show for the entire town," interrupted a new voice, "or just for me?"

Talfi broke off and glanced guiltily away. A woman was leaning against the palisade wall, arms crossed. Her auburn hair, caught in a long braid, contrasted sharply with her faintly greenish complexion and golden eyes. The muscles of a warrior coiled beneath her riding leathers and heavy boots, though her only visible weapon was a small knife sheathed at her belt.

"Kalessa," Ranadar said. "Are we done for the day?"

"I would say you were just beginning." She nodded at the other archers who were handing their borrowed arrows back to the old man who ran the range and unstringing their bows, all while pretending to ignore the two young men— *regi* men—who were carrying on beneath their noses. "It is near dark, and the range wishes to close. Shall we?"

"Sure, sure." Talfi unstrung his own bow, not bothering to hide the easy skill this time. Ranadar gave him a sour look. "It's your own fault, you know."

"My . . . ?"

"By now you should know I have all sorts of hidden skills."

"Good."

"Good?"

"It will make paying you back all the more interesting."

"We need to leave," Kalessa said. "Now." With that, she turned her back and strode stiffly toward the wooden gate. Talfi and Ranadar blinked after her.

"What did you do?" Ranadar gathered up his and Talfi's bows and hurried after her.

"Me?" Talfi said. "Why does it have to be me?"

"It is always you."

"It doesn't take much to piss off an orc," Talfi muttered as they exited. "It might have been that too many stars came out. Or too few. Or—"

"Shh! She will hear."

They emerged from the palisade at the edge of the market square of Balsia, the largest city on the South Sea. "Market square" was something of a misnomer, since the market actually started at a square but extended down dozens of blocks and side streets like a squirming octopus. Despite—or because of—the setting sun, more and more people were moving into the market. Talfi loved the market at this time of day. Thousands of voices rose in a colorful quilt of shouts and haggles and cries as people bought and sold everything from fish to flowers, from silver to saffron, from sugar to shovels. Anything he could think of, and many things he couldn't, came up for sale here, and something astonishing was always tugging at the corner of his eye. And lately it had just gotten better. Stalls that only two years ago had closed themselves up after dark now set out torches or lanterns and kept on selling while right beside them stalls that were shuttered for the day opened for business.

The difference was the Stane.

More than a thousand years ago, the Stane—dwarfs, trolls, and giants—had ruled the world with mostly benevolent intent. They had forged strong bonds with the Kin—orcs, humans, and merfolk—and they had brushed away the Fae—fairies, elves, and sprites. But over time, the Stane had grown corrupt in their power, stealing magic from the Kin and manipulating the Fae. Eventually, the downtrodden Fae had taken up arms against the Stane, and both sides called down terrible magics that sundered the continent itself and killed countless thousands. The Stane were banished to Glumenhame under the Iron Mountains, and the kindly Fae worked hard to restore the world. Folk said that Ashkame, the Great Tree of Life, had tipped, turned upside down, so that the Stane were at the bottom and the Fae were at the top, with the Kin always in the middle.

But in time, the Fae had also become corrupt, and the downtrodden Stane had risen up against them. Once again, their battle had nearly destroyed the world, but Talfi and his friends had put a stop to it. Barely. The Fae were pushed back into their own kingdom, and the Stane were released from their underground prison, once again able to walk in open air. But only at night—sunlight caused the Stane enormous pain.

That had happened not even three years ago. Until then, the city-state of Balsia had been a human country. But after the Stane emerged from under the mountain, Balsia's ruler, the young Prince Karsten, had started letting trolls and dwarfs into Balsia. At first they had been useful workers with strong backs, but the dwarfs were cunning craftsmen and many trolls were skilled merchants, and they had quickly woven themselves into the fabric of Balsian society.

But because of the sunlight pain, the incoming Stane did their work indoors or underground. Or at night.

Twilight at the market square was before the humans closed up and after the Stane opened, and it fascinated Talfi no end. Who would ever have thought Kin and Stane would work side by side? Short, twisted dwarfs with beards down to their knees sold intricately carved toys that sang and dolls that danced, silver teapots that kept water hot, and even full-fledged golems of stone and clay alongside human woolmongers, weavers, and apothecaries. Nine-foot-tall trolls with jutting lower jaws, swarthy skin, and night black hair trudged barefoot across the cobblestones with great baskets on their shoulders, their rumbling voices mingling with the higher-pitched ones of human men and women who also browsed the stalls, buying, gossiping, and arguing at the tops of their lungs in the lengthening shadows and flickering torches.

Not all humans were satisfied with the new arrangement. Even as Talfi watched, some merchants closed up their stalls or packed up their pushcarts in a tight-faced huff and left when the trolls and dwarfs opened for business. More than one gave Ranadar a wide berth as well until he remembered himself and pulled up the hood on his scarlet cloak to hide his pointed ears and cast his exotic features into shadow. Elves weren't well liked in Balsia, either—an elf's lingering touch was addictive, and turned humans into happy, willing slaves. Talfi was grateful to the Nine that he was immune to this effect. It would have cast his entire relationship with Ranadar into doubt.

"Where's Kalessa got to?" he asked over the noise. "She shouldn't be too far ahead of us."

Ranadar wore the tight look that often came over his face at the market—a great many merchants sold objects made with iron, and iron was as bad for the Fae as sunlight for the Stane.

"I do not see—there." He pointed. Kalessa was staring at them from a nearby butcher's stall, arms crossed. They threaded their way through the crowd to her.

"She still looks unhappy," Ranadar observed. "We need to defuse her before she explodes."

"We could just point her at someone we don't like," Talfi said.

"Are you shopping?" Kalessa said tartly. "Stopping to admire the view? Collect your favors?"

Talfi blinked at her. "We were looking for you, actually. We wouldn't have looked so hard if we'd known our heads would get bitten off."

"You can bite my—"

"Kalessa," Ranadar interrupted, "even orcs are not usually so snappish with their friends. And you look unhappy. Has something happened?"

Kalessa scowled. "I am not snappish. You are both sensitive."

Talfi caught the look in Ranadar's eye and snagged a wooden cup from a passing alewife, who had a tray of them around her neck. He dropped a half knuckle on the tray, and the alewife filled the cup from an ale pitcher, then waited patiently so she could get her cup back.

"Have a drink," Talfi said. "You look like you need one."

Kalessa looked annoyed but accepted the cup and drank. She was far from home herself. The prairies of Xaron, the orc lands, lay east, on the other side of Alfhame, and Talfi knew the city put her on edge, but her quick temper was rarely directed at her friends.

"What happened?" Talfi asked.

"I do not wish to discuss it." Kalessa held out the cup, and Talfi dropped another coin so the woman would fill it.

"As you like," said Ranadar. "We would not understand anyway."

"Yeah," Talfi chimed in. "We're just a couple of guys. Men wouldn't understand woman problems. You should probably talk to Aisa or something."

"Woman problems?" Kalessa drained the cup and held it out for a third, which Talfi also paid for. "Psh. My woman problems are ten times more difficult than your manliest man problems."

"I doubt it," Ranadar goaded, his tone overly airy. "Men and women cannot understand one another's problems. Women's problems are just too . . . too . . ."

"You were going to say *petty*," Kalessa said, thumping the cup on the alewife's tray.

"I was not."

"You were." Kalessa wiped her mouth with the back of one hand. "Understand this, then. I just heard from my mother. Word of my deeds before the Battle of the Twist and of the Great Golem reached the clans, and as a result, my clan has been promoted from Sixth Nest to Third Nest."

"Congratulations!" Talfi said in surprise. "Kalessa, that's great news!"

"It is and it is not." She waved away the alewife, who wandered off with her cups and pitcher. "It brings a lot of status and power to my parents, and it means my brothers and I do not have to worry so much about trying to marry up to a higher-ranking Nest."

"So why is it bad?" Ranadar asked.

"My mother is suddenly receiving a number of marriage proposals for *me*," Kalessa growled. "For the sake of the line, I must respond, and soon."

"You do?" Talfi shook his head. "But you have a lot of older brothers, yeah? There's no pressure on you."

"What do my brothers have to do with it?" she asked, genuinely confused. "I'm the only female in my family's generation. If I don't have children, our chieftain's line will end."

"Oh."

"Ah." Ranadar nodded. "That I *can* understand. I am the only child, and that puts me under considerable pressure as well."

"Uh . . . your parents . . . ," Talfi began, then stopped himself. The subject of Ranadar's parents was a touchy one, a subject Talfi had decided to avoid until Ranadar brought it up. Now that he had done so, Talfi found himself unsure what to say, especially since Kalessa was there.

Kalessa solved the problem for him with orcish directness. "Your parents put pressure on you?" she snorted. "How? You live in exile. The elf king is dead, and the elf queen has all but said you can never go home, now that you've sided with the people who killed your father. And you're *regi* anyway. How many children can you sire?"

Ranadar's face remained impassive, but Talfi bit the inside of his cheek. He knew Ranadar well, and noticed the tightening of the tendons at his neck and the way he drew his fingers along the hem of his cloak.

"Regardless of what you and my mother may think of me," Ranadar said quietly, "I am still a prince. Actually, I am *the* prince. If I have no children, the royal family line will end and another family will take the throne. The throne does not care about my mother's feelings toward me, or mine toward her. One day, she will die, and the throne will be mine to take or not. And if I do, I must have children. Therefore, she wants me to marry a nice elven woman and produce a number of nice elven children."

"Huh." Kalessa drew her knife and cleaned under a fingernail with it. "Bites Vik's balls, doesn't it?"

Ranadar remained silent for a split second, then gave a firework laugh. "It does. So maybe an orcish warrior princess who cannot decide on a man can share a problem with a *regi* elven prince who has already found one."

Talfi cocked his head, trying to work this out, then gave it up. "Maybe we should stop the love party and—"

A woman's scream tore across the market, followed by a crash. Glass shattered. All three of them came alert. The knife in Kalessa's hand flickered and changed into a long, thin sword. Two stalls over, humans and trolls scattered, though they didn't run away. The woman screamed again. Kalessa shouldered her way through the people with Talfi and Ranadar right behind her. In an empty half circle around a bottle maker's stall was a figure in a ragged cloak. He faced the stall with his hood down, but his back was to Talfi, so all Talfi could see was that he had dark brown hair, badly cut. One of the bottle maker's tables had tipped over, sending shattered glass in all directions. The plump woman who had screamed was cowering against one side of the bottler's stall, a large market basket clutched under her arm, while the bottler stared at the man with a startled expression.

"Hideous!" said someone.

"Is it a shape-shifter?"

"Probably a half-blood."

"Disgusting!"

"Someone call the guard!"

"What happened?" Talfi asked no one in particular.

"That creature scared this poor woman," replied a man, turning to look at Talfi. "It's not fit to walk the—hey! You're—"

But Talfi was elbowing his way through the crowd into the open circle. Glass crunched under his shoes. Ranadar and Kalessa came with him. The bottler and the woman still hadn't moved, and neither had the man. Or creature. Or whatever it was. The crowd kept its distance.

"It's all right, friend," Talfi said, approaching. "No one's going to hurt you. Everyone just got a little startled is all."

The man didn't move. Talfi, no stranger to odd occurrences, approached with calm caution. Hey, he had faced down ghostly *draugr*, wyrms, trollwives, and even Death herself. What could this guy possibly do?

As he stepped forward, Ranadar said, "Talfi, perhaps we should—"

At that, the figure turned. As one, the crowd backed up a step with a gasp. A cold wave of shock washed over Talfi and he froze on the cobblestones. Every nerve jangled and he felt his bowels loosen like water. This couldn't be. The left side of the man's face was malformed. Shiny, translucent skin stretched over bone and thin muscle as if it had been melted. A single, lidless eye stared out of its round socket, and the lipless mouth showed a grim row of yellow teeth. An equally malformed, clawed hand clutched the ragged cloak at his throat. But the right side . . .

The right side of the man's face looked exactly like Talfi's.

Chapter Two

The little boat drifted lightly on the rocking waves beneath a golden sun. Danr, in his human form, leaned over the gunwale to peer into the azure depths. The ocean lay cool and clean beneath the warm wood, and his head was free of pain, an advantage of wearing his human form. So far it was shaping up to be a fine day.

A shadow moved beneath the water. It started small, then ballooned to human size as it rushed toward the boat. Danr pulled back as a mermaid broached the surface. Aisa. With a wild cry, she arched over the boat, trailing silver water behind her long dark hair. A mask of fierce blue tattoos and seed pearls covered her face, and her muscular tail gleamed like a hundred jewels in the sunlight. Her breasts were bare and her arms were wide. A grin split Danr's face as Aisa passed over his head. She shouted again, a high, free sound, then landed in the water on the other side of the boat, drenching him in salty spray. He laughed, but there was a little desperation behind the sound. He had to enjoy every moment he could with her. Every second was more precious than a candle in a cavern, because one day, and he didn't know exactly when, it would all end.

Aisa's head popped out of the water with her hair floating all around her. Her mermaid skin was as dusky as

Danr's own, and her eyes were as wide and brown. The spiky blue tattoos gave her a proud expression, and they only enhanced her beauty. Aisa's simple appearance in the water gave a little flutter to Danr's heart. With a small laugh of her own, she reached out of the water. He took her hand, cool and wet.

"The water is beautiful and fine," she said in her lilting western accent. "You should try it, my love."

He shook his head. "I don't want to get wet."

"Really?" Her eyes danced with mischief. "Then why would you love a mermaid?"

She yanked hard and Danr went into the water with a yelp. The waves closed over his head. Salt water filled his nose and ears, and he started to splutter, but then Aisa was there. She put a hand over his mouth.

"Do not struggle," she said, and the water carried her voice perfectly well. "I will not let you sink."

They hung in the clear water. Her arm was under his, bearing him up. It was still a strange feeling. He was used to being the big one, the strong one, but down here, Aisa was the power.

"Here we go!" she said, and sped away with him.

Water rushed past him, so fast, so incredibly fast. The rushing sensation made his heart leap with a thrilling mixture of fear and excitement. They burst into a school of fish that scattered in a panicked rainbow of flashing scales and wide eyes. The warm ocean flowed over him like a silken lover, delicious and soft, and just when his lungs started to ache, Aisa pulled him to the surface. They both burst high into the air and fell back with a great splash. Danr resurfaced, flinging his dark hair out his eyes and blowing water like a dolphin. Aisa circled around him, lithe and agile, and his entire body thrilled with her very presence. He rolled over onto his back and floated, something he could only do when he was fully human. Danr was a half-blood, with a human mother and troll father. His normal shape was therefore big and muscular and dense, and any attempt at floating sent him straight to the bottom. Just last year, however, he had learned how to change his shape and become fully human when he chose. His human form was much smaller, with a whipcord build, straight jaw, prominent cheekbones, and slightly paler skin than his more trollish self. His hair, however, remained thick and black and shaggy above large brown eyes.

Sunlight didn't bother his human form, and he was able to float effortlessly on his back to enjoy the warmth and light without spears of pain drilling into his skull. Really, this was a delightful way to spend an afternoon, especially because none of it would have happened without Aisa, and it was the best way to spend their dwindling time together.

Aisa slid up beside him and murmured in his ear, "There, now. Is this not better than hiding in a boat?"

"I would never want to hide from you," he said.

"You are hiding something I want," she countered.

In response, he turned his head and kissed her, indeed, he did, and tasted salt on her lips while the waves rocked them both. At long last, she was here, with him. It was a perfect moment, and nothing should have ended it.

Which meant, of course, that something did.

A great bubbling came up from underneath Danr's feet. The water blooped and burbled, washing around them like a laundress's tub. A great green bulk rose from the ocean floor and burst to the surface just in front of them. It opened, revealing the biggest flowering lily pad Danr had ever seen. It spread across the suddenly still waters like an emerald carpet with a golden flower in the center the size of a cart horse. Danr furiously treaded water. Standing near the flower were two women. The first wore a cloak of pale spring green, and over her shoulder she wore a leather seed bag of the kind farmers used to sow fields. The second wore a rich green-brown cloak of summer and carried a gardening hoe over her shoulder. Their faces were neither pretty nor ugly, not old or young, and their hands were worn with work. Danr, of course, recognized both of them.

They were the Gardeners, the Fates who tended the Garden, which ordered all lives, mortal and immortal both. The woman with the seed bag was Nu, and the woman with the hoe was Tan. Their time was up.

"No," Danr whispered. "Not yet. You can't."

"We can," said Nu.

"We do," said Tan.

Danr's breath shortened and his throat thickened. He had wielded the Iron Axe, kissed Death on the cheek, and faced down Grandfather Wyrm, but this moment turned his entire body to ice. He looked at Aisa, and his own fear and sorrow were reflected in her eyes. All the things he hadn't said in the last eighteen months piled up under his tongue, but it was too late to say them.

"Great Ones," he said, and automatically tried to bow, even though he was still treading water.

"Is it . . . is it time?" Aisa asked. "Have you come for me?"

"We must speak," said the woman in spring green. Her name was Nu.

"Converse," added the woman in summer brown-green. Her name was Tan.

Danr, long conversant with careful truth, quickly noticed the Gardeners hadn't actually said they were coming to take Aisa away from Erda. Instead there was a long pause, as if the women were waiting for something. Danr tried to latch onto this small fact for reassurance, but had little luck.

Aisa hauled herself onto the edge of the lily pad and wrung water out of her hair. Danr's mouth was dry from both the fear and the salt water. He couldn't read her expression.

"Talk?" she said. "It has been six seasons since you came to us to say that Pendra disappeared, six seasons since you said you wanted me to take her place. Six seasons I have waited and wondered when you would come, and now you have. But you say you only wish to talk, Great Ones?"

Both Nu and Tan looked relieved. Nu said, "Indeed. Our sister Pendra is still missing, and the Garden weeps at her loss."

"Not the best news," Aisa sighed. "I was hoping you were coming to tell me she had returned."

"And now," said Tan, "we need you."

"We call on you," said Nu.

Another silence fell over the group. The lily pad rocked slightly, and the two Gardeners looked unhappy. Then Aisa said, "You require me."

This cheered them up. "You must come to the Garden and help us," they said together. "We will show you the way."

Startled, Aisa grabbed Danr's hand. There was a *wrench*, and the ocean and the lily pad were gone. The water vanished, the sunlight dimmed, and Danr stumbled as he found himself standing on dry ground. Nausea sloshed through his stomach, and he went to his knees for a moment, breathing deeply. No matter how many times he did it, Twisting made him sick, though if he was careful, he could at least keep himself from throwing up. After a moment, he got his stomach under control and pushed himself to his feet. Water dripped from his bare chest and the old trousers he'd worn on the boat, and he gaped at the lightly wooded field stretching before him. Tall trees poked up here and there, along with stands of smaller ones. But it wasn't grass that grew between them. It was a riot of plants. Thousands and thousands of different plants growing in a great mass. Carrots rubbed roots with wheat stalks. Peanuts tangled in pumpkin vines. Bean sprouts languished in the shade of gooseberry bushes. Unseen breezes made the leaves dance and writhe with soft sounds that hissed in Danr's ears. Or maybe it was the plants themselves, squirming to get loose, whispering to anyone who might listen.

Some attempt had been made at order. Danr noticed how the plants had been seeded in plowed rows, and the plants followed them, more or less, but even the original furrows dove and swooped like chaotic ripples on a sandy beach, and the plants themselves behaved badly, growing where they pleased and twining about each other in an orgy of golds and greens and scarlets and azure blue. It was tame wilderness. It was orderly chaos. It was ugly beauty.

It was the Garden.

The sight stole the breath from his very soul and twisted his heart around inside him. This was the most sacred of places. He was glad he was barefoot—and what a strange thought that was to cross his mind here and now; indeed, it was.

Aisa had told him of her visits to the Garden. It grew along the trunk and branches of Ashkame, the Great Tree whose roots drilled down to the dark realm of Glumenhame, whose upper branches cradled shining halls of Lumenhame, and whose trunk curled around Twixthame, where mortals lived. Every plant, every blossom, every fruit and seed was a mortal life somewhere in the mortal realms, and the way each tangled or twisted around the others showed how lives were intertwined.

And something . . . bothered him about the Garden. He couldn't put his dripping finger on it, but it was there, like an itch he couldn't scratch or a shadow at the corner of his eye. What was it?

"Danr came along, too," said Nu. "That is . . . interesting."

"Fascinating," added Tan.

"Delightful," said Aisa. He had lost his grip on her hand, and she was sitting beside him, her damp tail pressed against his legs. "My love, would you give me a hand to my feet?"

Automatically, he reached down and pulled her upright. It took effort, more than it should have. But he was human, and his human shape was considerably weaker than his birth shape.

As Aisa came upright, Danr felt a bit of his own personal energy leave him. It slipped down his arms, out his hands, and into Aisa. He shivered delicately. It was an intimate sensation, like pulling on a shirt still warm with someone else's body heat and fragrant with their scent. When Danr was in his human form, Aisa could and often did take energy from him to power her own magic. It wasn't much, but it was enough. With a faint glow and the sound of moving flesh, she . . . changed. Her tail split into a pair of legs. The scales and tattoos faded, leaving smooth, dusky skin behind. In a few soft moments, Aisa stood as a naked, bare-faced woman among the twisting plants of the Garden. Like Danr, Aisa herself was a half-blood, with a mermaid mother and a human father, though her ability to change her shape was much more extensive than Danr's. She stretched and ran her hands through her hair with a sigh.

Danr looked at her, and decided privately that she was more beautiful than anything the Garden might have to offer. Her long night black hair spilled down her back, complementing her dark eyes and slender nose and full red lips. Her breasts were high and round, and her hips tapered down to long, smooth legs. An incredible sight in an incredible place. It was hard to remember her as the slave girl he had known when they were younger, her body always layered in multiple dresses, her hands wrapped in rags, her face and hair hidden under scarves. At that time, he had thought himself an ugly, inhuman monster. But over time, she had changed. *They* had changed. Now it seemed foolish that she had ever hidden herself and that he had thought the Stane were ugly. Now he was standing in the Garden of the Fates, she stretching her naked body and he admiring it, and neither of them self-conscious.

"Perhaps you would join me in changing shape, Hamzu," Aisa said, using the nickname she had given him years ago. It meant "strong one."

Danr nodded once and stretched on his own. He closed his eyes, reached inside himself, and called to his birth shape. Aisa touched his arm, and some of her power came to him, though it was more difficult for her to share when she was in her own birth shape. Her power slid around and through him, boosting his spirit and making him feel almost buoyant, as if he might float away. His birth shape came easily to him, more easily than his human shape did. His back and limbs lengthened and grew heavy with muscle, splitting his trousers until they dropped away in rags. His chest grew thick and powerful. His jaw jutted forward, and his lower teeth grew upward enough to give him a pugnacious look. His own didn't become as large as a full troll's, but they tried. Shaggy black hair covered his head and fell a good way down his chest and arms, and his skin darkened. He towered over Aisa, with more than a full head of height on her. But his eyes remained the same—large and dark and liquid.

"Much better," Aisa said, taking his much larger hand in hers. "Your human shape is handsome, my Hamzu, but I like your true shape best. Especially when it has no clothes."

"We aren't alone, you know," he replied mildly.

"We have nothing the Gardeners haven't seen."

"I know. I just wanted to point it out."

"And we still need your assistance," said Nu.

"Aid," amended Tan.

"Help?" offered Aisa.

Nu nodded. "Look about you, sister. What do you see?"

"What do you observe?" said Tan.

There was a long pause. At last, Aisa said, "I do not feel comfortable in this role, Great Ones. It has been more than a year and a half now since Hamzu and I stopped the harbormaster's golem from destroying Balsia. Before then, I spoke with Pendra and even wielded her sickle. She said that every thousand years, one of you Gardeners steps down and a mortal takes over the role to keep you balanced and compassionate to mortals."

"Yes," said Nu.

"True," said Tan.

Aisa said, "Pendra said that because I lived first as a

slave and then as a woman of power, that because I had lived among the Fae and the Kin and was a friend to the Stane, that because I could wield the sickle and cut life without flinching, I was best suited to take her place. But then the two of you came to my and Hamzu's bedroom the morning after the golem's attack and you said Pendra had disappeared. And that was the last we saw of you. If you are not asking me to take Pendra's place, why are you coming to us now?"

"We were hoping to find her ourselves," said Nu.

"Keep up the Garden ourselves," said Tan. "But we could not. And so we need your help for the moment. Look about you. What do you see?"

Although the remark hadn't been addressed to him, Danr looked. The Garden stretched in all directions, until it curled downward and away to Danr's left. Behind him, the Garden crawled up a massive wall that vanished into the distance above, and the plants didn't seem to notice or care that they defied gravity. Danr felt he could have walked straight up that wall himself, and it was probably true. It wasn't actually a wall, but the trunk of Ashkame itself. The branch the three of them were standing on was so huge that it looked like a mountain covered with a riot of trees and plant life.

The branch Danr stood on was tilted a bit. Quite a lot, actually. It was like standing on a gentle but persistent slope, and he had to lean in order to stay upright. Even after everything he had been through, it was more than a little difficult to understand that someone who had grown up a half-blood thrall in northern Balsia was standing in such a powerful place.

The air was cool and crisp as a new daffodil, and a light spring breeze blew—Danr's favorite weather and favorite season. The sunlight was indirect, as if filtered through leaves high above, and it didn't hurt even his light-sensitive, trollish eyes. Really, despite the chaos and the splendor, it was the perfect garden for a half-blood onetime farmer, and he felt at once at home and relaxed in this fine and beautiful place, indeed, he did.

But that itch, that shadow, was still there, maddeningly at the edge of awareness. And then, cursing himself for an idiot, he closed his right eye and looked only with his left.

Nearly three years ago, Danr had encountered a trio of giants who had granted him—or saddled him with—the power of truth. The power prevented him from telling even the smallest lie and forced him to answer fully any question put to him, no matter how painful the truth might be. It also granted him the power to see the truth through his left eye. When he looked at the Garden with his right eye shut, it . . . changed. The shift was small and subtle, but now it was clear, and he couldn't understand how he had missed it before.

The Garden was dying. Leaves were curling up or turning yellow. Some were blackened and slimy. Danr's left eye spotted insects and disease—end rot that blackened tomatoes, downy mildew that yellowed lettuce, aphids that devoured roses, and rust that reddened grass. The breeze blew wafts of a thick musty smell now and again, and Danr wrinkled his nose in disapproval.

Nu and Tan noticed his expression, and they turned to him. "What do you see?" they asked together.

Danr couldn't help answering. "This place is falling into ruin," he said in his low, husky voice. "What's the cause?"

"It started in Twixthame," said Nu.

"It began in the middle," added Tan.

Then both women paused, as if waiting for something. Then Aisa stepped forward.

"It . . . commenced in the center," she finished in her lilting accent.

Nu and Tan looked visibly relieved.

"Our gratitude," said Nu.

"Our gratefulness," said Tan.

"Er . . . thank you," said Aisa.

"The sickness is the fault of someone in Twixthame using magic most foul and dread." Nu twisted the top of her seed bag. "We cannot see the source. Not without Pendra. But we need help."

"With what?"

Nu clutched at her seed bag. "The two of us cannot keep up with the weeds and tangles in the Garden. The two of us cannot root out disease and unease. With only two, the power is incomplete."

"We are Three," said Tan. "We are two who revolve around one in the center, a compass needle balanced on a fulcrum, a single-spoked wheel turning around a hub. Without the center, we cannot move."

"What is that to do with me?" Aisa asked.

"You are not Pendra," said Nu. "But you are close. You can help. When you are here, we work better."

"And you can work as well."

Here, Aisa looked taken aback. "I can? How?"

"Tend the Garden." Tan swept a hand at the distance. "Touch it. Feel it. Smell it. Become one with it. You will know what to do."

"But even if you do not, sister," said Nu, "your presence allows us to tend the plants better."

Danr swallowed hard. "So you're saying Aisa has to stay here now. Forever. Or until you find Pendra."

"No," said Aisa.

"Never," said Tan.

"Not yet," said Nu. "Mortals cannot survive in the Garden for very long. You cannot eat here. Or drink. Or sleep. Eventually, you will go mad and die. So no, you may only stay for a few hours at a time. But even that will help. As will any work you do, sister."

"And now we must work," said Nu.

"Labor," said Tan.

Another pause, and Aisa said, "Drudge."

The two Gardeners gave a pair of wan smiles and slid away. The Garden swallowed their cloaked forms up, and they were gone.

Danr watched them go, then sank to the ground with his forearms on his knees. He felt weak and washed out, and he was still naked.

"Well," he said at last, "what do we do now?"

She sat beside him. "I feel a great deal of power in this place," she said absently. "It did not take much energy for me to become human."

"Then why did you take mine?" he asked with a grin. He knew the answer.

"Because I like it, my Hamzu. It is like drinking fine wine, and it feels almost as good as when we share . . . other things." Her hand ran down his leg, and his body responded. He grinned again.

"I can't think of anything better to do in this garden," he said.

"Then we think the same way," Aisa said. "And I do love a man who knows my mind."

"Before you get too far, sweeties," said a new voice, "I thought we might have a chat as well."

They both twisted around. Standing behind them was a short, plump woman in a scarlet dress and a white lacy shawl. Her gray braids were coiled in a mass about her head and held in place with a pair of bone knitting needles. Even though the Garden light was steady, the woman's face was somehow thrown into shadow, not quite visible. She held one hand out before her, palm up, and over it hovered a glowing figure the size of a human head. The figure twisted and shifted, its shape never settling for long.

"Death," said Aisa.

"With a sprite," said Danr breathlessly. The day was proving more and more extraordinary, even for him.

"What are you doing in the Garden?" Aisa asked.

"Who is guarding your door?" Danr said at the same time.

"I haven't left my door, dear," said Death. "No need to stand. I've seen you naked already and don't need to see it again."

"Er . . . right," said Danr, wondering what would happen to some poor soul on Twixthame if he snatched a branch off a nearby bush and used it for modesty. "Sorry. We got caught in the middle of the ocean, and—"

"She does not care, Hamzu," Aisa interrupted. "My lady, you have a reason to interrupt us, I am sure."

Danr blinked at her, then made his face into an impassive mask. He and Aisa had met Death several times and had completed several tasks at her request, including killing a giant squid that had nearly killed both of them. Despite the number of times he had spoken directly with her, Danr had never lost his awe of Death, but Aisa seemed to find her more and more exasperating as time went on, a trait Danr found endlessly unnerving.

"Have you seen your sisters?" Death countered.

"You mean Nu and Tan?" Aisa said. "They are not my sisters quite yet. They were here a moment ago, but I do not know where they—"

"I found the reason the Garden is sick," Death interrupted, brandishing the sprite. "And I'm holding it in my hand."

Chapter Three

T he man with the melted face stared at Talfi for a long moment. Talfi stared back, unable to move. It was like looking in a twisted mirror. Talfi's first thought—

I have a brother?

—flickered and died like a firefly. Glass glittered in broken-diamond shards on the cobblestones, and the crowd behind him seemed to fade into nothing. All Talfi could see were the candle-wax features of the man who had half his face.

At that moment, a pair of guards in red and gold livery pushed through the crowd. "What's this, then?" one demanded.

Talfi was still staring at the melted features of the other man. "You—" he managed. "Who—?"

The man stared back from under ragged brown hair. His withered right hand clutched the cloak at his throat. "You—" he echoed.

Just behind him, Ranadar and Kalessa gave identical gasps. Ranadar said, "What in the name of the Nine Gods?"

"Vik!" barked Kalessa. "Who is that?"

The moment broke. The candle-wax man looked sharply around him and seemed to notice for the first time the gaping bottler and the gawking crowd. He pushed past Talfi, who was still too startled to react, and tried to lose himself in the mass of people. One of the guards grabbed his arm.

"Just a moment," he said. "Where did you—?"

The candle-wax man stiff-armed the guard in the chest. The guard flew backward and bowled into the people behind him. He went down in a red and gold tangle of arms, legs, and swearwords. Kalessa's knife leaped into her hand and flickered into a full-length sword while the second guard drew his own sword and lunged for the candle-wax man. The candle-wax man, moving with a cat's own speed, stepped aside and snatched the guard's sword out of his hand. With a screech of metal, he bent the sword in half.

Kalessa didn't pause. She leaped forward and thrust her blade straight into the candle-wax man's shoulder. There was a dreadful sound of metal sliding through flesh, and Kalessa came face-to-face with the candle-wax man's distorted features over her hilt. The candle-wax man blinked at her.

"You will not die today," she growled. "But you will come with us."

The candle-wax man grabbed the front of her tunic and lifted her free of the ground. Kalessa was so startled she let go of her sword. The candle-wax man flung Kalessa aside like a terrier tossing away a rat. She crashed into another booth. With another awful noise, the candle-wax man pulled her sword out of his own body. There was no blood. Talfi was too shocked to do anything but stare.

Now Ranadar lunged for the man, and his hand touched the candle-wax man's bare forearm. Talfi recognized what Ranadar was doing. A long, lingering touch would addict the candle-wax man to Ranadar, and the man would be unable to resist any command Ranadar gave until the day one of them died.

"Ran!" Talfi cried. "Don't!"

It was too late. A faint glow engulfed Ranadar's fingers as the glamour took hold. Kalessa's sword clattered to the cobblestones. Talfi took a step toward them, hoping to break them apart.

A mask of fear crossed Ranadar's face. He howled and snatched his hand away. The candle-wax man shoved Ranadar backward, and he fell against Talfi. Like Kalessa and the guardsmen, they both went down. A piece of broken bottle sliced Talfi's knee with red-hot pain.

"The Nine!" Talfi snarled. "Get off me!"

Ranadar rolled away, his cloak protecting him from more broken glass. Talfi got carefully to his feet, hot blood streaming down his leg. Nearby, Kalessa had also emerged from the booth. The candle-wax man was gone. The crowd slowly went back about its business in the twilight market.

"Are you all right, *Talashka*?" Ranadar asked.

Talfi put weight on his leg and winced. He'd been hoping to run after the man, but his knee hurt too much. "I'll be fine, but I won't be winning any races for a while."

Kalessa strode over, her face stormy. "Who the Vik was that?"

"I don't know," said Talfi. "Scared the shit out of me, whoever he was."

"My *Talashka*," Ranadar repeated, touching his face. "You can't—"

Talfi caught his hand. "Why did you try to addict him, Ran?"

"I—" Ranadar's face went pale under his hood. "I was not trying. I was only—"

"Who's going to pay for my broken bottles?" interrupted the bottler. "Half my stock is destroyed. Weeks of work!"

"I am sorry, friend," Kalessa said. "It was not our doing."

The balding man's face grew as stormy as Kalessa's, and orc and human looked surprisingly alike. "Someone has to pay! I have children to feed! A landlord who wants rent!"

Ranadar raised his hood to show his ears. The man flinched and raised his hands defensively. "Filthy Fae!" he said. "Just like all your muck-sucking kind. Did you enjoy destroying an honest man's living? Piece of shit like you isn't worth the—"

Ranadar, face impassive, flipped the man a coin. It was a gold hand, more than the bottler made in six months. Startled, the man snatched it out of midair.

"Go home and tell your children that not all Fae are cruel," Ranadar said, "and even a few are kind."

"I—yes, my lord." The bottler bowed and scuttled back to his booth.

"Ran," Talfi growled. "Why did you—?"

"Not here," Ranadar replied shortly. "We may as well end the day with one more explosion. Come along."

Heedless of the stares from nearby merchants and customers, Ranadar drew figures in the air with his fingers. They glowed for a moment, and disappeared quickly. When he was done, the elf was panting a little, and a faint shimmer marked the air in front of them.

"Really?" Talfi said.

"I would rather walk than Twist," Kalessa grumbled.

"Do not waste it," Ranadar said. "Go. Before I lose concentration."

Talfi sighed and forced himself to step through.

The *wrench* wasn't too bad. Then he exploded into a thousand, million, billion pieces that scattered all across the universe. He was a trillion seeds floating in a hurricane. After several frightening seconds, he was able to clutch at a twig and follow it to a branch, and then to a trunk. His body came together, and he burst back into existence.

For a bad moment, memory took over and he was lying on a grassy plain, screaming in agony with his right leg lopped off at midthigh. Smoke rose from the cauterized wound, and the stench of cooked flesh filled his nose. His breath came fast and his heart howled in his ears.

And then he was back in the right place, in the room he shared with Ranadar at Mrs. Farley's boardinghouse. Nausea swam through his stomach from the Twist, but it wasn't as bad as he had feared—the boardinghouse wasn't far from the market. A more distant Twist would have had him heaving up three days' worth of meals. He clutched at his leg and stared about the room with wild eyes.

Kalessa burst into the room a fraction of a second later, looking a bit greener than usual, and Ranadar appeared right after. The Twist snapped shut behind them. Ranadar pushed back his hood.

"That was not easy, with all the iron in the—Vik!" He caught sight of Talfi's face. "*Talashka!* What is it?"

"I . . . I almost forgot. And I remembered." Talfi was having a difficult time with words just now. "The Twist took my leg. I wasn't—I didn't—"

"Vik!" Ranadar swore again. He put an arm around Talfi and guided him to the bed. "What happened? Kalessa, bring some spirits. Mrs. Farley usually has some brandywine in the kitchen."

Kalessa dashed out the door while Talfi leaned against Ranadar and tried to sort himself out. Ranadar touched his face and examined his hands, and it took Talfi a moment to understand that Ranadar was checking him for injuries.

"What happened?" Ranadar asked. "Was it a stray memory? Something from a hundred years ago?"

Talfi shook his head. "Not even five. Vik! I'd almost forgotten. I *did* forget it. And then I remembered it. And then I remembered it again, but I forgot that I did." His hands shook. He knew he wasn't making sense, but he couldn't seem to pull himself together.

"It will be all right," Ranadar said, and he pulled Talfi close again. "It was just a memory. It was not happening again."

Talfi sighed and tried to make himself relax against Ranadar's body, but he couldn't seem to make his muscles unclench and his fingers were cold. After a moment, Kalessa returned with a clay mug, which Ranadar pressed to his lips. Talfi drank, and the brandywine burned all the way down.

Then, remembering something Aisa always did, he poured some over the bloody cut on his knee. That burned, too, and he sucked at his teeth. Ranadar gave him a handkerchief to press to the wound.

"How is it?" the elf asked.

"It's fine. Just painful."

"Mrs. Farley was a little startled to see me," Kalessa reported. "I believe she and the butcher are carrying on in some way, judging by what I saw when I entered the kitchen. I do not wish to see such a thing again."

"Good for her," Ranadar said. "Do you know where Aisa is? I would feel better if she examined Talfi."

"She and Danr went down to the beach with that rowboat," Kalessa said. "They are probably halfway to the Flor Isles by now."

"Nothing for that, then. But I do know Talfi will need food to ground him after a nasty shock like this. Could you—?"

"I was just down there," Kalessa protested. "Who knows what Mrs. Farley and the butcher are doing with that piece of meat he brought?"

"Just go, please."

Kalessa stumped away, muttering about orcish princesses being treated like servants. Meanwhile, the brandywine had warmed Talfi a little, and he was able to relax. Ranadar touched his hair. "Tell me what it was."

Talfi breathed out hard. "It was my leg."

"Your leg," Ranadar repeated.

"I told you about it. When Danr's grandmother Twisted him and Aisa and me from Glumenhame to Xaron, she made a mistake."

"Because the Twist was so distant," Ranadar said, remembering now.

Talfi nodded. "Danr and Aisa were all right, but the Twist cut my leg off. Aisa stopped me from bleeding to death, but then the orcs came and . . ."

"They sliced off your head." Ranadar hugged him again. "Barbarians. My *Talashka*. I am so sorry."

"I don't remember much about my head," Talfi said. "Kalessa's father pulled his sword out and the next thing I knew, I was sitting up next to a funeral pyre. My funeral pyre. And my leg was back. That doesn't bother me—I die and come back all the time."

"The boy who forgot how to die," Ranadar said with a small smile.

"The traitor elf," Talfi replied with a small smile of his own. "I just . . . when you Twisted us back here, the memory of my leg slapped me so hard, it was like I was there again, bleeding on the plains of Xaron."

"I've Twisted you since then," Ranadar said. "Death has, too. You didn't react this way then."

"I think it was the shock of seeing that guy with the melted face," Talfi said. "It just . . . unsettled me, and then I was pissed at you, and then we Twisted, and it was just a little much."

"Oh," Ranadar said. "Yes. Er . . . you . . ."

At that moment, Kalessa banged back into the room with a tray of food—bread and cheese and jam and fruit and even a pot of tea. "Will this do, Your Majesty?"

"Thanks," said Talfi, accepting the tray on his lap. Kalessa shut the door. "Ranadar and I are about to have an argument. Do you want to join in?"

Kalessa flipped a chair around and faced them over the back of it. "Always."

"An argument?" Ranadar edged away from Talfi on the bed. Talfi took advantage of the moment to spread a slice of bread with blackberry jam.

"We were going to have it in the market, but you pulled up a Twist so we could avoid it," he said, his voice flatter than he intended.

"Oh yes—you tried to addict the melted man." Kalessa's face was a hard mask. "And why was that?"

"Should we not talk about his strength? Or the way he failed to bleed when you stabbed him?"

"In time," said Kalessa. "Why did you do what you did?"

Ranadar snatched Talfi's brandywine mug from the tray and took a slug. "I was not thinking. It was . . . reflex. He would not run away if he wanted me."

"You would have addicted him to you for the rest of his life—or yours," Talfi said. "Just like Aisa used to be."

"Listen, I know what I did. Almost did," Ranadar said. "We need not—"

"I think we do need," Kalessa said from her chair. "A warrior controls his reflexes. I did—I attempted to wound, not kill. Clearly, you have not tried to control yourself. And why is that, I wonder?"

"It was an accident," Ranadar said shortly. "He frightened Talfi, and then he tried to flee without explaining who he was. We know so little about your past, *Talashka*, and anything we can learn is for the greater good, considering."

"And what would you have done with him once he was addicted to you?" Kalessa persisted. "Let him become your servant? Your slave?"

"Slavery is now illegal in Balsia," Ranadar snapped.

"The melted man would not care," Kalessa shot back. "He would love you. Like Talfi does."

"Not like I do," Talfi said.

"Actually—" Ranadar began.

"You know what I mean," Kalessa interrupted.

"I do not answer to you." Ranadar's face was set hard. "I am a prince of the Fae."

"And I am a princess of the Kin," Kalessa shot back.

"And I'm nothing?" Talfi said quietly.

Ranadar turned leaf green eyes on him. "What?"

"You still think of humans as less than the Fae, don't you?" Talfi said, trying and failing to keep a note of accusation out of his voice. "You see us as slaves."

"I—"

"Don't lie." Talfi hid his face behind his teacup for a moment. "Please don't. Danr can tell when anyone lies, but I can tell when you do."

Ranadar glanced between them like a trapped animal. He looked both sad and defiant. "You fail to understand. Even you, *Talashka*."

A cold hand slid down Talfi's spine. He had been half bluffing when he made the accusation, and Ranadar's words confirmed what he had only suspected. Talfi had been hoping he was wrong, and the realization he was right hurt more deeply than the memory of his missing leg. His muscles tensed, and his legs ached from sitting on the bed with the tray across them.

"What don't I understand?" he asked evenly.

Ranadar shifted on the bed and slid his fingers down the seam of his cloak. "I am three hundred and seventy-seven years old. For the first two hundred years of my life, humans were nothing but talking sheep. I did not think this. I *knew* this. It was much better for humans to serve the Fae, where they enjoyed the benefits of a civilized culture and where they did not squabble over land or their foolish honor, where they did not live in the shadow of the Iron Mountains and the Stane who lived beneath them."

"You mean it was better for humans to live as addicted slaves in Alfhame than with their families and friends at home," Talfi said.

Ranadar sighed. "Of course. My parents knew it, and my grandparents survived the Sundering to know it. You have to remember that after the Sundering, there were few humans left, and they lived in wretched poverty. There were no crops that first year, and everyone was starving. Humans *begged* to come live in Alfhame, where there was food and shelter."

"Because the Fae pushed the Stane into destroying the Iron Axe," Kalessa spat. "If it were not for your *squabbling*, there would have been no problems for anyone."

Ranadar spread his hands. "The Stane ruled Erda with a cruel fist, and the Fae fought to get everyone out from under it."

"And the Kin paid the price," Talfi finished.

"When the Tree tips, everyone pays the price," Ranadar said.

"The Kin pay more," Kalessa interjected.

"You are asking why I did what I did, and I am trying to explain," Ranadar said. "From the moment I was born, my mother and my father and everyone I knew taught me about humans. For two hundred years—twenty generations to orcs—I learned that Kin were lesser beings. Kin have weak minds and are easy to manipulate with even simple glamours. They loved us because they wanted to. I knew this. Here." He tapped his own chest.

"You fail to make yourself look better," Kalessa growled.

"And then, one day, a bright and merry slave who would not be cowed and who seemed immune to my father's addictive touch came into the palace and stole my heart," Ranadar continued, "and I began to wonder if the Kin were something better. Talfi showed me that humans had thoughts and feelings that ran as deep as my own, and I questioned what I knew. Then my father and mother found us out and cut his throat before my eyes. I was too cowardly to stop them, and could only watch his lifeblood spill a river across the floor. It crushed me like a glacier and drove my parents and me apart with a dagger of ice. I ran to the woods and became *mal rishal*, a forest lover who only rarely visited the city. Still, Mother and Father were sure I would eventually return and stay. To them, I was pouting over the loss of a puppy. And perhaps that would have become true in time. Perhaps I would have gone back to my old way of thinking."

Ranadar continued to draw his cloak through his fingers. "But only a hundred and fifty years after that awful day, I was visiting my birth home for the first time in decades when my Talfi appeared on the palace steps in the chains of an orcish slaver, and it was the most wonderful and terrifying moment of my life. When I saw you again, I knew I would never, ever give up this second chance. And I did not. I betrayed all my people, helped Aisa kill . . ." Here he paused for a deep, shuddering breath. "Kill my own father. I helped Danr repair the Iron Axe so he could slaughter my own people before they slaughtered the Stane. I did all this because Talfi had returned to me, and I would do it again." He sighed hard and twisted the cloak about his fingers. "But you and I have spent perhaps two years together, *Talashka*. It takes longer than two years to unlearn the lessons of three hundred and fifty-five others. I am trying, but I often fail, especially where you are concerned. I am sorry for my mistake today."

Talfi silently finished his food, feeling about six inches high. He touched Ranadar's hand, the same one he had used on the candle wax man. "I'm sorry, too, Ran. It can't be easy to—"

"Oh, cry a thunderstorm," Kalessa snapped. "The fact remains that you did your best to addict that man to you, and you thought nothing of the consequences."

"And what would you have me do, orc?" Ranadar flared back. "Should I fall prostrate before you and beg forgiveness? Go back in time and undo it? I suppose in your long and varied history as a murderer, you have begged forgiveness a number of times when you killed by accident."

"Murderer?" Kalessa looked horrified.

"How many Fae have you killed?" Ranadar said. "Did you check to see if they deserved it?"

"This is not about me," she said.

"You are not perfect," Ranadar said, "and yet you expect perfection from me."

"He apologized—" Talfi put in.

"To the wrong people," Kalessa said.

"—and we'll accept it," Talfi finished. "I think that's

enough talk about it. What we really need to know is who that man was."

"I already know that," Ranadar said.

"You do?" Talfi set the tray aside and turned on the bed to face him. "Why didn't you say something?"

"We went down a side road," Ranadar said. "There was a reason the man did not become addicted to me."

"And that is?" Talfi prompted.

"He was you."

Chapter Four

"You know you have a sprite in your hand," Aisa said in the quiet, dim light of the Garden.

"A dead sprite, honey," Death corrected. "His name is Grak-Lor-Who-Flits-Through-the-Emerald-Stars. He died seven minutes and six seconds ago and tried to sneak through my door, but I snagged him just in time."

"I hope this is an uncommon occurrence," Aisa said.

"Why did you snag him?" Danr put in quickly.

"He looked suspicious." Death waved the hand with the sprite above it, and the sprite bobbled uncertainly. "You develop an eye for this kind of thing after a while."

"And?" Aisa said. "Death herself stops a sprite from finishing his final task in life, so I assume it was at least a little important."

"Snippy, aren't we?" Death slid one of the knitting needles from her hair, and for a dreadful moment, Danr through she was going to skewer Aisa with it. Instead she poked Grak-Lor-Who-Flits-Through-the-Emerald-Stars. He squeaked, and his bright form flickered like a flame caught in a droplet of water, but he didn't speak. "Can you guess how this one died?"

Aisa sighed. "Let us pretend we cannot guess and that you will tell us quickly. It becomes tiresome when elder ones speak in riddles."

"Aisa!" Danr said. "This is Death! You can't talk to her like that."

"Why not?" Aisa shot back. "We know she will not come early for me. In fact, she will not come for me at all. Not if I will be taking Pendra's place one day."

"That's not entirely true, dear," Death said amiably. "I do enjoy our verbal sparring—so few people are willing to talk back to me, and I'd almost forgotten what it was like. Tikk does it, of course, but only when he wants something. At any rate, you aren't a Gardener yet, and I can come for you just like anyone else if you take an arrow to your heart or a sword to your neck. Besides, you have mortal tasks to complete."

"Such as?" Aisa said, unfazed.

Death cocked her head. "You do remember the reward I gave you after the Battle of the Twist, don't you?"

Here, Aisa did pause, and her hand went to her naked belly. She was remembering, and Danr remembered, too. Humans who remained among the Fae long enough lost their fertility, which was why the Fae needed a steady supply of slaves. Aisa's time as a slave among the Fae had cost her the ability to have children. Death had returned it to her. It wasn't something she and Danr had discussed. In fact, they had discussed very little since they learned Aisa would be . . . leaving eventually. Talking about it made it more real.

"I cannot forget," Aisa said softly.

"Just checking," Death said. Was she smiling in that shadow? There was no way to tell. "Anyway, as I was about to say, Grak-Lor-Who-Flits-Through-the-Emerald-Stars here died from wounds he received while capturing Pendra last year. Poor thing has been suffering for months."

Now Danr came fully alert. "Capturing her? Who captured her?"

"Queen Gwylph," Death said grimly. "Gwylph has imprisoned Pendra in a great ash tree at the foot of the Lone Mountain in Alfhame and she is draining Pendra's power for her own use. This sprite was wounded in the capturing, you see, and eventually died of his wounds. Now he sings for me." Death poked Grak-Lor-Who-Flits-Through-the-Emerald-Stars, and he squeaked again.

Danr cast about, feeling cold and vulnerable and very aware of his nakedness as chilly fingers slid down his spine. Queen Gwylph. He could still see her on the shore of Lake Nu, resplendent in her gleaming armor with her golden hair spilling down her back and her silver scepter in her hand. She gathered up power from thousands of *draugr*, spirits of the dead, and used it to decimate countless trolls, dwarfs, and giants until Danr faced her down with the Iron Axe in his hand. He had intended to kill her, but she had Twisted away at the last moment, and that was the last anyone had heard from her, though he supposed she was still ruling Alfhame. Now it was clear she was up to far more than that. How could she have captured one of the Gardeners?

"This is . . . outrageous!" Aisa sputtered. "Beyond filth!"

"For once, we agree, dear," said Death. "Queen Gwylph is using Pendra's power to create . . . life. New life." She poked the sprite again. "Isn't that true?"

"True!" squeaked Grak-Lor-Who-Flits-Through-the-Emerald-Stars. "Who knew? You blew true."

"Life?" Danr repeated. "But that's only possible for . . ."

"A god," finished Tan, sliding into view.

"A deity," said Nu, arriving with her.

There was a pause, and both Gardeners looked at Aisa hopefully. Death nudged her with one elbow. "You know it makes them unhappy, dear," she murmured, "and they've already been through enough, don't you think?"

"I am still becoming accustomed to the whole idea," Aisa murmured back, then raised her voice. "The Nine."

The Gardeners looked pleased for a fleeting moment, and lost the expression just as quickly. Nu said, "This is a disaster."

"A calamity," said Tan.

"A . . . catastrophe," said Aisa.

"Good one," put in Death. "You earn extra for the alliteration."

"Extra what?" Aisa shot back.

"Oh, I'm going to enjoy this for the next thousand years," Death trilled. "Listen, we have to do something, and fast."

"Quicky," agreed Nu.

"Speedily," said Tan.

"Not now," interrupted Death, then turned back to Danr and Aisa. "Look at the two of them. They're barely coherent without their third. The Garden is dying, the world is sliding into chaos, and soon everything will be gone, gone, gone. All because of that foolish queen. We need to work out what to do, my darlings."

Danr shook his head, feeling overwhelmed. He was a farmer, a former thrall, not someone who should be discussing the fate of the world with Death and the two remaining Gardeners. He shouldn't be—

Stop it, he told himself. He had reformed and wielded the Iron Axe. He had faced down this evil queen once and stopped her. He had faced Grandfather Wyrm and brought back the power of the shape. Royalty begged him to dine with him.

Even so. He had been born a farmer, he had lived a farmer, and a small voice inside him said he would eventually die a farmer. And what was wrong with that? He hadn't ever asked to be a . . . a hero. All he had ever done was trudge forward, always forward. What else could you do? And now all that trudging forward had brought him to this very strange and frightening place where Death herself was asking him for advice.

"Why don't you just . . . take her?" he asked. "The queen, I mean."

"I've tried, sweetie," said Death. "Oh, how I've tried.

But I can't touch her. I don't know why. And you've seen Nu and Tan here. They can barely keep the Garden from sliding off Ashkame into the void, let alone uproot the plant of someone who is feeding off the power of one of their own."

"Gwylph is powerful," growled Nu.

"Potent," snapped Tan.

"Er . . . divine?" finished Aisa.

"Not yet." Nu twisted the strap on her seed bag. "But closer and closer every day. She was one of the other choices, you know."

"Other choices," Danr echoed. "I don't understand."

"Aisa was not our only candidate to replace Pendra," said Tan. "We looked at other powerful women. Strong women who could also wield the sickle without flinching. Queen Gwylph nearly took the power of the Iron Axe for herself and would have ruled the world."

"If she hadn't destroyed it first," Death pointed out.

"But it made her a good candidate," Tan replied.

"She was an evil woman!" Danr protested. "She still is!"

"She thinks of herself as good, you know," said Nu gently. "She sees herself as a bringer of light and order. To her, the evil Stane need to be uprooted."

"The terrible Stane must be destroyed," said Tan.

"The filthy Stane have to be wiped out," said Aisa.

"Hey!" Danr said, affronted. "Whose side are you on?"

"Apologies, Hamzu," she said. "Something about this place."

"What poisons one plant fertilizes another," said Nu. "The only thing that matters is the overall health of the Garden."

"How could a mortal kidnap a . . . a Gardener?" Danr burst out. "Mortals can't interfere with gods and fate. It's the other way around."

Here, Nu, Tan, and Death all looked genuinely puzzled. "What are you talking about, dear?" Death said at last.

"The Nine, the Three, and I exist because mortals exist. And they exist because we exist. On the day the last living thing dies, I myself will cease to be."

"On the day the last plant sprouts, my job is done," said Nu.

"On the day the last row is hoed, my job is complete," said Tan.

"On the day the last weed is cut, my job is finished," said Aisa dreamily, and gooseflesh chilled Danr's arms.

"The Tree always tips," Death finished. "But eventually, it will cease to exist."

And something else occurred to Danr. "Why does it have to tip at all? Every time it tips, hundreds of thousands of people die. Why can't we just stop it from tipping?"

"It is the nature of the universe," said Nu quietly. "Two points revolve around a center, like a spoke around a hub."

"The Stane and Fae revolve around the Kin," added Tan. "Lumenhame and Glumenhame revolve around Twixthame. The Nine form themselves into three groups of three, and two groups revolve around the third."

"The Nine and the Gardeners revolve around me, dear," said Death. "So it is, so it was, and so it must be."

"That doesn't answer the question *why*," Danr persisted. "Why were the Kin chosen as the . . . the . . ."

"Nexus," Aisa said.

"Nexus," Danr repeated. "Why do the Kin pay the price when the Stane and the Fae go to war?"

"Someone has to," Death said in a voice that ended the discussion. But the question wouldn't leave Danr's mind. Perhaps it was the truth-teller in him, or perhaps it was the simple unfairness of it. He had seen the blood up close and personal, and the idea that more Kin blood would spill before all this was over made him alternately boil with outrage and freeze with sorrow.

"At any rate," Death continued, "making Gwylph a Gardener would have solved the problems she was creating in the mortal realm. We spoke to her about it, in fact, and she became angry when we told her we had chosen someone else instead."

Danr's eyes widened. "Is that why she took Pendra? Revenge?"

"That's probably part of it." Death waved her hand, and the sprite wobbled over her palm. "Really, you probably should have kept your mouths shut, sisters."

"She wants to become a Gardener no matter what you decide," Aisa said in a hushed voice. "She is taking a Gardener's power and she is usurping a Gardener's role."

"But she's still mortal," Danr finished, "and a mortal can't use that power, so she is destroying the world instead of helping it."

"Indeed," sighed Nu.

"True," murmured Tan.

"Yes," said Aisa.

"Who else were you considering?" Danr asked without thinking.

"Queen Vesha of the Stane," said Nu. "She was, in fact, our first choice."

"My aunt?" Danr said, amazed.

"She would have been perfect," said Tan. "A world-class magician. Experienced in the ways of the world. Willing to make necessary sacrifices, even when—"

"No!" Death's voice had gone cold as buried granite. She clenched her fist and Grak-Lor-Who-Flits-Through-the-Emerald-Stars vanished with a *crack*. The wind turned cold and the plants around her shriveled. Danr dropped to the ground with his heart shivering in his chest, and this time Aisa came with him. "Vesha chained me. Vesha took *my* power. I cursed Vesha, and cursed she will remain. The only Garden she will see is at the bottom of Halza's icy cesspool."

"Of course," said Nu.

"We agree," said Tan.

"Understood," Aisa whispered.

"Very well, darlings." Death's voice returned to normal

and she balanced the knitting needle point-upward on one fingertip. "But on other matters—there *is* a way to stop Gwylph and free Pendra."

Danr got cautiously to his feet. By now he was really wishing someone would conjure up a pair of trousers for him, or even just a blanket.

"What's that, then?" he asked, trying to sound amiable.

"A new weapon has entered the world," said Death. "One that, in its way, is nearly as powerful as the Iron Axe. It's called the Bone Sword."

The knitting needle lengthened until it was easily three feet long, and flat as well—a sword made of bone. The blade was shiny and so thin it was nearly translucent. A bloodred ruby was set into the pommel. It balanced on the tip of Death's finger, a tall sliver of ivory, and the air seemed to curl away from it.

"What does it do?" Danr asked warily.

"It will cut through nearly anything," Death replied, "including the ash tree that holds Pendra captive. It may also end Queen Gwylph's life. You'll have to travel to Alfhame to do it, and I shouldn't imagine it'll be easy."

"And where," Aisa asked wearily, "can we find this sword?"

The sword shrank back down into a knitting needle, which Death tucked back into her hair. Her voice hardened. "To learn that, dear, you'll have to talk to the sword's creator."

"And that is?" Aisa prompted.

"Queen Vesha of the Stane."

With a *wrench*, the Garden vanished. Danr found himself standing on a dusty road with Aisa beside him. His stomach heaved, and this time he couldn't avoid vomiting. The sight of it got Aisa started, and they emptied their stomachs together by the side of the road.

"A romantic finish to our day together," she said, wiping her mouth with a handful of grass. She was wearing an ivy green dress, and Danr realized with a start that he was wearing bark brown trousers and a sky blue tunic. A thick straw hat topped his head and kept out the worst of the evening sun. He held out his long arms.

"Why couldn't she have done this while we were in the Garden?" he groused.

"Why couldn't she have simply handed us the Bone Sword and Twisted us to Alfhame?" Aisa shot back. "Death's explanations come either too late or not at all."

"She brought us together." He put a thick arm around her shoulder. "If not for her, you and I would be . . . somewhere else."

"I will grant her that," Aisa agreed. "Grudgingly. But where are we now?"

Danr glanced around. They were at the edge of a wood. The road curved down ahead of them through farmland sectioned off by stone walls and hedgerows. The late sun slid sleepily toward the horizon to Danr's right. Behind them, the road vanished into the thick trees, where a cloak of night had already fallen. A few early crickets were already chirping in the leaves.

"I think we're about two leagues north of Balsia," Danr said. "Maybe three."

"Death gives us clothing but fails to put us closer to home," Aisa sighed. "Honestly, I think she enjoys making life difficult."

"You need to learn to get along," Danr said. "I think the Gardeners do a lot of work with her, and . . . and she gave you back your . . . your . . ." Unexpectedly, his throat grew thick.

"I need to sit a moment," she said, and spread her skirts under a tree at the side of the road. Sheep bleated in the distance, heading toward some distant paddock for the night. Danr sat beside her, big as a boulder. They both sat silent in the gathering summer evening as a warm summer breeze wafted the smell of soft clover and heather over them. Aisa's hand stole into Danr's.

"I do love you, my Hamzu," she said in a voice so soft he could barely hear it over the crickets. "But now—"

His stomach tightened. "I don't think I want to talk about this," he interrupted.

"We must, my love. We have avoided it for months and months."

"Then avoid it a little longer." A note of pleading entered his voice, and he hated himself for it. "It may never happen if we don't find the Bone Sword and cut Pendra out of that tree."

"And what will happen to us when this ends?"

The words, the forbidden words, hung in the air like a plague of locusts waiting to drop on Danr's heart and devour it raw. But Aisa had asked him a direct question, and the words were already piling up in the back of his throat. He knew what they were, didn't want to let them out for the locusts to destroy. For a tiny moment, he fought to keep them in. But in the end, he knew they would come out, and with a thickness in his chest, he spoke.

"When all this is over, if Queen Gwylph doesn't kill you first, you will go to the Garden and take Pendra's name. You'll become a Fate and you'll change the lives of everyone you touch. You'll stay young and beautiful forever, or maybe your face will change so that it looks ageless, like the other Gardeners. But mine won't."

Aisa tightened her grip on his hand, and he realized she had forgotten that he was a truth-teller, that when she spoke her question aloud, he'd have to answer it as completely as he could, no matter how much it hurt.

"At first, we'll see each other regularly," he went on in a voice hard as stone, "but after a year or two or maybe three, you'll become busier and busier, and it'll be harder to make time to see me. We'll miss a meeting and tell ourselves it was just once, but then it'll be another, and then another. Then you'll look at a plant and realize that several decades have gone by. I'll be old, and you'll wonder if you should just leave me alone." His eyes felt hot and scratchy and he sniffed hard. "The moment you become a Gardener, it ends for us. We both know it, Aisa."

She looked up at him for a moment with a naked fear and tenderness that tore his heart. Then her face hardened. "How can you say such things to me!" she snapped. "Such cruel, terrible things!"

Aisa started to scramble to her feet, her expression hard. A flash of hot anger flicked through Danr. Then he looked away and let it fade. "It's awful, Aisa. You can shout at me and get mad at me. You can keep things back from me like you used to. It won't change anything. It'll just hurt more, and I wish you wouldn't do it."

Aisa started to say something, then closed her mouth hard. Her posture eased, and she sank back to the ground. "You are right. I hate it, but you are right, and I am sorry." She sighed heavily. "I am not angry at you, you know."

"I know."

"How can I lose you?" she blurted out, and a pair of doves burst from the tree over their heads, their wings whistling as they fled. "I watched you die and helped you come back to life. After all the struggling we went through to find each other, how can I lose you now?"

"I don't know," he said truthfully. "You could . . . refuse the position. They can't make you take it."

"And who would they give it to?" she replied scornfully. "Queen Gwylph?"

"I suppose."

"Never," Aisa spat. "You know what she is like. That woman would turn the Garden and its people into her toys. She does not care about people."

"That's what I love about you, Aisa." Danr took her hand. "You won't give in. Even when it hurts."

They sat in silence for a long moment, watching the shadows lengthen, reflecting their somber mood. They were in no hurry to move along. To Danr's trollish eyes, the evening was perfectly well lit, and they didn't worry about finding their way back to Balsia in the dark. After a moment, something else occurred to Danr.

"Death said we had another task to complete before you'll become a Gardener. She hinted it had to do with—"

"A child." Aisa's hand went to her stomach. "I know. I have been thinking of it ever since she brought it up. How can I—we—have a child if I become one of the Fates?"

"Goddesses have children with mortals all the time in the stories," Danr pointed out. "Those children become great heroes."

"With mothers who play almost no role in their upbringing," Aisa said. "And the stories never say what happens to the . . . goddess who has to watch her offspring age and die."

"But our child could have children, and they could have children," Danr pointed out. "An entire grove might show up in the Garden just for us. And you could tend it."

"I do not know, Hamzu," she said. "It seems dark and frightening to me. It is nothing I expected or asked for, but I have it nonetheless."

"We don't get to be normal," Danr agreed.

"Can we decide later?" Aisa asked. "This is too difficult, too strange."

"Yes," he said truthfully. "But later will come awful quick. It might be better to start a baby now."

"Truly?" she said with an arch look. "In this very spot?"

He returned her look with a grin. "I can't lie, you know. We could start right—"

"Here!" said a new voice.

Danr turned and caught a glimpse of a man in a ragged tunic before the world bent and warped all around him. Danr's body melted and shortened, driving the breath from his lungs. Aisa shouted something, but her voice stretched high and thin. He landed with a thump in the grass by the side of the road, tangled in a pile of cloth. He fought himself free. The tree loomed above him, a thousand times its normal size. Aisa's face, also a thousand times its normal size, bulged above him. His field of vision was strange—flattened and rounded out, as if everything now fit on a huge plate. The Nine!

"Hamzu!" Aisa cried. "Rolk and Vik! What—?"

When Danr tried to answer, all that came from his throat was a strange croak. It came to him that he had been changed into a small toad. Above him, the ragged man laughed. He must have done it. Behind the man stood three other men with knives. They oozed forward, and the ragged man's hands gave off a golden glow behind them.

"Give me everything you have, girl," he growled, "or I'll squash your friend and change you next."

Chapter Five

"What do you mean the man was me?" Talfi demanded from the bed. "How could he be me?"

"If I knew that," Ranadar said, "we would know most of the answers we need."

"I think Talfi wants to understand how you know the man's identity," Kalessa said, interested despite her earlier animosity. She was still looking at them over the back of her chair.

"When I touched him and the glamour tried to take hold," Ranadar explained, "the magic . . . I cannot explain it very well. It seemed to bounce back at me, and instead of him becoming addicted to me, I nearly became addicted to him. That was why I . . . I . . ."

"Screamed like a kid goat?" Kalessa suggested.

"It was terrifying," Ranadar said seriously. "I caught a brief glimpse into his mind, and it was . . . you, *Talashka*. But also not you. He had some of your memories. He remembered things you have not mentioned to me."

Memories. Talfi stiffened and came quietly alert. His every nerve quivered with hunger. "What do you mean?" he asked in a careful, measured voice, as if anything louder might frighten Ranadar away like a skittish rabbit.

"I caught glimpses of a young boy—him—running through

an apple orchard. I saw him playing a pipe while he watched a herd of sheep under a sunny sky. I watched him bed a young man with black hair and gray eyes."

Talfi flushed a little but couldn't stop the questions. Every memory was precious, even if it was secondhand. "Who was the young man?"

Ranadar shook his head. "I know nothing about him, only that he . . . you . . . wanted him very much and that it was a long, long time ago. Do you remember him?"

"No." Talfi shook his head and slumped back. "I don't remember any of those things. Did my family have an apple orchard, then? Or sheep? Or did those things happen later, after the Sundering?"

"We also need to know the source of his strength," Kalessa said. "He tossed me as easily as a lioness tosses a kitten."

"And if he's me," Talfi said, "why didn't he bleed? Or seem to feel any pain when Kalessa stabbed him? I bleed. I feel pain."

"Until you die, *Talashka*, and come back to life," Ranadar pointed out. "Perhaps that has something to do with it."

"Discussion gets us nowhere," Kalessa decided. "We need to talk to that man. If we can find him. Can you see into his mind, Ranadar?"

"Elven glamour does not work quite that way," Ranadar replied. "Usually, we put our thoughts into *other* people and make them see or think what we wish them to. I have never been very good at it. You have seen me create simple disguises, and I can make people not see me—simple tricks like that. When I am close to someone—emotionally close, like my *Talashka*—the bond is more powerful. I recognize his mind, and I can feel what he feels when we touch. I assume that is why I caught glimpses of the candle wax man's mind." Ranadar shuddered. "It was very strange. There were two Talfis in my head."

"So what do we do now?" Talfi set the tray aside and

stood up, testing his leg. It took his weight, though he didn't look forward to running on it right away.

"We need to find the candle wax man and learn who he is," Ranadar said, also rising. "We should probably start by searching the market. Perhaps someone else there has seen him."

"No." Kalessa got to her feet and stretched. "It is nearly sunset, and I have to go see Slynd. It has been two days now, and if he does not see me, he will come looking for me. That would prove a disaster. And you must learn to ride, as you swore."

"But—"

"Disaster," Kalessa repeated with the ominous note only an orc could create. "Swore."

"We will watch for the candle wax man on the way," Ranadar sighed.

It was a long walk to the outer edge of the city, so they hired a carriage. As the wheels bumped over cobblestones or squished through mud, Talfi kept a sharp eye out for anyone resembling . . . well, himself, and wondered what he would do if such a person appeared. Grab him? Tackle him? Talk to him?

"We need to tell Aisa and Danr about this," Kalessa mused aloud as the people and buildings moved past them. "I wonder where in Vik's realm they are."

"Probably enjoying themselves," Ranadar said, "as we were trying to do before this came upon us."

They reached the edge of the city. In olden times, Balsia had been properly walled in, but the Sundering had brought down large sections of the original walls, and the city had since sprawled well outside the barriers in any case, so the edge of town was a nebulous sort of place where actual buildings faded into farmlands and estates of wealthy Balsians who couldn't afford to live within the truly fashionable Diamond District and who didn't want an ocean villa. Low stone walls and hedgerows snaked among the fields, marking boundaries. A few trees stood scattered among them. At Kalessa's direction, the carriage took them down a lane and toward what looked like a farm, complete with a house, out-buildings, and stone-lined fields and hedges of its own. How-ever, when Kalessa alighted from the carriage, a giant green blur burst from behind the barn and rushed straight at her. While the driver tried to calm the panicked horses, the blur halted near Kalessa and coiled frantically around her, hissing like the world's biggest teakettle.

It was a wyrm, a great emerald beast easily thirty feet long and nearly as tall as a horse. Its golden eyes matched Kalessa's, and its long tongue lapped the air. Huge coils all but hid Kalessa entirely, and she laughed within them until she was able to scramble out and drop in front of the wyrm's sleek head. Its—his—tongue flickered over her. She laughed again and scratched the underside of the wyrm's jaw. His tail whipped back and forth like a tree in a hurricane.

"Yes, Slynd, I have not forgotten you." Kalessa put her forehead against the wyrm's. "You are my first love for-ever, yes, you are!"

"He missed you." An elderly man with a bent back, a walking stick, and a straw hat emerged from the barn and approached. "You didn't come yesterday, and he was unhappy."

"Did you miss me?" Kalessa stroked Slynd's head. Slynd's coils writhed with happy excitement. "Mother is so sorry, and she missed her little one, yes, she did. Are you hungry, hmm? Come along, we will ride and then we will eat."

Slynd bobbed his head. Kalessa leaped onto his neck without even a saddle, and both of them rushed away. Kalessa raised her knife above her head and changed it into a sword with a whoop as they vanished into the dis-tance.

"Mother," Talfi muttered with a shake of his head. "Am I the only one who gets a little creeped when she says that to a wyrm?"

Ranadar laughed. "After a thousand years of life, *that* curdles your blood?"

"I'm just glad it's not mating season," said the old man, whose name was Neff. "These wyrms are difficult enough to handle without nesting time angrying up the blood."

"How many wyrms are you taking care of right now?" Talfi eyed the barn.

"Six at the moment, counting Slynd." Neff shook his stick. "Most of them from orcs who are travelin' through Balsia. Slynd is the only long-termer I have. Pays the rent, though, now that my sons and I—what is that?"

Neff pointed with his stick. Zipping over the fields came a little ball of golden light. It rushed at the trio like a shooting star, trailing sparks as it came.

"A sprite!" Ranadar put his hands up, but before he or Talfi could react further, the sprite cracked forward like a lightning bolt and struck Neff in the chest. The old man staggered and . . . changed. A golden nimbus surrounded him. His back straightened, his hat fell away, and his form puffed outward. In a blink, Neff had shifted from an old human man with a walking stick into a beautiful elven woman holding a scepter. Blond hair spilled in waves down her back, and her perfect, wide emerald eyes looked out imperiously from beneath a smooth forehead. Her ears came to graceful points. The early-evening sun sparkled off her silver gown and winked off her pearl-headed scepter. Her beauty was too perfect, too awe-inspiring, and Talfi knew it was a glamour, that she was trying to make herself so wondrous, but that didn't keep Talfi from wanting to kneel before her perfection. He found his knees starting to bend, and only sheer willpower kept him upright. He did recognize her, and so did Ranadar.

"Mother," Ranadar said, his tone halfway between anger and uncertainty. "What are you doing here? You better not harm Neff."

"Do you care about a single old man, my son?" said Queen Gwylph in a musical voice that made Talfi ache with hunger and delight. "An elf's lowest business is more important than the welfare of the highest Kin, and this Kin's life has nearly run its minuscule course."

"What do you want, Mother?" Ranadar said guardedly.

"And this," Gwylph said, turning to Talfi, "is the boy who forgot how to die. The first. Tell me, little one, what is it about you that made my son cruelly turn against his own mother and break her heart?"

Actual tears came to Queen Gwylph's eyes, and Talfi suddenly wanted nothing more than to comfort her, stop this lovely creature from weeping. Any world that would make her cry wasn't worth living in.

Then Ranadar touched Talfi's arm and blew warm breath in his face. The desire vanished like a burst soap bubble, and the queen seemed much less beautiful, to boot. He could see the fine spray of winkles on her face and the silver in her hair. Anger stiffened Talfi's spine.

"It's probably that I don't bed donkeys," Talfi said. "Or lick goat balls."

"How dare you!" the queen snapped out of reflex.

"That's what the goat said," Talfi replied.

"She is still my mother, *Talashka*," Ranadar said softly.

"I'd say I'm sorry," Talfi replied, "but I don't want to."

"You—" she began.

"The first time we speak in over a year, Mother, and you throw a glamour on my beloved," Ranadar interrupted. "Why are you here? You Twisted a sprite all the way from Palana, made it track me down, and ordered it to lay your image over this old man. That took a lot of power, so I assume you have a reason for spending it."

Gwylph recovered herself. "I am here for you, Ranadar."

"You will have to say more than that."

"Do you love me, my son?"

A pained look flickered across Ranadar's face before he managed to erase it. Talfi, who knew Ranadar well, wondered if Gwylph caught it, too. "That does not matter, does it? You have made your decisions, and I have made mine."

Gwylph dropped the scepter. It struck the ground and changed back into Neff's walking stick. She stepped forward and touched Ranadar's face. She was so close to Talfi that he could hear the illusory rustling of her gown and smell the flowery scent of her hair. Neither put a hold on him, but it was like standing next to the real Queen Gwylph.

"I miss you," she said with genuine grief in her voice. "You are my son, my only child. I do not care what your . . . friends or your beloved mortal have done. They may have killed your father"—here her voice choked a little—"but they are not you. I love you so very much, and I want you back where you belong. In Alfhame. At my side. Come home."

"I . . . cannot, Mother." Ranadar backed up a step and closed his eyes. "You know that."

"Is it because of the boy?" Gwylph persisted. "He can come. We will cast no glamours on him, I give you my word. He can stay as your playmate or your consort or whatever title you want to give him. He can stay until he dies that final time, and then you can move on."

"He will not die naturally, Mother," Ranadar said.

"Oh, my son." Here Gwylph seemed pained again, and Talfi wondered if it was real, or if she was just a very good actress. "That is not true. I have studied the matter extensively, and I know he was the vessel for the power of the Iron Axe. Its power was keeping him alive. Once the Axe was reformed, the power left him. He is a normal human now. He will die one day, and sooner than you think. It is always so with the Kin."

"There is more to the story," Ranadar said. "Did you know that Talfi died that final death when the Axe was reformed?"

"I . . . did not," she admitted. "He is still alive now, so I assumed—"

"You assumed wrong," Ranadar said. "Talfi was dead, forever. But I spoke with Death herself after the Battle of the Twist. Because I helped free her, she offered me a reward. I asked her to bring Talfi back to life, but there was only one way she could do it."

Gwylph thought only a brief moment. Her perfect features went pale. "No," she whispered.

"Indeed. Death said that for every day Talfi gained, someone else would have to give up a day of his or her own. I offered all of mine."

"You offered her all of them?" Talfi interrupted. "I didn't know that."

"You were dead," Ranadar told him. "Your *draugr* kept begging for release, and all I could think of was granting it to you. The pain tore me in half. But Death did not take all my days. She took only half and gave them to you."

"That much I knew," Talfi said, feeling a little overwhelmed. "Ran, it's like I told you in your parents' throne room—I didn't need more years. I've lived more than a thousand of them."

"But you remember almost none of them," Ranadar countered. "How fair is that? I do not want to live without you. The very idea pierces my heart with an arrow. Giving you half my days was a bargain."

Gwylph drew herself fully upright. "I did not know he had stolen your days, Ranadar."

"I gave them freely, Mother," Ranadar replied with some heat. "This was your doing, you know. If you and Father had not tried to slaughter the Stane, we would not have had to reforge the Iron Axe, and Talfi would not have *needed* my days."

"You—" Gwylph began, then bit back her words. "I do not wish to argue about blame. These events have ended, and this is where we are now. Your people need you. Alfhame needs you. *I* need you. With your father . . . gone, you are all I have left. Please come home. I am asking as a mother who loves you."

Ranadar set his mouth hard. "Mother, I—"

A great shout interrupted them. Slynd with Kalessa on

his back rushed into view. The wyrm skidded to a stop. Kalessa caught sight of the elven queen and, with an orcish war cry, vaulted over Slynd's neck, her sword raised. Queen Gwylph made a startled noise and backed away, but Kalessa was already swinging. The flat of her iron blade caught Gwylph square on the buttocks. With a yelp, she popped back into Neff, who went to his knees. The sylph hung in midair, spiky with surprise for a tiny moment. Then it fled with a thin shriek.

"Iron," said Kalessa. "Good against Fae."

"So please put it away," said Ranadar, backing up a step, "or change it to bronze."

Kalessa sheathed the sword—it shifted to its normal knife shape—while Talfi helped Neff to his feet.

"What happened?" the old man quavered as one of his sons came rushing out of the barn to see what was going on. "I don't remember any—"

"It's all right," Talfi soothed. "You just need some time to sit down."

"Why does my arse hurt?" Neff complained.

They gave vague explanations to Neff's son, who took the old man into the house. Kalessa patted Slynd's flank. "This is turning into a strange day," she said.

Ranadar picked up Neff's walking stick and leaned on it. His face was pale and his lips were tight. Talfi's stomach tightened and he put a hand on Ranadar's arm.

"Are you all right?" he asked.

"I did not know she still . . . cared," Ranadar said.

"She's still your mother," Talfi replied carefully. "Even after everything that happened." He paused for a long moment. "Do you . . . want to go back?"

Ranadar shook his head hard. "No. But . . . yes. I mean, I cannot. I should not. But I miss Alfhame. It is my home."

"Even though she helped your father kill your true love." Kalessa leaned against Slynd, arms crossed. "Even though she did her best to kill all of us."

"She also taught me glamours and how to live in the

woods and how to speak with sprites," Ranadar said. "She told the slaves to tuck me in at night while she told me stories of elven heroes and frightening ghosts. She is my *mother*."

"She is selfish and greedy and cruel," Kalessa continued relentlessly. "She thinks of no one but herself."

"She thought of me," Ranadar pointed out. "And she offered to allow Talfi to come back. That was . . . out of character for her."

"Are you defending her actions?" Kalessa asked.

"No," Ranadar sighed. "That is . . . I suppose it sounds like I am. It is not easy to turn away from my family. I did not betray my people because I hated her. I did it because I loved Talfi. Her actions were wrong, but she is still my mother."

"Why did she make that offer?" Talfi scuffed at the grass with one toe. "She has to know I wouldn't go. *You* know I wouldn't go."

"And I would never ask it of you." He put his head in his hands. "This is a hard place to stand, between my family and my love and my friends."

"Will you accept her offer?" Kalessa said. "Will you go back?"

"Certainly not," Ranadar said. "You are correct—she is greedy and selfish and that makes me wonder why she made this offer to me. It must benefit her in some way. It pains me to say it, but she does not want me. She *needs* me, and I do not understand why. I am nowhere near the magician she is, so she cannot be after my magic. She rules the entire kingdom, and will continue to do so for another two or three hundred years at least, plenty of time to figure out what to do about an heir, so it is not the bloodline. Why approach me now?"

"And where did she get the power?" Talfi mused aloud. "Didn't you say it takes a lot to do what she did?"

"I did," Ranadar said. "Mother is an expert at Twisting, and sending a single sprite that far would not tax her overmuch, but using it to take over Neff's mind and send a glamour that distance would take a great deal of power. If all elves could do *that* lightly or easily, there would be no need to conquer the neighbors with swords. So that leaves us with two questions—why does she need me at home, and where did she get the power to contact me this way?"

"And we still know nothing of the candle wax man," Kalessa sighed. "We need to talk to Aisa and Danr. Perhaps we should even talk to Death."

Talfi shuddered. "I don't like talking to Death."

"I like her," Kalessa said. "She promised me everyone would remember my name, and there is no greater reward in the world."

"Yeah, well, I'm always afraid she'll audit the days I have left or something," Talfi said. "We need to get back to the city and search for the candle wax man."

Chapter Six

Aisa blinked down at Danr the toad. He squatted on a pile of clothes on the side of the road, his goggle eyes wide with startled shock.

"You have money," said the ragged man. "Give it to me, or I'll turn you into a toad, too, and crush both of you."

He raised his hands. They glowed gold in the evening gloom and left light trails behind them when he moved. His three compatriots, each with a soot-blackened blade that would not gleam in moonlight, poked their knives toward her.

Aisa stared at the four men in genuine disbelief. For a tiny moment, an old fear flickered within her, and vanished almost as quickly. "Gentlemen," she said in a soft, measured voice, "do you know who I am?"

"You're the one who's going to give me her money, and right quick," the ragged man said. "And you're going to give me that nice dress so's I can sell it, and those boots, too."

"You do not know where you are standing," Aisa said.

"We're standing in the forest with a pretty girl in an expensive dress," said one of the men.

"That is where your perceptions are wrong." Aisa drew herself up and pulled her own power together, the power that had faced down the evil harbormaster and the biggest golem the world had ever seen. "You are standing on the edge of a cliff, and only you can decide if you will back away to safety—or fall into an abyss."

"Are you looking at this, girlie?" The ragged man swept his hands in an arc, leaving a swath of golden light behind. "Didn't you just see what I did to your friend?"

Danr croaked angrily from his pile of clothes.

"Will you try it on me next?" Aisa said, hands on hips. "Are you truly so foolish?"

"You gonna let her talk to you like that, Welk?" one of the knife men said.

The ragged man's face hardened. He gestured at Aisa, and a beam of golden light shot from his hands and caught her full in the chest. Or it would have if Aisa had not caught the beam in her own hand. She felt Welk's power rush through her, attempting to change her, mold her into what Welk wanted. But Aisa clamped down on her own shape and *held* it. The ragged man's power burned like fine brandy, and Aisa drank it in, molding it into what she herself wanted. She whipped off the dress Death had given her as her limbs shifted and thickened. Fur sprouted all along her body, her muscles stretched and grew powerful, and in less than a moment, a mountain lion faced the four men at the edge of the forest. She roared, and the smell of urine tanged the air around the band of bandits. Knives dropped from nerveless fingers.

Welk looked at his hands in astonishment. "I thought I could only do toads."

Feeling the strength of her new body, Aisa roared again, and the three men fled yipping into the woods. Welk tried to follow, but with a single leap, Aisa came down on his back and brought him down. She pressed a paw the size of a dinner plate on his head and brought her muzzle down to his cheek, so close that her fang slid across his skin, leaving a thin cut behind. A drop of his coppery blood slipped into her mouth. Behind her, Danr croaked again, and anger took Aisa. This man had changed her Hamzu into a toad, and how *dared* he? A growl rumbled low in her throat, and Welk's panicked panting beneath her only increased the rage. One little snap would end his wretched, worthless life. One small—

And then something touched her, gentle as a grain of sand sliding across her ear. Perhaps it was a new effect of the power she had drunk, or perhaps it was an increased connection to the Garden, or perhaps it was nothing but a new thought, but for a moment, Welk's life stood clear to her, as if she were examining the rings of a recently felled tree. She saw a child growing up in a poor family that scrabbled for a living at the edge of the forest, and the hard blows both his father and his mother dealt him. She saw him leave home and try his hand at laboring, at farming, at anything he could find, but unable to get decent work because of his ragged appearance and low station. She saw him pulling a plow in a field one day when a wolfhound raced across the freshly turned earth and, for no reason Welk could understand, bit him and then dashed away. She saw him accidentally change the man guiding the plow into a toad, and she saw people driving him away as a monster. All these things she saw in an instant.

Her anger faded. He was not that different from her, or from Hamzu. If things had gone just a bit differently, perhaps she would now have the same life he did. And she recognized the wolfhound. It was one of the former slaves to whom Danr had given his blood. The woman had become a shape mage, able to shift into a wolfhound shape and spread the shape magic with her own blood—or a bite, it seemed. Was this where the legends of werewolves had come from? The possibility bore more thought. At any rate, Aisa and Danr themselves had no small role to play in Welk's current state. If Danr had not given the slave woman his blood—at Aisa's request—Welk would not be turning hapless travelers into toads. Aisa pulled back and reclaimed her own shape, standing naked over him while he lay panting in fear on the road.

"You will change him back," she said. "Unless you want me to bite something off."

Welk scooted backward in the dust, eyes wide. "I can't. All I does is toads. Please, you have to believe me."

More angry croaking came from the side of the road. Aisa stepped on Welk's wrist and pressed hard. "Pray I do not become upset, Welk. I faced down the harbormaster and his golem. Crushing you will be simpler than stepping on a flea."

"That was you?" He flinched. "Aw, no. Please, my lady. I'da never done it if I'd known who you was."

"So you would have done this dreadful thing to someone else?"

"No! I mean, I did, but I don't . . . Look, everyone treats me like I have a disease. I'm starving, and I don't know what else to do for money." His voice shook a little. "Please help me, great lady."

"Hmm." Aisa could not say her heart melted with pity. He had power, but he had misused it. Even in her darkest moments, she had never done the things he had done. Well, perhaps she had, but she had done them to survive, and only to people who had deserved it. Well, perhaps . . .

She gave an internal sigh. She could not judge this man, even if one day it was—would be—her right as a Gardener. Did the Fates actually judge anyone? Now that she thought about it, she supposed they did not. How could they, when they themselves planted the Garden in such a way that individual lives were pushed in certain directions? How could they—she—judge a man when he was only reacting to the row in which he had been planted?

Still, he had turned Hamzu into a toad.

"Get up," she growled, "and come with me."

Welk scrambled to his feet and followed her meekly back to Danr, who was as puffed and indignant as only a toad could be. For a wild moment, Aisa wanted to pick him up and kiss him to see if that would change him back.

"We will fix this, Hamzu," she said. "While I am happy

to love a troll, I am not comfortable sharing my bed with a toad."

"Can't *you* just change him back, lady?" Welk asked.

"I can affect no shape but my own," Aisa replied shortly. "Give me your hand."

Uncertainly, Welk obeyed. His hand was both dusty and sweaty, and Aisa did not care for his palm against hers. "Hamzu, this man cannot change you back, and neither can I. You must do it yourself. Call to your own shape, and it will answer, just as it does when you change from a human back into a half troll."

"But, great lady," Welk said in a hesitant protest, "he's just a toad now. He won't have enough power to change his—"

The drop of blood Aisa had taken from Welk's body gave her an easy connection to him. She reached into his body, found his own source of power, and *pulled*. Welk gasped and dropped to his knees in the dust. Magic burned in Aisa, but she could tell it was not enough to return Danr to his own shape. She left Welk on the ground and knelt to touch Danr's head. Aisa and Danr had already shared blood with each other, creating an easy link, and it was simple enough to let Welk's power stream out of her and into him. For good measure, she added some of her own. For a moment, nothing happened. Then Danr exploded into his full shape. With a trollish snarl, he grabbed Welk by the scruff and hauled him, limp as a kitten, up to eye level.

"Who do you think you are?" he bellowed in Welk's face, and Aisa was ready to swear Welk's hair blasted backward. *"After everything I have done for the world, you touch me with your filthy magic? I should tear off your—"*

"Hamzu," Aisa interrupted with firm softness, "you sound very like White Halli."

At the mention of that name, of the man who had bullied Danr for years and whom Danr had finally beaten almost to death, Danr paused. Aisa could see him regain control of his temper, of that which he used to call the monster. Carefully, calmly, he set Welk down on his shaky legs.

"See that you don't do that again," Danr growled.

"No, great lord," Welk gulped.

"So. I suppose everything is all right now," Danr said with a cough, and turned to pull on his clothes.

"Thank you, great lord."

"I'm not a lord," Danr said shortly as his dark hair came through his tunic. "But we can't leave you here, turning people into toads and such. People already mistrust shape-shifters and shape magicians. You're making it worse by robbing people."

"I rob people because they won't give a shape magician honest work," Welk said with a flicker of spirit.

"Even so." Danr flexed huge hands. "We can't leave you here."

"Wait!" Welk put up a shaky palm. "If she's the lady what killed the harbormaster and his golem, that makes you . . . Danr. The hero from the Battle of the Twist! The Iron Axe!" He went to his knees again, and Aisa saw Danr trying not to make a face. "Please don't kill me, great lord! I won't never use my magic again! I swear!"

"Sure, all right," Danr said. "Get up. And I told you I'm not a lord."

"If it makes you feel better, you may call him Master Danr," Aisa said.

"Which still doesn't tell us what to do with him." Danr pointed at Welk, who tried not to flinch.

"I can think of a use for him," Aisa said suddenly. "One that will keep him out of trouble, help with the shape magician problem, and even let him earn his own money."

"Really, lady?" Welk scrambled to his feet, looking hopeful. "I'll do anything you say."

"Don't give her that kind of opening," Danr warned.

"Come with us," Aisa said. "We are going to Balsia to see Prince Karsten."

"Prince Karsten?" Danr said. "What for?"

"Is he going to execute me?" Welk squeaked.

"No," Aisa said. "I have a better idea, but I would prefer to explain when we arrive."

It was near midnight when they arrived at the outer edge of Balsia. Danr had no trouble seeing in nothing but starlight, and Aisa was happy to let him lead the way. Welk followed like a chastened puppy. A smaller city would have shut its gates after dark, but Balsia had overflowed its original walls centuries ago, and its gates had long since become decorations in the middle of busy streets.

Besides, the Stane were out and about after dark. Aisa, Danr, and Welk passed more than one troll on the street, tall and shaggy, or wide and blocky. All of them were dark-haired, with jutting lower fangs, long jaws, barrel chests, and muscular arms. They towered over Danr by two feet or more. They lumbered through the streets, pulling heavily laden wagons or carrying blocks of stone or just moving about. With them came the short, twisted dwarfs, moving about on business of their own. Danr remembered when he had gone under the mountain and seen trolls for the first time, how uneasy he'd been and how frightened for Aisa. Kin and Stane each saw the other as ugly monsters, as different as night and day. Danr's father, Kech, had smeared Aisa's forehead with a bit of his own blood to alert the trolls that she was not to be harmed, but even so, she had been nearly killed for being human. So had he, for that matter.

One of the trolls sniffed the air and deliberately moved to the other side of the street. "Half-blood, all stink," she said just loud enough to be heard.

Concerned and more than a little outraged, Aisa took Danr's hand. To her surprise, she didn't feel any tension in his huge grip.

"They'll learn eventually," Danr said in answer to her unasked question, "so what would be the point of getting angry now?"

"You have changed, my Hamzu," she said.

"For the better, I hope."

"Always that," she said. "Always."

As they approached the point where the houses thickened, the sound of arguing voices drifted down the dusty road ahead of them. Aisa listened.

"Is that—?" she began.

"Talfi!" Danr bellowed. "Ranadar!"

The arguing paused. It was following by running footsteps, and moments later, Talfi, Ranadar, and Kalessa emerged from the shadowy bend ahead of them. Talfi, the fastest of the trio, rushed at Danr as if to embrace him, then screeched to a halt. A troll pushing a giant barrow piled high with beer barrels rumbled past them. He sniffed the air and sped up to get past them.

"Halza's tits!" Talfi exclaimed. "You were human when you headed out this morning. What's going on?"

"You were supposed to be down at the ocean," Ranadar said. "Are you well? Did something happen?"

"And who is this?" Kalessa finished, her blade already in her hand. Welk raised his hands, and they glowed faintly.

"None of that!" Danr said sharply, putting himself between them. "This is Welk. He's sort of our prisoner."

"Prisoner?" Talfi repeated. "Why do you have a prisoner?"

"Why are you three out here at night?" Aisa countered.

"We were visiting Slynd at the farm and lost track of time after Gwylph showed up to talk with Ranadar," Talfi said brightly. "We couldn't find a carriage and had to walk back to—"

"Gwylph?" Aisa interrupted. "The elven queen?"

"What's she doing here?" Danr demanded.

"This is no coincidence," Aisa said. "It must have something to do with Pendra and the Garden."

"And then there's the candle wax man," Talfi put in.

"Enough!" Kalessa boomed.

Everyone, including Welk, turned to stare at her.

"Prisoners and queens, Death and the Gardeners, wyrms and candle wax—it is obvious we need to sit down and repeat our various stories to each other," Kalessa said. "But only back home and over something deeply alcoholic."

"Mrs. Farley and the butcher are going to love this," Talfi observed.

"The butcher?" Danr replied, scratching his head.

"Yet another story, I fear," Ranadar sighed, and made way for another troll.

"So let me get this straight." Danr pushed his cup aside. "You found a guy in the twilight market who looks exactly like Talfi, except for the melted half of his face, but he ran away before you could ask him anything, and then Ranadar's mother begged him to come home and be prince, even if it meant bringing Talfi along."

"That's about it," Talfi agreed.

"And you two," Ranadar said, pointing at Aisa and Danr with a shaky finger, "talked to Death and Gardeners, who said without Pendra, the other two Fates are unable to function fully. Death learned that my mother—my *mother*—kidnapped Pendra because she was unhappy about not being chosen as a Fate, and now she's using Pendra's power to create some kind of new life, which is corrupting the Garden beyond the Fates' ability to repair, so we need to ask Queen Vesha of the Stane—another former candidate for Pendra's position—for the Bone Sword, the only weapon that can free Pendra."

"And it all started with a picnic," Aisa said.

"Is this a normal day for you people?" Welk blurted out. He was sitting at the far end of the common room table, a little red faced from liberal applications of Mrs. Farley's home-brewed ale.

"You're a shape mage now," Danr said. "Get used to this."

"It seems clear," Aisa said, "that all this is connected—the candle wax man, Ranadar's mother taking Pendra, her appearance to Ranadar at the wyrm farm."

"Do you think she's responsible for the candle wax man?" Talfi said. "Did Gwylph . . . create him?"

"I do not see how or why," Ranadar replied. "She may have access to a Gardener's power, but creating a new Talfi . . . that would be beyond her. She would require . . . material. And she has none. Talfi is here."

"Aunt Vesha is involved in this somehow, too." Danr munched his way through a loaf of bread. "Did you get the feeling Death was sending us to her because she—Death—is angry at her?"

"I did," Aisa admitted.

"You've seen Death get angry?" Welk took another slug of ale. "I was going to ask if maybe you might want another shape mage to . . . you know . . . help out summat here and there, but now I'm thinking it would be smarter to join the army after all. Less deathy."

"We should secure this man," Kalessa said. "He is a thief and cannot be trusted. I can bind him so he will not move the entire night long, even to relieve himself."

"He did some regrettable things, my sister," Aisa said, "and he will work to pay for his crimes, but we need not be cruel to him in the meantime."

Danr crossed his thick arms. "He did turn me into a toad, you know."

"And you forgave him," Aisa replied.

"Mostly," Danr grumbled, and Welk gave him a sickly grin.

Ranadar said, "I will take care of him."

"You will?" Welk said warily.

In answer, Ranadar dipped his finger in ale and flicked several drops at Welk with a few murmured words. When the drops touched Welk's skin, they glowed faintly and vanished.

"What did you do to me?" Welk asked, eyes wide.

"If you wander more than one hundred yards from my person, you will die instantly," Ranadar said carelessly. "And if you use your magic, you will die a painful death that stretches out for more than an hour."

"Oh," Welk said in a small voice.

"I didn't know glamours could do that," Talfi said.

"Mind magic is more powerful than you think," Ranadar returned.

Danr closed his right eye and looked at Welk. He saw no glamour there. The truth came to him. Ranadar was lying about the magic. But what did it matter as long as Welk thought it the truth? Danr gave Ranadar a brief nod of acknowledgment. The elf's expression didn't change, but he sipped from his glass.

"Perfect," Kalessa said. "What do we do next?"

"In the morning, we need to deliver him"—Danr jerked a thumb at Welk—"to the prince. Then we need to track down this candle wax man and go ask Aunt Vesha for the Bone Sword."

"What if she doesn't give it to us?" Talfi asked.

Danr cracked his knuckles. "We'll take it."

Dawn woke Danr. The chill morning air hovering in the bedroom made him decide to stay in the warm bed just a few more minutes—a luxury he'd never been afforded as a thrall. Then he realized that Aisa was no longer beside him. In fact, she wasn't even in the room.

He tossed aside the blankets and pulled on his chilly clothes. "Aisa?"

No answer. Unease stole over him. The door was still shut and locked from this side. He cast about uncertainly. Where had—

"Good morning, Hamzu. I am glad to see you up and dressed."

He spun. Aisa was standing behind him, looking tired.

Startled, he swept her into an embrace. "You worried me for a minute," he said. "Where did you—?"

The top of her head was under his nose, and he sniffed her hair. It carried a different scent than usual, a scent he recognized. He gave a second sniff, then backed away and held her at arm's length.

"You were in the Garden last night," he accused.

She nodded. "I was."

He was wary again. "Did . . . *they* summon you?"

"In a way. I could hear them talking in my head." She rubbed her ear. "It woke me, and I felt a strong urge to go. And then . . . I was there. They *need* me, Danr. The Garden needs me."

"Why didn't you wake me first?" His voice was calm.

"It . . . didn't occur to me. I wanted to be there, and I just . . . went." She took his hand. "Are you angry? Please do not be angry. This is something I needed to do."

"I'm . . . a little angry," he was forced to say. "Not that you went to the Garden. It's that you went and didn't tell me."

"Yes. I am sorry." Her eyes went down. "I just did not wish to wake you, and it felt urgent to go. Please do not be angry anymore."

She was wrong, and he was right. For a moment, he wanted to hold on to the anger, the righteousness of it. For years, he had never been allowed to get angry at anyone, and now he had a chance to be both right and angry.

But then he paused. How small and stupid was that? This was someone he had quite literally died to save. Without thinking, he ran his hand over his chest, where the silver sickle had split him open, spilling the life's blood that had saved Aisa's life. The small, petty anger dissipated.

"There's no reason to be angry," he said with half a smile. "But I wish you'd've woken me up first. Did it . . . help? Was the Garden any better?"

"Not that I could tell," she sighed. "But neither did it hurt."

Downstairs, they found the others already at breakfast. Mrs. Farley was cutting bread and cheese at a side table while everyone ate. Welk hovered in the corner, refusing to take his eyes off Ranadar, who calmly downed cold meat and day-old biscuit. Kalessa gulped the strong tea she favored in the morning while Talfi doodled on his plate with a bit of blood sausage. Danr peered over his shoulder.

"A heart?" he said. "How sweet."

Talfi skewered the sausage with a knife and ate it. "I'm not awake yet, troll."

"Grouchy," Danr observed.

"How long will the glamour last?" Aisa asked Ranadar with an eye to Welk. Danr wondered if Aisa knew the truth, too.

"As long I wish it," Ranadar replied. "He should be pleased I do not plan to ride horseback to the Gold Keep."

They actually hired another carriage. Aisa made a caustic remark about Welk running behind it that made Welk blanch, but in the end he was allowed to sit on the floor. Danr, who had not at all enjoyed his time as a toad, didn't feel inclined to offer him a seat. The morning promised plenty of sun, and Danr clapped a heavy felt hat on his head to ward it off. It was nice to be in a position to afford felt hats and hired carriages.

The driver, a large man with green eyes and a close-cropped head of graying brown hair, perked up noticeably when Ranadar gave him the destination. Passengers who went to the Gold Keep would have money, and money would mean a good tip. He hopped down from the seat and bustled lap robes around them to keep their clothes free of flying mud and manure, a constant hazard in an open-topped carriage like this one. Welk's head poked out from the swaddles of cloth like an odd rock in a river.

"Get you there in a jiffy, sir!" he said. "My name's Joe. Joe Saylor. You need anything, you just let me know, good sirs! And ladies!"

"A sailor who drives a carriage?" Kalessa said.

"'S right, lady," he said, touching his hat. "Twenty years at sea, until that golem stepped on my ship during the Blood Storm. Now I'm driving a carriage. Never know where life'll take you, and that's a fact!"

"Tip him extra," Aisa murmured to Ranadar.

Joe gave Danr a quick look as he tucked in the final bit of robe. "You got any preference about the route, sir?"

"The route?" Danr repeated. "No. Why?"

"Only there's this group of people down by the temple of Grick. They're shouting and chanting about . . . certain types of folk."

"You mean half-bloods," Danr said evenly.

"And them new shape-shifters," Joe added.

"Grick's priests preach acceptance of all people," Aisa said in a tight voice. "This . . . demonstration is aimed at them."

"The temple is right on the way," Joe said, suddenly unsure of himself. "I only ask because there's another way to the Keep. We could avoid the whole thing, but it would take a lot longer. It's entirely for you to say, sir."

"Thank you for telling us," Ranadar said imperiously. "We are not concerned with such people and will take the shorter route."

Aisa said, "Perhaps we should take the—"

"We will take the normal route," Ranadar interrupted. "Drive!"

Joe touched his hat. "Right, sir."

"Why must every day be interesting?" Kalessa mused aloud.

And Danr was forced to answer, "Because it's us."

They heard the shouts before they saw the people. The temple of Grick was a wide, serviceable set of brown stone buildings tucked behind a wall that curved along the street. In front of the wall swarmed a hive of people, three or four deep. A few crudely made straw dummies poked up from the crowd on sticks. Some dummies were human shaped, others seemed to be animals. A few soldiers kept a wary eye on the people from a distance but otherwise stayed out of it. The imposing iron gate partway around the wall was firmly locked.

Danr closed his right eye and looked at the crowd with his left. Instantly, he saw the truth: pinched faces, tight bodies, curt gestures. These people weren't truly angry—they were merely afraid. But they put a mask of anger over their fear, which only made the anger burn brighter.

Joe turned the carriage down the street, his mouth tight. "We could go around, sir," he said over his shoulder. "I think the carriage could squeeze down one of those side streets if we're careful."

"Just drive," Ranadar said.

"What are they chanting?" Danr asked.

Aisa listened. "It sounds like 'Half-blood, half-dead.'"

"Some of them are shouting, 'Shift is shit,'" Ranadar observed.

"Imaginative," Kalessa said, touching the hilt of her knife.

"They're scared more than anything," Danr told them. "They're afraid of shape-shifters and half-bloods because both things are strange and different. And they're afraid of the Stane, too."

"They don't look very scared," Talfi said nervously. "Right now they're looking at us."

"Ranadar, my dear friend, why did you insist we go this way?" Aisa said.

"I am a prince of the Fae," Ranadar said, but with a hint of doubt now. "My business will not be delayed by common—"

"A half-blood!" someone shouted, and a glob of mud sailed straight at the carriage. It fell short and splattered the wheels. "He's riding in a carriage like normal people!"

"Who do you think you are?" shouted someone else.

"He thinks he's better than us!"

"Go back to Halza, half-blood!"

Danr felt the old anger stir, but it mingled with the truth he had seen earlier, which forced it back. Getting angry at

these people would be like getting angry at the wind—
there was no point. Clearly, they didn't recognize him as
Danr, the half-blood who had wielded the Iron Axe. Not
long ago, the greater danger would have been that the
crowd might overwhelm the carriage to touch Danr, even
tear away his clothes for souvenirs. He had been the only
human-troll half-blood in Balsia, and everyone knew who
he was. Ironically, his fame as the Hero of the Battle of
the Twist had encouraged more half-bloods to go public,
and now there were perhaps a dozen or twenty living
openly in Balsia alone. But instead of creating more acceptance, it had created a rift among the human population.
Some humans had indeed become more accepting, but
others had run in the other direction.

And some of those were currently running toward the
carriage.

"We should speed up," he called to Joe.

Joe was already clucking to the horses, but a contingent
of the crowd had moved to block the street in front of them,
forcing Joe to slow and stop. The people looked scared but
determined. Danr gritted his teeth. This wasn't going to
end well. He glanced at Ranadar and knew he and the elf
were thinking the same thing—they should have taken
Joe's advice and gone the long way. But here they were.
Kalessa grasped the hilt of her blade, her face grim, and
Danr swallowed. Welk's face was white amid the lap
robes.

"What now?" Talfi whispered.

In answer, Danr stood up and pulled off his hat. Hot
sunlight drilled through his skull, but he forced himself to
ignore the pain.

"My friends!" he boomed in his best public speaking
voice. "I am Danr of Balsia, Hero of the Battle of the
Twist."

Aisa stood up beside him. "And I am Aisa, who battled
the harbormaster's golem during the Blood Storm."

This startled the crowd into momentary silence.

"We are not enemies!" Danr said. "We are your neighbors and your children and your—"

"You crushed my house!" someone yelled.

"My wife died in that storm!" shouted someone else. "And my son!"

"She saved us from the harbormaster!" yelled a third person.

"They destroyed half the city!"

A chunk of the crowd surged toward the carriage. Kalessa started to pull her blade from its scabbard. Aisa put a hand on hers. "No!" she breathed. Joe snapped the reins, but people had already grabbed the horses' heads, preventing them from moving. Danr forced himself to stand tall before them and he sent a glance to Aisa. She met his look, and he knew they had the same thought. She could change shape—into a tiger, a bear, an elephant—and startle the crowd, but if she killed or even hurt someone, it would only make shape mages and shifters appear worse. If she did nothing, the people would hurt them. The front of the crowd reached the carriage. Kalessa drew her knife anyway, and it flicked into a double-edge broadsword. Danr drew himself up. He wouldn't let them hurt Aisa or anyone else, and he was strong enough to ensure—

"No!" Welk shouted, and golden light exploded in all directions.

Chapter Seven

The light drilled pain into Danr's skull, and he clapped his hands over both eyes with a throaty howl. When the pain died, he cautiously took his hands away and blinked rapidly to clear his vision.

The scene had changed. Kalessa was still standing in the carriage with her sword, but most of the crowd had vanished. The rest of the crowd stood dumbstruck outside the wall of the temple of Grick. Joe stared down in shock from the driver's seat. Everyone was silent.

Surrounding the carriage was a knot of toads. Danr counted perhaps forty or fifty, brown and warty and goggle-eyed. They hopped and skittered in a confused clump around the carriage, leaving behind small piles of their clothes.

"Welk!" Danr turned to him. "What did you do?"

Welk slumped in the bottom of the carriage, looking utterly exhausted. "I panicked," he moaned. "They were coming for me—for us!"

"And Ranadar's glamour—" Kalessa began.

Aisa was more pragmatic. "Run!" she bellowed at the people. "Or you may be next!"

The remaining demonstrators needed no further warning.

There was a sound of frantic footsteps and the street was clear.

Kalessa changed her sword back into a knife and sheathed it. "That was handled well."

"More important," Ranadar said, "what do we do with *them*?" He gestured to the knot of toads hopping about the carriage. "We cannot just leave them."

"The elf demonstrates compassion for the humans," Aisa said. "A greater wonder than the toad transformation."

"Hey!" Talfi said. "He shows a lot of compassion for me! Just last night, he—"

"Ranadar has a point," Danr interrupted quickly. "What *do* we do with them?"

Kalessa opened the low carriage door and crooked a finger at the toads. "Get in!" she barked.

"You can't be serious!" Welk protested, but his voice was little above a whisper.

"A true highborn mage takes responsibility for his actions," Kalessa said. "These people were not true enemies, so it becomes your task to take care of them." She gestured again at the toads. The toads, however, seemed more than a little wary. Kalessa sighed. "Do you want to stay on the street and be squashed by a passing lettuce cart, or come with the only person who has a hope of changing you back?"

The toads streamed into the carriage. They filled it with croaking and cold, leathery skin. Danr sat down before they could swarm his seat. Aisa didn't react quickly enough and had to sit on his lap. Welk sat amid them, his head a pale island in a sea of brown. The toads' rubbery legs and toes crawled over Danr's thighs, and he shuddered. Kalessa slammed the carriage door shut and leaped out of the carriage so she could cling to the side. Danr envied her forethought.

"Go!" she barked at Joe, who was only too glad to whip up the horses.

They made a strange procession—a half troll, an elf,

and three humans in a carriage filled with croaking toads and an orc hanging on the side. People turned to stare. Danr sat upright, his hands around Aisa's waist to steady her. He wasn't sure whether to laugh, or laugh, or maybe just laugh. What else was there to do?

"You look like you're going to eat a handful of these toads," Talfi observed from his place in the croaking pile. This only increased the croaking considerably.

"He will not," Aisa said. "Toads have a distinctly sour taste. Especially when they used to be sour humans."

The odd parade trundled into the high-class Diamond District, where great homes spread themselves behind stone walls like soft ladies collapsing within great skirts. The streets were wider, the cobblestones smoother, the people cleaner. But still the latter stared. People had been staring at Danr his entire life, but he couldn't seem to get used to it; no, he couldn't. Something about the eyes made him feel ungainly, clumsy, too big for his own skin. They were judging him, and even though he knew damn well it didn't matter what they thought, it still made him unhappy to be at the cold center of their thoughts.

"We seem to create an impression wherever we go," Aisa said.

"I think it's more of a crater," Danr sighed.

Ranadar, meanwhile, had fallen silent and was staring at nothing while toads crawled over his shins and ankles. Talfi looked at him for a moment, then touched his arm. "Are you all right, Ran?"

The elf remained silent a moment longer, then shook his head. His red hair tousled a little. "I was only thinking. So many people are upset, and so much of it can be traced back to my people. They trapped the Stane underground for a thousand years, they enslaved the humans, they skirmished with the orcs. Is it any wonder the people of Balsia are unhappy? They have never had an ally they can trust."

"So it has been for a thousand years," Aisa said.

"Now my mother is going out of her way to make

everything worse," Ranadar continued. "Perhaps we need someone to provide . . . an example. Someone to be trusted."

"What are you saying, Ran?" Talfi said, pushing a toad out of his lap.

"Now that I live among humans, I see many new things," Ranadar said. "I understand new ideas. Some have floated through my mind like morning mist for a long time, but after the argument we had over slavery yesterday and this demonstration today, the ideas have become more solid. For all time, we have not been the Nine People. We have been the Three People Who Fight. Someone needs to say, 'It is time to stop fighting and be the Nine People again.'"

"And that someone would be you?" Aisa set aside a toad that tried to climb her sleeve.

"Every one of you seems to have a purpose," Ranadar said. "Perhaps this is mine."

"A peace between orcs and elves, Fae and Kin, sprites and giants," Kalessa said. "That is a new idea indeed."

"I like it," declared Talfi. "And I think I want to claim my first favor."

"Favor?" said Aisa.

"He cheated three of them from me in an archery contest," Ranadar sighed.

"Why did you get into an archery contest with Talfi?" Danr put in. "He never misses."

"You tell me that now," Ranadar grumbled with mock severity.

"Fing!" Talfi agreed.

"What is this favor?" Kalessa asked curiously.

"Actually, it's both a favor and a reward for his proclamation about peace between the Nine People," Talfi said in airy tones. "I want a kiss."

Before he could make any bigger production out of it, Ranadar gave him one. The toads increased their croaking, though whether in approval or for some other reason, Danr couldn't tell.

"If there is a better way to begin peace between races," Aisa observed, "I cannot think of one."

They arrived at the blocky expanse of the Gold Palace, so named because the original stones had wide streaks of iron pyrite in them that glittered like the sun in full daylight. The center of the Gold Palace had been built for defense, and showed it—stone blocks crushed thin windows that peered over a stocky wall set with iron spikes— but over the centuries, each prince of Balsia had added something to it, another building, a courtyard, a wing, until the place had become a rambling, amiable fortress as fat as a dragon dozing in the sun.

Joe took them to the main gate, where Kalessa hopped free of the carriage and pulled the door open. A stream of toads poured to the stones while the guards gaped. Danr and the others stepped down, minding where they put their feet. Ranadar gave Joe a tip that made him gasp, despite the strange events of the day. He touched his hat and drove away as fast as propriety allowed.

Two humans and two golems stood guard on either side of the main gate. Spiky dwarfish runes crawled over the golems' baked brown skins, and a blue glow illuminated their eyes. Two streaks of blood smeared each of their foreheads. Someone had dressed them in the red livery that marked Prince Karsten's guards and servants, and in their blocky fists they held short pikes that matched the two human guards'. It showed the wealth of Balsia's prince that he was able to put a pair of expensive golems on light duty at the gate when elsewhere golems were on high demand for tiresome, difficult work once done by slaves. To Danr, however, the golems only brought back memories of that awful day during the Blood Storm when Aisa, grown to giant size, had sliced his chest open with Kalessa's blade and used his blood to take control of the enormous golem that threatened to destroy all of Balsia. Unconsciously, he touched his chest at the spot where the metal had split him open while the lightning flared and the wind howled around them both. Sometimes he could still feel the pain.

"Master Danr, Hero of the Twist, is here to see the prince," Kalessa told one of the human guards with a straight face. "Along with Aisa of Irbsa, Savior of Balsia and Bane of Golems; Prince Ranadar of Balsia, the Traitor to the Fae; Talfi of the Iron Sea, the Boy Who Forgot to Die; and Princess Kalessa, Master of the Mystic Sword. Oh—and Welk, the shape mage."

"And . . . the toads?" the guard stammered.

"What toads?" Kalessa said.

The croaking, hopping train of toads followed them through the palace. More than one servant approached with pained looks, but Danr returned a hard look of his own, and they backed away. The guards ushered them into a large meeting chamber—apparently someone had deemed the toads too tricky for the throne room—where a group of people awaited. Some looking annoyed, some looking curious, some looking angry, but all ducked their heads and murmured respectful words. Aisa had saved the entire city from the harbormaster and his giant golem, and both Danr and Aisa had restored the power of the shape to the Kin. And Danr had wielded the Iron Axe. For all these things and more, Karsten had offered them titles and land, but they had quietly refused, not wishing the responsibility. However, their status bought them an audience with the prince whenever they wanted one, and at the moment, Danr was only too pleased to trade on that.

"Danr! Aisa!" Prince Karsten came forward. He was young for his position, not yet twenty-one, and was still growing into a man's body. His dark hair and gray eyes gave him a rakish look that, Danr had heard, was already combining with his title to earn him a number of marriage proposals from highborn ladies. So far he had fended them off. "Never boring with you around. If it's not mermaids and magic, it's golems and dwarfs. And now . . . toads?"

Danr and the others bowed. It was a gesture Danr had learned to make with grace after long practice.

"It all makes sense when you hear the story, Highness." Danr introduced Welk, who was still looking pale and exhausted, and explained. His words echoed slightly in the large unadorned chamber. The room was furnished with nothing but a plain table and hard chairs with braziers spaced about for heat, but none were lit, indicating how hastily the room had been called into use. Danr didn't recognize the half dozen courtiers in the room, though he did recognize Lady Hafren, mother to Prince Karsten. She was a short, slender woman whose keen gray eyes missed nothing, and who shared Karsten's long nose and firm chin. Karsten's father, her husband, had died of blood poisoning from an infected cut, an accident that had left the throne unexpectedly empty, and Lady Hafren either hadn't been strong enough to overcome the Balsian prejudice against women to rule herself or hadn't been willing to try, for the then-teenage Karsten had been anointed prince only a few days after his father's funeral, with Lady Hafren as his primary adviser. She wore a thin circlet of silver on her brow as a symbol of her office, while the prince wore one of gold. So far, Karsten had weathered both the Stane immigration and the attack on the city by the harbormaster, and had shown himself to be a capable, if inexperienced, prince who was prone to a shockingly informal court that drove many of the older courtiers into conniptions.

"I'd already heard about the demonstration outside of Grick's temple," Karsten said toward the end of Danr's story, "but this—"

"You heard about it, but did nothing?" Aisa broke in.

Danr winced. Aisa had interrupted the prince. But as the city's savior, she was allowed a certain amount of latitude.

Karsten's face grew more serious and he looked more adult than Danr had ever seen him. "There's a lot of

resentment on the streets, Aisa. People—the human ones—
are nervous about all the changes. The Stane were a lot to
get used to, no matter how much we love Danr here. Now
we're adding shape magic and more half-bloods. People are
scared they won't know how to survive in this new world,
and it makes them want to shout and scream. If I let them
demonstrate, they feel they've been heard and they feel better. If I gag them, their anger builds. That leads to fights,
and fights lead to revolutions."

"And when people are hurt in those fights?" Aisa said.
"What then?"

"Someone will eventually be hurt, yes," Karsten said.
"It's the way it goes. Either the protesters will hurt some-
one, or the guards will hurt the protesters, or a riot will hurt
everyone. I'm trying to keep it to as few hurts as possible.
And," he added pointedly, "I don't need to justify how I run
Balsia to you."

"Of course not, Highness," Danr said quickly, before
Aisa could speak again. "And that's not why we're here. We
thought that the crown might want to handle this man Welk.
The toads were an accident." And Danr explained what had
happened while the knot of toads hopped and skittered
about the room, filling it with croaks and goggly eyes. Welk
looked very much as though he wanted to lie down. His
hands were shaky and his skin looked clammy.

"He changed all these citizens into toads," Karsten
repeated toward the end of Danr's story. "Can he change
them back?"

"Not that we've seen," Danr said, shifting a little.

"This . . . *man* changed more than forty innocent people
into toads?" Lady Hafren took up a spot beside her son and
folded her arms. "He should be imprisoned! Hanged in the
square for this horrible crime!"

Welk's already pale face went even whiter at this. Danr
became afraid the man might faint. Ranadar and Talfi
traded looks, and the croaking grew even louder.

"I do not believe killing Welk is really the best—" Ranadar began.

"This court does not take advice from the Fae," Hafren interrupted. "And certainly not from a traitor to his own kind."

"Now, look," Talfi said hotly. "It was thanks to this *traitor* that everyone in this room is alive right now."

"Says the *regi* boy who consorts with half-bloods and shape mages," Hafren retorted. "Our city is becoming corrupted with people like—"

"Me?" Kalessa also interrupted. "You forget yourself, lady. I am princess of the Third Nest, and I have feasted with Grick herself."

"Which means nothing in this room," Hafren snapped. "You wyrm-riders leave trails of slime wherever you—"

"Quiet!" Danr roared.

Shocked, the entire room fell silent. Even the toads stopped croaking. All eyes turned to Danr, as if only now understanding how close they stood to the tall and powerful half troll who had nearly torn the world in half. Danr's mouth went dry under all those eyes, but he wasn't going to back down now.

"We didn't bring Welk here to have him executed," Danr said in an even voice. "I don't know if changing someone into a toad is even a crime."

"If it isn't," Hafren said, sniffing, "it soon—"

Danr gave a half snarl, and she fell silent again. "I already said that the toads were an accident, and we'll figure out what to do about them. Meantime, we brought Welk here to help both him and the crown."

"How?" Karsten asked.

"Someone who can turn men into toads at a distance would be a great asset to the army," Aisa said. "Would he not?"

A small stir went through the court at that. Karsten frowned thoughtfully.

"General?" he said.

An older man dressed head to foot in Balsia ocean blue trimmed with gold stepped forward. "Obviously, he would. The army doesn't have any shape mages in it yet, and I've been wondering what'll happen if we go up against someone who has them."

"Then I believe you have your first volunteer," Kalessa said.

"He's a bandit!" Lady Hafren protested. "Like all shape mages! Untrustworthy!"

Aisa turned hard brown eyes on her. "Lady, are you saying that *I* am untrustworthy? I am the first shape mage, after all."

"I am saying—" Hafren said.

"This gets us nowhere, Mother," Karsten said, exasperated. "Look, I already said it's damn scary having shape mages and Stane and orcs and even Fae in the city these days. But it's also a damn good thing we still have a city to be scared in. Eventually, we'll sort it out, but for now I want these Vik-damned toads out of my court!"

"Very pragmatic, Your Highness," said the general.

"I may be able to help," Aisa said, "if Lady Hafren will not be too offended at shape mages performing magic in her august presence."

"Aisa," Danr warned.

When Hafren only pursed her lips, Aisa turned to Welk, who looked as though he would rather be trotting across hot lava just now.

"Welk," she said, "have you ever tried to turn one of your toads back into a human?"

He nodded. "Course."

"Why weren't you able to do it?"

"The power," he said simply. "It weren't enough. Changing into toads is easy, lady, but turning back takes more power, and I don't have it. I can change one or two, but after that, I'm dead. I'm about ready to drop right now."

"How did you change forty, then?" Karsten asked.

"I don't know, Your Highness," Welk whispered. "I panicked and got strong, but now I've got nothing. I'll be drained for days."

"Yesterday evening, you used your power twice, Welk," Aisa said. "That should have exhausted your magic, but I took a lot more from you to help Danr change his shape. And you turned more than forty people into toads when you panicked. You have more power than you are allowing yourself to use."

"What do you mean?" Welk asked in his soft voice while the court looked on with great interest.

Aisa touched his arm. "A great deal of magic is tied to your personal belief—your belief about what is possible, or your belief about yourself. You see yourself as weak and small, and this belief keeps your power weak and small. But there are times, such as when you fear for your life, that your true strength shows through. You need only find it."

"It sounds like a long and painstaking process," Kalessa said.

"Perhaps," Aisa replied. The toads had gone utterly still as little brown stones, watching the conversation in eerie silence. "But there is another way. Welk, there are two main sources of power for a shape mage. One is the shape mage's own self. This is very expensive and tiring, as you have already felt. Another is to take power from other shape mages from whom you have taken blood. Once a drop of their blood runs through your veins, you can borrow their power. It is easier if you are touching the other mage, and it is easier still if the other mage has changed shape. This is how legends of vampires and familiars began, and this is the best source of power."

"I didn't know this," Karsten breathed.

Aisa held out a hand to Kalessa, who used her mystic knife to prick Aisa's fingertip. Aisa showed Welk the scarlet drop. "We will use this."

"Aisa!" Danr stepped between her and Welk. "We spread the first form of shape magic with our own blood."

"He has already become a shape mage through contact with someone else's blood," Aisa said. "This will not change that."

"Is that how it happened?" Welk burst out. "That dog who bit me was a shape mage who gave me this power?"

"Only because you have shape magic in your blood already," Kalessa said. "Some distant ancestor who could control shapes before the Sundering. The blood of another shape mage woke it up, and now you have it. You can spread it yourself, if you like."

"Why doesn't anyone tell us these things?" Welk cried.

"We are telling you now," Aisa said. "Open."

Reluctantly, Welk opened his mouth. Aisa let a single blood droplet fall on his tongue.

The room exploded with light. Pain lanced through Danr's head again, and again he threw up a hand to shield his eyes. The prince and the court shouted and shrieked. Danr blinked hard. When his eyesight cleared, he saw Welk, now standing tall and strong. Aisa was next to him, looking surprised. And in the corner huddled a frightened group of more than forty naked men and women, the people who had charged the carriage.

A silence filled the room. The court stared at the naked folk. The naked folk stared at the court.

"Wow," said Talfi.

Chaos broke through the room. The naked people frantically tried to cover themselves. Some members of the court tried to toss them cloaks or other loose articles of clothing while other courtiers babbled excitedly. At Karsten's quick command, two servants bustled about the room, herding the men one way and the woman another to find clothing for them and escort them out of the Gold Keep.

"I believe you now have both your court magician and an invaluable new recruit for your army," Aisa told the slightly dazed prince.

The group of them made hasty excuses and fled. Karsten and Lady Hafren didn't try to stop them.

Once they were outside and a safe distance from the keep, Ranadar and Kalessa both halted and rounded on Aisa. "What happened?" they demanded in one voice.

"I am unsure," Aisa said slowly.

"I know," Danr said. "Without even using my true eye, I know."

"Then spill it," Talfi said.

"She's becoming a Gardener," Danr said in a sad voice. "Slowly, but it's happening, yeah? Her blood is more powerful now than it ever was. Welk tasted it, and boom! His power leaped ahead. He doesn't need to borrow from Aisa—she gave him a lot of it permanently. And she isn't even tired."

"But I can feel him still," Aisa said.

"Can he . . . feed off you?" Kalessa said, worried.

Aisa shook her head. "The blood bond is powerful, but not omnipotent. I am still stronger than he, so Welk cannot take power unless I allow it." She took Danr's hand. "We will work through this, my Hamzu."

"Will we?" he burst out. "It's coming. Every day it's coming closer, and I don't see any way to solve it."

"What are they talking about?" Talfi muttered to Kalessa.

"They're worried that if Aisa becomes a Gardener, they will be unable to remain a couple," Kalessa said, and caught Danr staring at her. "What?"

"We only talked about it last night for the first time," he said.

Kalessa said, "You do know that Aisa tells me everything. Often before she tells herself."

"What is *that* supposed to mean?" Danr demanded.

"Vik!" Talfi smacked his forehead. "*That's* why you're worried. Aisa will be immortal, and Danr will be . . ."

"Not," Danr sighed.

"It does seem unfair," Ranadar said. "For the two of you to go through all that you have and then lose each other in the end."

"Maybe we can ask Death," Talfi said. "It's not like she doesn't like us. Or owe us."

"Death has limited power here," Aisa said. "She can take life but cannot grant it. You and Ranadar, of all people, know that."

"What if once you become a Gardener and have infinite days, Death gives you half of them, like she gave me half of Ranadar's?" Talfi persisted. "Half of infinity is still infinity, right?"

Danr snorted. "I don't think it works that way for an immortal."

"We are getting nowhere with this," Ranadar said. "In the meantime, we have other problems to solve. We must find Talfi's candle wax man, and also fetch the Bone Sword from Queen Vesha."

"We can't do both at the same time," Talfi objected.

"Why is it so urgent that you find the candle wax man?" Aisa asked. "He could wait."

Talfi violently shook his head. "He looks exactly like *me*. And I'm the only thousand-year-old person in the world. He might know something about my past, or somehow be . . . me. I need to find him. Before he leaves town or runs away forever."

"And I will aid him," Ranadar added. "In any case, as a Fae, I would not be welcome in Queen Vesha's kingdom, so I cannot seek the Bone Sword with you."

"Are you saying we should split into groups?" Danr asked.

"It looks wisest," Ranadar said.

Danr thought about that. "We would be dividing our power."

"But doubling our speed," Ranadar replied.

"The entrance to Vesha's kingdom is in northern Balsia," Danr said. "It'll take weeks to get there."

"Perhaps Ranadar could Twist us," Aisa began hesitantly.

"That distance is beyond me," Ranadar said. "You would almost certainly arrive without an arm or a leg. Or a head."

Danr shuddered. "Thanks, but no."

"We will ride Slynd," Kalessa said. "He can easily carry three. On wyrm-back, it will take a week, perhaps less."

"That decides it, then," Aisa said. "Ranadar and Talfi will stay here and try to find this candle wax man. Learn where he came from and why he is here. Hamzu and Kalessa and I will take Slynd to see Queen Vesha about the Bone Sword."

"Let's just hope she's gotten over that whole cursed-by-Death thing," Talfi said.

"And that we can find one man in a city of more than a million," Ranadar added.

Talfi spread his hands. "How hard could it be?"

Chapter Eight

"All right, it's pretty hard," Talfi admitted.

Ranadar set down the arrow—bronze-tipped— and picked up another. They were sitting in the walled courtyard beside Mrs. Farley's boardinghouse, where she kept a small garden and even a struggling rose arbor. Several quivers' worth of arrows lay spilled across the dirt at the foot of the latter. Ranadar sighted along the second arrow, checking for imperfections.

"What is hard?" he asked.

Talfi chewed a thumbnail. Normally, he would have liked sitting in the shade of the arbor, doing nothing truly important, as long as he could do nothing important with Ranadar. The soft afternoon light gave the elf's scarlet hair a startling luminescence, and his ivy green eyes sighted down the arrow with inhuman concentration. He was handsome and kind and it pierced Talfi's heart when they were separated. He liked nothing more than to slip into bed at night with him and let their bodies mold together. Sometimes he felt he could stay like that for days. And now, for the first time in his life, he had managed to keep a long string of memories, and many of them in some way involved Ranadar—or Danr. But he wasn't in love with Danr.

Lately, he had been wondering what it would be like to spend multiple centuries gathering memories. Elves were born ready to live eight hundred years or more. Humans . . . weren't. Talfi was the longest-living person on Erda, but he remembered very little of his thousand-plus years, and he supposed that was how he had coped. Now that he didn't lose his memory every time he died, would he be able to handle living until Ranadar died? And how long would that be, anyway? Ranadar was just under four hundred years old and had—what?—another four hundred left, so with Death dividing time between him and Talfi, the two of them probably had two or two and a half centuries left.

That didn't actually seem very long, when Talfi considered it. Not when he considered living over a thousand, or the fact that Aisa would live only the Nine knew how long as a Gardener. Still, two hundred fifty years was more than Talfi had any right to hope for. It was way more than any other human got.

But none of this found them the candle wax man.

They'd been looking for three days now. They had hired people to help look, had offered rewards, had personally scoured the streets until Talfi's legs ached and Ranadar's lips pursed with frustration. Nothing. Today, Ranadar had decreed they would take a few hours to themselves, though in Ranadar's case, that seemed to involve checking equipment as well as sitting quietly in the garden. Ranadar seemed to have trouble doing nothing, something Talfi never understood.

He drew a heart in the earth by his knee, then made a face and stabbed it with one of the arrows.

"You will ruin the tip," Ranadar admonished. "And what is hard?"

Talfi churlishly stabbed the heart one more time, then set the arrow down. "All this searching. I'm getting tired of it."

"Patience was never one of your strong suits," Ranadar said. "Perhaps the Nine are trying to teach you some."

"Sure. After a thousand years of being a plaything of the Nine, I'm ready to learn more from them."

Ranadar looked nervously about. "You break my heart when you speak that way. We of all people know the Nine have a way of—"

"Let's go." Talfi stood up and dusted his hands.

Ranadar glanced up at him, then meticulously gathered up the arrows and hung the quiver from his belt. He took up one bow and handed the other to Talfi.

"What are these for?" Talfi asked.

"After we search at the market, we can try more target practice." Ranadar smiled his quiet, woodland smile, the one that always went straight through him. "Perhaps this time you can teach me."

The market was its usual bustle and rush. Ranadar wore his hood up to hide his Fae heritage as they moved from stall to stall, pretending to shop but actually watching for anyone with odd features. They saw spice sellers and salt-mongers and bakers' carts and merchants who sold a dozen kinds of cooking oil. They paused at a man who was trying to sell a rune-encrusted clay golem—"Barely used! Transfer control with just a bit of Stane blood! Take any reasonable offer!"—and moved on. They passed the old slave market, with its stalls and its iron rings driven into the walls and stone floor. No one used the space. Not yet. Slavery had become illegal in the city-state of Balsia just last year, and to everyone's surprise, the economy had not collapsed. It had instead thrived. The former slaves were now hired workers who earned money, which they spent freely at the markets. This, in turn, made the merchants wealthier and allowed them to expand their businesses and hire more employees. The only people who weren't happy were the former slave owners, who were forced to pay people they had once given nothing but food and shelter, but Prince Karsten had once pointed out to Talfi that they, too, would feel the positive effects of former slaves who spent money. It would just take a little longer.

* * *

The colors, smells, and sounds of the market square swirled in a cacophony that made Talfi a little dizzy. After an hour of fruitless searching, however, he pulled Ranadar into a space between two stalls for a breather. The quiver of arrows banged at Talfi's waist.

"We'll never find anyone this way," he said. "We need to narrow it down, even just a little."

"How?" Ranadar countered.

Talfi chewed the inside of his cheek. "When you touched the candle wax man, you felt his mind and knew he was me."

"I did," Ranadar said slowly.

"Can you find him that way? Feel his mind?"

"I am . . . unsure," Ranadar said. "Touching his mind was a surprise. It was like touching yours, and it caught me off guard."

"When did you touch my mind?" Talfi said in surprise.

Now Ranadar looked surprised. "I always touch your mind. Whenever I touch you, I touch your mind."

"You read my *thoughts*?" Talfi spluttered. "You—"

"No." Ranadar shook his head. "That is, I *could*, if I pushed, but I would not without your permission, and you would probably know I was there. Anyway, touching is not reading. My mind recognizes you when you are near me just like my eyes see you coming and my ears hear your approach. Iron and other barriers can stop this, but I cannot shut it off any more than I can stop my ears."

"Oh." Talfi touched his arm. "So you know this is me?"

"Of course." Ranadar blinked at him. "How do you Kin go through life half-blind? I cannot imagine not being able to sense the people I know this way."

A little excitement grew in Talfi's chest. "Does this only work with people you know, then?"

"Yes."

"What if you pushed?" Talfi persisted. "What if you

pushed hard and looked for . . . me? Could you find me? Other versions of me?"

"Oh! I could try, though there is a great deal of iron about, and that makes it difficult."

"Try!"

Ranadar closed his eyes. The shouts and cries and rumbles of the market square continued past the stalls. The merchant to their left got into a heated debate with a customer over the price of a bottle of scented oil.

"Can I do anything to help?" Talfi asked.

"Just be silent," Ranadar replied with a look of intense concentration hardening his face. After a moment, he held out his hand. Talfi took it without hesitation.

The world Twisted. Everything, including Ranadar, vanished, and Talfi was floating in cool velvet darkness. For a dreadful moment, nothing happened. Lights flickered and flared all about him. Human-shaped lights. Hundreds of them. Thousands! Talfi could see through them like ghosts, and he couldn't recognize their features, or even tell if they were male or female. A few beneath his feet flared dark blue—Stane. Wonder washed over him. Was this how Ranadar saw the world when his eyes were closed?

One light flickered in the distance, drawing Talfi's attention. He stared at it, and all at once Talfi *knew* it was . . . himself, in the same way he knew his own reflection. That flicker must be the man they were—

Another light flared to life, this one closer and off to the right. Talfi spun. That light was also Talfi. Another flared. And another. And another. They popped into existence like flowers bursting open across a spring meadow. Talfi stared in a mixture of fear and disbelief. Were all these lights versions of him?

He felt a vague tug on his hand. The darkness twisted again, and Talfi was standing next to Ranadar between the market stalls. Ranadar's green eyes were wide and wild.

"How many of you are there?" he said.

"That was my question." Talfi twisted around, as if he might see one of . . . *them*. "Where—?"

"There's one—two—this way." Ranadar grabbed Talfi's arm and towed him through the market. They threaded their way through the crowd—all human, since the sun was still up—until they came to a dark alley so smelly with garbage and urine it made Talfi's eyes water.

"The trolls can't dig those new sewers fast enough," he muttered, trying to peer into the gloom. "And have you heard the rumors? That they're digging all the way to Glumenhame?"

"Just go," Ranadar said, and pushed him forward.

Talfi stepped in something that squished. His heart fluttered fast in his chest, and tension knotted his stomach. The bricks slipped beneath his feet, and the still air hung heavy around him. This was stupid. What was he afraid of? He knew how to fight, and anyway, he couldn't die. Not yet.

But he could be in for a hell of a lot of pain. A broken leg or a dislocated jaw wouldn't kill him, but it would knock him flat for weeks of agony.

Two ragged figures loomed in the shadows. Curiosity overpowered dread. Talfi moved toward them. "Hey!" he called.

The figures spun, tense. Then they caught sight of Talfi's face and instantly relaxed. One of them moved closer, into a ray of sunlight that illuminated half his face. Talfi's heart skipped and he heard Ranadar gasp behind him. It was like looking in a mirror. The man looked like—was—him. The brown hair that curled over his forehead was Talfi's. The sky blue eye was also his. The firm chin, the long jaw—all Talfi's. They were exactly the same height and build. Even his ears were shaped the same. Or the ear that Talfi could see was the same.

"What is it?" the young man asked. He had Talfi's voice.

Talfi's tongue froze in his mouth like a block of ice. Chills ran ghostly hands up and down his skin. He couldn't think. His mind had utterly stopped.

The young man moved forward, and the light illuminated more of his face. His melted face. Talfi touched his own face, half expecting to feel unnatural, stretched skin. The second figure remained in the shadows, but his height and build were Talfi's as well. Talfi's own skin crawled around his body like cold worms.

"What is it?" the first man asked again.

"I . . . ," Talfi managed. "Are you . . . ?"

The head of an arrow slid over Talfi's shoulder. Ranadar was aiming straight at the man's heart. "Who in Vik's damned name are you?"

Both men froze. The second man made an inarticulate gargling sound. The candle wax man's mouth fell open. "Ranadar?" he said. "Ran?"

"Ran?" echoed the shadowy second man. His voice was rough as a cat's cough.

The arrowhead jerked. Talfi's hands and feet were ice. "Who are you?" Talfi said hoarsely. "How do you know us?"

"Know you?" the candle-wax man said, clearly himself shocked and puzzled. "We're . . . wait. You're . . . you're *Talfi*."

"I know who I am," Talfi said. "Who are you?"

More gargling sounds emerged from the shadowy man's throat. He slid forward into the light. His face was scarred even worse, and his body was more twisted. Still, it was clear he was also Talfi. One of his eyes was melted shut, but his good eye, wide and sky blue, stared at Ranadar with something like adoration. Talfi's stomach twisted.

"Who *are* you?" he demanded yet again. "Both of you?"

"I'm . . . you," the candle wax man said. "Talfi."

"Where did you come from?" Ranadar's arrow had steadied now, and his voice carried steel. "Speak, or this arrow will find your heart."

The second man abruptly spun and fled, trailing his

ragged cloak. His footsteps squished and thudded into the dark distance. Ranadar's fingers tensed around the arrow, but he didn't loose it.

"You won't shoot him," the candle wax man said. "Any more than you would shoot me. It would be putting an arrow in your own heart, Ran."

"Stop calling him that!" Talfi burst out.

The candle wax man reached out and took Talfi's unresisting hand in his own. It was a moment of perfect symmetry, like holding his own hands but being unable to feel them. It was the strangest sensation of Talfi's life, and he recalled getting his neck broken by a giant squid. "I remember you. I know you. I *am* you. Talfi. My name is Talfi."

"How?" Ranadar withdrew the arrow but didn't relax his guard. "Talfi was born before the Sundering. He has died countless times and come back to life. You cannot be him."

"I . . . remember that," the man said, his hands still gripping Talfi's. "I remember being held down on the altar, and I remember my father turning away and I remember the trollwife raising her knife."

Talfi's knees felt like rotten bread dough. "How do you know that?" he whispered. "No one knows that. No one except—"

"Danr and Aisa and Ranadar," said the other man. "And Grandfather Wyrm."

Ranadar sheathed the arrow and set the bow across his shoulders. "I need to examine you. And I do not wish to do it in a urine-soaked alley."

Talfi became aware that he was still holding the other man's hands, and he snatched them away. "Where, then?"

"Our room at the boardinghouse," Ranadar stated firmly. "For privacy."

"What makes you think I'll come with you?" the other man countered.

"You will come." Ranadar turned and stalked away. A

moment later, Talfi followed. A moment after that, the candle wax man followed, too.

Talfi sat on the bed and watched while Ranadar examined the other man. It was like seeing a road accident. He didn't want to watch, but he couldn't help it. The other man stood a few paces away, his dirty, ragged clothes hanging off his body, and he looked, moved, and even breathed like Talfi his own self. And yet . . . he didn't. There was the melted look of his face, of course, but there was another quality about him that Talfi couldn't quite put a finger to. Perhaps it was the pulse jumping at his throat seemed a little off, or that his hair didn't curl quite right, or that his left arm seemed a fraction longer than his right. Or maybe it was just Talfi's imagination. His stomach turned.

Ranadar, meanwhile, conducted his examination with a strange thoroughness that seemed almost . . . intimate. He didn't actually touch the other man, but he ran his palms over the man's body a bare inch above his skin with his eyes closed. His hands glowed with a faint yellow light, and his breath stirred the other man's hair. Talfi felt hot and scratchy and tense. The other man met Talfi's eyes, and Talfi wanted to crawl away. The mirror was looking back at him and telling him that he himself was the reflection.

"You need to tell us where you came from," Talfi said. "No more of this 'I am Talfi' garbage."

"I have gaps in my memory," the candle wax man confessed in Talfi's voice. "I remember—"

"No," Talfi interrupted. "I want to know how you're so strong and why Kalessa's sword didn't hurt you in the market square and how you came into existence. You and . . . the other one of you. Of me."

"I . . . want to tell you," said the candle wax man. "But I can't. I'm not allowed."

"Not allowed?" Ranadar repeated. "By whom?"

"I can't say that, either," he said. "I wish I could, but I can't. You can threaten me or hurt me or do anything else you want, but I can't say."

Talfi didn't like the sound of that at all, and from the looks of it, neither did Ranadar. Best to try from another angle, then.

"You know Danr and Aisa and Ran," Talfi said. "And me."

"Well, yeah. I didn't expect to see you in the market like that, though," the other man said as Ranadar, tight-lipped, knelt to run his hands down one leg.

"Who were you expecting to see?" Talfi countered.

"No one. I mean . . ." He shook his scarred head. "It's confusing. I remember a lot about my life. Our life. But I know that I'm not you. Except I *am*, because I remember everything."

Talfi had no idea what this meant, so he changed the subject again. "Who were you talking to in the alley?"

"I was talking to . . . I guess he's my brother." The other man seemed genuinely puzzled, as if he had never put these concepts into words before now.

"He looked like you—me—us," Talfi said. "But even more melted. And Ranadar saw a lot of others just like you both."

"Yes." The candle wax man swallowed. "Look, I know this is confusing. It's confusing to me. I'm in this city, and I know my friends Danr and Kalessa and Aisa are here somewhere, but they don't know me."

Talfi forced himself to get up and look the candle wax man straight in the face. Ranadar continued his own examination. Talfi stared at the man's eyes, the man's hair, his stretched and glistening skin. The candle wax man bore this in silence. Then Talfi noticed something. The skin on the scarred left side wasn't as taut as he remembered. The cheek muscles had filled out a little bit, and the scars on the ear had definitely smoothed out.

"Is your *face* healing?" Talfi said incredulously.

The candle wax man put his unscarred right hand to his face. "I don't know. Is it?"

"Your scars are definitely getting better." Talfi didn't know whether he should be fascinated or horrified.

"That's good, right?" The candle wax man held up his left hand. It had improved as well.

Talfi sat back on the bed. "How did you get the scars?"

"I've always had them." He sighed while Ranadar ran a hand over his foot. "I don't know where they came from or why I have them. But I know my name is Talfi because *your* name is Talfi and you're the First."

"The First?" Talfi repeated.

"The first one of us," the man explained as Ranadar, now looking pale, came up his leg.

Talfi was ready to hit something in disgust and frustration. "What does that *mean*?"

"It means," Ranadar said standing up, "that this man is a golem."

Then he snatched up the chamber pot and vomited into it. Startled, Talfi handed him a glass of water from the pitcher on the washstand. The other Talfi moved to help Ranadar to a chair, but Ranadar waved him away, and the other Talfi dropped his hands, looking awkward.

"Are you all right, Ran? What do you mean he's a golem?" Talfi asked.

"Made of flesh instead of clay," Ranadar said. "But a golem, nonetheless. The runes that grant him life are drawn with blood vessels under his skin, and the blood smear that binds him to his owner is hidden with a glamour that I cannot break, so he looks human, but he is definitely a golem."

"That's why you're so strong," Talfi said. "And why Kalessa's sword didn't hurt you."

The other Talfi shrugged.

"He would have all those abilities," Ranadar said, his

face still a little green. "The flesh is not quite alive. It is
a . . . copy. Stabbing it is like stabbing dead meat. Watch."
With elven quickness, he drew his bronze knife and
stabbed the other Talfi in the side. Talfi gasped and touched
his own side in unconscious sympathy.

"Hey!" the other man said. "What was that for?"

Ranadar pulled out his knife. There was no blood—
only a soft sucking sound that turned Talfi's stomach and a
hole in the side of the other man's tunic. Through it, Talfi
saw the bloodless slit in the flesh. Ranadar sheathed his
knife. "See? The magic gives him life. Of a sort. I think
the magic that made him was imperfect, but it is healing
him bit by bit even as we speak."

"And why did you throw up?" the other man asked, running his fingertips over the small opening.

"The magic." Ranadar closed his eyes a moment.
"Touching it was like . . . dragging my tongue through
manure. I would rather climb into that chamber pot than
do it again."

"Gosh, thanks," said the other man in an exact echo of
Talfi's own voice and tone. His words were glib, but Talfi
caught a hint of pain behind them, and the other man's sky
blue eyes softened when he looked at Ranadar. Talfi set his
mouth.

"I do not blame you," Ranadar said to him. "You are
who you are, through no fault of your own."

"And who is that?" Talfi demanded.

"I'm me, but I'm made out of you, Talfi," the other Talfi
said. "It's why I look like you and sound like you. The
same's true of the others."

Talfi was glad he was already sitting down. His legs
wouldn't have supported him if he'd been standing. "How
can you be made from me? Who made all of you?"

But even as he asked the question, he realized he knew
the answer. It slid down the back of his head, cold and
sharp as an icicle. His eyes met Ranadar's, and the horror

in them told Talfi that the same cold idea had come to
Ranadar as well.

"He can't tell us," Ranadar said slowly. "His maker forbade him to say. But I think we both know who it is."

"Your mother," Talfi whispered. "Queen Gwylph of
Alfhame."

Chapter Nine

A red moon was just rising over the monastery walls when the first creature leaped at Danr. It illuminated the darkening village road that slipped past the monastery and gleamed off the feathers and scales of the beast. It had the head of an eagle and the body of a mountain lion. A hissing snake grew from between its shoulder blades. Behind it stomped a seven-foot tree with human arms covered in bark. A bull with the hindquarters of a giant wolf bellowed and pawed the earth while an entire flock of red canaries with ferocious teeth and long, shiny claws swirled toward them, tearing the air with high-pitched shrieks.

With a grunt, Danr caught the eagle-lion and fell backward. The eagle-lion snapped the air with its beak. Danr kicked hard with his knees. The creature flew over his head, but a sharp pain pierced his shoulder—the snake bit him as it shot by. The eagle-lion flew several yards down the village street, screeching and hissing as it went.

Kalessa's blade flicked into a gleaming great sword. Her battle cry rent the early-night sky as she charged the bull monster. It bellowed again, lowered its horns, and charged in turn. The two thundered toward each other, horns and sword held high. Seconds before they would have smashed into each other, Kalessa leaped high and somersaulted between the beast's horns. Her sword stabbed down, catching the creature between its ribs and spearing its heart. It bellowed in pain and crashed to the dusty road. Unfortunately, the motion wrenched the hilt out of Kalessa's grip. She stumbled away from the convulsing corpse without her weapon.

Slynd was having difficulties of his own. The fifteen-foot tree thing stormed at him while the red canaries swooped down in a chittering horde. The tree swatted at him with a heavy, branchlike arm. Slynd curled out of the way, but the canaries also slashed and sliced his hide with their razor claws and teeth. The tree brought down a massive foot before Slynd could eel aside, and it caught him behind the head. His body lashed and squirmed, but the tree was too heavy.

"The abbess wants their blood!" shouted a woman's voice from atop the monastery wall. "Bring them inside, precious ones!"

Danr didn't spare the monastery wall a glance, but he noted the words. Whoever was up there wanted them alive, and that gave him an advantage. He rolled to his feet, his arm burning where the snake had bitten him. No time for fear. No time for thought. Leaving the unbalanced eagle-lion behind, he charged at the tree. With a great roar, he crashed straight into it. The shock jarred his spine and creaked his ribs. The tree stood still for a moment with Slynd's neck pinned beneath its knobby foot. Then it creaked slowly backward. Its great arms made slow circles, but balance eluded it. The tree crashed to the road. Its arms waved helplessly in the air.

"Aisa!" Danr clutched at his burning shoulder. Was the poison deadly, despite the woman's orders? "Aisa! Where are you?"

Slynd snapped at the canaries, which continued to slash at him. Kalessa leaped back to the dying bull-wolf and reached for her sword hilt, but the creature's death throes wrenched the blade back and forth. She couldn't catch it. A hissing screech behind Danr told him the eagle-lion had recovered and was readying itself to pounce again. He spun to face it.

"Aisa!" he shouted.

"Get the orc!" called another voice, a man's this time. "Bring her!"

Why did the monastery want them? The eagle-lion leaped again, but this time it was going for Kalessa, who was a few paces away. Danr waited until it was nearly on him, then punched it between the eyes. Or tried to. Even as he swung his fist toward the eagle's head, the strength drained out of him. The punch missed entirely. Danr went to hands and knees, recognizing the feeling.

"Aisa," he gasped. "Not now!"

But it was too late. His strength was nearly gone.

The eagle-lion's arc carried it toward Kalessa, but she saw it coming. She managed at the last moment to grasp the sword hilt. Instantly, it flicked into its knife form, freeing it from its prison of dead monster flesh. Kalessa flung herself to the ground. The eagle-lion sailed over her, missing her by inches. But just as it had for Danr, the serpent's head lashed down and stung her shoulder.

Slynd was still snapping at the red canaries that tormented him. They opened up weeping wounds on his side and back. He had managed to dispatch perhaps half of them. The ground shook with his rumblings and squirmings.

Aisa burst from between two village houses in the form of a tusked elephant twice as tall as Slynd and heavier than any creature Danr had ever seen. Darkness gathered at the edges of Danr's vision, and his limbs grew heavy. Aisa trumpeted and thundered toward the eagle-lion. It gathered itself. Kalessa staggered, looking as tired as Danr felt. What was going on? If Aisa had taken power from him, they shouldn't both be—

The poison. The poison was sending him to sleep.

Aisa rushed at the eagle-lion, and this time the creature gave ground. It scrambled aside, dodging her trampling feet. Aisa overran and whirled in an impossible move that sent her sprawling. In midfall she changed into a great falcon that swooped in a tight arc and shot back toward the eagle-lion. Slynd continued to lash at the flock of red canaries. Sleep came over Danr in warm waves. He tried to fight it one more time, but his eyes were heavy, so heavy. They slid shut just as Aisa reached her foe.

The soft light of late-afternoon sat pleasantly on Danr's head, and he sighed with relief as he pressed his back against the rough bark of an ash tree. He could still smell the foul undercurrent of rot in the Garden, but it was still beautiful in its strange chaos. It felt as if he could sit here forever. Infinite colors both bright and muted exploded in all directions. Vegetables mingled with flowers mingled with leaves mingled with vines, and it was all just as it should be. Except for the rot, of course. Without giving thought to how he had come to this place or why, Danr leaned down to examine some of the plants at his feet with the experienced eye of a farmer. Root rot had invaded some of them. These two were in danger. That one was a lost cause. Perhaps if he uprooted it, he could stop it from infecting the ones around it. He pulled it out with a sharp jerk, revealing slimy, dying roots. A tiny scream thinned and died in the still air.

"Is someone here?" It was Nu's voice. She was only a few yards away, around the other side of the tree with her bag of seeds.

"Is someone there?" That was Tan, nearby with her hoe.

Danr froze, the plant still in his hand. He was a farmer, the son of a thrall. What business did he have mucking with the Garden?

"It is I." Aisa stood up from among the plants, holding a small sickle. "I am working."

Danr stared. What was *she* doing here? For that matter, what was *he* doing here? He tried to remember what he had last been doing, but nothing came to him.

"That is good, sister," said Nu.

"That is helpful, sister," said Tan.

"That is true," said Aisa.

"Have you found the Bone Sword yet?" asked Nu. "Our vision is so clouded now we can barely see beyond our noses."

"Our hands," added Tan.

"Our feet," said Aisa, "are carrying us to see Queen Vesha even now. But . . . something has happened to delay us. A bit. Though what it is, I cannot remember."

"Recall," said Tan.

"Recollect," finished Nu. "You are mortal still, and the Garden plays tricks. And you are asleep, so this seems much like a dream."

"A vision," added Tan.

"A hallucination," breathed Aisa.

"Yes." Nu shifted her bag, and several seeds fell from it, unheeded. Tiny plants sprouted at her feet, but half of them turned black and died. "In a dream, you know what you need to know and nothing more. We are so glad to see you, sister. But now it appears you will leave us."

"Leave?" said Aisa. "I do not understand. Why would I—"

Icy water sloshed over Danr. He bolted awake with a gasp. Cold stones ground into his back. He tried to get to his feet but found he was chained to a wall by both wrists and ankles. A man in a dark cloak was standing over him with a bucket.

"He's awake, Abbess," the man said.

Danr shook his head, trying to clear it. The last thing he remembered was being in the Garden. No. The last thing he remembered was fighting monsters with—

"Aisa!" he shouted, pulling at the heavy chains. "Where is she?"

The man pointed. A few yards away stood a cage made of layers of heavy bars and wiry mesh. The bars were too heavy for any animal to bend and the mesh was too fine for any creature to slip through—a cage made for a shape-shifter. In a motionless heap in the center lay a naked Aisa. A few feet to Danr's left, Kalessa was also clamped to the wall, though her chains weren't as heavy. In front of her was a great bundle wound in canvas and tied down with ropes. It looked like a giant dumpling. The bundle trembled and shuddered but otherwise was clearly unable to go anywhere, and it took Danr a moment to realize that the thing was Slynd, wound up and tied down. Aisa, though, wasn't moving.

"If you've hurt Aisa," Danr snarled at the man, "I'll rip both your arms off and beat your skull in with them!"

The man backed up a step but otherwise failed to respond. They seemed to be in a ring of great ash trees whose papery leaves reached upward for the silver moon that coasted far above them. Little ropes and chains hung from the trees, testament to the animal sacrifices made there, and small piles of fragrant ashes among the roots told of old prayers burned with incense. Cut grass within the ring formed a velvet carpet and threw up its springtime scent. The night air was chilly, and the full moon had climbed high into a starry sky. The monastery wall formed one side of the grove, and it was to this that Danr was chained.

In the center of the grove sat a . . . thing. Danr could see it only now that the bucket man had moved out of the way. The thing was the size of a cart horse, and it had no shape. It seemed to be a messy, mottled blob of flesh. It had no eyes, no ears, no arms or legs. Just pale, blotchy skin and a few stray hairs. The thing quivered and made a squelching sound like someone stepping on moldy grapes. Danr's stomach turned over, as if he had put his hand into a pile of dog manure.

"What in Vik's name is that?" he said.

"Patience, child," said a new voice. "It is the truth-teller's duty to answer questions, not ask them."

The voice twisted a chill down Danr's back. Vik's balls, it wasn't possible. From between the trees came a woman in a long dark cloak in a style similar to the bucket man's, but hers was also sprinkled with silver stars and edged with brilliant white. Her braided dark hair, aging face, and soft figure made her look almost motherly, but Danr knew she was anything but. The woman was flanked by two other people in dark robes—other priests—and by a golem, scratched and battered but limping gamely along. Beside the woman padded the lion-eagle. Both its heads hissed at Danr until the woman put a hand on the eagle head. The creature stilled.

"Sharlee Obsidia," Danr spat. "So this is where you ended up."

"Crawling among the insects and the filth," Kalessa growled. Last year, Sharlee Obsidia and her husband, Hector, had captured Kalessa and Ranadar, kept them chained up for days, used that leverage to force Danr and Aisa to bring the power of the shape back to Balsia and ultimately start a civil war. Danr knew damn well Kalessa loathed Sharlee and regretted the fact that she had escaped. Her feet lashed in Sharlee's direction, though her hands remained shackled to the wall.

"The lizard speaks with a forked tongue," Sharlee said softly.

"I will fork your tongue, coward," Kalessa snarled.

"Kalina and I forgive your impertinence," Sharlee said. "You can't help being what you are."

"I was found by Grick herself," Kalessa said. "You would not find your own sphincter if not for the smell."

Sharlee's face tightened, and she aimed a kick at Kalessa. Kalessa snapped out her own leg and trapped Sharlee's ankle in the bend of her knee. She yanked, and Sharlee went down. The eagle-lion shrieked but seemed uncertain what to do. Kalessa managed to drag Sharlee closer with a dreadful inevitability before the monks grabbed Sharlee and pulled her free. They set her upright and tried to smooth her robe.

"You'll pay for that, you scaly bitch," Sharlee snarled, brushing at the mud on her clothes.

"Are you not required to forgive?" Kalessa said sweetly.

Sharlee hardened like frozen venom. She put a hand on the eagle-lion's head, and it looked up at her with strange golden eyes. After a moment, Sharlee turned her own eyes up to the moon, and the silver light played across her face and her expression cleared. "But of course, child. You were right to remind me. I forgive you. With all my heart." She wet one finger with her pink tongue and drew a shiny circle on her forehead. "I beg the forgiveness of Lady Kalina, mistress of the moon. May Kalina shine evermore!"

"May Kalina shine evermore!" chanted the other monks in unison. They drew forehead circles of their own.

"She shines out your ass," Kalessa said.

"Blasphemer!" said one of the monks flanking Sharlee in horror. "The lady chose you for an honor, and you spit on—"

Sharlee quieted him with a touch on his arm. "Kalina forgives all, Lif. We have only to ask." She came around Kalessa, safely away from her kicking legs, and knelt next to her. "You must also ask for Kalina's forgiveness, child."

"At your behest?" Kalessa snorted. "Never."

"Child." Sharlee tutted. "The price of disobedience is high."

"I can afford it."

"Perhaps you can," Sharlee said amiably, "but what about your wyrm?" She nodded at Lif, who drew a long knife and strode for the quivering canvas bundle of outrage that was Slynd. Before Kalessa or anyone else could say a word, Lif thrust the knife through the canvas. Danr cringed. A bellow of pain boomed from inside the canvas.

"Slynd!" Kalessa struggled against the chains. "I will kill you! I will slice you in half and drain your blood!"

"The child hasn't learned her lesson," Sharlee said. "She must earn her penance. May Kalina shine evermore!"

Lif pulled the knife out and thrust it in again, deeper this time. Slynd hissed and bellowed, but he couldn't get away from the knife or the pain.

"May Kalina shine evermore!" repeated the other monks.

"Stop it!" Danr cried. "You're hurting him!"

Kalessa's face had lost all color. "All right. It is as you say. I . . . I beg Lady Kalina's forgiveness."

"For?" Sharlee prompted, and Lif raised the knife again. Thick blood ran down the blade.

"For . . ." Kalessa was breathing hard, and she swallowed. Every word was wrung from her. "For wronging you. For committing blasphemy."

"And?"

"And?" Kalessa repeated, confused.

Lif thrust the knife back into the second wound and twisted it. Slynd made a hissing scream that raised the hair on Danr's neck and twisted his guts. It went on and on until Lif pulled the knife back out.

"Vik! What do you want?" Kalessa cried.

Sharlee leaned in close, and Danr barely heard her. "Ask forgiveness for being born a crawling wyrm not fit to lick the moon lady's feet."

Rage flared in Kalessa's eyes. "You . . ." Lif raised the knife again, and Kalessa bit her lower lip until it bled. Danr silently pleaded with her to go along with it. They were only words, empty ones. But to Kalessa, an orc who would be remembered for her words and her deeds, every syllable was blood. Kalessa panted hard with fury, but finally, with aching slowness, she said, "I ask the lady's forgiveness for my birth."

Sharlee's smile was both triumphant and beatific. She spat on Kalessa's forehead and drew a circle with the spittle. "You are forgiven, child. May Kalina shine forevermore."

"May Kalina shine forevermore!"

"And more than that," Sharlee continued, "I must *thank* you. All of you."

"For what?" Danr asked with a wary eye on Lif.

"If you hadn't tried to kill my sweet husband, none of this would have happened." Sharlee gestured at the monastery and the grove and the eagle-lion. "I would not have found the blessings of Kalina and I would not have been chosen as the abbess. Kalina's will would go undone." She pressed her palms together above the eagle-lion's head. It slitted its eyes. "We are all nothing but tools in her blessed hands."

"Your mouth makes words that your heart does not believe," Kalessa said.

"If I did not believe," Sharlee said, "Kalina would not have blessed me with her power. Or my sweet husband. Or the brothers and sisters of her monastery."

Lif raised his knife over Slynd again. Danr thought about changing his own shape, using his smaller human form to slip the bonds so he could go for Lif or even Sharlee, but Danr was badly outnumbered and he was bound to lose. Instead he spoke up. "Why do you talk about Hector as if he were alive, Sharlee? We watched him turn into a piece of slime and die."

At Sharlee's gesture, Lif strode over and gave Danr a good sideways kick in the stomach. The air burst out of him, and hot pain exploded across his belly. At least Lif wasn't stabbing Slynd. "You will address her as Abbess, half-blood bastard."

"We must not lay blame, Lif," Sharlee said mildly. "He can't help that his mother was a troll's whore. Though perhaps this one should also ask forgiveness. He'll probably need persuading, too."

"Stop it!" Aisa pushed herself groggily upright within her cage. "Do not . . . touch him, you piece . . . of filth!"

Sharlee turned. "Not your best insult, child. It shows a rotting intellect."

"The poison . . . makes it a challenge," she said, and a troll's rage built in Danr at the weakness in her voice. It burned the pain away. He pulled at the shackles, but they were too solid, even for him.

Aisa managed to turn herself all the way to face Sharlee. "You cannot . . . cage a shape mage . . . woman."

"That is the cage of humility and pride, child," said Sharlee. "We use it for novices who are coming into their power. The mesh is too fine for even the most humble shape you might take, and the bars are so heavy that you'll crush yourself if you take a proud one."

"I am the . . . first shape mage," Aisa panted. "Mere . . . poison and iron bars . . . will not contain me." She flowed into a wolf shape and back into a human shape, forcing the last of the poison's weakness from her voice and body. Danr gave a private sigh of relief. Changing shape always healed a shape mage, though no one knew exactly why. Danr privately suspected it was because the body naturally changed into its original, unwounded shape. The difficulty lay in having enough power to change shape when your energy reserves were already low from being wounded.

"Always full of pride, aren't you, child?" Sharlee said. "Not that I'll underestimate you again. You nearly destroyed me last time. Me and Hector."

Danr worked his jaw. He had the feeling it wouldn't do any good, but he had to say it. "We didn't kill your husband, Shar—Abbess. You forced me and Aisa to hunt down the power of the shape and bring it back to you. He died because of that, not because of us."

For a moment, his mind flickered back to that dreadful day, when he and Aisa and Talfi had met Grandfather Wyrm at the bottom of the ocean. Grandfather Wyrm, the most powerful shape mage the world had ever known and the only person besides Talfi to survive the Sundering. He had done so by changing from a human into a wyrm and over the centuries had grown massive—and forgetful. He had forgotten what it was like to be human. But in the end, he had given both Aisa and Danr some of his blood. It woke a tiny amount of shape magic in Danr, and rushed a tidal wave of it through Aisa. Anyone who ingested their blood and who also possessed the Kin's dormant shape magic would experience the same thing. Except for some people, the experience turned deadly. Some people lost all control of their bodies and died in a dreadful jumble of shapes. Hector and Sharlee Obsidia had both taken

Danr's blood. Danr still shuddered at the memory of Hector falling to the ground, wrenching around and pissing himself, extruding wretched limbs and even wings, until he died.

"I know, child," Sharlee said. "You didn't kill him."

"Really?" Danr blinked in surprise. His troll's eyes saw perfectly well in the bright moonlight, and her face was the picture of calm. He shut his right eye and gazed at her with only his left. To his further astonishment, she changed very little. The darkness he had expected to see simply wasn't there.

"Ah. The truth-teller gazes at me with his true eye. Look all you like, child." She approached and leaned down to pat his cheek while the eagle-lion watched. The blob thing shuddered with a squishy noise. "Troll magic is nothing to the eye of Kalina herself."

"Nothing can keep out the truth, Sharlee," Danr said. "You've just . . . changed."

"The woman has not changed," Kalessa snapped, regaining more of herself now that Lif wasn't waving the knife at Slynd anymore. "She has only donned a set of robes. You can coat wyrm shit with sugar, and it will still be wyrm shit."

Sharlee's face flushed, but she made an obvious effort to keep control and turned back to Danr. "Do you know what has happened to me in the last year and a half you gave Hector your blood and twisted his body through pain and terror, child?"

"I don't know," Danr was forced to say. "And Hector *took* my blood. I didn't give it to him."

Sharlee ignored him. "I lost everything. You and your friends smashed all my golems but this one and destroyed my fortune. I fled north and ended up at this monastery, half-starved and dying of exposure. The good brothers and sisters of Kalina the Moon Woman took me in. They taught me simplicity and balance, child, and when I discovered that your blood had given me the power of the shape after all, they became convinced I had been blessed by Kalina herself."

"You learned you can change the shape of other things," Danr said, trying to keep her talking until he could figure out what to do.

"Other *living* things," Sharlee agreed in a cold, amiable voice. "The lady lets me melt flesh like beeswax, mold it and shape it into anything I like." The tip of her tongue glided over her upper lip, and her voice lowered to a hiss. "It's why they made me abbess. Would you like a demonstration?"

She reached for Danr's chest, her hands glowing with faint golden light. Horrified, Danr tried to back away, but there was nowhere to back to.

"Do not touch him!" Aisa shouted.

"The lady commands it, child," Sharlee whispered. A small line of saliva slid from the corner of her mouth and she touched Danr with her glowing hands. More pain ripped through him, squeezed his heart with a red-hot fist. He kicked and squirmed, but he couldn't get away from the awful pain. Danr was aware that Aisa was screaming and rattling at the bars of her cage, but the searing pain was too powerful for him to do more than writhe and gasp.

"Abbess," Lif interrupted. "The ceremony? Our lady moon is nearly at her height."

Sharlee glanced up. The moon was almost directly above them. She pulled her hands back, and the pain ended with an abruptness that left Danr dizzy. He sat shuddering in the chains.

"Thank you, Lif," Sharlee said. "We must begin. May Kalina forgive my slight."

"Kalina forgives all," the others said, all together.

Danr panted in his shackles. His insides felt like scrambled eggs. Had she done anything permanent to him or had she just wanted to hurt him? Vik! What now? The blobby thing in the center of the ring shuddered again, and some kind of sharp-smelling goo oozed down the sides.

Drums beat like a dozen hearts. Other robed men and women and even a few children were filing into the grove now and taking places among the ash trees. They carried a number of sharp weapons—knives and swords and sickles—and they gleamed soft silver in the moonlight. The eagle-lion settled on its haunches.

"What ceremony?" Danr tried to demand, but it came out more as a hoarse grunt. "What is this about?"

Sharlee was shrugging into a silvery outer cloak that another monk was draping over her robe. Dark, heavy runes skated around the edge.

"This isn't a story, child," Sharlee said. "I'm not going to recite a poem or chant a little song that tells you what my plans are. You'll just have to find out."

Danr shut his right eye again and stared at her again, more carefully this time. He saw the power of the shape coiled within her like a blacksnake ready to strike. It was different from his own power, and from Aisa's. In her, the shape magic was a poison. Something drew his eye aside, and he saw the same poison within the eagle-lion. Sharlee had created the eagle-lion. Well, he knew that. But when he looked a little closer, he saw the faint outline of . . . a person. His stomach tightened. The eagle-lion wasn't several animals crushed together as Danr had assumed. It was a human being, altered so totally it was unrecognizable. Vik! Had the other creatures also once been people?

He glanced at the other monks, now fully encircling the grove. A number of them were shape mages, but their power was weak, no more than a flicker. Sharlee must have shared her blood with them, and—

Then he knew.

"Your blood isn't very powerful, Sharlee," Danr said in a slow, measured voice. "I can see it. You gave it to these monks, but it hasn't wakened much magic in them. You've made promises to them. Promises of magic, promises of power. Promises you can't keep. They're afraid of you because you can change their shapes, but you know eventually they'll overcome that fear. They'll overcome *you.* But now you're thinking, *I have the firsts. I have their blood.* You're dressing it up in a ceremony, but all you're planning to do is cut a vein and give our blood to them so you can keep your position as abbess."

He raised his voice. "Those who take the blood of the first sometimes die. Their bodies twist and break. It's painful and horrible, and it takes a long, long time. That's the truth."

Some of the drumming faltered. Sharlee's smile, wooden and unyielding, returned to her face.

"You know nothing, child," she said. "It's not my blood they carry."

"Then whose—?" Danr began, but then his eye went to the blobby thing in the middle of the grove. His voice went shaky as a feather in a windstorm. "No."

"After you left me and my home in a wreck, I crept back to it," Sharlee said. "You'd left Hector's body to rot like a dead dog in the gutter."

"A dead dog in the gutter would have been an improvement," Kalessa put in. "Your husband needed to bathe to qualify as a slob."

Sharlee ignored this, or seemed to. Danr saw the vein throb at her forehead. "After you left, I went back and found he wasn't dead. My own magic came to me then. I . . . changed him. Stabilized him."

"Using the magic you took from us," Aisa called.

"And now you still have Hector," Danr finished. "You keep him here because his blood is actually stronger than yours. His blood gives your people at least a little magic."

"Yes." Not seeming to care that the ring of monks was waiting on her word, she stepped over to the blob and stroked it. It shuddered. "My dear Hector."

Danr forced himself to look at both Hector and Sharlee with his left eye as the moon climbed overhead and the

drums droned and eagle-lion stared. He saw the pale image
of the man Hector had been, saw him writhing in pain,
deaf and blind and dumb within the shape Sharlee had
given him. Danr's heart sickened. Hector had earned no
sympathy. He had done terrible things to countless people,
had sent countless people to their deaths. Yet Danr couldn't
help feeling sorry for him. And Sharlee. A thick red band
tied them together, a love that was as deep and true as his
love for Aisa. Deeper, in its way—it'd had years to mellow
and thicken, years Danr and Aisa hadn't had yet.

Danr cringed. A love so thick and so heavy Sharlee
couldn't let Hector go. A love that drove her to transform
him into this . . . wreck. His and Aisa's love would never
turn into something like this. Would it? A sudden fear drove
him to stare even harder, look deeper at the bond between
Hector and Sharlee while the drums battered the air.

Threads of darkness, stinking black rot that blotted the
insides of his nose curled through the bond. Almost against
his will, Danr followed them as they spiraled downward
like roots, down into the ground, into the dark, sucking
depths that hid teeth and claws and rotting corpses. The
Garden. Now that Queen Gwylph had tainted the place, it
was tainting Sharlee and her magic, had curled its new filth
around Hector, had even threaded through the others in the
monastery. That was why the shape magic was poison to
them. But the bond itself was still strong, could still be a
source of strength.

Danr's right eye popped open and the vision vanished.
"Sharlee," he said hoarsely. "You have to stop this. It isn't
you. It's the Garden—warped shape magic—that makes
you think this way. It's affected you and the entire monastery. But you can turn it around. You can—"

Lif kicked him, in the ribs this time. The pain wasn't as
bad, but it ended Danr's plea in a grunt. "We follow the
great Lady Kalina," he growled. "We are one with the
moonlight and we share in the stars. Your words mean
nothing to us!"

"But your blood," Sharlee said, "is something else entirely."

"You intend to keep me around to feed your people," Aisa said flatly.

"You are the First," Sharlee agreed, and raised her voice. "All hail the First!"

"All hail the First!" the monks shouted.

"And you, my friend," Sharlee said to Danr, "we will keep as our oracle. You speak with the voice of Kalina. You will spend your days telling truth for me while we bleed Aisa for the good of the monastery. Eventually, we will all be shape mages, and we will spread the word of Kalina throughout Balsia. And the world."

"I'll tell you nothing!" Danr spat.

"You can't help it, truth-teller," she said. "I have complete power over you and your slave bride."

"You have no power," said Kalessa next to him. She leaned forward as much as her bonds would allow, and her voice hissed into Sharlee's ears. "You only have what you steal from others. You are a common thief. A shit-stealing thief who feeds on dung. Even the place between your legs has to steal its pleasure because no one will give it to you. Even your husband and his soft, tiny member knew that, and he got what he deserves."

That did it. Rage filled Sharlee's face, and she turned on Kalessa with a roar. "Orcish whore! You'll become the worm that you are!"

Danr tried to shout as golden light flared from her hands, but at the moment Sharlee flung her magic at Kalessa, another bolt of pure power blasted from Aisa in her cage and struck Kalessa as well. Danr shied away but shut his right eye to understand what was happening. His true eye saw it all, as if time had slowed. Sharlee was sending magic that would twist Kalessa's shape into a worm, as she had promised. Danr could already see her body shifting and moving.

Aisa's power, including her growing power as a Gardener,

filled Kalessa like the way sunlight filled a prism. The power tore through the orcish woman, exploded Sharlee's own meager shape magic, and amplified her spell. The magic that struck Kalessa burst into her with a thousand times the intended power. With a shriek, Kalessa burst free of her bonds, and instead of shrinking, she grew. Her body twisted and ballooned, until a great wyrm half again as large as Slynd writhed before Sharlee.

What came next happened so fast Danr could barely follow it. Sharlee stared openmouthed up at Kalessa for a tiny moment. Kalessa struck. Sharlee was gone. Kalessa raised her head up to the sky and jerked her jaws once, twice, three times. Swallowing. A squirming lump wriggled down Kalessa's long throat and vanished into her body.

Chaos burst through the grove. The drumming abruptly ended. Monks and nuns scattered with shrieks and screams. The eagle-lion lunged at Kalessa, but she swatted it easily aside with her tail. It hit a tree and slid motionless to the ground. Lif and the other monk snatched up crossbows and aimed the weapon at Kalessa. Danr used the moment to gather his own power and flow into his human body. His wrists and hands easily slid out of his bonds, and he lunged at Lif. His human form was light and scrawny and the tackle was clumsy, but it was enough to ruin Lif's aim. Danr and Lif went down with Danr on top, and Danr rushed back into his true form. Lif gasped under Danr's full weight. Danr punched him, and he went limp.

"Look out!" Aisa shouted.

Danr tried to twist aside, but not fast enough. Searing pain hit him as the other monk's crossbow bolt caught him in the spine. Danr lost all sensation in his legs. They buckled beneath him and he landed facedown in the dirt. The world went dark.

Chapter Ten

"**Q**ueen Gwylph made you," Talfi repeated slowly.

The other Talfi let out a long, relieved sigh. "I can't say it, but you can."

"That can't be." Talfi's legs wobbled and he sank to the bed. "The elven queen . . . how could she *make* you? A whole bunch of you?"

The other Talfi shrugged. "Not allowed to talk about it."

Ranadar straightened and took the other Talfi's head by the chin to peer into his face, and the other Talfi sighed. "Even his eyes are the same, *Talashka*. I don't know how this was done."

"Aren't the dwarfs the only ones who can make golems?" Talfi said.

"Yes. But this—he—is no ordinary golem. I have never heard of a golem made of flesh until this moment, nor have I heard of one that heals itself. It would require powerful magic of the kind the world has not seen since . . . since . . ."

"The Sundering," Talfi finished, more than a little hoarsely. "How does it work?"

"I'm standing right here, you know," said the other Talfi.

Ranadar said, "I do not fully understand it. I am a minor magician, a spark to my mother's inferno."

"You're really good at archery," Talfi said, trying to lighten the mood. "Fing!"

"And you're good in the bedroom," the other Talfi added. "And the hammock. Remember that one time when—"

Talfi socked him in the stomach. He hadn't meant to. His hand balled up on its own, and his fist flew out before he could stop it. The punch came from his sitting position on the bed, so there wasn't much power behind it, and the other Talfi only gasped a little and stumbled backward a step.

"What was that for?" he asked.

Anger he didn't know he was carrying suffused Talfi, red and ugly. "You don't remember *anything*," he said.

"I do remember." The other Talfi backed up to the washstand table and leaned gingerly against it. "I'm *you*."

Talfi's face flushed and his stomach roiled. "You're not me!"

"But I remember," he protested.

"Calm, *Talashka*." Ranadar put a hand on Talfi's shoulder. "This is a strange situation for all of us. We will work out what to do." He turned to the other Talfi. "What do you remember? What is the earliest thing for you that you can tell us?"

The other Talfi thought. "I remember . . . sitting on a table in a huge room. The room has a ceiling as high as the sky and a fireplace that's big enough to eat me, but they probably only look that way because I'm small. A lady with a wrinkly face is cutting my hair with a big pair of scissors, and I'm scared because I don't like the noise the scissors make—*snip, snip*—in my ear, but I don't run away because the table is really high up."

"I don't remember that," Talfi said quietly.

"I remember being mad at my sister and holding her doll over the well. It's soft and made of quilt patches. My sister is yelling at me, and just before I drop her doll, Mother runs out and snatches the doll away. She swats me on the butt and I cry." The other Talfi blinked at Ranadar and Talfi. "I remember hugging Danr right after he was exiled and watching him disappear into the darkness at the foot of the mountain. I remember helping Ranadar dress in the palace at Alfhame on a warm summer morning and he keeps changing his mind about what to wear, so I call him an uppity elf because I know he won't punish me. He laughs."

Talfi was on his feet again, fists clenched and heart pounding and nausea twisting his stomach. "I only remember that I always called him an uppity elf, but not how it started. Why do you remember these things and not me?"

"I'm *you*," the other Talfi repeated. "We all are. All the other ones."

Ranadar was beside him now, his arm around Talfi's shoulder. "It's all right, *Talashka*. We can handle this. Together."

Talfi looked at this mirror image of himself, the one who knew as much as he did but in different ways. He trembled under a terrible curiosity. He hungered for the memories locked inside the other self's mind, hundreds or even thousands of fragments that might piece together more of his own past. He wanted to devour the man alive, force him to give the memories over. Give them back. But this demand also made him angry. He shouldn't want these things. He shouldn't *need* to want them. They should be his already. The crying need repulsed him and frightened him at the same time, and with that came anger, and the emotions tangled themselves into a terrible dark ball that swallowed up his insides and made him tremble.

"Talaskha?" said Ranadar. "What is it?"

"How many of you are there?" Talfi demanded, ignoring him. "Why did Gwylph make you? Why are you here?"

The other Talfi shrugged. "I can't talk about it."

"We need more information," Talfi said, and turned to Ranadar. "How can we get it? Can you look into his mind?"

Ranadar shook his head. "I already explained that. But . . . there may be another way. It is drastic and horrible, but . . ."

"What is it?" Talfi said. Snapped, really. "Spit it out."

"It involves doing something awful to a fellow Fae," Ranadar said softly. "I have never done such a thing, but I know how it works."

"And your mother has done such nice things to Kin?" Talfi shot back. "To me?"

"I know how Danr feels now," Ranadar muttered. "Always caught between."

The other Talfi cleared his throat, and Talfi thought, *That's what it sounds like when I do it.* "Listen, Ran," the other Talfi said, "you betrayed your people and helped save the world. What do you have to lose now?"

"Don't call him that," Talfi said through clenched teeth.

"Call him what?" said the other Talfi, looking surprised.

Talfi couldn't stop himself from snarling, "I call him *Ran* and *uppity elf*. Not you."

"But I—" the other Talfi began.

"You what?"

Other Talfi looked away. His voice dropped. "Nothing."

"All right, all right." Ranadar kept his hand on Talfi's shoulder. "I will try this thing. This new thing. But you will have to fetch a few things for me, because I cannot get them myself."

"Like what?" Talfi said warily.

"All the knives and spoons from Mrs. Farley's kitchen," Ranadar instructed. "And we will visit the market, and find another place to work. We should not do this in Mrs. Farley's house."

"I know a spot we could use," Talfi said. "Down in the Rookery."

"What are we doing?" the other Talfi said.

Ranadar said, "We will summon a sprite."

Assembling everything Ranadar needed actually took a few days and several trips to the market, where Ranadar visited merchants who revealed unexpected back rooms in their stalls or hidden drawers in their chests. Scandalous amounts of money changed hands. Talfi didn't ask how Ranadar knew about these people, and Ranadar didn't comment. During that time, Talfi refused to let Other Talfi stay with them in Mrs. Farley's boardinghouse, even in a different room. Talfi neither knew nor cared where he slept and how—or if—he ate, but he seemed content to follow Talfi and Ranadar around most days. Or maybe he was just following Ranadar around.

His face continued to heal as well. After a few days, his skin had lost its stretched look entirely, and the muscle filled out. Only a little pebbling remained, and then only if you looked closely. His left hand got better more slowly. His forearm muscle smoothed, and his thumb and first two fingers lost their clawlike appearance, but his last two fingers remained shiny and twisted, and the other Talfi developed the habit of keeping his left hand closed in a fist to hide them while he, Talfi, and Ranadar moved about the city.

More than once, they also caught sight of the other man from the alley, though he kept his distance, and now that he was alert for it, Talfi saw other versions of himself here and there, always just a glimpse, and always too far away to do anything about it, even if he wanted to. Many of them were malformed in some way, and people treated them like beggars, barely giving them a first glance, let alone a second. Talfi wondered if they were healing, too, but he couldn't get close enough to tell. Did they also have pieces of memory that were lost to Talfi himself? Talfi wanted to know, but also didn't want to know.

If they had his memories, what good would it do him? He had no way to put them into his own head, and hearing about them from Other Talfi only made him unhappy and upset, like watching someone else wear his own clothes or eat his own food.

And what did they remember about Ranadar? The question always made him cold.

Why were there so many of him? What was their purpose? It seemed that if enough of them—of him—were
scattered across the city, someone would eventually notice.
Or would they? How often did you notice individual people on a crowded street or the malformed beggar on the
corner?

One day, he saw another Talfi limping through an intersection when a carriage bolted past. It rammed into the
other Talfi, who went flying. Talfi reflexively reached out a
hand to help, though he and Ranadar were many yards
away. Several onlookers gasped. They gasped even more
when the other Talfi got up and limped quickly away as if
nothing had happened. Talfi remembered how Kalessa had
stabbed the other Talfi in the market to little effect. Was it
related to the way Talfi himself didn't die? There seemed
to be no way to know without asking Other Talfi, and Talfi
couldn't bring himself to form the question, so he remained
silent.

Eventually, Ranadar announced he had everything he
needed from the market and was ready to summon the
sprite. They headed out, with Other Talfi in tow, mostly
because he wouldn't leave them alone.

Talfi led them through the Rookery, the windward side
of Bosha's Bay. The Tenner River meandered through the
city here, but unlike the deep, fast River Bal, which ran
through the city from the north, the Tenner was slow and
shallow, and as it coasted west to empty into the bay, it
split into an even slower, shallower river everyone called
the Niner. The area south of the Tenner was prone to tidal
flooding, especially during storm season, which meant the
only people who lived there were the ones who were forced
to. For reasons lost to time, the area was known as the
Rookery. For reasons that were more obvious, the area
between the Niner and the Tenner was simply called the
Sludge, and Talfi doubted even Danr would walk there
after dark.

Oddly enough, the only way to get to the spit of land

that jutted across the mouth of Bosha's Bay and sheltered it from the ocean proper was through the Rookery, and since the temples of the warrior twins Belinna and Fell were on the tip of that spit of land, a wide road cut through the Rookery leading to it, and that road was reasonably safe, even after dark, in part because the priests of Belinna and Fell patrolled it. This was the road the trio walked now.

They went in silence. The sluggish, shallow Tenner smelled of sea tide and bad algae and dead fish and garbage and the filth the tanners threw into it, for by law all the tanners and their smelly businesses were housed down here. The buildings varied wildly, from cut stone, to ragged wood, to piles of mud. The streets were a horror. Talfi didn't see a well or a fountain anywhere, and he wondered where the people found water to drink. It was clear enough what they did with their waste.

The inhabitants of the Rookery themselves stayed close to the shadows, as if they were afraid of getting caught in the early evening sunlight. Hollow, hopeless eyes stared from rags and patches as the trio passed, and misery hung in the stinking air like a dark mist.

And yet there were bright spots. Taverns were open for business down here, just as they were near the market square. A number of houses along the patrolled road even seemed prosperous, though the women hanging out the windows made it obvious what kind of business they were conducting. One house was populated with men, and Talfi caught Ranadar's eye at that. The elf simply shrugged. Small groups of well-dressed people also walked the patrolled road, or rode in carriages along it. Slumming, Talfi decided, or looking to visit one of the prosperous houses.

The image of the carriage and the distorted version of himself flying in a rag-doll arc across the intersection nagged at Talfi, and he finally spoke to Other Talfi.

"So you're all basically unkillable," he said.

"I don't know about that," Other Talfi said, in his

maddeningly familiar voice. "Though I've never watched one of us die."

"The seat of a flesh golem's magic is his heart," Ranadar said. "If you cut it out, he would probably die. The same would be true if you cut off his head."

Talfi snorted. "Isn't that true for everyone?"

"I suppose it is," Ranadar said with a little laugh.

"Maybe we should test it," Talfi said, giving Other Talfi a grim look.

"All right!" Other Talfi stopped and crossed his arms, forcing Talfi and Ranadar to halt as well. "Maybe we should have this out right here."

"Have what out?" Talfi crossed his own arms.

"Why you hate me so much," Other Talfi said.

"I don't hate you," Talfi objected.

"Sure you do. And I know why. You're afraid of me because you think I love Ranadar as much as you do."

Talfi's face grew hot. "That's a lie!"

"I do love him, though," Other Talfi said softly. He dropped his arms. "I remember it. I remember loving him."

"Take it back." Talfi cocked a fist. "I'll beat your damn face in, even if it looks like mine!"

Ranadar stepped between them, creating a strange mirror image—an elf between two identical men, while pedestrians paused to stare. "We do not need an argument here."

"You can't love him," Talfi almost shouted. "You're not even alive!"

"I *remember*," Other Talfi repeated, and shifted his focus to Ranadar. "I've slept with you and kissed you and made love with you a hundred times. I remember walking through forests in Alfhame with you and sneaking away from your parents with you. It happened." Tears stood in his blue eyes. "I missed you every second we were apart, and then when I saw you here in Balsia, I thought we could—we could—"

"But you also knew that you were just a copy of my *Talashka*," Ranadar said slowly.

"A copy of a memory is still a memory. A copy of a feeling is still a feeling." He reached for Ranadar's cheek. Talfi's heart twisted inside him.

Ranadar brushed Other Talfi's hand away. "It is hard to hear blunt words, but I have no feelings for you one way or the other, and I will not give up what I have with the real Talfi to explore anything with you—or any of the other flesh golems, come to that."

Talfi gave a heavy internal sigh and his muscles unwound like great springs. He'd been tense but hadn't realized how tense until Ranadar spoke those words.

"The real Talfi," Other Talfi murmured. "Yes. Cut out my heart."

"Drama suits you badly," Ranadar said.

Other Talfi looked up sharply, then flashed a quicksilver grin. For a tiny second, Talfi saw how good-looking they—he and Other Talfi—were, and it was disconcerting. "Worth a try," Other Talfi said.

"What's going on here?"

Startled, the trio looked up. Two men on horseback had approached, both of them in the red and gold livery that proclaimed them members of the prince's guard. Behind them came a clay golem, also in livery. Stane runes crawled over its exposed "skin." The streets had become noticeably emptier. Dogs barked some distance away.

"We're just having a conversation," Talfi said, a little bewildered. "Is something wrong?"

One of the guards leaned down, apparently to get a better look at Talfi's face. His horse danced a bit. "The prince is looking for your type."

Type. A small icicle of fear slipped through Talfi's heart, and a word—*regi*—flicked through his head. The response was automatic. In some places, men who loved other men were persecuted, even executed. Talfi pulled himself together. Balsia was not one of those places. *Regi* were not particularly well liked here, but neither were they rounded up and arrested. Or so Talfi told himself.

"What's my type?" he asked, keeping his voice steady.

The guard ticked features off with his fingers. "Brown hair with a curl, blue eyes, looks about seventeen, boy's build, favors red clothes. And"—he gestured at Other Talfi—"there's more'n one of you."

"Oh," Talfi said. "That. We're . . . brothers."

"Not how we hear it." The guard, an able-bodied man with dark hair and thick arms, drew a truncheon and dismounted while his companion remained on the horse. The golem came forward. It was unarmed, but Talfi knew from experience that it would be stronger and faster than it looked.

"What is this about, sir?" Ranadar asked. His hood was still up.

With the tip of his truncheon, the guard lifted Talfi's chin in a way Talfi disliked very much. "We're getting a lot of reports about trouble being caused by someone of your description."

"What kind of trouble?" Other Talfi asked quietly, though Talfi heard the tension, and he wondered if the three of them could take on two guardsmen and a golem in a fight.

"Disturbing the peace, mostly," said the guard. "Though more'n one've said something about stealing food. And we're hearing about a whole lot of so-called brothers. After that incident with the toads, the prince is starting to wonder what's going on. Shape mages, maybe, who've learned to look like other people. We're looking hard at people like you, and right now I'm thinking you both need some up-close looking."

The guard intended to take him—them—in. And Talfi had the feeling that any protestations that he knew the prince would fall on deaf ears. Talfi glanced about, wondering if they should run for it. The guard noticed and drew back the truncheon. The other guard's horse danced now, and the man riding it had to work to calm it.

"What's wrong with these damn horses today?" he muttered.

"I wouldn't be trying to go anywhere," said the guard with the truncheon. "In fact, I'm thinking we should haul you down to the keep for some questions."

"Good sir." Ranadar pushed back his hood, revealing his ears and Fae features. "I have business, and you are interrupting it."

The guards, one afoot and one mounted, blinked at him. The guard with the truncheon said, "What's an elf doing in the Rookery, then?"

"My business," Ranadar said coolly. "These young men belong to me. We will be on our way."

"Slavery's illegal in Balsia these days," the guard said. "You got no authority. We'll be bringing you in, too. For questioning. Golem!"

"Sir?" said the golem.

"Give me the iron shackles. For the Fae."

Ranadar pursed his lips. "Talfi, shake your sack and set it down by that wall, would you? And then I will show this good guardsman exactly why he should let us go about our business."

"Shake and—?" Talfi began.

"Just do it," Other Talfi said.

Talfi shook the sack hard. The objects inside clanked and rattled even as the golem got the shackles from the first guard's horse. Both horses tried to rear, and only quick work from the guards kept them steady. Talfi stepped over to the wall to set the sack down. Both guards were now watching him and their horses, and not Ranadar.

"Here, now!" said the guard on the ground to Talfi. "Don't you be going anywhere!"

Out of the corner of his eye, Talfi saw Ranadar's hands and lips moving, and he understood what was happening. The air near Talfi took on a soft shimmer.

"Look, this is just a misunderstanding," Talfi said loudly. He pointed. "What you're looking for is in that sack."

The guards turned to look at it.

"Now!" Ranadar said.

Talfi dove into the shimmer. So did Other Talfi. The Twist snapped around him, pulled him in an infinite number of directions, then snapped him back together. He stumbled out into the street, a different one. Nausea rocked his stomach, but he held himself together. They must not have gone very far.

Other Talfi also appeared on the street. A split second later, Ranadar popped into being, and the Twist snapped shut.

"Oi!" the guard shouted, and his voice came from only one street over. "Find them!"

Hoofbeats and some shouting trailed off, then silence. Ranadar looked a little pale.

"Are you all right?" Other Talfi asked before Talfi himself could.

"I had to Twist us quickly, and it was a drain," Ranadar said. "Just let me rest a moment until my head stops hurting from the clang of all that iron."

"Why did you tell the First to shake the sack and put it down?" Other Talfi said. "It has everything in it."

"The sack has iron in it," Talfi said. "Ran couldn't Twist it. The shaking was to upset the horses and distract the guards. Run back and get it. Quick—before the guards come back."

Other Talfi dashed off while Talfi helped Ranadar to a sitting position on the noisome street. "You were brilliant," he said.

"As were you," Ranadar replied with a wan smile. "I cannot think of anyone else I would rather trick guards with."

"You know there's another meaning to that sentence."

Ranadar pretended to hit him, and Talfi pretended to shy away. "I love you forever, you know," Talfi said.

"I know," Ranadar said. "And coming from people who truck with immortals, that is a promise indeed."

Talfi was leaning down to kiss him when Other Talfi returned with the sack. "I got away pretty easy," he said. "But we're all good runners. Always have been."

The words ruined the moment, and Talfi's ire rose. "Don't say that," he snapped, and helped Ranadar to his feet. "I'm not *we*."

Other Talfi slung the sack over his shoulder. "Look, if you're going to take everything I say to mean—"

"Perhaps we should just keep moving," Ranadar interrupted.

A pair of cats raced out of an alley with their tails at full brush, and the distant dogs set up their barking again until someone yelled at them to stop. The trio moved down the street in silence. After a while, Other Talfi said, "I don't like this one bit."

"Besides the obvious," Ranadar sighed, "what do you not like?"

"Don't you feel it? Something in the city is . . . off."

"Off." Ranadar stopped again, annoying passersby who were forced to stream around them. "What do you mean *off*?"

"The air," Other Talfi said, looking nervous now. "The water. The sky. I don't know. Off."

Talfi cocked his head, listening in spite of himself. The city seemed normal to him. The heavy smells of waste and rotting food and horsehair and unwashed skin, the press of moving people in motion like dirty ocean waves washing through the streets, the shouts and yells and screams and hollers, the clang of iron tools that made Ranadar wince. All of it was . . .

Wrong.

"I do not see what you—" Ranadar began.

"No," Talfi said. "He's right. I don't want to say it, but he is. Something's off. I can't put my finger on it."

"Then how can we know what it is?" Ranadar asked.

Other Talfi cocked his head. "It's . . . what is it?"

Talfi thought a moment, then snapped his fingers. "The animals! Do you hear?"

All three of them remained where they were and listened. The sounds of the city rose and fell in the normal—no, not quite normal—cacophony. Dogs barked, but with a frantic note. Alley cats yowled in a panic. A flock of pigeons circled the sky, unwilling to set down and rest. A goose girl's flock honked and flapped its wings restlessly while a shepherd fought to keep his bleating sheep under control.

"The animals are unhappy," Ranadar said after a moment.

"Exactly," Talfi said. "Even the guard's horses were restless. Did you notice?"

"Hmm," said Ranadar.

"What does it mean?" Other Talfi asked. "You're an elf. You're supposed to know this stuff."

"Yeah," Talfi said. "You ran in the wilderness for almost two hundred years after we—" He caught himself. "*I* died." He hurried on, though Other Talfi gave him an interested look. "What was the phrase you used? *Many rushes?*"

"*Mal rishal,*" Ranadar corrected. "An elf who lives apart from the others. Animals become restless when they are fearful or unhappy, but if that is the case, what could frighten every animal in the city at the same time?"

Talfi looked hard at Other Talfi. Other Talfi edged away from him. "I didn't do anything."

"That we know of," Talfi said grimly. They reached the building he had in mind, an unprepossessing, two-story building with a lower story of stone and a second story of battered and blackened wattle-and-daub. The roof was long gone, as was the front door.

"What happened to this place?" Other Talfi asked.

You don't remember? Talfi almost said, then swallowed the words. "It used to be a brewer's place, but it burned during the Blood Storm and the owner left town, so it's been empty ever since. We might have to chase out some squatters, but we can use it and no one will ask questions."

"Let's go," Other Talfi said.

"First," Ranadar said, "we must decide what to do about him." He cocked a graceful thumb over his shoulder. Talfi, who was reaching for the tavern door, glanced around. Behind them on the muddy street came a twisted figure, his face hidden under a ragged red cloak of the color Talfi favored. Talfi's fingers chilled. It was the second man from the alley all those days ago, the one who had run away.

"He's been following us for a while," Ranadar said as a cart laden with empty barrels rumbled by, spraying mud. "There is another one of him two streets over, and I think more are coming."

"Why didn't you say something?" Talfi hissed.

"I did not wish to alarm you."

"I'm alarmed," Talfi said. "Highly alarmed."

"He won't hurt you," Other Talfi said. "*We* won't hurt you. You're the First."

Talfi set his mouth. "I'm not worried he'll hurt me. I'm worried . . . I'm worried . . ."

"What?" Other Talfi said.

"I'm just worried." Talfi stormed inside the building. He couldn't seem to sort this out, and the world wasn't giving him the chance to do it. How many other versions of him had Gwylph created? Were they all here in Balsia? How was she doing it? *Why* was she doing it? And why *him*? The questions swirled inside him like lava and ice, and he couldn't seem to keep his bearings. Now he was also learning that Other Talfi—and, by extension, the *other* Other Talfis—had memories of his own past that Talfi himself did not. Even worse, some of those memories involved Ranadar. It was like discovering his greatest treasure had been stolen by a hundred thieves before he had even known he'd owned it. Worse was the thought that the memories he had lost had been somehow locked inside him all this time, then snatched away and given to these . . . golems of himself. If only he could have figured out how to unlock the memories, he would have known, really *known*, who he was, instead of having the snatches and patchworks of himself.

Perhaps the memories were still there, locked inside him even now. Or perhaps they had been removed and handed to the other Talfis. But how and why? The helplessness and anger and fear nipped and sliced at him with a thousand knives, and he had no idea how to handle any of it.

Ranadar touched his arm in the doorway. "I know, *Talashka*."

Talfi paused. "Know what?"

"I know you are unhappy and upset. Over the flesh golems and what they represent. Over the memories they have . . . stolen from you."

"Hey!" said Other Talfi. "I didn't—"

"Are you reading my mind now?" Talfi almost snarled.

Ranadar shook his head. "I told you I do not have the power for that. But I know you better than I know anyone, and it hurts me to see you in fear and pain. We will learn what is happening and we will handle it. Remember, we speak with Death, and we changed the world. We can handle my mother and a few golems."

Talfi barked a short laugh. "I don't know who's worse— Death or your mother. But thanks. Let's go in."

"I didn't steal your memories," Other Talfi said stubbornly.

"What shall we do about him?" Ranadar gestured at the other flesh golem wavering in the crowd several yards away.

"He doesn't seem to be healing," Talfi said.

"It's not his fault," Other Talfi said defensively. "I think he's an early one, and *she* was still learning when she made him."

"Will he interrupt us?" Ranadar asked.

"Probably not," Other Talfi said.

"Then let's leave him and go in," Talfi growled, and did.

The building's interior was a wreck, but the heavy wooden floor was solid, and the stone walls seemed steady. Even after months of exposure to the elements, the heavy smell of soot hung in the air. They did have to chase away half a dozen startled squatters, and Talfi felt bad about that, but they could come back shortly, and Ranadar promised to leave them a few coins.

The back wall sported a chimney and hearth, and they decided to set up there. The plaster and whitewash had long disappeared from the walls, and someone had made a serious effort to dig some of the stones out of the chimney's masonry. Ranadar built a tiny fire in the hearth with some charcoal he had brought with him while on the other side of the room Talfi and Other Talfi silently laid out a partial ring of iron utensils—knives, spoons, tongs, skewers, and others—four feet across. One side of the ring was open. There was one spoon left over when they were finished, and Talfi stuffed it into his pocket.

"The sprites are airy, difficult creatures," Ranadar said as he lit the fire. "They do not always concern themselves with the affairs you and I might, much in the way giants and merfolk have concerns that differ from those of the rest of the Stane and Kin."

"Is that why they talk funny?" Talfi asked.

Ranadar took from his pack half a dozen bottles and jars he had bought at the market, along with a bundle of dried herbs. He also laid out a supply of food—cheese, sausage, bread, three pears, and a bottle of wine. "Their minds are only half in this world. But the royal family has always had a special rapport with the sprites. I fear Mother is exploiting it. I must do the same." He breathed out heavily. "This will drain me considerably. I will need this food and your help to eat it when I am done."

"What exactly are you doing?" Talfi said. "You haven't explained very well."

"I will open a Twist to Alfhame and use it to summon a sprite," Ranadar said. "When it arrives, you will have to put it into the ring of iron and close the circle so it cannot escape."

Talfi blinked at him. "You aren't that good at Twisting. You said so yourself. You also said it takes a lot of power to Twist something from that far away."

"I know." Ranadar took another breath. "That is what all this material is for."

He set about pouring and mixing from the bottles. The mixture itself he put into a small pot on the fire. It boiled quickly. Ranadar put on a leather glove and with it, he crushed a small amount of the dried herbs into the mix. The herbs had a sharp, oily smell that crinkled the insides of Talfi's nose. Other Talfi sneezed. Ranadar removed the glove and shook it carefully to remove all the herb dust.

"You know I'm going to ask what that stuff is," Talfi said, "so why don't you just explain and save us the trouble?"

Ranadar took the little pot off the flame with the look of someone about to drink spider venom poured over broken glass. "The infusion is brandy and highly illegal painkillers. The herb is Tikkscock."

"Oh." Talfi's eyes grew round and nervous. "That's poisonous."

"Not if it's prepared properly," Ranadar said. "And not if you're Fae. Among the Fae, it boosts magic power. It also has a number of difficult side effects. Tikk is more cruel than kind."

Other Talfi said, "Especially when you crush his—"

"How bad are the side effects?" Talfi asked.

"Most of them are ameliorated by the painkillers and brandy." Ranadar sat next to the tiny fire and stared into the pot, a bird hypnotized by a snake. "I will be hungry when we are done. And I will want more of the herb. Do not give it to me."

"Why?"

"It is addictive, and easy to overuse. This is why the Fae use it only rarely."

"Ran," said Other Talfi suddenly, "is this a good idea?"

Talfi, who was feeling much the same thing, could only nod, even though he wanted to push Other Talfi aside. "I don't want you to get hurt. We can find another way to learn what we need to know."

"There is no other way. I love you, my *Talashka*."

Talfi barely had time to notice the flicker that crossed Other Talfi's face before Ranadar closed his eyes and drank the potion.

There was only a small moment. Ranadar's body stiffened. A golden glow started in his center and spread softly through his body like a candle flickering to life and steadying as the wick drew. Ranadar opened his eyes. The cornea and iris were filled with the pure blue of a noon sky. Talfi moved to go to him, but Other Talfi put a hand on his shoulder.

"Don't," he whispered. "I know we want to, but we shouldn't."

Talfi wanted to shake Other Talfi's hand off, wanted to go to Ranadar, but after a moment, reason prevailed. He set his mouth and stayed by the iron circle.

"Incredible," Ranadar said in a low, rich voice Talfi had never heard before. A small spasm warped Ranadar's features, then passed. The pain he had mentioned. "I feel it. Ashkame. The branches that Twist through the world. Yes. I can see them now. And . . . more."

"More?" Talfi said. "What do you see, Ran?"

"The roots," Ranadar said in that strange, low voice. "They are rotting. The magic twists them. The Tree tips, and this time it will fall."

He rose to his feet, graceful as a young tree, and made a complicated set of gestures. His hands trailed bright golden light, leaving strange curved runes in the air. A rushing sound followed them. Ranadar's face was gleeful,

thrilled in a way that frightened Talfi more than a little. A
bit of spittle ran from the corner of Ranadar's mouth. Talfi
exchanged a look with Other Talfi and he knew that the
other man felt the same way. Perhaps they should stop him.
But neither of them knew the repercussions of interrupting
a spell like this, and the memory of losing his leg in a previous Twist was always fresh in Talfi's mind. So he chewed
his lip and said nothing.

"Come to me, you little bastard," Ranadar murmured.
The golden trails glowed brighter. "You cannot resist me.
Come to me *now*."

Ranadar punched the air and the golden light vanished.
With a *pop*, a sprite appeared in midair before him. Its
chaotic, ever-changing form went spiky with fear and surprise.

"You!" Ranadar snapped another gesture, like a man
capturing a fly, and the sprite froze. Ranadar made a throwing motion. The sprite arced across the room through the
opening in the ring of iron. It hit the open air at the back of
the ring and bounced as if it had hit a physical barrier.
Quickly, Talfi nudged a knife and a spatula into place, closing the circle.

The sprite bobbled in midair, recovered itself, and tried
to flee, but when it hit the edge of the iron circle, it
rebounded—once, twice, three times. A mewling sound
filled the air. The sprite reminded Talfi of a small child
pounding its fists on a locked door.

"No! No! Let me go!" it cried. "It hurts in spurts."

Ranadar faced it from across the room, well away from
the iron circle. His eyes kept their eerie blue. "Answer my
questions, sprite!"

"Mired in iron! A dark day for royal Fae to command
this way," the sprite whimpered in a pain-filled voice. "A
cruel tool to blind one of your own kind. How could our
one-day king do this dreadful thing?"

The words seemed to strike Ranadar with the force of
closed fists. He flinched hard and his hands shook. The

sprite's final sentence rang in Talfi's ears as well. Ranadar was still a prince of the Fae, and the sprites cared less for what was happening in the physical world than other Fae did. A sprite would see Ranadar as the up-and-coming king of Alfhame, no matter what he had done in the past, and it would be as confused by Ranadar commanding it with iron as a cat would be confused by its owner trying to drown it in a well. Iron was a terrible weapon to use against the Fae. Its merest touch disrupted their magic and confused their minds. The ease with which the Kin used iron was the only thing that kept the Fae from invading Balsia and taking it for their own, in fact. Imprisonment within an iron circle had to be one of the most painful, dreadful things one Fae could bring upon another, and even after everything Ranadar had done, he was still their prince.

"Answer quickly my questions and the questions of my friends," Ranadar said, "and you may go."

"Ask your task, Prince Ranadar, you are," said the sprite.

Ranadar first said, "What is your name?"

"Bel-Jan-Who-Caroms-Over-Trees-by-Scarlet-Sunrise," said the sprite.

"Did my mother, the queen, create these flesh golems?"

"Yes, yes!"

"How did she create them?" Talfi put in.

"With power from the late Fate." Bel-Jan-Who-Caroms-Over-Trees-by-Scarlet-Sunrise flickered, and yet another Talfi was standing inside the circle. Talfi involuntarily backed up a step. "She—I mean the queen, long and lean—used a stream, a dream, a gleam, of your blood."

Now Talfi's legs went weak and he had to sit down. Other Talfi went with him.

"My blood," Talfi whispered. "She's creating the flesh golems, the other versions of me, from my own blood. Where did she get my blood?"

But even as he formed the question, he knew the answer. His mind fled back to the awful day in the throne room of

Palana. Danr was holding the newly reformed Iron Axe and they had just realized that the third piece they needed—the Axe's magic—was the same power that kept bringing Talfi back from the dead, and the only way to release the magic back to the Axe was to kill Talfi with it. Permanently. And at that moment, a piercing pain ripped through Talfi's back. He'd had just enough time to look down and see the spear point emerge from his chest before he'd collapsed and died. In a pool of his own blood. What had happened to that blood after Danr had all but destroyed Palana in the Battle of the Twist? He had never given it a thought. Until now.

"Explain further," Ranadar ordered. "Be quick!"

"The sky makes it hard to try," Bel-Jan said in Talfi's voice, and Talfi's skin prickled. "The essence of the self is blood and bone, and from that is all the flesh grown and sown. We cower before the queen's new power, and the ash—dash, mash, flash—tree—flee, sea, key—contains the Fate—late, date, create the flesh." The sprite popped back into its own form, twisting and writhing in midair. "Oh! Regain pain flame disdain!"

"What's he saying?" Other Talfi said. "I can't follow him."

Ranadar set his jaw. The eerie blue in his eyes was fading. "My mother got hold of Talfi's blood. Blood and bone contain the essence of who we are, and my mother is using that essence to create flesh copies of Talfi. Normally, she could not dream of doing such a thing—no one in the world could—but she has Pendra trapped in that ash tree. That gives Mother more than enough power to do this. I would guess that the reason some of the flesh golems are disfigured is that the process is imperfect."

"Yes!" whimpered the sprite. "A mess. But it improves, moves. She makes more, Talfis galore."

"Why me?" Talfi said, but he realized he knew the answer. "It's because I don't die. My flesh and bones regrow, and that's why she can make hundreds of golems out of the tiny bits she got."

The sprite bobbed an assent.

"What is she making them for?" Ranadar demanded. "Speak!"

Bel-Jan spun unhappily within the circle. "She has forbidden, rid and bidden that no one say, nay."

"Then you can sit in that circle until Death calls for you," Ranadar said in a soft, cool voice Talfi had never heard before. The blue glow was nearly gone.

"I cannot, may not, will not." Bel-Jan spun madly in place, so agitated he failed to rhyme. "Must not."

"We won't let anyone know you told, Bel-Jan-Who-Caroms-Over-Trees-by-Scarlet-Sunrise," Talfi said. "No one will ever find out. Besides, you'd be telling your future king."

"That is true, do," said Bel-Jan-Who-Caroms-Over-Trees-by-Scarlet-Sunrise.

"You can tell," said Other Talfi. "Your future king wants to know."

Bel-Jan hesitated one more maddening moment, then said, "The orders will be to invade, blade. Destroy and redeploy the Kin from within."

"Oh," Talfi said. His mouth went dry as he thought about the crowd of selves Ranadar had seen. "There's already a bunch of . . . me here, and if they suddenly attack the city, it'll catch everyone by surprise."

"They could easily destroy a large part of Balsia," Ranadar agreed softly. "Even if they did not capture the city, they could damage it enough for my people to invade it without trouble. My mother is intelligent."

Bel-Jan said, "Hail the queen!"

"Hail the queen!" said Other Talfi automatically.

"What?" Talfi stared at him as a dreadful thought crawled through his mind. "Are you obeying Queen Gwylph right now?"

"I . . . I . . . ," other Talfi stammered. "I can't . . ."

"She forbade you to speak of it," Ranadar supplied.

Other Talfi remained silent, but his expression spoke

the truth. Talfi swallowed as the full implications stole over him. The flesh golems were immensely strong, incredibly difficult to kill, and they didn't feel pain. And they had already been seeded throughout Balsia.

"Bel-Jan," he said, "how many of . . . me has the queen sent?"

"A nifty four hundred fifty."

Talfi felt the blood drain from his face, leaving cold skin behind. "There are four hundred and fifty copies of me in the city right now?"

"More to come, all mum," said the sprite.

"The Nine," Talfi breathed. "We need to tell someone. The prince. Or the—"

The ground rocked beneath him. Talfi lost his balance. The floor seemed to rumple like a blanket, sending Talfi tumbling to the floor. His breath smashed out of him.

"Earthquake!" Ranadar shouted. "Out! Get out of the house!"

Talfi tried to scramble upright, but the shaking floor kept knocking his feet out from under him. Panic overtook him. The ground wasn't supposed to move. It was a solid thing. Forcing fear back, he pushed himself upward again, and failed. The floor rocked. Iron utensils flew in all directions, breaking the circle. Bel-Jan-Who-Caroms-Over-Trees-by-Scarlet-Sunrise fled out of a window in a trail of light. The walls groaned like angry ghosts. In front of Talfi, a spiderweb of cracks rushed up the chimney. A hand grabbed his arm and steadied him a little, letting him get to his feet. It was Other Talfi.

"Come on, First!" he shouted. "Let's—"

The chimney collapsed. Talfi had enough time to throw up a hand before a ton of rocks landed square on him.

Chapter Eleven

Danr sat up in the Garden. He was naked, in his human form, and pain blazed through his back and shoulder. The Garden's gray light soothed his eyes, and the smells of the plants stretching in all directions calmed him, slowed his racing heart, despite the awful pain. The soft sound of water dripped somewhere nearby. This place was comforting and quiet. Why had he been so upset? How had he gotten hurt? He couldn't remember.

He didn't want to be in his human form. It was injured and too small. He concentrated, pushing the pain aside, and found the power within himself. His form expanded, his jaw and teeth lengthened, his muscles bulged, and he was in his familiar, comfortable half-troll shape. The pain slipped away, and a crossbow bolt dropped to the ground behind him. He blinked at it. Where had that come from? And what did it matter, anyway?

Another smell, the smell of rot, assailed him. He hoisted himself to his feet and came to a set of plants all tangled together. One of them was a half-dead climbing rose that had tangled itself around a rotting blob of mushroom. The rose's roots were infected with more rot, and its thorns had snagged a number of plants around it. The mushroom was also dying, and in pain to boot. This wasn't right. They both needed to come out. Danr reached down for the rose with one large hand and the mushroom with the other.

"Why are you here, friend?"

It was Nu with her seed bag. She was staring at him from under the hood on her green cloak. Tan was nowhere to be seen.

"I'm . . . just here," he said, putting his hands behind his back.

"Hmm." Nu pulled the drawstring on her bag shut. "Tan and I sensed someone else was here earlier, when our new sister came to visit. Was that you?"

Danr thought a moment. "I don't know," he said truthfully. "It may have been. Where is Tan?"

"We aren't joined at wrist and ankle," she replied. "What were you going to do with the rose and mushroom?"

"Pull them out," Danr said promptly. "The rose is tangling itself in everything around it, and the mushroom is dying. It's in pain, somehow."

"Indeed," Nu agreed. "But have you thought that if you pull the rose out, you will also damage the plants it has entangled?"

"No," said Danr the truth-teller. "Should I try to work it free instead? That might take a long time."

"Sometimes speed is more necessary than care. Other times, we must take care for the surrounding plants before we remove a tangle." Nu narrowed her eyes. "Which is more important here, care or speed?"

Danr examined the mass with a farmer's critical eye. "The rose is getting more and more entrenched," he said. "The longer she stays, the more tangled the other plants get. And the mushroom is trying to eat everything around it and spread its pain farther. Every moment that passes makes it worse for everything else. So, speed."

"Interesting choice," Nu said. "Just the sort that Aisa would have made."

The name triggered a rush of memories. The monastery.

The animals. Sharlee. Victor. Kalessa transformed into a wyrm. "Aisa!" he said. "Is she—?"

"First, your task, child," said Nu. "You named it. You must complete it."

"I—"

"Your task," Nu repeated firmly.

There was more here than Danr understood, but his worry for Aisa overrode everything else. He reached down to grab—

—and bolted upright. The giant wyrm—Kalessa, he remembered—was running off the last of Sharlee's followers. He was in his clothes, and the moon had passed its zenith above the ash grove and Aisa's cage. The great bundle of cloth that was Slynd continued to tremble in outrage. For the second time, Danr scrambled to his feet. Kalessa would have to be all right. Right now Danr needed to see to Aisa.

He dashed past Slynd to the cage and found a key hanging on one corner of the door, not reachable from the prisoner because of the mesh inside. He snatched it down and, with shaking fingers, unlocked the door.

Aisa lay in an exhausted heap on the cage floor. Danr picked her up and carried her out. She struggled out of his arms once they were clear of the bars and mesh. "I am well," she insisted. "Are *you* all right? I saw you shot with a crossbow and my heart stopped."

"I'm fine," he said. "I changed my shape and it healed me."

Kalessa's jaws made *clop-clop* noises as she bit the air behind the last of the fleeing monks.

"You turned her into a great wyrm," he accused.

"No such thing," Aisa shot back. "Sharlee tried to turn her into a tiny wyrm. I just . . . helped."

"She ate Sharlee," he said mildly as Kalessa twisted back on herself to return.

"Transformation can be hungry work," Aisa replied. "But there is still Slynd to deal with. And Hector."

"Which one do you want?"

Danr sighed. "You free Slynd. I'll take Hector. I should have done it the first time around, so it's my job."

Aisa didn't object to this. She took Danr's knife and headed toward the canvas bundle while Danr caught up Kalessa's blade. He had never actually held it before. It was tiny in his hand, and he wished it were larger, easier to handle. Instantly, it was—sharp, heavy, and over six feet long. If Danr hadn't seen Kalessa do the same trick a thousand times, he would have dropped the sword in surprise. He made himself stride to the center of the ash grove, where the blobby horror squelched and quivered. Danr closed his right eye and gave it a glance with his left. At such close range, he could almost feel Hector's pain. It hung like a red shroud over the blob that had been Hector Obsidia, and he also saw terrible hatred—hatred for the world, hatred for what he had become. Hatred for himself.

Danr's stomach swam with nausea, and acid burned the back of this throat. He swallowed, and for a moment he was . . .

. . . in the Garden, with Nu looking over his shoulder. *Speed or care?*

Had he really been there, or had that been a dream when he lost consciousness? It felt like a dream, but one more real than any he had ever experienced.

Speed or care?

Speed. The truth-teller in him knew there could be no more delay. The pain and rot and hatred emanating here had to end, and it had to end quickly. Danr raised the sword. The blob quaked, and angry ripples spread across its mottled skin. Before he could hesitate further, Danr slashed down with the sword. It cleaved the blob in two.

Pus and blood exploded in all directions, covering Danr with warm goo. It got in his eyes and mouth. An awful, rotting smell burst from the blob. Danr choked. He dropped Kalessa's sword and threw up. The two halves of the blob oozed flatter and flatter as the noisome liquids drained out of it. A few bubbles burbled and died.

Aisa, meanwhile, slashed open the canvas that bound Slynd. He exploded free, hissing angrily, looking for someone to bite. Aisa backpedaled.

"Calm, Slynd," she said. "We are friends. I released you after the bad people tied you up."

But Slynd was having none of it. The fury in his yellow eyes made them all but glow. He hissed like a thousand kettles and reared back to strike at Aisa, who was too tired to change shape and escape. Horrified, Danr tried to wipe the rest of the gore from his eyes and help her, but he was still half-blind and couldn't do much.

"Slynd!" Kalessa slid into the grove and reared up behind Aisa. "Stay!"

Danr froze. He hadn't expected that Kalessa would be able to speak. On the other hand, Grandfather Wyrm, who had also once been human, was able to speak, so why shouldn't Kalessa? Her wyrm voice was deeper, almost thunderous, and it halted Slynd in his track. He backed away and coiled around himself, hissing and muttering.

"He will calm down in a few minutes," Kalessa said, bringing her own head down to ground level. It was as big as a horse.

"Thank you," Aisa said, blinking up at her. "Are you . . . well?"

"I am in no pain, if that is what you mean," she replied. "And I am not agitated or unhappy. Did you see the look on Sharlee's face? I have been waiting for my chance at her ever since she chained me up."

Danr wiped the last of the blob fluids from his face, though the stench still covered him in an eye-watering miasma. Hector and Sharlee had kept Kalessa chained to a tree for days and days as a hostage against the good behavior of Danr, Aisa, and Talfi, who were to bring back the power of the shape. Now, at last, that power had killed both of them—and altered Kalessa herself.

"It worked, sister," Aisa said.

"It worked?" Danr squelched over to them, and both of them drew back at the smell. Kalessa's tongue flickered in disgust. "You mean you—"

"Goaded her, yes," Aisa said. "We knew if we made her angry enough, she would try to change Kalessa into something cruel, and then I would merely . . . add to it."

"You worked that out together while Aisa was in the cage and Kalessa was chained up?" Danr said incredulously. His clothes were sticking to him now.

"Not in exact words," Aisa said, "but the sentiment was there. Kalessa and I are blood sisters, after all. That was also the bond that let me add power to Sharlee's spell."

Danr spread his hands. "How are you going to change back?"

There was a long, long pause. Aisa and Kalessa exchanged glances. "I . . . do not know," Aisa said at last. "I cannot change anyone but myself."

"Maybe Welk could do it," Danr said.

"I doubt it very much." Aisa chewed a thumbnail. "The only animals he can transform into humans are ones he changed himself. It takes a powerful and skilled magician to undo someone else's spell. Even I cannot do it yet. And Sharlee herself is . . . well, you know where she is."

"She tasted like incense," Kalessa said. "Do you mean this could be permanent?"

Aisa's face tightened. "I fear it may be, sister."

"Hmm." Kalessa twisted around to look at herself. Her scales gleamed like liquid emeralds and hissed against one another in the cool moonlight. "There are worse fates."

This took Danr by surprise. "It doesn't bother you?"

"Bother me?" Kalessa raised her head and roared like a cannon exploding. Slynd raised his own head and joined her. The sound drove Danr's ears flat against his skull. The ash trees shook, and even the stone walls of the monastery trembled. "Not one person in the world will forget me now."

"Oh." Aisa shot Danr a glance. "What do you think, Hamzu?"

He had to laugh a little then. "If a problem becomes a solution, I say let it lie. Right now I need a wash."

Aisa caught up Kalessa's sword and Danr squelched down to the village, where they found a well. Danr's clothes were judged beyond salvage, so he simply ripped them off. The pails he and Aisa hauled up from the well were icy cold, but Danr welcomed the shock. Each bucket washed away a little more of the horrific memory of blood and pus, of Hector Obsidia himself, and what he and Sharlee had done to Danr and his friends all those months ago. After more than a dozen buckets, he finally felt clean.

Kalessa and Slynd stood guard over them during this process. Kalessa glared around the dark village with her new eyes the size of dinner plates. "No one seems interested in coming out to see us," she observed.

"That could not possibly be due to the two enormous wyrms writhing around this courtyard." Aisa set the bucket down. "Or it may be that they are unsure of what has happened at the monastery and do not know how to find out."

Kalessa raised her head and flickered her tongue at the village. She seemed to relish new sensations. On a whim, Danr closed his right eye and looked at her. Instantly, he saw Kalessa both as an orc and as a wyrm at the same time. *That* was even stranger—it meant Kalessa's wyrm form was just as true as her birth form.

"Should we at least tell the villagers what happened?" he wondered aloud.

"I think they will figure it out," Aisa said. "More than anything, I want to be free of this place. Tonight."

"All of us can see in the dark except you, sister," Kalessa said. "And you will be riding. We will travel a good distance up the road and then find a place to rest."

Danr felt a vague pricking at his hand, and for a moment he was holding a dead climbing rose. A voice echoed in his head. *Sometimes speed is better than care.* Then both sensations were gone. He shook his head and accepted the dry clothes Aisa had pulled from their packs.

Slynd was still wearing the saddle. After a moment's discussion, they decided that Danr, the largest, would ride Kalessa while Aisa continued to ride Slynd. Kalessa's back was much broader than Slynd's, and Danr had to cling to the horns protruding from her neck ruff to keep from sliding off. It was distinctly odd, knowing he was on a friend's back, and he tried not to think too deeply about it.

The two wyrms and their passengers fled the village, and the night swallowed it behind them. Kalessa rushed up the rough road with a surprisingly smooth . . . gait? Slither? Danr wasn't sure what the correct term was. In any case, it was clear she was pushing her new shape to see what it could do, and Slynd was hard-pressed to keep up. Even though it was night, they traveled far faster than they had when it was three of them riding Slynd.

"Such speed! Tikk himself would be jealous," Kalessa said over her shoulder in her new, low voice. "We will reach Queen Vesha's lands days faster at this rate. You did not lose my sword, did you?"

"I have it," Aisa called from the laboring Slynd.

"Grick would approve." Kalessa fell silent and slithered onward.

Dark trees and fields flowed past them beneath the now-setting moon. The chill air bothered Danr not at all now that he was dry. Cold rarely bothered him—even in winter he went barefoot. Trolls, of course, lived underground, and it wasn't particularly warm there, so Danr—

"I did not enjoy that," Aisa said, breaking into his thoughts.

Danr gave her a quick glance. He had to look down because Kalessa's back was so much higher than Slynd's and Danr was already so tall. "Enjoy what?"

"Killing them," Aisa said. "I have thought about Sharlee and Hector often since they took our friends hostage. If it weren't for them, my grandmother and Ynara would still be alive. The merfolk would not be angry with me. I would not feel so much guilt and anger. But now that I have killed them—or arranged for their deaths—I do not feel particularly better."

"It doesn't seem fair, does it?" Danr said. "It was just, and it needed to be done. Hector was in pain and he wanted to hurt more people. I saw it." He tapped his left eye. "The only way to stop them was to kill them. I should feel good about it, too, but . . ."

"Yes," Aisa sighed, and Danr wanted to hold her very much right then, but they were on different wyrms. Why were they so often separated by a gulf? He set his jaw. That separation would soon become permanent. He'd been trying not to think too much about that, but the knowledge crowded his mind at bad moments. They hadn't talked about their impending loss—or about a baby—since the night Welk changed Danr into a toad. The topic was too raw yet. But sometimes, late at night when he couldn't sleep, he turned the problem over in his mind, searching for a solution, a way for him and Aisa to stay together even after she became a Gardener.

"I noticed rot in Sharlee and Hector," Aisa said. "Just like in the Garden."

Now Danr looked at her full-on. "So did I. In my true eye. Did the Garden corrupt them, or did their actions corrupt the Garden?"

"I think they were already rotten, and their corruption allowed the Garden to make it worse," Aisa said. "That is the way of it—corruption is drawn to corruption, rot to rot. You saw how easily Hector and Sharlee blackened the people around them."

Danr shuddered. "Yeah. It was . . . yeah."

"But there is something you are not telling me, Hamzu. I can hear it in your voice."

The question was unasked, which meant he could choose how and when to answer it. He felt grateful for this small courtesy, even though he was going to tell her anyway.

"That injury knocked me out, and I felt like I was in the Garden. It was like a dream, or something."

"Hmm. A hallucination when you were injured?" she hazarded. "Or perhaps you went there like I go when I sleep. But you are not a Gardener, nor are you in line to become one."

He turned to peer ahead into the night, though there was nothing to see but empty road. "I keep waiting for everything to make sense, but it only gets worse."

She shook her head. "We need to get the Bone Sword from Queen Vesha. Then all of this can end."

"That's what I'm afraid will happen," Danr muttered.

The rest of the trip continued without real incident. Kalessa relished her new form. Every day, she rushed down roads both smooth and rutted, clearly enjoying the near invulnerability her scales granted her. She reported being able to taste incredible new sensations on the air, and couldn't imagine how she had missed them before. She hunted deer and elk with Slynd for food, and didn't seem to mind devouring them raw in the slightest.

"I would not have done this as an orc," she said after one meal, "but as a wyrm, I cannot imagine eating any other way. The bones crunch, and the blood adds a perfect tang to the meat."

"It certainly saves time cooking," Aisa said dryly.

And the likelihood that she would never become an orc again seemed to bother her not at all. "All my life I have ridden wyrms," she said. "I have long thought it must be wonderful to be so big and fast and powerful, and now I have that wish. Nothing is better!"

"Do all orcs feel that way?" Danr asked. They were riding past a herd of sheep that panicked and fled across their paddock as the wyrms passed with their two riders.

"Many do," Kalessa said. "Many old stories tell of orcs

and wyrms exchanging shapes. You know that. Perhaps this is why we feel so close to our wyrms."

"And now those old stories are coming true," Aisa mused. "Shapes are so . . . fluid. In the right hands. I wonder . . ."

"What?" Danr asked. "When someone who is fated to become a Gardener wonders something, the rest of us tremble, you know."

Aisa made a face that wasn't quite smile and wasn't quite grimace. "You remember that legend Grandmother Bund told us, the one that says the Fae and the Kin and the Stane were made out of three different kinds of clay?"

"Yeah." Danr's eyes grew distant as his thoughts went back to his grandmother's aged, powerful voice telling the story in the dark under the mountain. "The Stane came from rich, dark clay. The Kin came from smooth, fine clay. The Fae came from white, weak clay. Though probably the Fae tell the story a little different."

"I also have a different story for you," Aisa said from Slynd's back. "Long, long ago, when fire was a new discovery and living in a cave was the height of wealth, there was only one race of people, and there was only one god. Let us call him Tikk, the trickster. And Tikk the trickster told the people he would give them a gift, if they wanted it. The people gladly accepted a gift from their god, not realizing that Tikk was laughing behind his hands at them, for the gift was the power of the shape. Some people wanted nothing to do with this new power, and kept their shapes. Other people learned to change their shapes, and the shapes of other people. They changed their shapes a little bit, and then a little more, and then a little more.

"One group of people, the ones who lived in caves, changed their shapes so much that they no longer wished to come aboveground except at night, and their eyes became sensitive to light, and they twisted their magic until they could shape the shadows and the earth itself and forgot the power of the shape entirely.

"Another group of people, the ones who lived in the forests, went into the trees and into the air above until the heavy iron became painful anathema to them. They twisted their magic until it became all light and air and glamour and forgot the power of the shape entirely.

"Another group of people, the ones who farmed and fished, became close to the beasts they husbanded. They kept the power of the shape pure, and learned to change into any animal they pleased. Some went into the ocean and never came back. Others went to the grasslands and learned the power of the wyrms. And still others remained where they were, learning the power of eagles and lions, bears and boars.

"And over time, the groups of people changed so much that they forgot they had once been a single race of people and remembered only a time when they had been the three groups of three, the Nine Races. And once that happened, the trickster god discovered he had himself been tricked, for he was split into nine gods. But a piece of him flew away and remained himself, which is why the Nine are actually ten. And so the world spun out—one becoming three, three becoming nine, while two always revolve around a third, in the mortal world and among the gods and among the Fates, with the one trickster gadfly remaining a little apart.

"The Fates?" Danr said.

"Three and a trickster," Aisa said. "Three Gardeners and—"

"Death," Danr finished. "Oh. Shit."

"She did say Tikk likes to talk to her," Aisa finished.

Silence fell over the three of them and Slynd. Danr tried to digest what Aisa had said. It made a strange sort of sense. Certainly more than the clay story. He thought about Death in her chair with her knitting needles with the three Fates beside her and he shuddered. Three and one. Everything was three and one.

Then Kalessa made a hissing snort and the moment passed. "Really, sister! You do have strange ideas."

"Hmm," was all Aisa said in response.

Three days and nights passed. Every morning when Aisa woke up, she reported working in the Garden, but Danr slept undisturbed beside her through the night, and they decided his trip there must have been a hallucination brought on by shock and injury. All three of those nights, Aisa slid her body against Danr's and he wordlessly accepted her lovemaking within the fortress of the two wyrms that coiled around their camp. No words traveled between them about a child. If one came, one would come, and Danr realized that he wanted a child, a piece of Aisa to keep with him. And if Aisa left to become a Gardener, he would raise the baby as best he could.

But on the third night, Aisa lay on his chest and said, "You and . . . the little one will not be alone, you know."

"No?" he said, knowing what she meant.

"You have two great wyrms to guard the both of you, and two near-immortal men who will probably be better mothers than—"

"If you finish that sentence," Danr interrupted, "they will both hunt you down with bows and arrows."

She laughed lightly. "In any case, you will have help. And I will be there, too, in whatever way I can be."

Talking. They were actually talking about it. Danr raised his head up gingerly, as if he might frighten the topic away like a shy rabbit. "Maybe the child will stay with you in the Garden. Or maybe it will be able to travel back and forth and be with both of us."

"I . . . hadn't thought of that," Aisa said. She brightened. "I have been assuming the child will be mortal and always in this world, but why should that be? As a Gardener, I will be running the universe. Why should I not have what I wish?"

"I feel sorry for anyone who doesn't give you what you wish," Danr said.

"Hmm. Let me show you what I wish."

*   *   *

When they reached northern Balsia, they briefly considered a trip through Skyford and the village where Danr had grown up and Aisa had lived, then decided against it. Neither of them had many good memories of the place, and they had no desire for the earl to make a fuss over them as Skyford's most famous former residents. However, they did stop at the top of hill where the road looked down on Skyford, which lay at the bottom of a river valley. It was the very spot where Danr, leading a skin-and-bones steer, had paused to look down at the city more than two years ago, with no idea how much his life and the world were about to change.

"It looks different," Aisa observed from Slynd's back.

Danr squinted beneath his hat in the afternoon sunlight. The last time he had visited, Skyford was enclosed on three sides by a great palisade of wood and stone while the river formed the fourth side. Later, the earl, now dead, had brought armies from all over Balsia, and they had set up a camp across the river that had nearly dwarfed the city. Now it looked as though the city had expanded into that camp and become permanent. Stone buildings had risen like blocky mushrooms and spread across the slanted valley floor.

"Those are Stane buildings," Danr said.

"The trolls and dwarfs have come calling, just like they did in Balsia," Kalessa the wyrm said. "Whether the Skyford folk accepted this by choice or by force, I am curious to see. Perhaps we should stop in after all."

"Let's not," Danr said. "I don't want to add to any tension."

They skirted both Skyford and the little village beyond it and headed into the mountains. Danr had expected to find the path with difficulty, but instead they discovered a clear, well-maintained road that twisted upward through forest and foothill.

"The road makes sense," Danr mused. "The Stane build

with stone right handily, and if they're in and out of Sky-ford, they'd want a nice path."

"It is easy to climb," Kalessa said. "Come, Slynd! And do not eat any trolls you encounter, no matter how tasty they appear."

"They won't come aboveground during the day," Danr reminded her. "Sunlight bites them harder than it does me."

As Danr predicted, the road remained deserted. Only the great green trees and heavy boulders stood guard along the way as it climbed up the mountain. Danr sighed with relief when the shade blunted the sharp sunlight. In a short time, they found themselves at the Great Door. It was just as Danr remembered it—an outcropping of rock that jutted from the side of the mountain and didn't look at all like a door. But when he slid off Kalessa's back with a stiff groan, he saw the cunning handles carved to look like part of the outcrop-ping, and the faint outline of the door itself. Unbidden, Danr's memory called up the first time he had come here. A troll named Kech had threatened to eat Danr and Aisa alive if Danr couldn't prove he was part troll by opening the Great Door. It took three bone-cracking tries, but Danr had done it. Kech had been forced to admit Danr under the mountain—and eventually admit that he was Danr's father.

"This will not be fun," Aisa said. "It nearly killed you to open this door last time."

Danr looked at her, then set his feet, grasped the hidden handles, and *heaved*. The door ground open and flipped aside with a crash. Slynd whipped himself backward into an S at the sound. Danr raised a shaggy eyebrow at Aisa while Kalessa gave a laughing little hiss.

"How?" Aisa said, covering her mouth with one hand.

"I was sixteen back then," he said, "and still a boy. Come on."

They strode forward and slid down into darkness.

Chapter Twelve

Silence rang in Ranadar's ears and he stood blinking in shock at the mound of rubble piled in front of him. He couldn't seem to get his mind working properly. Dust choked his nose and throat. As always, he was aware of the iron all about him. Painful, dreadful iron. Iron forges in the distance, iron tools in the houses, iron utensils scattered about this very room. The heaviness dragged at him, grated on his nerves, put a bad taste into his mouth. The feeling was always there in this awful city, this place where iron horseshoes rang harsh on cobblestones and iron hammers bashed on awful anvils. It never quite went away, a headache that wouldn't end.

And he was also *hungry*. His stomach roared its emptiness, and his hands shook with ravenousness. He snatched up the sausage, bread, and pears from the floor and, heedless of the dust, crammed them into his mouth in greedy bites, then washed it all down with the wine. Vik, he wanted more of that Tikkscock. The power that had washed through him was like drinking pure sunlight. The memory turned the wine to Stane piss in his mouth. He had to find—

Talfi! Where was Talfi! How could he have forgotten? Ranadar shook his aching head in the dusty air. The food helped clear his mind a little. The earthquake! What had happened? Someone coughed and hacked nearby, and it came to him that he was standing in the building where he had summoned the sprite and forced it to talk. He turned, trying to understand, but his head would not come together. The dust settled a little. The figure coughing a few paces away was Talfi. Relief flooded Ranadar. He realized he was still holding half a pear in his hand, and he stuffed it into his mouth.

"Talashka," he said, and moved toward Talfi. The Nine! There had to be some Tikkscock left somewhere. He found himself scanning the floor for a leaf, a steam, even a seed. Then Ranadar saw the hand. It protruded from the great pile of debris that had once been the chimney and a good part of the ceiling above it. Ranadar recognized both the hand and the wrist of the tunic. It was Talfi's.

The world snapped into place. Ranadar remembered. The earthquake, the fleeing sprite, the cracking chimney, the collapsing wall. The man coughing near him was not Talfi, but the flesh golem. Talfi was dead.

Panic fluttered at the back of Ranadar's throat and he forced it down. It would be all right. Talfi was not dead. Talfi could not die. But neither could he come back to life. Not with a ton of rock grinding him down. Was he even now trying to revive and dying again? Ranadar's heart wrenched and the panic returned, quick and tight. He shouted Talfi's name and fell to pulling at the debris with his bare hands. He clawed at the stones and beams. But they were heavy, and he was weak from the damn iron. He no longer wanted the Tikkscock.

"First!" The flesh golem joined in. Ranadar thought little of the creature, even though it looked exactly like his *Talashka*, but in that moment, gratitude overtook him and he would have done anything in repayment. Together they shifted several stones and managed to pull aside a beam. The golem's great strength was a powerful asset, and he tossed aside rocks like pebbles. From outside erupted sounds of terrified screams and panicked shouts and other cries. Ranadar ignored them and kept working. Moments later, however, they found themselves unable to shift a boulder-sized rock with a beam resting atop it. Talfi lay directly beneath.

"Try harder!" Ranadar gasped. Dust and sweat streaked his hair and itched under his clothes, but he didn't care. He and the golem grabbed and heaved. Nothing moved. Talfi's hand stuck out, a grisly and pitiful petition. Blood oozed across the palm. Despair crawled over Ranadar, and he wanted to creep under the rocks himself and die. He grabbed again, ignoring his own scratched and bruised hands.

"Can you create a Twist to get him out?" the flesh golem asked.

"He could not step through it," Ranadar said through clenched teeth. "Lift!"

The flesh golem shook his head. "We can't do it."

"We must!" Ranadar tugged at the beam again. Splinters tore at his skin. "Come on! We must not . . . must not leave him."

"We can't do it," the other Talfi repeated. "Ran, it's impossible."

Rage filled Ranadar, and he whirled on the golem. "You want him dead! You want him dead so that—"

"What?" the golem asked. "So I can have you?"

"Isn't that the reason?" Ranadar tried to lift the beam again. The iron nails inside it nipped at him like cold claws, but he could not stop. "You think that if he is unable to come back, I will turn to you."

"I'm him," the golem said in that maddeningly familiar voice. It was both comforting and horrible at the same time, and the sound of it made Ranadar feel both relieved and sick. "It's *me*. You know that, Ran."

"Do not call me that!" Ranadar barked.

"It's what I remember calling you," the other Talfi said. "This flesh and blood are the same. The memories are the same. We're the same! I love—"

"Stop it!" The bolt of mental energy flashed from Rana-dar's head and struck the other Talfi square in the face. The other Talfi went to his knees with a cry of pain in Talfi's voice that wrenched Ranadar's heart. What had he done? Without thinking, he ran over to Other Talfi and put a hand on his shoulder. "I am sorry. I did not . . ."

"Vik! Where did you learn to do that?" Other Talfi gasped. "You've never done it before."

"Does it hurt?"

"Like a troop of dwarfs are pounding hammers in my head," he groaned. "I think I'm going to be sick." And he threw up.

Ranadar rubbed his temples, feeling even worse. "I am sorry. I did not mean . . . that is, I did know I could . . . maybe the Tikkscock brought it out. That and being angry."

"I don't want you to be angry at me." Other Talfi got unsteadily to his feet. "I hate it when we argue."

"You and I do not argue," Ranadar said.

"That's not how I remember it." Other Talfi's voice was quiet. Hesitatingly, he reached for Ranadar's hand. When he touched it, however, Ranadar pulled away.

"We need to find a way to save Talfi," he said.

Other Talfi closed his eyes in either pain, resignation, or both. It disturbed Ranadar that he could read the emotions because he had seen the exact same expressions on Talfi's face. And for a moment as small and quiet as the footstep of an ant, it flickered through his mind that if they could not find a way to pull Talfi out, perhaps it would be possi-ble to find happiness with someone who was his Talfi's double, and perhaps, over time, he would forget that this Talfi had ever been anything but the real Talfi.

He flicked the dreadful thought away. It was not true, would never be true. But the ghost of the idea remained in his mind, the way someone at the edge of a cliff wonders what it might be like to jump over the side.

More shouts and screams rose from outside the building.

These sounded a little different from the earlier ones. The devastation to the city must be terrible, but Ranadar had given it little thought.

"We can save him," Other Talfi said. "All of us."

Another figure lurched into the room, stirring the dusty air. It was the other flesh golem. His twisted face was covered in dirt, whether from sleeping outside or from the earthquake, Ranadar could not tell.

"Help . . . First," it—he—said.

Before Ranadar could react further, more figures pushed into the building—two, four, a dozen, twenty. All of them wearing ragged clothes, most of them badly disfigured, all of them Talfi. Ranadar found himself in a room filled with curly brown hair, sky blue eyes, and faintly crooked smiles. Some of them seemed intelligent; others were clearly feeble-minded. Ranadar's heart pounded in his chest, a bird trying to escape. He could not take it in, not fully understand what he was looking at. It was like standing in a forest that suddenly pulled up its roots and walked toward him. With cold certainty, Ranadar knew that this crowd of golems was the reason for the fresh screams outside. All these men shared Talfi's flesh and blood. Did they share his memories and . . . feelings as well?

Without a word, they moved toward the rubble and together they grasped the great, heavy beam. It easily wrenched aside under the inhumanly powerful strength of the flesh golems. The stones beneath it melted away, and no time, Talfi's crushed and broken body slid free of the rubble beneath the warped hands of his duplicates. His skull was crushed and misshapen and one of his legs was folded at a sickening angle beneath him. Ranadar's insides twisted.

"Talfi," he whispered. His entire world narrowed to that broken body. Ranadar touched the bloody face. He looked so much smaller when he wasn't alive. Ranadar had seen Talfi die a dozen times, and each time it stopped his own heart. Even with Death's promise, he could not seem to quite believe that Talfi would come back. And now Talfi had been crushed beyond all recognition. What had it been like? Sudden guilt racked Ranadar. Talfi had died in agony because Ranadar had brought him to this place. If Ranadar had not decided to summon the sprite, or if they had done it somewhere else, Talfi would never have gone through this. He would still be alive. Ranadar was cruel and selfish, just as everyone said.

"Come on, *Talashka*," he begged. "Wake up. You have to wake up."

But Talfi did not move. His body was growing cool.

"He's gone, Ran—Ranadar," Other Talfi said quietly. His palms were bleeding from a dozen cuts, and one of the fingernails had torn off from the scarred little finger of his twisted left hand. The other flesh golems stood in a Talfi crowd behind him. Some looked frightened, some looked solemn. Several were weeping quietly. It looked as though a hundred twisted spirits of Talfi were mourning his loss. Ranadar could not bear to look at them. He concentrated on Talfi—the real Talfi. But Talfi did not move.

A heavy lump grew in the back of Ranadar's throat, and his arms felt heavy. Hot tears pricked the backs of his eyes. "He will come back. He has to. Death promised."

"Some things not even Death can undo," Other Talfi said. "Let's . . . let's take him back to Mrs. Farley's. It isn't safe to stay here."

"No. No!" Ranadar insisted. He pulled Talfi's body tighter against him. "He will come back. He always comes back!"

"Ranadar." Other Talfi squatted next to him. "Ran. I'm sorry. I know you've lost him so many times. And maybe there's a reason for that." Other Talfi took a deep breath. "Maybe the reason he can't come back now is that . . . we're here."

"What?" Ranadar stared at him, and it was the most disconcerting thing imaginable to be cradling the body of his dead love while talking to a man who looked and sounded and acted exactly like him. Even his mind felt the same. This man was not a simple brother or a twin. This man was the same flesh, the same blood. "What are you talking about?"

"What if . . . I'm him now?" Sympathy and love filled Other Talfi's eyes, and they were Talfi's eyes. "You don't have to cry. I'm back. It's me!"

For an achingly long moment, Ranadar wanted to reach for him and leave the pain behind. It would be simple. This Talfi would be the same as the other Talfi. If the other Talfi was dead, what difference would it make?

The other Talfi. Ranadar closed his eyes. How could he ever have let his *Talashka* become an "other Talfi"? The pain did not matter. Talfi did. Ranadar got to his feet.

"It is not safe here," he said, forcing himself to ignore Other Talfi's aching, disappointed look. "We should bring him to Mrs. Farley's."

Other Talfi wrapped Talfi in his ragged cloak, picked up the body—at that thought, Ranadar had to force himself to remain stoic—and headed for the door. The other flesh golems made way for him like an honor guard. Ranadar followed.

Out on the street, Ranadar blinked and shied back. Chaos had spread everywhere. A number of houses and other buildings had collapsed in the earthquake, sending panicked people into the streets. Their cries and shouts and frightened chatter filled every corner, and the streets themselves were a bumbling press of people. Some were wounded and bloody. Children cried, babies wailed. Crowds gathered around some of the collapsed houses, desperately clearing away rubble to get at victims underneath as Ranadar and Other Talfi had done. Other, wealthier sections of the city must have been equally hit, and those sections no doubt had the prince's guard and houses with clay golems and—once the sun set— trolls to help. But guards and golems did not come to help the poor. He turned to the horde of flesh golems that streamed out of the building behind him.

"If you want to show your humanity," he said, "help these people!"

Without a word, the golems split up and spread out. They moved up and down the street, stopping at places where people were digging through rubble, and they helped. They pulled aside beams and cleared away fallen walls. No one seemed to notice the disfigured flesh, not in the crisis. It occurred to Ranadar that if Mother wanted to use the flesh golems to invade and take over the city, now would be the time.

"She won't do it now," Other Talfi said, as if reading Ranadar's mind. "There aren't enough of us yet, even with the city in a mess."

"You can simply refuse," Ranadar said. "Look at how much good you—you all—are doing."

Other Talfi shook his head above the sad, ragged bundle in his arms. "If *she* commands it, we have to do it. We're built that way."

"Then you are less human than I thought." He turned sadly to go, and missed the look of shock that crossed Other Talfi's face.

The trip back to Mrs. Farley's house was filled with more stress and pain. The earthquake had been relatively mild, but Balsia wasn't prone to them, and the city was not built to withstand them. A number of structures had simply fallen in on themselves, while others showed cracks or other damage and yet others showed no ill effects at all. The animals, which had become agitated in the moments before the quake, Ranadar realized, were now even louder and more panicky than their owners, and the sounds of horses, waterfowl, chickens, dogs, and other animals mixed with the yells of their owners. Some places had caught fire, and bucket brigades hastily rushed water from city wells to put them out. More than once, Ranadar and

Other Talfi encountered the prince's guard in their red and gold uniforms, looking harried and trying to keep order. Silver-shirted followers of Fell and Belinna, the warrior twins, joined them. Green-robed priests and priestesses of the goddess Grick, known for her aid and mercy, were out and about with sacks of medicine and worried expressions on their faces. Ranadar did his best to slip through the noisy crowds with his hood up and avoid thinking about Talfi. He had to get home to Mrs. Farley's. That was all that mattered. Just get home.

They passed a large shop that had completely caved in on itself, and Ranadar found himself thinking how foolish it was to build with dead wood and stiff stone. If such an earthquake had struck Palana, the trees would have swayed a little, but the flexible houses built into them would have gone undamaged.

"Fae!" The word came from a potbellied man in an apron standing outside the shop with two younger, shorter, thinner versions of himself. He pointed a blunt finger at Ranadar. "A stinking elf! Did you cause the earthquake, stinking elf?"

Ranadar halted, taken aback. He had forgotten to raise his hood or throw up a glamour, and his elven heritage was plain as the overhead sun. His thoughts fled back to the market, where the bottler had called him names as well, and he thought of how he always had to hide in this place—hide his heritage, hide his love, hide his grief—and he thought of how he himself had to hide—hide from iron, hide from fear, hide from humans. Bile and acid washed his stomach. He yanked his hood up and turned his head away.

"Funny how he shows up right after it happened," said a jowl-faced woman.

"Leave him alone," Other Talfi snapped over Talfi's bundled body. "He didn't cause anything."

But it was too late. Other people standing nearby had noticed and were whispering and pointing. Some were talking openly. "Go home!" one of them said suddenly. "We don't want your kind here!"

Others glared along with him. More than one fingered iron knives at their belts with hard looks on their faces. Ranadar stood there with his dead love in the arms of a flesh golem, and his knees buckled under the injustice of it all. He had given everything he had so these people could live. He had helped rid this country of slavers. Now the Fae—his own people—were planning to invade the country, starting with this city, and he was trying to find a way to stop it. And for what? So they could spit on him in his grief.

"Fae filth!" One of the men balled up a fist. "I'll show you how we treat garbage in Balsia!"

The man rushed forward, and anger burned inside Ranadar. The power he had felt before gathered in his mind. If these people thought he was a monster, he would show them what a monster could really do. He would—

Other Talfi leaped between them, bundle and all. The man slammed into him with an *oof*. Startled, Ranadar let the power dissipate. He expected both Talfi and the man to fall to the cobblestones in a tangle of limbs, and he was steeling himself to seeing the dead Talfi spill out of the cloak, but Other Talfi remained rigid as a tree. The man bounced off him and landed flat on his back.

"You won't hurt him," Other Talfi said in a deadly even voice.

"Vik!" The man scrambled backward while the crowd gaped. "What are you?"

"The real threat to this city, apparently." Other Talfi shifted the sad, ragged cloak in his arms so it lay over one shoulder and put his free arm around Ranadar. Ranadar noticed the torn fingernail and the way he smelled like Talfi. Ranadar was too upset to push Other Talfi away, and the familiar touch calmed him, even as it reminded him of his recent loss.

And some shame came, too. Had he not just been thinking that someone needed to stop the fighting between Fae
and Kin? These people were not angry at *him.* They were
angry because they were frightened, and Ranadar was a
target. It was hard to remember, but he should try. Someone had to take the first step to make things better, and
sometimes the best way to stop a fight was to walk away
from one. Even in anger.

"Let's go, friend," Ranadar said. Other Talfi's arm was
still around his shoulder. "Before someone gets hurt."

"Regi!" the man on the ground spat. "That's why you're
defending him. Pair of *rassregi*! Does the elf drill your
hole at night, *regi*?"

A sharp retort automatically came to Ranadar's tongue,
but he swallowed it and walked away. Other Talfi, however, didn't feel such constraints.

"You've obviously given it a lot of thought," he called
over his shoulder. "You should ask that manly wife of
yours to strap one on for you. Then you won't have to fan-
tasize so much about elves."

The other people in the crowd looked just as outraged
as the man on the ground, and a couple of other men
seemed ready to attack again, despite Other Talfi's show of
strength. Other Talfi bristled, but Ranadar shook his head.

"Talash—my friend," Ranadar said, "please walk away.
For me."

Other Talfi gave him a peculiar look, but obeyed. Dark
looks from the people followed in their wake, but Ranadar
ignored them. Other Talfi continued to carry the red-
wrapped bundle over one shoulder and kept his free arm
around Ranadar.

"Assholes," Other Talfi muttered. "Vik-sucking assholes. Don't they know who we are? What we did?"

Ranadar wanted to react to this, he truly did, but it was
overwhelming to watch a living copy of Talfi call his attackers names while carrying the cooling corpse of Talfi himself.
His throat thickened, and he forced a wan smile to his face.

"Thank you for the help," he said, coming out from under Other Talfi's arm. "I am fine now."

A flicker of disappointment crossed Other Talfi's face, but Ranadar was too unsettled to do more than register its presence. "Just as long as you don't use that mind-smashing thing again," he said. "I could tell you were getting ready."

Ranadar nodded and concentrated on moving forward. That was Danr's philosophy, correct? Just keep moving forward, always forward. He tried it now.

They passed more people and heard more rumors and stories. The Gold Keep had fallen. No, it was barely damaged. No, it had not been damaged at all. A tidal wave was moving toward the city. No, it had already struck, but the spit of land that protected the harbor had stopped it. No, the coast to the west had been flooded. No, everyone should move to higher ground to avoid the tidal wave. No, the priests of Bosha had said there would be no tidal wave.

Through it all, Other Talfi kept Talfi's body close against his chest and followed Ranadar without further comment. Ranadar was sweating now, both with effort and with grief. With every step, it became clearer and clearer that Talfi was really gone. Grief gave way to more anger. Death had promised! She had taken half his life away and given it to Talfi, but Talfi was dead. What kind of universe allowed—

A chill came over Ranadar, and he halted so quickly that Other Talfi nearly bumped into him from behind. What if the reason Talfi had failed to come back was that Ranadar's days were over? Death had not actually said how many days Ranadar had left. Today might be the end. Today Ranadar must be fated to die as well. It made perfect sense. He certainly did not wish to live.

"What is it?" Other Talfi asked.

Ranadar silently took Talfi's body from him and pressed his face into the ragged cloak. Before the sun set, they would be together in Vik's realm—and he would pause at Death's door to tell her what he thought.

"My *Talashka*," he whispered in a choked voice. "We will always be together, one way or another."

He wondered how it would happen. Another earthquake, perhaps. Sorrow might overcome him and he might simply end it himself. Or he could just fall down dead. He wondered how Mother would react when she learned of it. A strange calm came over him. Soon it would be over, and he would no longer have to worry about dying Talfis or his mother's machinations or rescuing the Great Tree.

"What's wrong?" Other Talfi said. They were only two streets away from Mrs. Farley's house. This part of the city was showing little damage, though the streets were still filled with uncertain, worried people.

"I have realized something important," Ranadar said. "Something that should have occurred to me earlier."

"Uh . . . can it wait until we get to Mrs. Farley's?"

"Probably not," Ranadar replied with a grim smile. "At any moment I will—"

The bundle in his arms squirmed hard and gave a loud gasp. Ranadar's heart jerked. With a cry, he set the bundle on the filthy cobblestones and pulled the cloak away. Talfi blinked up at him, his head healed and his hair crusted with blood. His sky blue eyes were confused, and he worked his jaw back and forth. Ranadar gave an unprincely shout as his heart soared.

"You are alive!" Ranadar shouted. "The Nine! You are alive!" He yanked Talfi into an embrace of wild delight and disbelief as tears sprang to his eyes.

Talfi, for his part, seemed a little bewildered. He hugged Ranadar in return and patted his back. "I'm all right. I always am. What's the big problem?"

"You've been dead a long time." Other Talfi leaned laconically against a wall with a few fresh cracks in it, though there was tension in him. "We were beginning to wonder."

"Wonder?" Ranadar backed up a moment and held Talfi at arm's length. "*Talashka*, we thought you were truly dead."

"Oh." Talfi patted himself as if making sure everything

was in the right place. He pulled a spoon from his pocket and looked at in confusion. "I always come back, Ran. Death promised."

Ranadar floundered, not sure how to respond. Just a moment ago, he had been ready to die, *sure* he was going to die, and now his reason to die was alive again, and the world was a fantastic place. He felt as if he might fly to pieces or shout or leap into the air and punch the sun, all because the world had returned to normal.

Talfi slipped the spoon back into his pocket, and it struck Ranadar as such a mundane gesture that he nearly laughed with giddiness.

"How did I get out from under the . . ." Talfi's handsome face paled a little, and he swallowed a little. "That is, I remember the chimney falling and . . . then I was here."

"Ranadar dug you out with his bare hands," Other Talfi said lightly.

"Did you?" Talfi sighed. "Gods, Ran. Thank you. That was a bad one."

Ranadar snatched him into a long embrace again and privately wondered if he would ever manage to let go. It was the most wondrous thing simply to hold Talfi in his arms, feel Talfi's cheek against his own, touch his hair. But eventually he did let go.

"We'll call that your second favor," Talfi said with a shaky laugh. "Fing!"

"Oh!" Ranadar laughed himself. "I had almost forgotten. That should not be a favor."

"It's mine to use," Talfi replied. "Shut up and let me use it."

"Took you long enough to come back," Other Talfi said lightly. But Ranadar heard a hint of strain in the voice he knew too well. "We thought Death had reneged."

Talfi stretched his arms wide and grimaced slightly as his joints popped. "When Kalessa's father chopped my head off, I didn't come back for several hours. I don't know why you're so surprised."

Ranadar grinned and caught him in a third embrace. "I

am just thrilled to have you back, *Talaṣhka*. Hurry! We should check on Mrs. Farley. We will tell you everything else on the way."

Mrs. Farley's house had ridden out the earthquake with minimal damage, though the lady herself was sitting on a bench outside the front door, clearly reluctant to reenter the house. She started off it with a small cry when she saw them. "Good Grick! You're covered in blood, Master Talfi!"

"It looks worse than it is," Talfi said. "I'm all right. Just need to wash."

"The well water's all cloudy, but it'll do for a rinsing," Mrs. Farley said uncertainly. "I don't dare go back inside for any brandy if you've cut yourself. What if there's another quake?"

"I doubt there will be another, Mrs. Farley," Ranadar said, feeling suddenly tired now. It had been a horrifically long day. "Though I suppose a great many people will be sleeping in the streets tonight. It will be a sporting day for thieves."

"That's why I have my courtyard," Mrs. Farley said. "I'm glad to see you boys are all right. Did you bring back my kitchen things?"

"Damn. I think they were lost in the earthquake." Talfi showed her the spoon from his pocket, then put it away again when Ranadar drew back. "That is all that survived. We'll replace everything, we promise."

"It'll make eating difficult until then, Master Talfi," Mrs. Farley sighed. "I—oh! You must be Master Talfi's . . . brother?"

This last she directed at Other Talfi. He stepped forward and took Mrs. Farley's hand. "Sure am. Arrived just now and wham! The quake hit."

"I see." Even during a crisis, Mrs. Farley played the good landlady. "Will you be staying long? Your brother has rented the entire place with his friends, and there's plenty of—"

A sprite flickered through the sky. It shot down the street and struck Mrs. Farley full in the chest. She made a soft sound of surprise, and then standing in her place before the house was the grand and beautiful form of Queen Gwylph of the Fae.

Chapter Thirteen

Just as Danr remembered, the tunnel abruptly widened into a cavern so great and wide and tall, a hawk could have flown across it and not realized it was underground. Mushrooms of sizes ranging from thumbnail to oak tree grew everywhere, and many of them glowed with a soft green luminescence that provided Danr's troll eyes with more than enough light, but were dim and gloomy to Aisa and Kalessa, though perhaps Kalessa's new serpentine vision was more sensitive.

A great stone staircase descended into the cavern ahead of them—the tunnel came out some distance above the cavern floor—and the tall risers were difficult to descend, built for trolls and giants as they were. Though now that Danr thought about it, the dwarfs, who were much shorter than even humans, had to have some way of getting out. There must be a different staircase somewhere else.

In the distance flickered more lights, an entire cityful of fireflies. Danr inhaled the damp, mushroom-scented air and remembered the last time he had visited Glumenhame, the kindgom under the Iron Mountains. Here he met Kech, his father, and Bund, his grandmother and a powerful trollwife. Danr had liked Bund a great deal, and her death still caused him sorrow. His father, Kech, on the other hand, was someone Danr had little respect for. Kech had fallen in love with Danr's mother, Halldora, and she with him, but when Halldora had become pregnant, Kech had been too weak to acknowledge his half-blood child, and he had turned his back. Years later, Danr had threatened to reveal their blood ties, and Kech had begged him to stay silent. In the end, Danr had agreed, though many people, including Kech's wife, Pyk, and their son, Torth—Danr's half brother—knew Danr's origin.

Also in the know was Bund's sister Vesha, queen of the Stane. She had seen the value of having a nephew who could move freely between the sunlit upper world and the gloomy underworld and had appointed him temporary ambassador to Skyford and the Kin in general. Vesha, however, had also been instrumental in chaining Death and using her power to break the Fae spells that had kept the Stane trapped and starving underground for centuries. For this Vesha had paid a price. Death had escaped and laid a terrible curse on her: Vesha would be immortal—until she set foot aboveground. Then Death would come for her personally. Danr hadn't seen or heard from Vesha since then, and he still didn't know whether to live in awe of her accomplishments or in horror of her foolishness.

Danr paused at the top of the great staircase for a moment, remembering all this, until Kalessa nudged him with her nose. "Are we standing here all day? We have a sword to find."

They trooped down the stairs. The two wyrms had less trouble than Danr had expected, but the risers were difficult for human-sized legs, and Aisa finally clambered onto Slynd's back. At the bottom, a great wooden bridge trundled across a noisome, eye-watering pool of bat droppings that slithered with multilegged insects. When Danr had last been here, the bridge was creaky and more than a little nerve-racking, but someone had rebuilt it firm and strong. At the front of the new bridge, a troll stood guard. It—he—was more than a head taller than Danr, and his massive body was thick as a pile of boulders beneath a rough-and-tumble suit of dwarf-built armor. Thick black hair stuck out from the huge helmet that covered his head, and he carried a bronze-shod club with spikes in it. His jaw jutted pugnaciously forward, pushing his small nose back into his face and letting long white fangs poke upward. Trolls would find him handsome, Danr was certain, even if humans did not. The troll looked to be about eighteen, though Danr hadn't spent a great deal of time among his father's people and wasn't very good at estimating the ages of other Stane. The troll guard raised his great club at them as they reached the bottom of the stairs. Kalessa, Slynd, and Aisa drew back from the troll with literal hisses, but at this distance, Danr was able to recognize him.

"Torth!" he said. "I haven't seen you in some time!"

The troll stared down at Danr uncertainly. "Do I know you, human?"

"I'm Stane," Danr said blandly. "I visited our—your—father just before Grandmother Bund died. Aisa here came along. Remember?"

Recognition stole over Torth's face. It warred with fear and more than a little anger. "I remember. It was because of you my grandmother died."

Another pang went through Danr, and a weight settled on his shoulders. He remembered with pain Bund casting the spell that opened the Twist to send him, Talfi, and Aisa to Xaron so they could look for the Iron Axe and persuade the orcs to join in the fight against the Fae. The spell had cost Bund the last of her fading strength and killed her. It had also cost Talfi his leg and his life, though that situation had ultimately improved.

"None of us knew she was going to kill herself when she sent us to Xaron," Danr said quietly. "If I had known, I wouldn't have let her do it."

"No one could stop Grandmother Bund from doing anything she decided to do," Torth grumbled in the dim cavern.

"That is certain," Aisa put in. "I think of her often, and remember her strength and power. You must be proud to be her grandson."

Torth seemed a little mollified at that, and he shifted his club with a clank of armor. "So, why are you here? Have you come to see . . . my family?"

"In a way," Danr said, and on impulse added, "Look, Torth—you're my brother. My only brother. I know we aren't supposed to talk about it because Father's a prince who fathered a bastard child with a human. But everyone knows what happened. Everywhere else in the world, people toss me gifts and throw me parades. Down here, can't you and I at least be friends?" He put out a hand and held his breath.

Torth hesitated, then brought up his own hand. Abruptly, he pulled back. "You're after the queen."

That caught Danr flat. He dropped his hand. "What?"

"You're right—everyone knows who you are. You wielded the Iron Axe and saved all of us. I was there, too, remember?"

"You were at Palana?" Danr gasped. "I didn't see you."

"We were all somewhat occupied," Kalessa said.

"I had put on my armor—this very suit of it," Torth said. His voice was deep and rumbling, though the cavern was too big for an echo. "And I was put in command of a regiment of trolls, dwarfs, and giants, just like Father. The horns sounded to announce sunset, and we marched out the Great Door. Except something went terribly wrong. A Twist wrenched us across the continent, made us all dizzy and sick and scattered our soldiers. The Fae fell on us then and we couldn't stop the slaughter. Only a few of us had iron armor and weapons, and even those of us who did were too unsettled to use them well. I saw my friends cut in half and their blood ran in black rivers."

"I'm sorry," Danr said softly. "I tried—"

"Then you showed up with that Axe," Torth continued as if he hadn't spoken. "You called fire and stone from the sky and made the earth shake and cut the Fae to ribbons. I had thought I couldn't be more afraid when the Fae Twisted us to Alfhame, but I was wrong. You were the most terrifying, fearsome thing I'd seen in my life. Vik himself would have hidden in his bucket of souls when he saw you coming. I pissed myself in my armor.

"You faced down the Queen of the Elves, and she fled like a coward. The queen!" Torth thumped his club on the cave floor, and the sound rang hard. "And then we were suddenly back in Glumenhame, as if none of it had ever happened. Except a great many of us were dead, and our own queen is cursed. And all the doors are open and we are free to come and go. We have food and we have trade with the Kin now. The sacrifice of our people was painful, but not in vain."

"Er . . . good?" Danr hazarded.

"And now you've returned," Torth said. "You're the hero of the Stane. Everyone celebrates who you are and what you did, and they call you a prince. Father could publicly acknowledge you now, and it would make him an even bigger Stane than he is now. But it would shame Mother."

"Hmm!" Kalessa put in. "He is celebrated and she is shamed, even though he is the one who strayed outside his marriage. You Stane live underground because everything about you is backward."

"Hey, look," Danr said, "we don't need to—"

"You want the crown!" Torth burst out.

This silenced everyone. Water dripped, and Slynd's scales scraped against stone as he shifted position. Finally, Danr said, "The crown?"

"You're my brother, which makes you a prince," Torth spat. "Aunt Vesha has no children, which puts Father in line to be king after she dies—if Death ever takes her—and me in line after him. But now you're here. You saved us all. The moment you arrive in the city, they'll throw a great celebration that'll last for nights. And then Aunt

Vesha will have no choice but to put you in line for the throne. First in line. Half-blood or not." He spat again.

"I thought the Stane disliked like half-bloods," Aisa said.

"It's more complicated than that," Torth said. "Some half-bloods are better than others."

"To become a full-blood, all you must do is save the world?" Aisa said.

"I don't want to fight," Danr interrupted. "And I don't want the crown."

Here, Torth paused warily. "You don't?"

"Up there"—Danr pointed at the ceiling—"I've been made a knight and a baron and, when I wasn't paying attention, a priest. I've also been crapped on, spat at, and hit with big sticks. All I really want is to be left alone on a farm somewhere. The last thing I want is to rule over a bunch of people who half love me and half hate me for the way I was born."

Torth chewed his tongue. Danr felt a strange pain at his hesitation. He'd barely thought of Torth until this moment, but now that he was facing him, he wanted to feel a greater connection. Everyone else he'd grown up with had siblings, but never Danr. Being an only child had accentuated how different he was to the humans around him. Now that he had a brother, he wanted to *have* a brother. For real. But Torth saw him as a rival, not to be trusted, not to be—

"All right." Torth held out his hand.

Danr stared down at it stupidly. "What?"

"You're my brother," Torth said, still holding out his hand. "It shouldn't matter, I guess, whether you want the crown or not. Blood is blood. I'm more worried about Mother, but—"

"Brother!" Danr shook Torth's much larger hand in his own. It was strange to shake hands with someone bigger and stronger than he was, but this was his brother. He had a brother. A small bit of elation feathered through him.

"Just hug him," Kalessa said, flicking her tongue. "Truly!"

Torth and Danr embraced, a little gingerly because of Torth's size and armor, but fully. For the first time in his life, Danr was hugging his brother, and he wanted the moment to go on for a while, even though he had to surreptitiously wipe at his eyes.

"Well," Torth said, and his voice was a little thick, "I suppose I should bring you into the city. Get the parade started."

"If it's all the same to you," Danr said, "I think we'd rather skip all that. We're a little pressed for time, and we need to see Aunt Vesha. Can you arrange it?"

"Yeah, course." Torth cocked a thumb. "There's a back way into her caverns. I can take you. Brother."

"Brother," Danr echoed with a grin.

"Oh, brother," said Aisa, but Danr caught the soft note in her voice.

Danr had not visited the royal caverns the last time he had come under the mountain. They were a series of tunnels dug through the rock that wormed in a thousand directions. Each was polished smooth and overlaid with marble and granite, often shot with veins of gold or silver. Mosaics of precious stones showed scenes from ancient stories— Bosha and Kalina warring with the Fae, trickster Tikk in the shape of a fly landing on Grick's vulva as Brinna and Fell were born and adding himself to the Nine, Urko being split in half as a punishment and living partially in Glumenhame and partially in Lumenhame. The stones refracted the luminescent light of the ever-present mushrooms, amplifying it and brightening the caves without hurting sensitive trollish eyes. They passed sumptuous rooms with intricately carved stone furniture and even some of precious wood. A great kitchen bustled with a dozen trolls and gave off strange smells that nevertheless made Danr's mouth water. Torth led them past this room before the huge cooks noticed them and left them in a

small side chamber, though *small* was a relative term—
the room would have housed three human families com-
fortably.

Torth said, "Wait here. Brother." He left.

"How long does he intend to do that?" Aisa asked.

"Oh, leave it alone. Sister," Kalessa put in while Slynd
explored the room.

"I am only teasing." Aisa put her hand into the crook of
Danr's arm. "I am glad the two of you have decided to get
along. And it will make one part of the Garden that much
less of a tangle."

A moment later, Queen Vesha strode into the room. She
towered over everyone there, including the wyrms, but she
wore an elaborate dress of night blue velvet embroidered
with gold thread. Like with all trolls, her jaw jutted forward, showing plenty of teeth, and she wore her dark hair
in a long, thick series of braids wrapped around her head.
Torth came behind her, wearing a more straightforward
tunic and thick trousers. Both trolls were barefoot—Danr
had never met a Stane who went shod except into battle.
Vesha went straight to Danr and hoisted him off the floor
in a tight embrace. Danr's breath rushed out of him and his
ribs creaked.

"Nephew!" she grumbled in his ear. "It's been too long!
And Aisa!"

Aisa stepped back out of hugging range. "I would rather
not be crushed," she said, "pleased as I am to see you,
Highness."

Vesha set Danr down. "And Torth tells me you brought
friends from the orcs. Hail, good Kin."

Kalessa dipped her head. "Hail, Queen of Trolls."

"Extraordinary," Vesha murmured. "If I hadn't heard of
it already from Torth, I'd be shocked. An orc with the
power of the shape! The old stories are coming true again."

"And trolls are allying with humans in Skyford and the
city of Balsia, I see," Aisa said. "I never thought to see
that day."

"Isn't it wonderful?" Vesha said. "The new earl in Sky-ford gets along with the Stane very well, and so does young Prince Karsten. Trolls like to dig, you know. We're nearly done with the new tunnels."

"Tunnels?" Danr said.

"We're working on connecting Glumenhame and Balsia. Soon, trolls and dwarfs and perhaps even giants will be able to travel freely to Balsia and back without ever worrying about the sun. It's a wonder. The dwarfs have been gloating about the engineering for months."

"And Prince Karsten approves of this?" Aisa said.

"It was his idea," Vesha replied. "Bringing the Stane and the Kin together, and everyone profits. Once you get past his mother, you find an extraordinary young man. He'll be a great king one day."

"Hmm," said Kalessa. "All we need now is someone to bring in the Fae and we'll have world peace."

"As if that would happen," Vesha snorted. "How is your friend Talfi, by the way?"

"Talfi? Still alive and kicking," Danr said.

"And will be for some years to come," Aisa added.

Vesha scratched her ear. "Good to hear, good to hear. Did he come with you?"

"He had to stay in Balsia," Danr said, a little puzzled at this turn in the conversation. As far as Danr knew, Vesha hadn't said more than two words to Talfi. "Listen, I should say that what we've come for is a little delicate, Aunt, and we're pressed for time."

"Of course, of course," Vesha said, then added without thinking, "What's it all about?"

There was a pause, and Aisa had time to say, "Oh dear," before the direct question forced Danr to speak.

"The Garden that grows in the shade of Ashkame is rotting because Queen Gwylph of the Fae has imprisoned one of the Gardeners, and Gwylph is stealing her power, kind of like the way you stole the power of the *draugr* and corrupted yourself—sorry—and the only way to get her out is with the

Bone Sword, so you have to give it to us right now—sorry—otherwise everything and everyone in the world will die and we're hoping you're not that stupid—sorry."

Torth sucked in his breath at this, and the silence returned. Danr gritted his teeth and looked away. Vesha worked her tongue around the inside of her mouth for a long time.

"After living with Bund," she said at last, "I should know better than to ask a direct question of a truth-teller. No apologies are necessary. It was my fault for asking."

Danr breathed a sigh, and Kalessa hissed faintly behind him. "Thank you, Aunt," he said.

"But I can't give you the Bone Sword," Vesha finished.

The silence returned a third time. Finally, Aisa said, "You know we will ask the obvious question."

"Come with me," Vesha replied, "and I'll explain."

Danr was about to comply, then spread his feet and folded his arms. "Aunt, I think you should explain now."

Torth took in his breath and Vesha the queen drew herself up. "What do you mean, *nephew*?"

Her emphasis on the last word was meant to point out his lower status, but Danr had had enough. "We're trying to save the world. Again. Last time I looked, the world included the Stane. Death herself said we need that sword to do it, and I intend to take it, no matter what you say. I didn't kill my best friend before the Battle of the Twist and die myself during the Blood Storm just so you could stall me over some petty problem." Danr tapped his left eye. "If you don't tell me, I'll look for myself. And I'll tell. *Aunt*."

"And if the Sword is the only thing that can prevent my death?" Vesha countered.

Danr set his mouth. He'd had a feeling it had something to do with that. "Your life won't mean much if the world ends. Tell us. Please."

Vesha hesitated, then nodded. "At least walk while we talk."

She took them deeper into the caverns, down spiraling stairs and sloping ramps. The decorations faded away, until they were tromping through bare, living rock. They passed other trolls, all of whom leaped aside, startled at seeing the queen herself, let alone the queen accompanied by a human and a pair of wyrms. Vesha ignored them, and Danr took his cue from her.

"The moment I set foot aboveground, Death will come for me," Vesha said as they went. "I thought Death might do something like that to me when we first bound her. It was a necessary sacrifice, and I thought I was willing to accept it." She sighed. "I wasn't. All my life I've wanted nothing more than to walk under the moonlight and feel open air around me. Now it turns out I'm the only Stane who can't."

"Where does the Bone Sword come into this?" Kalessa asked.

"I carved it from living bone, with help from the dwarfs," Vesha said. "The sword is alive, which makes it the only weapon that can ward off Death."

A chill ran down Danr's spine. "You want to fight Death herself?"

"The moment I cross that threshold," Vesha said with a firm nod, "I will challenge her to personal combat. When I win, I will walk the world above as I please."

"You cannot mean to kill Death," Aisa protested.

"Of course not!" Vesha said. "I will vanquish her and force her to lift the curse."

"Then why haven't you done it already?" Danr asked shakily as they came to the bottom of another staircase.

"Truth?" Vesha said. "Because I am . . . cowardly. I am working up the courage. I will only have one chance, and if I lose, Death will drag me through her door. It frightens me."

"Then let us have the sword," Kalessa said, "and when we are finished with it, we will return it so you may continue working up your courage."

"I don't think I can do that," Vesha said. "You might not return it, and I would lose my chance forever."

Aisa narrowed her eyes. "Whose bone is it?"

The earth moved. It rumbled beneath Danr's bare toes. A faintly sick feeling stole over him, and he had to swallow hard to keep his gorge down. Dust sifted down from the ceiling. Then the movement stopped. Aisa and Kalessa exchanged confused looks. Vesha paled.

"The Nine!" Danr swore, trying to keep his stomach down. "What was that?"

"So you felt it, too," Vesha said.

"Of course we felt it," Aisa said. "It was an earthquake."

"No," Vesha said. "It was more than that. It felt like someone ran a dirty hand over my soul." She withdrew a ridiculously small key from her belt and handed it to Torth. "Run ahead and check the vault. Tell the guards we're coming."

Torth dashed off. Danr leaned against the cave wall and breathed deeply of the cool air. His nausea faded. "Cave-ins?"

Vesha closed her eyes, and Danr could almost see her reaching out with her mind. "No," she replied. "It was minor here. Farther south it was much more powerful, but here it's fine."

"Good news, then," Aisa said. "Whose bone was it?"

Still Vesha didn't answer.

Danr closed his right eye. The world flickered and he saw . . . truth. Vesha was walking through a stone tunnel illuminated by quiet mushrooms, but she was also standing over her sister Bund's body while a Twist slammed shut before them both. Also lying on the cavern floor was . . .

"Talfi," Danr said in a hushed voice.

Everyone stopped, including Vesha. She turned to stare at him with eyes as hard and unblinking as brown granite. "The truth-teller knows," she said.

"When the Twist cut off Talfi's leg, you kept it." Cold horror slid all around Danr's body like chilled dog vomit.

"You took it to the dwarfs, and you stripped the meat off it and you forged a sword out of the bones. That's why the Bone Sword can fight Death. Not because it's made from a living thing, but because it's made from a living thing that can't die."

"Yes," Vesha said simply. "My sister was dead, and the leg was there, and I sensed its magic. I kept it. My sister was dead, but your Talfi was still alive. Keeping his leg seemed fitting somehow. And then when Death cursed me, I knew exactly how to use it."

Danr shook his head hard. This explained Death's reaction to the Bone Sword and Vesha's asking after Talfi. Vik! She had Talfi's leg bone down here—and Death wanted him to use it. What kind of world had the Nine created?

Kalessa looked agitated, and Aisa seemed ready to fight, but Danr stepped ahead of them. "Let's just get the Sword, all right? We'll talk about ethics later."

"I still haven't decided if I'm lending it to you," Vesha said with deceptive mildness. "You saved us all, but you also killed my sister."

That still hurt. At one time Danr would have backed down, but that time was past. "Grandmother Bund let herself die because she loved me and because she loved you," he said. "She chose to sacrifice herself just like you did, and I know sacrifice, yes, I do."

Vesha's face was made of iron. Was it going to crack? Before Danr could find out, Torth rushed up to them, eyes wild.

"The vault!" he panted. "Fairies have gotten into the vault!"

All of them bolted forward. They clattered down one more staircase and came to a plain stone door. When Danr got closer, he realized the door hadn't been carved so much as forged. It was solidified lava, polished smooth. A tiny keyhole was in the middle, and the door itself hung open. Without further words, they shoved their way inside.

Beyond the door was a great vault the size of a small castle. Ledges and nooks lined the walls, and huge shelves hung on chains from the ceiling. Bound chests and metal boxes and knotted sacks bulged on every surface, and great piles of gold and silver coins gleamed on the floor.

In the center of the room, a short pillar twisted up from the floor. It wasn't made of stone or wood, but of solid darkness, an ebony that sucked in all light around it. The pillar moved and squirmed like a living thing. Cradled atop the pillar was a simple glass case, narrow and sleek, and inside the case was a long white sword that stood out against the black pillar like the finger of a ghost floating in a dark room. Actually, the sword wasn't quite white. It was more translucent, like a bone that had been stretched thinner than a leaf, and looked as though it might slice through a heart, or a soul. A bloodred ruby was set into the pommel, and the cross-guard was heavy ivory, carved in thousands of runes. More runes curled up and down the blade. The sword looked both delicate and deadly.

Unfortunately, also in the room were hundreds of fairies, the small, earthy Fae. Fairy chitter-chatter filled the air like autumn leaves. Each creature was no more than waist-high on a human, with nut-brown skin, knobby joints, a bald head, a wizened face, large eyes, and sail-like ears. A group of them had formed a pyramid that reached the top of the twisted pillar, and the fairy at the top was cutting through the glass with a strange blade of a kind Danr had never seen before.

A few steps away from the pillar, the air rippled and distorted, as if a small heat wave had been trapped there, and the distortion had a night black border. An open Twist.

"They are stealing the Bone Sword!" Kalessa shouted. She shot forward with Slynd beside her. The fairies, however, had seen them the moment they entered, and every one of them vanished. Kalessa and Slynd snapped at empty air.

"An invisibility glamour!" Vesha shouted. "Watch your-selves!"

Aisa pulled Kalessa's blade from her belt and flicked it into a great iron sickle that she swept back and forth in front of her. There was a screech, and a fairy popped back into view, clutching its bleeding arm and howling in pain. It skittered up a wall. "You can't stop us!" it shouted.

"I would tell you to leave now or die," Aisa shot back, "but I think no one wants to let you live!"

Kalessa whipped about. She lashed treasures off their shelves. Coins scattered in a golden rain. A number of thumps and screams said she made contact, but the fairies remained invisible. Slynd snapped at empty air again and made swallowing motions. A small bulge went down his throat.

Vesha raised her arms. Darkness flooded from her sleeves and flowed over the room, effectively extinguish-ing most of the light from the mushrooms. Danr's trollish eyes, however, were unaffected.

"We can't see you," Vesha barked, "but now you can't see anything!" She strode into the vault, lashing about with her massive arms.

"Aisa!" Danr called. "Hit that Twist with your iron weapon!"

"How?" Aisa yelled back. "I cannot see it!"

Danr closed his right eye. Every fairy in the room snapped into view. The one at the top of the pyramid had finished cutting the glass and was already reaching into the case. Its hand closed over the hilt of the Bone Sword, still hidden by the glamour.

"They've got it!" Danr bellowed. He bolted forward and bowled straight into the pile of fairies. The impact crashed his teeth together. He went down. Fairies flew in all direc-tions. The fairy with the Bone Sword lost its grip and went flying. It whirled through the air, sheared through a metal box, and clattered across the floor. A thousand gold teeth spilled from the broken box. The Sword's ruby pommel stone gleamed like red anger, even in the darkness.

"I see it!" Torth dashed over to snatch it up, but almost immediately cried out in pain. Two fairies had latched onto his arm and sunk their sharp teeth into his hand. He howled and dropped the Sword. A third fairy snatched it up and fled straight toward the open Twist. Torth wrenched his arms around. One of the fairies slammed against the wall. There was a *crunch*, and the fairy went limp. The second fairy kept a death grip on Torth's hand, however, and the fairy with the Sword was only a few steps away from the Twist, which was right behind Aisa. But Aisa couldn't see it.

"Vesha," Danr bellowed, "cancel the darkness so Aisa can see! Aisa, kill the Twist behind you!"

The darkness vanished. Aisa spun, but it took her several seconds to find the Twist, barely visible as a black-bordered distortion in the air. The fairy with the Bone Sword was already leaping toward it. Without thinking, Danr lunged for the creature. With the tips of his fingers, he caught the fairy around the ankle just as it entered the Twist. In that moment, Aisa spotted the Twist and slashed the sickle through it.

A thunderous explosion knocked Danr backward. Light smashed his eyes, and noise boomed against his very bones. He slammed against a wall, and pain crushed his back. Dazed, he slid to the floor, both blind and deaf. The world rocked and spun, and nausea heaved in his stomach. The pain throbbed up and down his spine. All he could do was lie there and try to breathe.

Eventually, the pain lessened and he was able to push himself into a sitting position. His ears rang, but his vision was clearing. With aching slowness, he grabbed one of the stone niches above his head and used it to pull himself upright, wincing at every movement.

The room was devastated. Piles of worked gold and

silver lay everywhere. The boxes and cases were scattered and broken, their gilded contents strewn about the room. Hundreds of fairy corpses had been flung everywhere, motionless as broken dolls. The room smelled of hot metal and mangled mushrooms.

Kalessa and Slynd were wound together in an emerald tangle. Torth and Vesha were collapsed in heaps near the door. And Aisa! Where was Aisa? Fighting the pounding pain in his back, Danr desperately scanned the room, looking for her. She lay half-buried in a pile of platinum armbands. Danr hobbled over to her, heart pounding. She had to be all right. She couldn't be dead. She couldn't be—

Aisa coughed and tried to move, but the load of silver was too much for her. Relief so powerful it made him giddy swept over Danr. He leaned down to help free her and noticed for the first time what he was holding in his hand. It was a fairy's leg, sheared off and cauterized at the upper thigh. Danr dropped it with a shudder. It landed with a small, sad thump at his feet. Still wincing at the hot pain coursing across his back, he helped clear the silver away from Aisa. Carefully, she sat up.

"Can you hear me?" he asked, and his own voice was faint to himself.

She pointed to her ear, shook her head, and flinched from pain of her own. That was when Danr noticed her arm jutted at an unusual angle. She looked down at it as if puzzled, then looked back up at Danr. Vik, his back hurt. And now that he had time to take stock, he noticed it was hard to breathe. The explosion must have cracked a rib, or even two. He tried to kneel down next to Aisa, but this caused a fresh wave of pain that made him dizzy.

Aisa held up her good hand, halting him, then closed her eyes for a moment. A soft golden light slipped over her, and she changed into a small white cat. The cat squirmed out of her clothes and almost immediately changed back into a naked Aisa. She held up her broken arm, which was now whole.

Vik! He had forgotten. Danr reached inside himself for his own power and took his human shape while Aisa scrambled back into her dress. The pain vanished. His vision cleared completely and his hearing returned. His clothes collapsed around him like a bad tent, so he quickly pulled the power a second time and changed back.

"That's better," Aisa said, retrieving Kalessa's blade, which had fallen nearby and reverted to its default knife shape.

Danr took a moment to revel in the absence of pain, then put his arm around Aisa. "I was afraid you were—"

"I know," she said. "So was I. I am glad we are unhurt. But we should see to everyone else before we celebrate."

Torth and Vesha, with their solid troll bodies, had fared better and were only stunned, as were Kalessa and Slynd, though it took some time to untangle them. The fairies were all clearly dead.

"What happened?" Vesha said. "Where's the Sword?"

Danr cast about. The Sword was nowhere to be seen. Only the forlorn fairy leg lay bent on the floor, as if in trade.

"I think the fairy and the Sword went through the Twist at the same time the sickle touched it," Danr said. "It slammed shut and cut off the fairy's leg."

The implication hung heavy in the room. Queen Gwylph had the Bone Sword.

"Vik!" Vesha turned and slammed the wall with her fist. Magic blasted from the blow, and the entire vault shook. Danr nearly lost his balance. Vesha slammed the wall again and again, and each time the vault shook. Danr stumbled forward and grabbed her arm.

"Aunt Vesha!" he shouted. "You're bringing the place down!"

Vesha started to hit one more time, then visibly forced herself to regain control. Her breath came in short gasps and her eyes were wild with volcanic fury. "This won't stand!" she snarled. "It will *not*!"

A mass of frantic-looking trolls and dwarfs appeared at the vault door. Vesha whirled on them. "Get out!"

They fled, slamming the door behind them.

"We'll get it back from her, Aunt," Torth said. "We will."

Vesha started to snarl again, then turned her back for a long moment. The tremors in the cavern died down as her magic subsided. When she turned around again, she had regained more composure.

"How did those fairies get in here?" she said with deadly calm. "We're deep under the Iron Mountains. Iron. No Fae has ever been able to Twist through them, let alone do it all the way from Alfhame *and* find the power to hold a Twist open for so long."

"The power is easy enough when you have a Gardener all to yourself," Danr pointed out. "Pendra's power isn't limited by distance. Or iron."

"Then why did the touch of iron collapse the Twist?" Kalessa countered. Her tongue flicked the air with agitation.

"Hmm," Aisa said. "I do not like to say."

"Spit it out," Vesha said.

"I think the iron sickle did nothing to the Twist," Aisa said. "Rather than let Hamzu pull the fairy back or allow him to follow the fairy through, Queen Gwylph slammed the Twist shut the moment she had the Bone Sword in her hands. The explosion was to shove us back—and keep the fairies from revealing her plans."

"She killed her own people to ensure their silence?" Kalessa gasped, deeply offended and horrified both. "This is beyond monstrous!"

"The Elf Queen is wielding power she does not understand," Aisa said with a shake of her head. "And she is using it in terrible ways. Now that she has created life, death means little. She will only become worse as her power grows."

"Monstrous," Kalessa repeated, flicking her tongue again. "Was the Twist related to the earthquake?"

"I can't imagine it wasn't," Vesha said. "That would

explain why I felt sick. The earth itself is being corrupted, and that affects Stane everywhere."

"There is more," Aisa added. "The Twist was not created with a Gardener's power or with Fae magic. I felt that the moment the sickle touched it. The iron had no effect because it was yet a different type of Twist."

"What kind was it, then?" Vesha said.

"Did you not recognize it?" Aisa countered. "The black border. Its easy ability to punch past iron." She took a breath. "The Twist was Stane, my queen."

Silence dropped across the vault. Vesha worked her long jaw back and forth. "That's not possible. Gwylph is a master of the Twist, but she can't use Stane magic. Not even with the help of a . . ."

She trailed off and looked at Danr. Danr met her eyes. A terrible thought crossed his mind, and he knew she was having the same thought.

"What happened to the box I gave you?" she asked evenly.

Danr had to speak, but since he didn't readily know the answer, the truth-teller in him allowed him a few moments to think. When Vesha had appointed him ambassador to the Kin, she gave him a box that was actually a Twist in solid form. It allowed him to pull gifts—bribes, really—from the Stane treasure vault from wherever he happened to be. He had given coins, golden goblets, and the gilded, bejeweled skull of Bal himself to the humans, and to the orcs he had given more coins and gems and gleaming swords and runic daggers, all in the hope of creating allies with the Stane.

"I couldn't bring it with me to Palana in Alfhame," Danr said. "We were disguising ourselves as slaves, and slaves own nothing, so I left the box with the orcs in Xaron. Kalessa's father said he'd hold it until I could come back for it, but I never had the chance."

"Gwylph has been a step ahead of us," Aisa breathed. "She used Pendra's power and her own mastery of the

Twist to warp the box to her own purposes and steal the
Bone Sword."

"How did she even know the box existed?" Torth asked.
"Or where to find it?"

Aisa gave him a scathing look. "Pendra knew."

"Father!" Kalessa said suddenly. "The elf queen took
the box from my father! What happened to him? And my
family? And my Nest?" Her body quivered. "We must find
out! We have to go to Xaron! Can you Twist us there?"

"Let me think," Vesha said. "I have to think."

Dark guilt settled on Danr's shoulders and made his
stomach into a black hole. If the Fae had hurt Kalessa's
family, it would be his fault for leaving the box with Kalessa's father. He should have known better, should have kept
the box with him.

Vesha paced to the center of the vault, to the spot where
the Twist had stood. The crushed mushrooms that illuminated the ruined room were beginning to fade, and shortly
the room would be in total darkness. Vesha put out her
hands, and more velvet darkness flowed from them. Danr
remembered the way Grandmother Bund had commanded
the shadows, but this was no picture show. These shadows
twisted in ways that nothing should twist. They formed
fractals—patterns within patterns within patterns that made
Danr dizzy to see. Without thinking, he closed his right eye
and looked only with his true eye.

The shadows snapped into focus sharp as knives, hard
as dark diamonds. They writhed and twisted, seeking the
branches of Ashkame itself—the source of all Twisting.
Awed, Danr understood what Vesha was doing. She was
following the Twist. It was delicate work, like creating art
with hummingbird feathers. Sweat broke out on her wide
forehead, but she ignored it, concentrating on following the
faintest traces of magic. The shadows turned through nothing, but also through everything, touching the entire universe for a bare moment. Then Danr saw a presence, a
female figure made of golden light with threads of darkness

running through it and a black hole in her chest where her heart should be. Vesha's fractal threads touched the figure, and the figure whirled around. The threads snapped back into Vesha's hands. She staggered a little, and Danr opened his right eye with a strange mixture of amazement and pride. This was *his* family. Then a bit of nervousness came to him.

"That was Queen Gwylph, wasn't it?" he said.

"I followed the Twist back to its origin," Vesha said with a nod. She looked as though she might like a glass of water. "It started in Alfhame with Gwylph, but she's not in Palana."

Vesha gestured in a way that reminded Danr of Grandmother Bund. The deepening shadows flowed from the corners of the vault and gathered in the center where they were all standing to create a contoured map of the continent. Danr blinked at it. The more he looked at it, the more he saw. It wasn't like reading a map in a book. It was like staring down at the actual world from high in the sky, and if he focused on one spot, he saw great detail. There was Balsia, sculpted in shadow on Bosha's Bay. Streets crisscrossed every which way. Tiny houses lined the streets, and—here he squinted hard—people and horses and carts and carriages moved up and down them. For a moment, he thought he saw Talfi and Ranadar. Talfi was carrying a large, long bundle. Or perhaps it was just his imagination. Then Danr's eyes watered and he was looking at the entire map again.

"Gwylph is here." Vesha pointed at the spot where the Silver River flowed south and hit a single mountain. The mountain forced the river to fork, splitting itself into the Otra River and a secondary branch of the Silver River. "The Lone Mountain was pushed up during the Sundering and it divided the Silver River. The original riverbed behind the mountain dried up, which is why it's called the Sand River now."

"It lies directly on the borders of Balsia and Palana," Kalessa observed. Her great head hovered over all of them, and she was obviously doing her best to keep her agitation under control. "An ideal staging area for an invasion."

"How can she invade Balsia?" Aisa said. "The Kin have too much iron. And now that everyone knows how to break the Fae addiction, they do not have the strength. Not against an army encased in iron."

The answer, the truth, struck Danr with an electric jolt. "It's Talfi," he said. "Vik, Tikk, and the Nine—it's Talfi!"

"I don't understand," said Vesha.

"Talfi found that strange duplicate of himself in Balsia," Danr said. "It had to come from somewhere. And if there's one, there can be two. Or a dozen."

"Or a thousand," Kalessa breathed.

"Flesh golems," Vesha said. "Vik! She's creating flesh golems!"

"What are flesh golems?" Danr asked, though just the term gave him a pretty good idea, and it wasn't a pleasant one.

"The dwarfs make golems by creating a statue, drawing the right runes on it, and smearing the runes with blood. The blood is a conduit for life, and the runes are a conduit for magic. The two combine to animate the golem, make it seem alive." Vesha wet her lips. "You can animate anything this way—clay, wood, stone, metal, even ice, if you're very skilled."

"And . . . flesh?" Aisa looked a little sick.

"Also possible. And strictly forbidden." Vesha shuddered. "You could make it look like the dead have come back to life. Or you could piece together random pieces of—"

"That will do," Kalessa said. "I eat many interesting things now that I am a wyrm, but this turns even my stomach."

Vesha nodded. "But it becomes worse. No magic will heal—"

Here, Danr and Aisa traded glances.

"—but the right magic can create a . . . copy. Theoretically. If you have a piece of something that was once alive, you could grow an entire new being from it, like a seed sprouting into a tree. A hand or a leg . . ."

She trailed off and looked a little guilty.

"Do not halt on our account," Kalessa said grimly. "We know what happened here."

"It could grow into a whole person," Vesha finished.

"The Fae do not possess such magic," Aisa objected. "The queen does not possess such magic. Ranadar reminded us. She and other Fae can manipulate the mind and the Twist. Not the flesh."

"But Gwylph has the power of a Gardener," Danr said, jaw tight. "And the candle wax man Talfi saw could have been a badly done first job, yeah? She's practicing. On living beings."

"She won't stop at Balsia," Vesha said. "Once she has Balsia, she'll take the rest of the world. Except this foul magic is forbidden for a reason. It pollutes Ashkame itself, and if she's creating an entire army of flesh golems, she could easily poison the entire Great Tree."

"We are aware of that problem," Aisa put in. "But if it is true, that Gwylph is creating an army of . . . false Talfis, the big question is, where is she getting the material?"

"Material," Danr repeated.

"Ranadar said she needs a piece of Talfi to grow these flesh golems. Remember? So where did she get it? That was the main reason we decided she was not behind this."

And Danr remembered. He remembered watching the pain on Talfi's face as Ranadar's father, King Vamath, ran him through with a spear. And he remembered the blood pooling scarlet on the throne room floor. A cold feeling stole over him.

"Talfi died in Alfhame," he said. "He left material behind. He left his blood."

Kalessa sucked in a breath. "That is true."

"It would be enough." Aisa let out a long breath and gestured at the vault of dead fairies. "All of this and more because the Fae and Stane possess Talfi's blood and bone."

Kalessa couldn't keep still any longer. "I want to know what is happening in Xaron. Will your map tell me?"

Vesha waved her hand through the map, and it vanished. "Alfhame stands between Glumenhame and Xaron, and I can't see that far. In any case, our first priority is to get the Bone Sword back."

"What about my people?" Kalessa demanded, and Danr looked away, unable to meet her eyes. "My Nest? My family? The Fae must have attacked them in order to get that Vik-sucking box."

"If that happened," Vesha said, "there's nothing we can do to change it. I'm very sorry to be cold, Lady Kalessa, and I'm sorry this happened, but we have a bigger concern. The world—"

"You were not so concerned about the world a moment ago," Kalessa snarled. "You wanted to keep the Sword for yourself."

"All right, all right." Danr forced himself to step between them. "We don't have time to argue. Aunt Vesha, can you Twist us to Alfhame? Or . . . Xaron?"

Vesha thought a long, long moment. "It wouldn't be safe. I accidentally alerted Gwylph to my presence just now, so she'll be watching for me and the other trollwives. We might be able to raise the power to Twist you there, but if Gwylph intercepts the Twist—and believe me, it would be easy for her—she could tear you to pieces in a blink."

Danr glanced at the fairy leg lying on the floor and shuddered. "Then we'll have to run for it."

"We can go north," Kalessa said firmly. "Up and around Alfhame, then south through Xaron to the southern coast, which we can follow to the Sand River. That will actually save us time."

"How?" Aisa asked. "It is many miles longer."

"Balsia is wooded, and there we must follow meandering roads," Kalessa pointed out. "Also, people have attacked us for being strangers. These things slow us down. Xaron is grassland. We can travel in a fast, straight line, and no one will hinder wyrm-riders. Along the way, we can also find out what happened to my Nest."

"Very well," said Vesha.

"And what will the Queen of the Stane be doing to help?" Aisa asked pointedly.

"If Gwylph is planning to invade Balsia with this army of flesh, Glumenhame won't be far behind," Vesha said. "I will have to raise my armies once again, though we're scattered far these days. The trouble is always the same with us—we can't do anything aboveground during the day. But we may have a way to deal with that. I just need to have a word with the giants and the dwarfs."

"What kind of word?" Danr asked.

Vesha gave a thin-lipped smile. "Dig."

Chapter Fourteen

The sun shone golden in Queen Gwlph's hair and sparkled off her perfect green gown. "My darling boy," she said in her low, musical voice. "I am so glad to have found you."

"Mother," Ranadar said. "What are—"

"You better not have hurt Mrs. Farley," Talfi interrupted sharply.

"And what will you do if I have?" Gwylph countered with a raised eyebrow. "I am hundreds of miles away."

"I'd tell you to fuck yourself and the horse you rode in on," Talfi said blandly, "but I can tell you already have."

"Now, look, you little—"

"What are you going to do?" Talfi interrupted. "I am hundreds of miles away."

"Mother," Ranadar said, "what do you want? And be aware that if you want something, hurting my landlady is not the best way to persuade me."

"I know how much you care about your pets," Gwylph said. "It is good for you to keep a hobby, and they might learn something from you."

"Am I being insulted?" Talfi said. He clutched dramatically at his heart. "The Nine! Whatever will I do? Oh, wait—I'll just imprison a Gardener, use her power to create some flesh golems, invade Balsia, and threaten to destroy the world so I can take the Gardener's place. That'll make me feel better! Afterward I can go back to my horse brothel and wear out a few stallions."

Gwylph pointed to Other Talfi. "You. Hit him."

Lightning quick, Other Talfi backhanded Talfi across the face. Pain cracked. His head snapped back and he stumbled. Blood trickled from his nose.

"Again," Gwylph said, and Other Talfi punched Talfi in the chest. Talfi's feet left the ground and he landed more than a yard away. More pain exploded through Talfi as he hit the unforgiving cobblestones. Other Talfi's expression remained flat as a stone. He raised his fist again.

"Stop!" Ranadar ordered in a shaky voice. Other Talfi hesitated.

"The golem will obey only me," Gwylph said. "I could order him to kill, but from what I hear, your pet would only recover. So perhaps a good beating would be more in order."

"Stop it, Mother!" Ranadar said again, trying to move between Other Talfi and Talfi, who panted on hands and knees on the ground. The awful pain pounded at his back and ribs and face like a thousand dwarfs with hot hammers. Other Talfi backed up a step. "What do you want?"

"This is just a demonstration, my son," Gwylph said in her low, fluid voice. "The flesh golems obey me fully. They will even destroy their First, as they like to call him."

Still panting, Talfi pushed himself upright on hard, unyielding stones. The city closed in around him, laughing at him. Hot sunlight poured down on his back, uncaring and cruel. The queen gave him a mocking smile, and his fists clenched to hit her, even though he knew it would only hurt Mrs. Farley. A growing resentment bloomed inside him like a black rose. The world was kicking him around, and no one seemed to care. His eyes grew hot and his ears rang.

"Do you have something to say, little *regi* boy?" Gwylph said pleasantly.

Talfi glowered at her. A thousand demons clawed anger inside him. Every slight, every injury screamed to be let out. But he kept silent.

"I have seeded this human city with hundreds of flesh golems now, my son," the queen said as if Talfi suddenly weren't there, and that made the heat behind his eyes grow even hotter. "You have just seen what one of them can do, how fast they can move, how hard they can hit. Now think of an army of them."

"What are you going to do, Mother?" Ranadar asked evenly.

She raised a perfect eyebrow. "You already know that. We will crush Balsia and take it for our own. Once we have the city and its resources, we will conquer the Stane again, as is proper. The flesh golems will destroy them easily— my flesh golems can hunt the Stane during the day, and they do not mind iron in the slightest. The Fae will rule."

"Why are you telling me this, Mother?" Ranadar said. "You have to know I will tell the Balsian prince. He is already hunting down your flesh golems."

"Is he? Goodness, I had never guessed." Gwylph laughed, a delightful, musical laugh that Talfi was forced to find adorable, even while his ribs ached from Other Talfi's punch, and that brought up another black wash of anger. He loved the queen even while he knew she was manipulating him with magic. He wanted Ranadar to breathe on him and dispel the glamour as he had done back at the wyrm farm, but Ranadar should have known to do it without his asking, and so Talfi gritted his teeth and tried not to see the queen as so lovely on his own, and resented that Ranadar wasn't helping him. Other Talfi, meanwhile, kept his eyes on the queen, utterly ignoring everything else around him.

"You *want* the prince to arrest the flesh golems?" Ranadar said guardedly. "What are you up to, Mother? What do you really want?"

Here, Gwylph's face softened like honeyed butter, and

Talfi wanted nothing more than to cast himself at her feet and listen to her speak. Talfi concentrated on the dull hammers thumping across his back and chest to keep the illusion at bay. Why wasn't Ranadar doing anything about it?

"I want you to come home, my son," Gwylph said with a note of pleading. "Leave before war strikes the city around you. Leave, or I will put all your pets to the sword. Return to Alfhame where it is safe. We will welcome you. I never wanted you to leave us." A single, diamond tear slipped down her cheek. "I love you. Come home, or I will destroy the humans."

The sun's heat vanished and every ache on Talfi's body stood out in a hot lump. He stared at Gwylph. Was it true? The queen was willing to slaughter hundreds, thousands of people just to bring Ranadar back to Alfhame? One street over, shouts from a passing group of children came to him. If Ranadar didn't return, those children and their parents would be dead in a few days, and they had no idea. Talfi felt sick. He tried to catch Ranadar's eye, but Ranadar remained focused on his mother. This horrific conversation was growing worse and worse. Talking with Death was more pleasant. In desperation, Talfi plunged a hand into his pocket.

Ranadar had come to the same conclusion as Talfi. The color slipped from his face, and he gestured at the half-ruined city. "How can you say that, Mother? How could you kill all these people on the chance it will make me return?"

The queen looked genuinely surprised. "I would move the world to bring you home, my son."

Ranadar swallowed hard and he swayed a little. "But you already have the war ready to begin. You already plan to invade."

"If you return, I will merely occupy Balsia and the human lands," said the queen. "The Fae will take treasure instead of slaves as tribute." Her voice hardened. "If you do not return, all the humans will die."

"That is a lot to hear," Ranadar said slowly. "I must consider this."

Relief cascaded across Gwylph's face. She leaned down and kissed Ranadar's forehead. "You have no idea how happy that makes me, my *Ranadka*. If you wish to speak to me again, simply call on me three times and this kiss will send your voice to my mind. But do not consider long. We must—"

Talfi darted forward and smacked the queen with Mrs. Farley's last spoon. The iron disrupted the glamour cast over Mrs. Farley by the sprite. Gwylph's image wavered and warped, then popped like a soap bubble. The sprite, its form spiky with pain and surprise, fled into the sky. Other Talfi shook his head as if waking from a light doze. Mrs. Farley, now herself again, cast about in confusion.

"What just happened?" she asked. "I feel very strange all of a sudden."

"It's probably the aftermath of the earthquake," Talfi said. "Why don't we get to the courtyard and find some water?"

The butcher, a blocky man with pale, receding hair, hurried up at that moment. He had been caught down at the animal pens when the quake hit and he had only now been able to make his way to his home neighborhood—and Mrs. Farley. She received him gratefully, and he was glad to bring his lady to the well in the back courtyard for something to drink, leaving Talfi, Other Talfi, and Ranadar at the front stoop. Once they were alone, Talfi turned to both Ranadar and Other Talfi, angry, but not sure who to confront first. He finally settled on Other Talfi.

"What in the name of the Nine are you doing?" He jabbed a finger into Other Talfi's chest. "I thought I was the First or whatever the Vik you call it."

Other Talfi flushed and backed up a step. "I'm sorry," he said, and his voice sounded truly contrite. "If the queen gives an order, I have to obey. All of us do. Except . . ."

"Except what?" Talfi snapped.

"Except for when Ranadar speaks," Other Talfi said. "He told me to stop hitting you, and I did. I was surprised."

"The Nine!" Talfi swore. "You still obey an elf!"

"Not just any elf," Other Talfi shot back. "Him!"

Talfi started to answer, but Ranadar intervened. "There is no point in arguing, *Talashka*. He is what he is. We may as well argue with a carrot for being orange."

"That isn't fair," Other Talfi said hotly. "I'm no different from you. If you get hungry, you have to eat. When you get thirsty, you have to drink. You need air to breathe. It's built into you by the Nine."

"Obedience is not," Ranadar said.

"Isn't it?" Talfi said in a low voice.

Now Ranadar looked on his guard. "What do you mean?"

Talfi didn't want to ask the question. He wondered if this was how Danr felt when someone forced him to tell the truth. "Are you going back to Alfhame?"

Ranadar paused, a little too long, and every moment was a spear in Talfi's heart. "Would it be a bad idea?"

"How could it be good?" Talfi burst out.

"Our people have been fighting for millennia," Ranadar said. "Look at us! We have all but destroyed ourselves twice in as many years, and now we are working on a third. Someone has to stop it!"

"What are you *talking* about?" Talfi demanded.

"Ever since the day of the demonstration, I have been thinking," Ranadar said softly. "And while we were bringing your . . . body back here, I was thinking. And now that my mother has reappeared to speak with me, I have been thinking. If I returned to Alfhame, I would be king one day. I could make changes. Even as the heir apparent, I could make changes. The orcs and the humans and the Stane know I am friendly to them. Some of them even trust me. Instead of brandishing a closed fist, I could extend an open hand."

"We can fight. We don't know that she'll win," Talfi

shot back, though the words sounded empty, even to him. "Let's warn the prince, get Balsia ready for the attack."

"After that earthquake?" Other Talfi said. "She could take the city any time she wants. The only thing holding her back is that Ranadar is still here and she doesn't want him to get hurt."

"Come *with* me, *Talashka*." Ranadar took him by the shoulders. "I *need* you. Be my chief adviser, the one who knows how the Kin think, the one who can tell me when I am uppity." He laughed. "If I am king, I can create new laws that allow humans and elves to marry. Even when they are the same sex. What of that?"

Other Talfi shifted uncomfortably but showed no signs of wandering off. Talfi shot him a pointed look to make him go away, but he stayed where he was. And the anger still squatted inside Talfi like a bloated toad.

"And what are you forgetting, uppity elf?" The words came out harsher and more bitter than Talfi had intended.

"Forgetting?" Ranadar tried to touch Talfi's shoulder, but Talfi batted his hand away. "*Talashka*, what—?"

"How can you *forget*," Talfi growled, "what it would be like for *me* in Alfhame? I wouldn't be your beloved husband. I wouldn't be your happy little consort. I'd be a fucking *slave*."

"I could *change* that." Ranadar's voice rose as well, and his ears were turning red. "This is the point! I cannot change a thing when I am *here*, in this stinking, lazy, iron-ridden city! Have you forgotten what it is like for me *here*?"

"Tell us," Other Talfi said.

"Shut up," Talfi snarled. He knew he was overreacting, knew he was making things worse, but he couldn't stop. A black miasma curled within him like rotted roots, poisoning his words and filling him with more anger. For a tiny moment he thought he actually smelled rotting plants, but he flung the sensation away with a shake of his head. He was too angry.

"Every moment in this pig-sucking city is nausea," Ranadar said, ignoring the exchange. His voice rose. "Every day is sand under my skin. Every second is a headache. I wish I could have gone with Danr and Aisa and Kalessa. At least then I would not live with filthy iron and dirty looks and wondering which human is hating me."

"Oh, but you just want to help!" Talfi's own voice rose to match Ranadar's. More pain and fear and frustration spilled out. The smell of rotting plants returned. "You just want to go back to your little kingdom and make things better for everyone!"

"I do!" Ranadar snapped. "And I can get away from this cesspit at the same time!"

"So humans live in a sewer!" Talfi shouted. "And you airy-fairy perfect *slave-owning* elves live in crystal palaces in Valahame with the Nine! The Fae shit and stink like the rest of us."

"My kind does not burn *regi*," Ranadar said. "Remember that when you are rutting with your dark-haired boy."

The remark landed like a punch to the gut. Other Talfi gasped. Talfi stared at Ranadar for a long moment, mouth open. Ranadar wavered, then firmed his chin and looked away. Talfi spun and marched away.

"Where are you going?" Ranadar called after him.

"To find another bed to sleep in," Talfi shot back over his shoulder. "Maybe one with a dark-haired boy in it."

Other Talfi hurried after him. "You shouldn't be out by yourself," he said. "You might—"

"Get killed?" Talfi finished. The anger still burned hot and red inside him. "You're a bigger danger to me than anyone else."

"You'll calm down," Other Talfi said. "You'll come back."

"Will I?" Talfi rounded on him. They were barely in sight of Mrs. Farley's house. Ranadar was still standing on the doorstep, but Talfi couldn't tell if he was watching. He told himself he didn't care. He *didn't*. Let the uppity elf stew for a while. Maybe they needed some time apart anyway. They'd been together nearly every moment for the last two years, trying to make up for two hundred years of separation, and maybe that was a mistake. Maybe they weren't supposed to be together like this. Ranadar was an elf, and elves didn't think the way humans did. They didn't live the way humans did. They didn't love the way humans did.

And they were both men.

Their relationship was doomed from the start. Talfi just needed to get used to the idea. Maybe, if Ranadar wasn't around, Talfi would forget all about him the next time he died anyway.

"When are you coming back?" Other Talfi asked.

Talfi set his jaw and walked away, ignoring the hot tears that pricked the back of his eyes.

Ranadar bolted awake, and he was in the wrong place. He glanced frantically about, trying to remember where he was. Above him, instead of a ceiling, thousands of stars coasted gently across velvet darkness. He lay in a tangle of blankets on the ground. For a confused moment, he was in the forests of Alfhame. Then memory returned in a flood. Talfi and the flesh golem had not returned, and eventually Ranadar had crept into the rooming house for blankets so he could make a bed in the courtyard beside the rooming house amid the noises of people in neighboring streets who were doing the same thing. Mrs. Farley had gone to sleep at the butcher's, leaving Ranadar utterly alone for the first time in months. Ranadar's heart beat fast in his chest. Something had wakened him, but he could not make out—

Shouts and grunts and the clank of the metal came from the street. Protests. Screams. More shouts. Rumbling troll voices. Ranadar listened from his blanket, trying to learn what was going on, but the sounds were too garbled, and the noise of iron crashing on iron made him wince. For a moment he considered leaving the walls and seeing for himself, then scolded himself for being foolish. He did not need to become involved in every altercation in the entire city. Already he had caused enough trouble.

More shouts, this time with the sound of fighting. The voices sounded familiar, but the clashing iron made identification impossible. It could not be Danr or Aisa or Kalessa—they were nowhere near Balsia.

Tense again, Ranadar forced himself to lay back on the hard ground and automatically he reached toward Talfi for comfort before he remembered that Talfi was not there. Instead he made himself lace his fingers behind his head and work his jaw back and forth as he stared upward at the bejeweled sky, still exhausted but unable to find sleep again.

Talfi was gone. Gone. When Ranadar had brought blankets down from the bedroom to spread in the walled courtyard, he had automatically created a place for Talfi. And when he had realized what he was doing, he could not bring himself to change it. Changing it would be admitting that Talfi was not returning, and anyway, how would it look if he *did* return and Ranadar had created a single bed?

Except Talfi had not returned. An ant ate a tiny hole into Ranadar's heart and gnawed it steadily larger every moment Talfi stayed away. In some ways, this was worse than thinking Talfi was dead. When Talfi was dead, there had been a finality. Now Ranadar could only wait and hope, and hope was slipping away like sand between his fingers, a few more grains, and a few more, and a few more. Soon, he would be left with a handful of nothing.

Ranadar sighed and held his head. He had been a fool. Again. The argument itself had been idiotic, born of tension and fear and misdirected anger. He should have seen that. Once his own anger had died down, Ranadar went out to look for Talfi, not sure whether he was planning to berate him for being an idiot or beg his forgiveness. But he had been unable to find Talfi anywhere. Now Ranadar lay in lonely blankets on rocky ground by himself because his temper had gotten away from him.

The iron in the city poked at Ranadar with sharp fingers, and he rolled over, trying to ignore it. His room in the house was above ground level, where most people kept iron implements, and that blunted the impact somewhat. Down here, the feeling was always worse. At least the commotion had ended, and with it the mind-spearing sound of iron clashing against iron. The constant dull headache, however, remained with him, and he wanted nothing more than a cool forest and an absence of the awful metal. And Talfi next to him. He missed his form, his voice, his eyes, the way he called Ranadar an uppity elf. He missed—

"Ran," said a quiet, familiar voice. "Is that you? I can barely see."

Ranadar twisted, getting tangled in the blankets, and managed to sit up. Talfi was squatting next to him. Ranadar had not even heard him approach. His heart swelled and even the iron headache abated. Even Talfi's mind was there, sharp and familiar. Shaking, he reached for Talfi's hands. Talfi took them with a wry grin that made Ranadar want to leap into the stars themselves.

"I am sorry, *Talashka*," he said quickly. "I do not want to argue with you. I do not—"

"No, Ran." Talfi put a hand over Ranadar's mouth, halting his words. "I'm sorry. Look, we were both tired and upset and angry, and we said a bunch of stuff we didn't mean." He smiled again, a slice of moonlight in the darkness. "One of us has to be mature, right?"

"One of us," Ranadar said with mock seriousness. Then his throat thickened. "Vik! I am so glad you returned, my *Talashka*! I could not live without—"

Talfi kissed him, halting the words again, and sank to the blankets next to him. Tears of joy leaked from Ranadar's eyes, and he ran his hands through Talfi's hair, so glad to feel it under his hands again, to smell Talfi's scent, to hear his voice. He could drink those sensations and never need to eat again.

Eventually, they parted. "I do love you," Talfi said. "Even when I'm angry at you, I love you. I'll never do that again. I promise. We'll work out what to do about Alfhame and everything else."

Ranadar's every muscle went limp with relief at those words, and he swiped at his eyes. "Then come lie with me."

The sly grin returned. "You mean you want to—"

"Sleep," Ranadar said with a grin of his own. "I am exhausted. But now that you are here, I will be able to rest again."

They curled around each other under the blankets, and the distant sounds of iron did not bother Ranadar one bit.

Morning came, bringing with it more noise than usual. Most people were already outdoors, so voices and calls and iron clanks came early. Booted footsteps marched past and faded. The guard out on patrol, no doubt. Ranadar's stomach rumbled. When had he last eaten?

He looked down at Talfi, a deep sleeper and never a morning person. Oh, what a relief to wake up beside him! Ranadar reached down to touch the brown hair that curled just a little, then ran the back of his finger down Talfi's faintly scratchy cheek. Talfi shifted in his sleep and brought his hand up as if to shoo away a fly. Ranadar smiled and teasingly touched the end of Talfi's nose. Talfi sniffed and brought his hand up again. Then Ranadar saw the missing fingernail and two twisted fingers.

The chill of Halza's entire realm flashed through him. Ranadar jerked his hand back as if he had plunged it into ice water. "No!" he whispered.

Talfi—no, Other Talfi—opened sky blue eyes. "Morning," he said sleepily, then caught Ranadar's expression. "What's wrong?"

A serpent's nest of emotions tangled up inside Ranadar. They slid around, leaving slick trails across his ribs. Acid boiled bitter at the back of his throat. He had spent the night with a flesh golem. He had held the creature in his arms. He had kissed the lips. He had run his hands across the skin, all the time basking in the relief that his *Talashka* had returned, when all the time Talfi was still out there, still angry at him, still gone. His relief had been as false as this creature's love. It was like finishing a fine meal and learning the cook had first urinated into the pot. Thank Rolk they had not shared their bodies.

"Halza spawn," Ranadar spat. "Vik filth."

Other Talfi understood. His face fell. "I'm real, Ran."

"Saying it does not make it true, creature," Ranadar said. "Leave!"

"My blood is real!" Other Talfi pleaded. "My memories are real! My love is—"

"You are not Talfi!" Ranadar barked. He closed his eyes for a moment, trying to calm down. "I know how you think you feel about me and how you—"

"I *do* feel about you," Other Talfi interrupted. "Why is that so hard to understand?"

"Your emotions were given to you by someone else." Ranadar was trying to hold on to his temper, but it was difficult. And he wanted a bath. "You only exist because my mother created you."

"The same can be said about you," Other Talfi countered. "And you loved me last night. I'm the same person I was then. You just know more about me now."

"Last night I thought you were someone else." Ranadar straightened, his jaw tight, and took a deep breath. Other Talfi looked up at him with those maddening blue eyes, and a small inner voice asked Ranadar what would happen if Talfi did not return. "Look, you said your emotions are legitimate and I should recognize them. If that is true, then you must also recognize mine. I do not wish to cause you pain, but I feel no love for you." He chose his words carefully, making them fall flat and hard as granite. "I cannot love you, and I do not wish to. Even if you were not a flesh golem, I would not love you. It is because I love Talfi. The . . . first Talfi. And you are not he."

The sun cleared the courtyard wall, throwing a waterfall of Rolk's golden light across the little courtyard. Other Talfi drew his knees up to his chin just as the sun struck him, and he looked so handsome that Ranadar held his breath and reminded himself hard that this was only a golem.

Could golems actually be people? He did not want to think about it. It had been difficult enough to work his mind around the idea that humans were more than simple sheep. Golems were animated objects of clay and stone, or even flesh. They did not live.

Or? Where was the dividing line between life and non-life? Other Talfi was made of flesh and he spoke and acted like a human. How indeed was that any different from how a real person acted? Ranadar could even sense Other Talfi's mind, something he could not do with clay golems. Were the Nine Races merely flesh golems created by the Nine?

The question was too complicated to unsnarl right now. Right now Ranadar had more important problems to solve. He strode for the courtyard gate. Other Talfi struggled out of the blankets to follow him.

"Where are you going?" he asked.

"To find the real Talfi," Ranadar said. "I need his forgiveness, and I need his help to stop my mother. And I do not need company."

To Ranadar's relief, Other Talfi did not follow.

The city was still chaotic, though cleanup was already under way. Ranadar even found a street vendor selling boiled eggs and was able to feed himself. Life had to go on.

Worry continued to gnaw and nag at him. Once his stomach stopped bothering him, he closed his eyes and felt about with his mind, searching for Talfi—or anyone who felt like him. Talfi and the flesh golems all appeared exactly alike to Ranadar's mental eye, which was how he hadn't

realized last night's substitution. Another cold shudder
came over him at the thought, and he pushed it aside, trying
to concentrate. He found Other Talfi, still in Mrs. Farley's
courtyard, easily enough, and lots of other humans and
many Stane beneath his feet. He got a flicker of an idea, the
image that they were digging, digging toward the east.

Ranadar shook his head—he needed to find Talfi, but
there was no trace of him, or of any other flesh golems.
However, his range was short, and all the iron in the city
kept fences around his mind. Searching this way was frus-
trating and painful both. He wished he were more powerful, like his mother, able to push his mind further out so he
could find Talfi quickly with thoughts alone. But he was
not his mother.

He shook this idea away. The trouble was, he had no
idea where to find Talfi, and Balsia was a large place. He
could try some of their more favorite haunts—inns and
taverns where Talfi liked to drink and Ranadar liked to
eat—but he was not sure they would be open for business,
or even left standing. Then he remembered the guards
from before the earthquake, the ones who had tried to
detain Talfi and Other Talfi because the prince was becoming nervous about the flesh golems, though Prince Karsten
did not know the true nature of the creatures. What if Talfi
had gotten arrested last night? Maybe he and a lot of other
flesh golems were down at the Gold Keep right now. That
would explain why Ranadar had not felt any of them.

The Gold Keep. Ranadar chewed his lower lip. Prince
Karsten needed to know the truth about the flesh golems,
and Ranadar had intended to discuss the matter with him,
but the earthquake and Talfi's protracted death and the
argument afterward had flung the idea right out of his mind
until now. Mother had made it clear that Ranadar needed to
hurry.

He changed direction and trotted down the street.
Along the way, he came across a knot of humans speaking
in hushed tones and thought he heard one of them say

arrested. Ranadar halted and, for safety's sake, spun a small glamour that blurred his features and made it difficult for anyone to see under his hood.

"Excuse me," he said, "but did you just say something about an arrest?"

"I did," said the human, an older woman running to plump. "You hear about the trolls, too?"

"Trolls?" Now Ranadar was confused.

"They was out last night," said one of the others, an older man. "Stomping around, grabbing young men. Those tusks of theirs was shining in the torchlight like iron spikes. I saw 'em myself. Didn't you hear 'em? It was noisy, it was."

Ranadar remembered hearing them, but he had been thinking about Talfi. Who had probably been in the neighborhood when all this happened. His mouth went dry. "The trolls were arresting young men?" he repeated. "Why?"

"That's what I want to know," said a third human, a blond boy not even eighteen. "Those Stane move into our town and cause this earthquake, and now they're grabbin' people off the street! Vik! Someone needs to teach them a thing or five."

"What do you mean, the trolls caused the earthquake?" Ranadar asked, confused.

"Now, Seb," the woman scolded. "We don't know that. That's just rumor, it is."

"So why were the trolls grabbing people?" Seb demanded. "They hungry?"

"Way I heard it, Prince Karsten sent 'em out," said the older man. "Those strange men we've been seeing around town, they're real strong, right? We've seen 'em haul stones and throw men."

"My cousin's neighbor said she saw one throw a man over the wall of the Gold Keep," said the blond man.

"So Prince Karsten got the trolls to take the . . . strong men?" Ranadar's heart was beating hard again. "Why?"

"Only the trolls are strong enough," said the older man. "And the trolls know what these men smell like, see, so they can tell who to arrest. The human guards have a harder time of it. I used to have a dog that could—"

"No," Ranadar almost snapped. "I mean, why is the prince doing this?"

"Oh! You ain't heard?"

"Heard *what*?" Ranadar nearly screamed.

"Prince ordered their heads off. Only sure way to kill 'em."

"That can't be right," said the woman. "I heard the strong men are carrying plague and the prince is killing them in order to stop the—"

But Ranadar was already running for the Gold Keep.

Chapter Fifteen

A isa had been in the Garden for only a few minutes when the monster attacked. The earth beneath her feet felt as soft and rank as mushrooms left in the sun for too long, and everywhere around her, the plants and trees were drooping. Above her, Ashkame seemed heavy and tired, carrying the thick weight of air, and cracks ran up the great wall of bark.

So many of the plants were rotting, their roots only loosely in the soil. Several were so far gone they were poisoning the ones around them. Flies buzzed, drawn to the rank smell. In the mortal world, this meant people were more prone to fighting and arguing, to mistrust and depression, to discord and strife. Husbands cheated on their wives. Wives abandoned their husbands. Parents beat their children. Lovers argued. Neighbors started vicious rumors, stole, and vandalized. Small slights escalated into family explosions or even clan warfare.

Aisa took Kalessa's sword from her belt and flicked it into a sickle, and with it she cut out some of the worst plants, the ones that were corrupting the plants around them. Outraged flies buzzed around her head. When she regretfully cut the offending plants, the poisoned ones perked up, but only a little. And in many places, the corrupted plants were so numerous it would take cutting wide swaths to accomplish anything, and that would cause more problems than it solved.

"We are moving toward war," she muttered to herself, waving away a fly. "A bad one. Beneath a rotting world tree. Gwylph must be stopped."

Aisa glanced about, looking for Gwylph's plant. Death and the other Gardeners had said they could not uproot her, however hard they tried, but perhaps Aisa could—

An angry buzzing behind her made Aisa turn. Warm, humid air and the sweet smell of rotten meat burst over her. The blood drained from Aisa's face and her fingers went numb. Behind her hovered a fly the size of a cottage. Purple ichor dripped from the proboscis that dangled obscenely between its eyes, and Aisa could see the stiff black hairs that covered its body. But they were not hairs, were they? They were themselves flies. The creature's outer skeleton crawled with flies. The entire creature was made up of flies, thousands and millions and billions of them all clinging together. Fear, pure and black, speared Aisa and her feet rooted themselves to the ground. The fly spat greasy ichor on its forelegs and rubbed them together with the sound of a thousand rubbing files. Then it slapped Aisa aside. Aisa flew sideways and plowed into a patch of wintergreen. Terrified, she rolled aside just in time to avoid a belch of ichor that splattered the plants where she had been. An eye-watering stench of vomit choked her, and the wintergreen dissolved with a hiss. The faint sound of screams reached her as a hundred people on Erda died.

Aisa cast about, looking for something, anything to fight with. Nothing was nearby, not even a branch, and Kalessa's blade—now a knife—had fallen several yards away. She gathered her power, intending to change shape. A walrus, or even an elephant, could smash this thing.

The fly's proboscis snapped at her like a tentacle and snatched her by the waist. Thousands of flies vibrated filth against her skin. Aisa's concentration evaporated. The fly dragged her forward. Aisa screamed and grasped at her power, desperately trying to pull together enough to change into something, anything that could slip free—a cat, a raven, a goat—but the terror would not let her focus. Where were Nu and Tan? Where was Death? She could not imagine they were unaware of this thing. The fly stood over her now. Hundreds of flies crawled over Aisa's body. The creature's wings, filmy clouds of flies, fluttered, and its mandibles opened to crush her. Flies slid up her nose and into her ears. Aisa desperately tried to force the fear away, but it would not—

And then Hamzu was there. With a troll's roar, he bowled into the creature. It released Aisa, who rolled away in a cloud of flies. The creature tumbled away, tangled with Hamzu and trailing yet more flies. Still roaring, Hamzu punched and pounded at the thing and dragged out great handfuls of insects, but the flies simply flowed back into place, leaving the creature largely unaffected. It struggled against him, managed to shove him away, and got airborne, leaving Hamzu flat on his back on the ground. The creature spun, formed a stinger that pointed straight at Hamzu's heart, and dove toward him.

Aisa snatched up Kalessa's blade. It automatically flicked into the sickle shape. She threw it. The sickle whirled through the air, metal gleaming, and sliced straight through the creature.

For a moment, it appeared that nothing happened. The creature dove forward another foot or two while Hamzu tried to scramble out of the way. Then its front half divided neatly from its back half. The two halves tumbled end over end, crashed into the ground, and collapsed into two clouds of flies that themselves dissolved into smoke and vanished.

Aisa dropped to the mushy ground. Hamzu lumbered over and caught her up in his big arms. "Are you all right?" he rumbled. "The Nine! That thing was—"

"I am fine," she said. "It barely touched me. You can put me down."

He did, and they both sat down again. The Garden twilight settled over them, and the soft shade of Ashkame
spread in all directions.

"My heart almost stopped when I saw that thing attack
you," Hamzu said. "What was it?"

"I think it was a symptom of the Garden's corruption,"
Aisa said. "Everything is becoming worse."

"You're still coming here at night to work, I see," he
rumbled.

"Of course. I am never quite sure if I am in some way
dreaming this or if I am fully here. It is confusing." She
paused. "What are *you* doing here?"

He pushed his dark hair out of his eyes with thick fingers. "I'm not sure. It's happened more than once now. I'm
just . . . here. Maybe I'm just following you, like Talfi fol-
lows Ranadar." Hamzu stretched and Aisa heard his shoulders pop.

"Hmm." She took his hand. "Whatever the reason, I am
glad you were here. That creature—"

"Would have been your death," said Nu, hobbling out of
some bushes.

"Your doom," added Tan, following her.

"My end?" Aisa finished. "Can anyone truly die here?"

"Of course they can." Nu's face was shockingly pinched
and pale, and she was leaning on Tan, who was, in turn,
leaning on her. Nu's seed sack was slack and empty. Tan's
hoe was rusted and cracked. It turned Aisa's stomach to
see them. "We are all dying now. We offer an apology. We
tried to help against the creature, but we were so far away
and we move with such slowness."

"Such difficulty," whispered Tan.

Aisa started to speak, to add the third phrase, but Hamzu
interjected first.

"Such a long way," he put in with a kind nod. "But
everything worked out. It's all right."

Aisa gave Hamzu an odd look, but he didn't seem to
notice. The responsibility of finishing the Gardeners'

three-way conversations had fallen to Aisa, and she had woven herself into the pattern only reluctantly. Hamzu had just done it without realizing it. What was going on here?

"I . . . would like to ask you something, Great Ones," Hamzu continued, breaking Aisa's train of thought. She knew what he was going to ask, and her heart quickened. She begged him with her eyes not to do it, but he avoided her gaze.

"Ask if you wish," Nu whispered. "But these days our vision is often clouded."

"Blocked," Tan croaked.

"It is hard for them to see," Aisa warned, before he could say anything. "There is no need to bother them."

Still Hamzu avoided her gaze, though she could see the tension in his jaw. He intended to ask. She could see it in his face. Her own body tensed and she wanted to clap her hands over her ears like a child. Oh, that man could be stubborn! She braced herself, and the question came, falling from his mouth like a jagged stone.

"Is it possible," he said, "for a mortal and an immortal to . . . marry and stay together?"

Just hearing the question was painful. It lay there between them, a trap ready to spring shut. Aisa wished he could take it back. She knew what the answer was, what it had to be: *no*. The immortal would outpace the mortal. The mortal would grow old and die. Such a relationship was impossible. But not asking the question meant there was some hope, some possibility that one day they could find a solution. Asking the Gardeners meant getting an answer from the most powerful entities in the Nine Worlds. If they said it was impossible, hope died. Aisa could not bring herself to face the death of hope.

"Ah," Nu said with a small nod. "This question does not require vision. Only knowledge."

Aisa found she was holding both her breath and Hamzu's hand. Might as well get it over with. Her voice was tiny. "What is the answer, then?"

"It is no," said Nu firmly.

"Impossible," said Tan.

"Never?" said Hamzu.

The two Gardeners remained silent and Hamzu's hand tightened. He made a small sound. The weight of it all crashed over Aisa. The day she released Pendra with the Bone Sword would have to be the day she would bid Hamzu good-bye. Aisa looked at Hamzu, at his warm brown eyes and strong face and big hands and tousled hair. He looked back at her, and she could see a sorrow in him that crushed worlds. This wonderful and powerful man, who had been through so much with her, *for* her, was lost to her forever. And that was the way it was. She firmed her jaw. Very well, then. She had been making sacrifices her entire life. This was just one more. To save the world, she would—

"No!"

Hamzu gave her a startled look, and Aisa realized that she herself had been the one to speak. More words came out of her in a rush. "I will not! I am tired of hurting myself and sacrificing that and destroying my own life for the good of all. I will *not* give up my Hamzu. I will *not* give up my love. I will become a Gardener, and I will find a way."

"It has never been done," said Nu.

"Not been—" said Tan.

"Oh, shut up!" Aisa snapped. "You are filled with power, but you whine like puppies. What is the point of being a Fate if you cannot change the rules to suit yourself? Come along, Hamzu. We are leaving."

She snatched at his elbow and found herself lying on her back beside a dying campfire. Slynd and Kalessa were still curled in a great wall all the way around them, dozing softly, nose to tail. Hamzu sat up and scratched his head.

"Was that . . . did I just dream . . . ?" he said.

"You did not," she said. "I was there, too."

"Did you just tell the Fates to shut up?"

A bubble of laughter escaped Aisa's throat. "I believe I

did. Oh my!" A snort burst from her, and she clapped a hand over her mouth so as not to disturb the slumbering wyrms. "I! An escaped slave girl from Irbsa telling the Fates themselves to halt their tongues!"

Hamzu gathered her into his arms while she shook, both with laughter and with the aftereffects of the fight and her confrontation with the Fates. She felt safe there, safer than in the Garden, safer than anywhere else in the universe. His heart beat against her ear. For just a moment, she leaned into him, let his strength shelter her, let herself be the weak one. She looked up him and reached up to touch his face.

"I want to have a child with you," she whispered.

"What, right now?" he said, not sure if she was joking.

She pulled him down for a long kiss. "Right now."

Two days later, they crossed the border into Xaron. They had gone north of Balsia and skirted Lake Nu, the northernmost of the Three Fate Lakes. The grasslands up there were hot and arid, and no one wanted to live there, so the area was largely ignored by both Fae and Kin. The dark forests of Alfhame ran straight south, side by side with the Xaron grasslands all the way to the South Sea, so they decided the safest course would be to stay a league or two east of the forests to avoid elven mischief. Once they reached the ocean, they would have to either risk sneaking along the southern coast of Alfhame or, more easily, hire a ship, to get to the Sand River. But they still had no idea how they would get the Bone Sword away from Queen Gwylph or use it to free Pendra.

"We found the Iron Axe," Danr said stoutly. "We can find the Bone Sword."

But when they crossed from the northern grasslands into Xaron, they found devastation. The grasslands ahead of them were blackened and burned as far as they could see, and the dry smell of smoke hung heavy on the air. To their right, the distant green line of the Alfhame forest marched into the distance, a sharp contrast against the black prairie.

Kalessa trembled in agitation beneath Danr's body. "What happened? How far does this go?"

"Stay here," Aisa ordered. "I will look."

Before Danr could respond, she changed into a hawk and, leaving her clothes behind, swooped into the distance. Danr dismounted. Kalessa coiled and uncoiled her body, her tongue lashing the air, while Slynd slithered in a circle around them, his great body leaving a trail in the ashes. Danr remained silent. There was nothing for either of them to say. Danr gnawed his upper lip, trying not to let the guilt overwhelm him. But he couldn't help worrying about Kalessa's family. Her father, Hess, had been a great help to Danr when he and the others were looking for the Iron Axe, and now Danr felt so guilty about leaving the box with them that his stomach became a stone in his middle. He paced about, unable to stop. Kalessa and Slynd ignored him. Some feelings were too raw to share.

After what felt like a week, Aisa dropped from the sky, landed, and took back her own shape. Her face was tight as she snatched up her cloak and wrapped it around herself.

"Well?" Kalessa demanded.

"It is bad," Aisa said. "The burning goes on for miles and miles. I saw no orcs in any direction, but I did see several encampments of Fae."

"Fae?" Kalessa reared back in shock. "In the orc lands? They never venture outside their forests."

"They appear to have expanded their boundaries," Aisa said grimly. "We will have to swing east to avoid them."

Kalessa was trembling with the effort of keeping herself calm. "My family's lands are near the fork in the Great Wyrm Rivers to the south and east," she said. "Near the breeding grounds. It is on our way to the South Sea. We must hurry."

Danr wordlessly climbed onto Kalessa's back. The

moment he was settled, she vaulted forward, and he barely kept his seat. Slynd rushed to catch up, and Aisa fled into the sky as a falcon again. They rode grimly onward without speaking past mile after mile of dead and scorched grassland. More than once, Aisa dove at them and shot to the east, telling them to swerve aside and avoid a Fae encampment. Danr saw plenty of little fairy tracks.

"How did they do this?" Danr asked at one point. "The orcs have iron weapons."

"I am unsure," Kalessa hissed without checking her pace. "The Fae have powerful magic and are better archers than we, but orcs are warriors, and the Fae have not ventured outside their forests for a thousand years."

In order to remain unseen, they decided to travel at night and hide during the day. Danr could see perfectly well at night, and Aisa could fly ahead as a scout in the form of an owl. Wyrms, it turned out, depended on smell from their tongues and vibrations in the ground to navigate as much as they used their eyes, so darkness gave them no trouble. They slid forward as fast as they dared under eerie summer skies, speaking only when they had to, and then in low murmurs. Twice they encountered Fae on patrol— sprites and fairies and once a company of elves—but they ignored Aisa, who appeared to be a simple owl, and Kalessa merely curled around Danr to hide him while Slynd hissed at the passing Fae, as if he and Kalessa were a mated pair of wild wyrms. The Fae paid no attention to them.

Their food gave out. Aisa was forced to widen her range and hunt small game. She brought rabbits back to Danr, who ate them raw. Kalessa and Slynd could go a week or more without eating, though it wouldn't be comfortable for either of them, and Kalessa said she wanted no food.

The ride was difficult and exhausting. Danr slept restlessly during the day, his hat pulled low over his face against the relentless prairie sun. When not in animal form, Aisa almost never wore clothes and instead preferred to go naked beneath a simple cloak. "Easier by far to get into and out of," she explained as she pulled the cloak around herself one morning. Her face was pinched and tired.

"Is it harder to come back to human shape?" he asked. "You spend the entire night as an animal, and I'm afraid you might lose yourself."

"This does not happen." She yawned and curled herself under the cloak as Kalessa and Slynd wove their usual ring around them. "I am myself, no matter what shape I take. The same happens to you."

The next night, they found orcs. They had just crossed a river—part of the Great Wyrm, Kalessa said—and the grass and flowers had returned. Kalessa was showing some relief at this. Danr could feel that her muscles were a little more relaxed as he rode her. He smelled the campfires before he saw their glow, and Aisa swooped back to lead them. Kalessa put on a burst of speed, and in moments they found themselves at a great wall of woven wyrms. They hissed menacingly until Kalessa hissed back and snarled at them, whereupon they fell silent and unwove to let Kalessa and the others through.

Beyond was an encampment of orcs. Dozens of tents of all sizes were scattered among small fires. Already several orcs were emerging from them. Their greenish complexions and golden eyes looked strange in the firelight, and the sharp, curved swords they bore gleamed in the flickering light. They seemed a bit confused. Danr was clearly not an orc, but he was accompanied by two wyrms. Aisa the owl silently landed and burst into her human shape. Danr tossed her the cloak while the orcs shouted an alarm and raised their weapons.

"It's all right!" Danr called. "We're—"

"Mother!" Kalessa shot forward and nearly bowled over a particularly tall orcish woman with graying auburn hair in a long braid down her back. She looked, in fact, very much like Kalessa. Or would have, if Kalessa hadn't changed her shape.

Xanda recovered herself quickly. She recognized her daughter's voice, if not her shape. With a gesture, she told the rest of the orcs to stand down. "Kalessa! What in the name of the Nine? Are you all right? What has happened? Is that Danr and Aisa with you?"

"I had an encounter with a shape mage," Kalessa said. "But I am fine."

"This is . . . unbelievable." Xanda reached out to touch her daughter's face, both exploring it and expressing a mother's tenderness. "Can you change back?"

"Not yet." Kalessa's tongue flickered out, not quite touching Xanda. "Where is Father? And Jaxo? And—"

But Xanda's face told the story. Aisa gasped, and Danr's insides twisted. He glanced around. The other orcs of the Nest had grim faces, and Danr saw many empty spaces among them. Slynd made a soft sound. Kalessa froze, then drooped all the way to the ground. Her voice fell to a whisper. "All of them?"

Xanda touched Kalessa's face again. "Oh, my little princess wyrm. We wanted to send word but did not know how to reach you, or if it would get past the Fae. I am the chief of the Third Nest, and you are my sole heir."

A long moment of silence hung in the air. The campfires snapped, and insects chirped in the grass. Then Kalessa threw back her horned head and bellowed to the sky. The sound was agony given its own form, purified sorrow and anger in one long scream. Tears gathered behind Danr's eyes to hear it. Kalessa's grief roar grew louder and louder until Danr and the others clapped their hands over their ears. Kalessa's body writhed and thrashed, forcing Danr, Aisa, and Xanda to leap back. To Danr's shock, she started to glow. The glow intensified, coruscated across her body, combining with her roar to pound the air with thunder and lightning. A great flash seared Danr's eyes with pain. He buried his face in his hands, but he could still see the awful light.

It ended. The silence returned, but it took several

moments for Danr's eyes to clear and the pain spike to leave his head. When it did, he found he was standing a few paces away from Kalessa. She lay naked on her side on the ground. Tears streamed from her eyes.

"Daughter!" Xanda helped her up. Another orc flung a blanket around her. Kalessa blinked and stretched out her hands beneath the blanket.

"I have . . . changed," she said in a bewildered voice. It sounded so strange to hear her normal tones after weeks of the hissing rumble of the wyrm.

Xanda gathered her daughter into her arms, and the two of them wept the heavy tears of their Nest while all around them the other orcs raised their arms and shouted defiance to the stars. Danr joined them, and after a moment, so did Aisa. Danr didn't know or care if anyone heard. They bellowed their outrage to the Nine, to the Gardeners, and to Death herself. The release brought him both a feeling of power and of weak relief.

When the noise finally subsided, Xanda guided Kalessa to one of the fires while two orcs brought food and drink. Danr and Aisa joined them.

"Mother," Kalessa said, "what happened?"

"It was the box," Xanda said, and her words put a black hole in Danr's heart. "The Fae wanted it. Why, we do not know. They attacked us at the breeding grounds during incubation, before the wyrmlings came out of the ground. They Twisted in and caught us by complete surprise. Our iron usually stops the Fae from Twisting through our lands."

Aisa said, "Queen Gwylph is drawing on the power of a Gardener these days, and the Gardeners are not bound by the Fae weakness for iron." She gave a quick explanation.

Xanda's face hardened. "The elven queen attacked us with an army of . . . men. But they were not men. They did not show pain or fear when weapons struck them. The sprites, fairies, and elves who came with them hung back until the strange men had wounded or killed enough of us, and then they all went for your father and brothers. Our family fought as bravely as an army of a thousand orcs, but in the end, it was too much. I saw him fall from a distance, and could do nothing. A sprite flicked into his tent and emerged with the box Danr had given him, and the moment it did so, they set fire to grasslands and retreated. They burned it all and set patrols to hold the land. I later learned that the other Nests were attacked as well, damaged or even destroyed. The worst of it is the loss of the breeding grounds. All the wyrmlings were killed in the fire, and we lost many adult wyrms in the attacks."

"Wyrms do not mate every year," Kalessa explained sadly to Danr and Aisa. "And when they do, it is lucky if they lay more than a single egg. It will take decades to recover."

"I am very sorry all this happened," Aisa said. "It is a crime, and it shows how far Queen Gwylph's corruption has gone. She no longer cares about anyone but herself, no goals but her own. We must—"

Danr burst out, "It was my fault. Everything that happened here was my fault."

"Was it?" Xanda turned to look at him with narrow golden eyes.

"A strange thing for a truth-teller to say," said Kalessa.

"It's true," Danr said, trying not to choke. "I left the box with Chief Hess. If I hadn't done that, none of this would have happened."

"Oh," said Aisa. "Hamzu, you—"

"If we are going to go that route," Xanda interrupted, "we may as well blame the dwarfs for creating the box in the first place. Or Queen Vesha for giving the box to you. Or my husband for agreeing to keep the box." Her voice hardened. "Do not blame yourself, boy. That trail is for weak-hearted fools. The person to blame is the one who sent that army here—Queen Gwylph herself. I want to watch my own wyrm bite her head off and swallow it while she still screams."

There was a moment of silence broken only by the soft crackle of the campfire. At last, Aisa said, "I can see where Kalessa got her way with words."

Xanda snorted. "We need to decide what to do next."

"You are a chieftain among the orcs now," Aisa said, "is that right?"

"I am chieftain of the Third Nest," Xanda replied with a nod.

"Could you call the orcs up to war?" Aisa asked. "Again?"

"Now?" Xanda sighed. "Normally, the orcs would happily go to war against the Fae, but they have hurt us badly. Morale among the tribes is low, and my status as chieftain of the Third Nest is new. I do not think all the tribes would listen to me."

A thought came to Danr. "Kalessa," he said slowly, "can you take the wyrm shape back again?"

"I . . . do not know," Kalessa said while Slynd writhed in the darkness behind her.

"The old legends say the orcs have a strong connection to the wyrms," Danr said. "Orcs became wyrms, wyrms became orcs. Orcs were even able to see into the minds of their wyrms. Now that the power of the shape has returned, Kalessa, maybe you can bring all that back to the orcs, starting now."

"Slynd?" Kalessa turned and her wyrm slid forward with his chin on the ground. Kalessa put an arm around his massive head. "Can you feel what I think? Can you see into Mother's mind?"

Slynd's tongue flicked the air and his golden eyes reflected the fire. Otherwise he gave no response.

"Try it," said Aisa. "Welk did it. I am sure you can. Use Slynd. Touch his scales. You need only remember what it was to be a wyrm and you can become one again."

"Hmm." Kalessa closed her eyes and ran her hands over Slynd's head. A long moment passed, and Danr held his breath. "I feel something, but it is faint. Not powerful enough to use."

"Here, sister." Aisa slashed her palm with Kalessa's blade and held it out to Kalessa. "I do not know why this did not occur to me before."

Without hesitation, Kalessa swiped up a few drops with her fingertips and let them fall onto her tongue. Danr gave an inward wince. No matter how often he shared blood or watched Aisa do it, the process still put him off.

Xanda watched in fascination. "What is happening?"

"Danr and I are shape mages," Aisa said. "We shared blood with Grandfather Wyrm himself, and that unlocked our own ability to change form. Anyone else who has a latent ability for the same can find it if they share our blood, or the blood of someone else whose power has been wakened. But there is a price. If Kalessa changes form after she takes my blood, she will be able to draw magical strength from me."

Xanda sucked at her teeth. "This would create a powerful bond in a tribe! Shared blood that allows a tribe to share strength and shape! I cannot imagine."

Kalessa, meanwhile, had closed her eyes. Slynd rubbed his head against her like a cat asking for its ears to be scratched. "The feeling is stronger now," she said, "but still I can do nothing with it."

On impulse, Danr closed his right eye and looked at her with his left. Kalessa . . . changed. She was still herself, but also standing in her place was a great wyrm, the powerful wyrm whose shape she had worn for the last several weeks. Kalessa and the wyrm were the same in much the way Danr's half-troll and fully human forms were the same. The wyrm, however, writhed behind a wall inside her, unable to get out. Kalessa was calling to the wyrm, and so was Aisa's blood within Kalessa, and the wyrm tried mightily to squirm through the barrier, but still it could not get out. It flicked its tongue in anger.

Anger. Hmm. Danr ran his tongue around the inside of his mouth. *I'm sorry, Kalessa.*

"Your father is dead, Kalessa," he said. "Maybe if you'd

been here, he would be alive. And your brothers, too. Instead you threw in with a half troll, a human slave, and a *Fae*. What kind of daughter does that?"

Xanda and Aisa gasped. Kalessa's eyes popped open. "How dare you!"

"How dare *you*?" Danr countered. He felt the pain his words were causing her, felt the acid teeth as if they raked across his own skin, but he kept going. "You left your people behind when they needed you most. What could that magic sword have done in defense of your tribe? How many enemies went unslain because you chose outsiders over your own people? What kind of chieftain will you make?"

"Hamzu!" Aisa hissed. "What—?"

Kalessa shot to her feet, her face a fury. Behind her, Slynd reared back with an angry hiss. Xanda's face was pale.

"You dare speak to me that way after everything I have done for you?" Kalessa snarled. A faint golden glow limned her body. "After the enemies I have slain for you? When I have endured endless torture and pain for you?"

"You don't know what pain is!" Danr shot back, also on his feet. "No orc does. You even let yourself be chained up by Sharlee Obsidia. Twice! Some warrior."

"I will slay you where you stand, Stane!" Kalessa boomed. But her body was already changing. The blanket fell away. She thickened and grew. Her voice deepened. Scales sprouted and coruscated across her skin. In moments, Danr found himself facing a great horned wyrm. Two of them—Slynd was right beside her.

"Now you die," Kalessa snarled, and lunged at him.

Shit, shit, shit. Danr dove aside at the last moment. Kalessa missed, but Slynd was there. He caught Danr around the waist before he even hit the ground and flung him into the air. Sky and ground blurred into a sickening mess as Danr spun through nothingness. He flailed wildly, but there was nothing to grab. The world jerked to a stop.

A terrible pressure was crushing his midsection. He couldn't catch his breath. Kalessa had him sideways in her mouth like a cat with a mouse. Her teeth dug into skin and muscle. Danr struggled but got no leverage. The pressure increased and Danr let out an involuntary groan.

"Sister!" Aisa barked. "Look at yourself! Look at what you are doing!"

The pressure let up, but only marginally. Danr's bones creaked, and he prayed to the Nine. Puffs of air—Kalessa's breath—rushed past him in a dreadful kind of wind.

"You did it, my daughter!" Xanda exclaimed from somewhere behind Danr. "You changed like the orcs in the old legends!"

"Now let him down," Aisa added. "You know he meant no harm."

There was a long, long moment when Kalessa didn't move. Danr, heart pounding in his ears, forced himself to remain limp. Kalessa finally opened her mouth and let him drop to the ground. Danr stumbled and went to one knee. Aisa rushed over to him.

"Are you well?" she demanded.

"A few bruises, I think," he said, "but I'll live."

Kalessa lowered her head and glared at him with heavy golden eyes. "You said those things to make me angry."

"I saw it." Danr tapped his left eye. "You needed a push, and anger was your fuel. I'm sorry. You're a good daughter, Kalessa, a warrior who frightens the Nine themselves, and the best orc I know."

"You do not know more than a dozen," Kalessa accused with a small laugh. "I apologize for my outburst, my friend, and I am glad you are uninjured. Your words took bravery. Though . . ." She twisted around to look at herself. ". . . they seem to have worked."

"Can you change back yet again?" Aisa asked.

In answer, Kalessa's body glowed and in a moment, she stood naked before them all. This time, Slynd snatched up the blanket and dropped it over her.

"I feel him," Kalessa said in awe. While she spoke,
Slynd brought his head down and Kalessa stepped onto it.
He raised her higher and higher, a look of adoration on his
face. "His mind speaks to me and mine to his. Not in
words, but in . . . concepts. Slynd and I are one!"

A roar rose. Startled, Danr spun and saw that the rest of
the tribe had emerged from their tents, attracted by the
commotion. They crowded around Slynd and Kalessa,
their green skins and golden eyes making a strange and
boisterous crowd beneath the starry sky. All of them
wanted to touch Kalessa. Slynd lowered his head carefully,
and Kalessa put out her hands to every orc she could reach.
Danr felt a pride he hadn't known he could feel. Kalessa
was a strange sort of sister to him, and to see the orcs rally
around her like this made his heart swell. Kalessa had
Slynd raise her again.

"My sisters and brothers!" she called, still wrapped in the
blanket. "This magic can come to you, just like in the days
of old. We can find our strength! We can regain our power!"

Wild cheers broke out among the assembled orcs. Aisa
tossed Kalessa's blade to her. She caught it, changed it
into the great curved sword orcs favored, and raised it
above her head, never minding that the blanket fell away.
She made a stark and powerful picture, standing naked on
the head of a great wyrm with the gleaming magic sword
describing an arc above her head.

"We can rebuild the Nesting grounds, overcome our
enemies, regain our lost lands!" Kalessa boomed. "Who is
willing?"

Every orc shouted and howled and yelled. Danr realized he himself was roaring like a troll.

"Then share in the power!" Kalessa finished. "Share in
your wyrm!"

A celebration began. The orcs broke out drums and rat-
tles, creating a heart-thumping rhythm that pulsed in
Danr's veins. More food and drink appeared. Orcs danced
and shouted in equal measures around the fires. A green-

robed priestess appeared, and Danr wondered if she was the same one they had encountered back when they were searching for the Iron Axe. He hadn't seen her face beneath her hood, so he had no way to know, and this woman showed no signs of recognizing him. She quickly took charge of doling out dollops of Danr's and Aisa's blood to a line of orcs, waving a sweet-smelling bundle of burning sage in blessing over each and calling on the power of Kalinda, the shape-shifting moon, on each orc. Kalessa, still naked, stood atop Slynd's head and looked on with glittering eyes. Danr had to remind himself not to stare at her and her fierce beauty while the priestess squeezed another drop of blood from the cut on his hand.

To everyone's disappointment, especially after Kalessa's rousing demonstration and speech, none of them were able to change shape, even Xanda. At least none of them turned into chaotic blobs and died. Perhaps orcs weren't prone to that. Kalessa, for her part, remained unfazed by the failure. She stepped down from Slynd's head and donned a cloak, as Aisa so often did. Danr wondered how quickly nudity and cloaks might become the custom for shape mages.

"Danr, my friend," Kalessa said, "would you look at the Nest with your true eye?"

Danr did. Every orc in the tribe—man, woman, and child—showed at least a small affinity for connecting with the wyrms, and inside many of them he saw a trapped wyrm, just as he had seen inside Kalessa. He reported this to her with more than a little wonder.

"It is as I thought," she said with a firm nod. "They only need learn, as I did. And we must spread blood to the other tribes."

The party continued, even though everyone was tired. "They need a reason to celebrate," Xanda said. "It is good to *have* a reason."

Eventually, Danr and Aisa retired to a tent Xanda ordered set up for them, and it was a fine, fine thing to

stretch out on soft furs and wyrm-skin leather after so
many weeks of cloaks and cold ground.

"Do you every wonder if we are doing the right thing?"
Aisa asked from the crook of his arm.

"I don't understand the question," Danr was forced to
say truthfully.

"We are mortals making decisions like gods," Aisa
said. "Look at what we have done! We have changed an
entire tribe of orcs, and through them, all orcs everywhere.
We gladly interfered with the way a prince runs his kingdom. Rather than execute a man who turned people into
toads for robbery, we increased his power and turned him
over to the army as a weapon. Everywhere we go the world
becomes wildly different, and this will affect the Nine
Races in ways I can scarcely comprehend! Now we are
exhorting the orcs to go to war again—more changes."

Danr sighed. The dark tent was warm, and Aisa was
warm against his body, and the furs were warm under his
skin, and these things combined with the long day and
night were making him drowsy. "Gwylph is making even
bigger changes," he said. "We're only trying to repair the
damage she's doing."

"I haven't even *seen* her," Aisa said, "except that one day
you faced her down with the Iron Axe. Even then, she had
little to say to me. And here I am, working hard to stop her.
It feels so strange."

"It'll be even stranger when you're a Gardener, won't it?"
he said. "You'll change even more lives than we are now."

"Yes," she said seriously, "but I will do my best to
ensure that the changes are the best for all and try to leave
everyone as much free will as possible. I . . . I make a poor
judge, Hamzu. I remained angry at Welk for turning you
into a toad even after I learned how he arrived at such a
place in his life. I will be setting events into motion that
make people do dreadful things in order to survive. I can
see this. Every thousand years, the Tree tips, forcing such
things to happen, and I will be a part of it. It frightens me."

"You can still turn the position down," Danr said. "Let someone else do it."

"Do not say that aloud," Aisa cried. "I think of it every day. But Death and the Gardeners said there is no one else in the world except Queen Vesha and Queen Gwylph. Death will never accept Vesha, and Gwylph as a Gardener would be disaster."

Danr sighed again and hugged her closer. "That's what I love about you. You can't give up, even when you should."

"I am with child," she said.

Danr froze in the dark tent. His mind stopped working and tried to run in a hundred different directions but staggered about as if drunk instead, and his tongue became a block of wood in his head. A baby! Aisa was going to have a baby! *His* baby! Suddenly, the Tree tipping seemed small and insignificant.

"The child will be yours, you know," Aisa said when he didn't respond.

His tongue freed itself. "The Nine! A baby! That's wonderful news! Aisa, I can't believe . . . well, I can definitely believe it, but I'm . . . Vik, I don't know what I am!"

"The term is *father*, I believe," she said, but there was a smile in her voice.

"My Aisa!" He kissed her, trying to tell her in that single gesture how he felt. A new life would enter the world soon. Iron Axes and Bone Swords were lumps of metal and slivers of ivory compared to this. The sun and the moon and a thousand stars blazed inside him, and he reeled with the enormity of it.

When they separated, she was breathless. "Perhaps I should become pregnant more often!"

They lay for a moment in silence, enjoying their own company and the thought of impending parenthood.

"I wish I could tell my mother," Danr said at last. "She would be so happy to know about this."

"So would mine," Aisa said.

"Though Kech the troll will be a grandfather. A grand-troll." Danr laughed a little. "I wonder what he'll think of that. Oh! And my brother will be an uncle!" The world seemed to tilt a little at the edges.

"Hmm," said Aisa, and squeezed his hand.

"Now I have a hard question," Danr said.

"Where the baby will live," Aisa replied, "after I become a Gardener."

"You read my mind like an orc reads a wyrm." Danr was trying to keep his tone light, as Talfi would, but it came across as heavy anyway.

Now Aisa sighed. "We do not have enough information to decide," she said. "If the baby is mortal, it will not be able to live in the Garden, where no mortal can survive long. But I . . . I will be there every day. I do not care what Nu and Tan might say, or what Death might think. I will be there for my child." She rubbed her belly, perhaps in unconscious anticipation. "Not only that, but he or she will anchor me to this world so I do not forget what it is to be human."

"And if the baby is an immortal?" Danr said.

"That opens up an entirely new line of thought, does it not?" Aisa said. "She—or he—will outlive you, but all children do that, and I will not see my own child outlive me. How is that in any way a bad thing?"

"Now you sound like me when someone asks a direct question," he complained. "The baby isn't even born yet, and already you're looking ahead to the day I die."

"You did ask, my Hamzu," she laughed. "But truly— what if we brought another immortal into the world?"

It was half a question, which allowed Danr some freedom in answering it. "I don't know. I don't think it's ever happened before. Except for Tikk. He changed into a fly and landed on Fell's knee just as Grick was birthing him and Belina, and then he changed into a baby so the Nine would think she had triplets instead of twins."

"In the version I heard, Tikk landed on her vulva," Aisa

said with a shudder. "When I go into labor, I am giving you the job of guarding against insect incursions."

"Should I swat?" he asked.

She smacked him on the shoulder. "I suppose we can only wait and see."

"And stop Gwylph," Danr added. "If we don't, the baby won't be born at all, because there won't be a world for him—or her—to be born into."

Aisa fell quiet. Then she said, "I wonder what would happen if you looked at my belly with your true eye. Perhaps you can tell if the baby is healthy. And see if it is a boy or a girl."

He sat up, surprised. Aisa was sensitive about Danr's true eye, and he had long ago sworn to her he would never use it on her without her express permission. "Do you want me to look?"

"No," she said, rubbing her stomach again. "And yes. I only want good news from you, but in that case, hearing nothing is just like getting bad news."

"I won't look if you don't want me to," he said.

She breathed out heavily. "Now that the thought has occurred to me, it will bother me greatly if you do not look. Get it over with."

"We're only going to see if it's a boy or a girl," he said, forcing his voice into a calm he didn't feel. "Probably nothing else."

"Just look."

Danr closed his right eye and looked. A long silence stretched through the tent.

"Huh," Danr said.

Chapter Sixteen

Ranadar arrived at the Gold Keep with his lungs burning and legs aching. The two red and gold guards were standing outside the main gate along with the two golems. On the spiked wall above them in a cloud of flies were three impaled heads. Their swollen tongues hung grotesquely from their mouths and their hair was streaked with dried blood and their eyes were already milky, but all three were easily recognizable as Talfi. Ranadar's guts turned to water. Was one of them the real Talfi? Ranadar was panting now, and not from exertion. Talfi had been unable to return to life when he was crushed under the chimney stones. He would not return to life with his head separated from his body. Ranadar tried to keep himself under control, but it was difficult under the dead gaze of three men who looked exactly like Talfi. Who might *be* Talfi.

He forced himself to look up at the dead heads. The left ear on the first one looked partly melted. It was not Talfi. The bloody hair on the second one was ragged and badly cut. Also not Talfi. The third one . . . the third one had no flaws on his face. His hair was cut the same way as Talfi's. He was missing a front tooth, but that could have been knocked out during the arrest. Ranadar's throat caught. It could not be. Ranadar told himself to be calm. All the flesh golems looked like Talfi, and this one—

Ranadar caught sight of a blue strip of cloth around the head's severed and bloody neck. It was the remains of a high shirt collar. When he left, Talfi had been wearing a pale red shirt—his favorite color. This was not Talfi, either. Ranadar's knees went weak with relief and he leaned against the wall of the Keep for a moment.

"What do you need?" asked one of the guards at the gate.

Ranadar dropped the glamour so the guards could see his face. "Tell the prince that Ranadar of Alfhame demands an audience," he barked.

The guard summoned a page, who escorted Ranadar inside the gates and into an antechamber, then dashed off to deliver the message. Ranadar waited impatiently. At last, the page returned to the room. Following him came Lady Hafren, accompanied by two ladies-in-waiting. The ladies closed the door. The room had no furniture in it, forcing all of them to stand.

"What is your business with the prince?" Hafren asked without preamble or civility. The thin silver circlet she habitually wore as a symbol of her status as the prince's chief adviser had been replaced with a thicker one of iron, an unsubtle warning for Ranadar to keep his distance. The metal put a putrid taste into his mouth and made his head ache.

"I wish to speak with your son," Ranadar said. "Prince to prince."

"In this kingdom, we do not recognize the Fae as royalty," Hafren replied waspishly. "What you wish to say to him you will have to say to me."

Ranadar stared at her. It was not difficult to see that she was creating a barrier between him and Prince Karsten. She had no intention of letting him speak with Karsten or even of letting him know Ranadar was here. Still, he had to try.

"The . . . men you are holding in the cells," he said. "I have information about them, and the prince needs it."

Hafren made an imperious gesture. "Go ahead, then."

"They are a kind of golem," he said. "Made of flesh instead of stone or clay. But one of them is not a golem. He is human, and you have falsely imprisoned him. I have come to ask for his release."

"This man looks exactly like all the other . . . flesh golems, does he?" Hafren said. "Even though he smells the same as a flesh golem to the trolls?"

Ranadar nodded. "He does. But—"

"Then how do you know this man is not a flesh golem?"

Vik! "My lady," Ranadar said in a deliberate, even voice, "you have met this man and know him. It is Talfi. I cannot imagine your son would authorize the execution of a friend!"

"I am overseeing this, not my son," Hafren said. "He has other duties, and there is no need to worry him with this problem."

"The *problem*, lady," Ranadar said through clenched teeth, "is that you are executing an innocent man. And the flesh golems themselves have done nothing to earn such treatment."

"What does it matter to you what happens to a golem?" Hafren said, spearing Ranadar with an arrow of guilt. "They aren't alive. They don't think. We put their heads on spikes outside the Gold Keep so other people can see what they look like and find the rest for us."

Ranadar clenched his fists. The idea of slaughtering all the flesh golems wholesale felt wrong, but he could not explain how or why. Had he not himself just argued that the flesh golems were nothing but animated piles of meat? He should not be upset at the thought of their deaths. As Hafren said, they were not quite alive.

Quite alive. That word *quite* made a great deal of difference. There was doubt. And Ranadar had never advocated destroying the flesh golems. Was it possible to be alive and not know it? Was it possible to only *think* you were alive and actually be . . . not? Ranadar was not sure, but he *did* know that it was wrong to kill something that might not be alive in order to find out if it was dead.

And it was not right to kill Talfi.

"Why have you executed only three so far?" Ranadar found himself asking.

"They're strong and difficult to hold down while we cut off their heads," she said dismissively. "This evening we will bring in some trolls to speed up the process. Though I hear the dwarfs can build a machine that drops a blade to cut off a head quickly and without fuss. Perhaps we'll hire them to build one for us."

A thought came to Ranadar. "How many do you have in the cells right now?"

"Perhaps eighty or a hundred," she said with an airy wave. "The cells are bulging, which is why we need that dwarfish machine."

You want *the prince to arrest the flesh golems? What are you up to, Mother?*

The truth came to Ranadar now. Thanks to the arrests, the Gold Keep was stuffed full of flesh golems, freakishly strong beings who were almost impossible to kill. Beings who could bend iron bars and were unfazed by swords, knives, or iron bars. Beings who would obey the command of his mother and boil up under the very feet of Prince Karsten. Mother could destroy the Gold Keep and everyone in it with a mental word. The flesh golems being arrested was not a flaw in her plan to rule Balsia. It was *part* of it.

And what was Ranadar to do? He could not let Hafren execute Talfi and all the golems, but was it any better to let them loose in the city, still under his mother's control? His insides twisted. Above all, he had to get Talfi out.

"This is . . . a wrong, my lady," Ranadar said carefully. "These creatures . . . men . . . have done nothing wrong." *Yet,* he thought. "You cannot kill them just because you do not understand what they are."

Harfen looked at him askance. "Can I not? Are the Fae once again telling the Kin how to run their own affairs?"

"They are alive," Ranadar said. "I have seen their minds. I have touched them. They do think, just as you and I think."

"Ha! Trustworthy Fae magic has the answer."

Ranadar pushed down the rising panic that was creeping into his voice and agitating his body. "My lady, I beg you—let me at least visit the cell and show you the one I am seeking. You will see that he—"

"Is your true love?" Hafren finished. "I know all about you Fae and your *regi* ways, how you seduce humans with a touch. Perhaps I should just kill you now and end his addiction to you. Or are they *all* addicted to you? My prince." She spat the last two words.

Red outrage mingled with pale panic now. Ranadar drew himself up, and the ladies-in-waiting shied back. "There is no addiction between us. I am a prince of the Fae, and what we have is—"

"You and your kind have no right to exist," Hafren interrupted again. Her voice was a hiss. "You are an affront to the Nine, and your seed should be burned from Ashkame itself."

Ranadar was struck speechless. It wasn't just the flesh golems, then. Hafren had another agenda. She hated *regi*, and she was willing to commit murder over her hatred. Ranadar's heart moved between despair and outrage. The outrage won. He thrust a finger into Hafren's face, but she did not flinch. "I came here to find a peaceful solution. I came here to find a way to work with humans and see how we are more alike. You call yourself humans, but I see only monsters."

He pushed past her and stormed out of the room, out the gates, out of the Gold Keep. He refused to look up at the awful heads. When he got to the street, he was shaking. *Regi*. All his life, people had told him how wrong it was to love men, to be himself, to do anything but what *they* decided was right for him. After Talfi died that first time, he had worked hard to ignore other people, to live as best he could without worrying what they thought. He had paid for it, but in the end, the Nine had rewarded him for it, reunited him with Talfi. Now he was going to lose Talfi again because of hatred toward people like him. The anger and outrage thundered through him even as the iron headache pressed against his temples like lead clamps. He made a fist. Perhaps it was time for this *regi* to fight back.

"Mother," he said, and pushed mental effort behind the word, calling her as she had instructed, as her kiss allowed. "Mother! *Mother!*"

Moments later, a sprite appeared above the city. The chaotic ball of light skittered down from the sky, rushed around the corner, and vanished from Ranadar's view. There was a shout of surprise from the keep gate, and Mother came sedately around the corner in her golden gown. Ranadar decided the sprite must have taken the body of the page—the guards all carried iron weapons. He was only vaguely curious about what she had done to stop the guards from pursuing her.

"My son," she said in her low, musical voice. "Have you made a decision?"

"I will come home, Mother," Ranadar said.

She clasped her hands together and touched her thumbs to her lips. "*Ranadka!* You have no idea how much that thrills me! These humans have—"

"But"—Ranadar raised a finger—"I have two requests first."

People in the street stared as they passed, but Mother ignored them in the way a shark ignores minnows. "Anything. Name it! I have power you cannot imagine."

"First, the humans have arrested most of the flesh golems, and they took Talfi, too," Ranadar said. "They are in the cells beneath the Gold Keep, and the humans intend to kill them all. Can you get Talfi out so he can come with me?"

"Easily done, and gladly," Mother said. "What is your second request?"

"I want you to call off this invasion," Ranadar said.

"You must promise not to invade Kin territories—human, orc, or merfolk—with flesh golems or Fae ever again."

She fell silent. Her perfect face showed a number of conflicting emotions. Ranadar held his breath. At last, she said, "I will do as you ask, Ranadar. If you will swear to come home to me immediately."

Ranadar swallowed. "I swear, Mother."

"That is fine news, indeed!" Her eyes grew distant and her voice changed. Ranadar heard it inside his head. *My army! My prince and heir has sworn to return to me. Break free of this prison. Then scatter and hide yourselves, more carefully than before.*

The queen turned her attention back to Ranadar. "The golems must stay in Balsia until you come to me, as you swore you would. The moment you arrive, our bargain will be sealed and you will have what you asked for. I am waiting for you at Lone Mountain in Alfhame. Oh, my son, how I have missed you!" She stepped in to kiss his forehead as she had done before, and Ranadar smelled the daisy scent in her hair, a smell of childhood and home. Then she was gone and a very confused page was standing in her place while a sprite fled to the sky.

"What—?" began the page.

A low rumbling started under their feet. It grew louder. Shouts and screams rose within the Gold Keep. The page ran back toward the gate. Ranadar waited, pacing a little. More shouts and screams, punctuated with occasional crashes and thumps. Someone shouted an order to lower the portcullis. But this apparently came too late. Moments later, a herd of Talfis in ragged clothes thundered around the corner. Ranadar smiled and prudently crossed the street. A startled, bruised-looking set of guards followed them, along with a clay golem that hopped on one leg and carried the other in its hand. The people on the street scattered. Horses neighed and reared. One of the Talfis saw Ranadar and pointed.

"Ran!" he shouted. "Vik! It's Ran!"

The Talfis scattered in a hundred directions, running with Talfi's easy, loping speed and flummoxing the guards, who did not know which way to turn. It was breathtaking, in a strange, stomach-wrenching way. Ranadar always forgot how fast Talfi could run, and it made sense that his duplicates would share the trait. Hafren came up behind the guards. Her hair was in disarray, her iron circlet was missing, and her dress was torn. Ranadar wanted to laugh aloud.

"Catch them, you idiots!" she screeched. But the Talfis were already gone. Except for one, the one who had pointed out Ranadar and the only one who was not required by Mother's command to scatter and hide. This Talfi, the true Talfi, flung himself into Ranadar's arms.

"Ran!" he said breathlessly into Ranadar's ear.

Ranadar's entire body sagged with thrilled relief, but he had the presence of mind to spin a glamour. It would not make the two of them invisible, but it would make people reluctant to notice them.

"You are safe," he said. "Thank the Nine you are safe!"

"I'm sorry about last night!" Talfi blurted. "I would never leave you! Never! I was just mad, and—"

"I am also sorry," Ranadar interrupted. "But we should move. I cannot hide two people under a glamour for long."

"Where are we going?" Talfi asked as they moved down the street together.

"Back to Mrs. Farley's to get some things," Ranadar said, avoiding the long-term answer for now. It was so good to have Talfi back he did not want to ruin the moment with the news of his promise to Mother. "What happened to you?" he asked instead.

"After we . . . fought," Talfi said, "I ran into a bunch of trolls. They were looking for me . . . for the flesh golems. They didn't believe me when I told them I wasn't a golem, and I guess I wouldn't have, either. They threw me in a cage on a cart with a bunch of other versions of me, and that had to be the strangest thing I've seen in a while. They could have broken out of the cart any time they wanted to, but no one gave them the orders. I told them to do it, and they wouldn't, even though I'm the First."

Because Mother wanted them arrested, Ranadar thought. He led them around a knot of carts and narrowly missed a goose girl with a herd of geese. "What happened then?"

"They hauled us down into the cells and left us there. It was cold and wet and they didn't feed us or empty the shit bucket, so it stank to make your eyes water. I was scared you didn't know where I was. Eventually, a bunch of guards came in and dragged three of them away. We didn't know what was going on, but we could guess. And then all of a sudden, the golems went berserk. They smashed down the doors and stampeded up the stairs, right over a bunch of the guards. I wasn't going to stay! When I got out the gates, I saw you."

"Lady Hafren was going to execute all of you," Ranadar said grimly.

"And Karsten went along with this?" Talfi's eyes were wide.

"Karsten doesn't know. I think he's too busy dealing with the earthquake."

"But why?" Talfi said.

"A combination." They turned another corner, and Ranadar judged they were safe enough to let the glamour drop. "She does not like *regi* men, and she does not like the Fae and she does not like a Fae prince living in Balsia and she does not like flesh golems, so she would rather kill them. And you."

Talfi halted and caught Ranadar in another breathless embrace. "I'm sorry about everything I said," he whispered into Ranadar's ear. "I was stupid, and I don't ever want to fight with you again. I can't live without you. Not a century, not a year, not a day."

"I feel the same, my *Talashka*," Ranadar whispered back, but he was tense with the words he still had to say.

They continued on their way. Life was returning to

normal in the city. People were already repairing or rebuilding damaged houses, and the streets bustled with business.

"The big question is why the golems decided to revolt," Talfi said. He turned to look at Ranadar. They were nearly at Mrs. Farley's now. "Did you have something to do with it?"

"I?" Ranadar temporized. "What makes you think I had—"

"You were right there when it happened. That's too big a coincidence to swallow. Don't get me wrong, Ran—I'm insanely glad it happened. But what did you do?"

"I—"

Ranadar was saved from answering further by Other Talfi, who barreled out of Mrs. Farley's door to greet them. He nearly knocked Talfi over with a hug.

"First!" he said breathlessly. "You're all right! Well, of course you're all right. You can't be anything else. It's just good to *know* that—"

"You're babbling," Talfi said, disentangling himself. "What's wrong with you? You've never acted like this."

"Just glad to see you." Other Talfi ran a hand through his hair and kept his eyes away from Ranadar. "Yep. Really glad."

"Were you not ordered to scatter and hide?" Ranadar said.

"Yeah," Other Talfi said. "I hid here. She didn't say how long we had to hide, so now I'm coming out."

"Hide? She?" Talfi said. "What's going on?"

"The queen ordered it." Other Talfi tapped his temple. "I heard her in my head."

"Why would she order that all the way from Alfhame?" Talfi said, bewildered. "*How* did she order it from Alfhame? Does it have anything do with the escape?"

"Well, yeah," said Other Talfi brightly. "Ranadar promised Queen Gwylph that if she called off the invasion and broke you out of the cells, he'd go back to Alfhame."

The blood drained from Talfi's face and Ranadar felt as

if he had been punched in the gut. "You promised what?" Talfi whispered.

"It is not quite like that," Ranadar said quickly. "I did not—"

"Did you promise her you'd go back to Alfhame?" Talfi interrupted.

"Yes, but—"

"Vik's balls!" Talfi turned his back in a fury. "After everything we argued about, you went to your mother and promised this while I was in prison? Did you also promise I'd come as your slave?"

"Damn you!" Ranadar hissed at Other Talfi.

"I'll go with you," said Other Talfi. "She won't notice the difference unless she looks closely, and she won't."

"Talfi." Ranadar put a hand on Talfi's shoulder. "Please, listen. I swore to her I would return, yes, but only because it was the only way I could get you out of the cells. They were planning to kill you. And the invasion! I got her to call off the invasion!"

"I can't die, Ran. You didn't need to promise anything." The red anger in his voice rang harsh against Ranadar's ears. Only moments before Ranadar had been worried that he would never see Talfi again, and now they were fighting again. What was wrong with them? A faint smell of rotting plants drifted past, and he wrinkled his nose, trying to ignore it.

"We do not know that entirely," Ranadar said. "What if they cut your head off and put it on a spike outside the gates like they did with the others? Would you come back then?"

Talfi turned back around. "Spikes?"

"You did not see—we were trying to get away." Ranadar swallowed. "I was angry at the way Hafren treated me and at what she said about you, and I did not want all the golems to be executed. So I promised my mother I would return if she would call off the invasion and get you and the others out. She did, so now I have to go to Alfhame."

A silence stretched between them. Ranadar wanted to speak, but the silence was too heavy, and he could not break it. At last, Talfi sighed and rubbed his nose with the back of his hand.

"Well," he said, "I suppose we would have had to pop over to Alfhame next anyway."

The shift was so abrupt it made Ranadar sway. The rotten plant smell vanished. "We would?" he said.

"Yeah. Danr went with Kalessa and Aisa to find the Bone Sword while we stayed here to find out what the candle wax man was about. And we did—Queen Gwylph was planning to invade Balsia with him and the other golems. But she called it off, and now we have to go to Alfhame."

"Why?" asked Other Talfi.

"The invasion may be off, but Pendra is still caged up," Talfi pointed out. "Aisa and Danr and Kalessa are heading to Alfhame with the Bone Sword to stop the queen once and for all. We can't let them do it alone."

"I'm coming, too," said Other Talfi. "You'll need help."

Talfi snorted. "Sure. And the minute the queen tells you to stab us in the back, you'll do it."

"Not if Ranadar tells me to do something different," Other Talfi said. "Do you think I *like* having to obey the queen? She's beautiful and I feel that need to obey her, but I don't . . . I don't . . . you know."

"Love her?" Ranadar said.

Other Talfi glanced away. "Yeah."

Ranadar shook his head. He felt nothing for Other Talfi. Did not wish to. But he did feel bad for him. It was not his fault—

"I wonder what would happen to all you golems if the queen died," Talfi mused aloud.

Other Talfi's head came around. "What?"

"You know." Talfi spread his hands. "Elves addict humans with a touch. Mind games and glamour. I wonder if something like that's what makes you obey her. I mean, elven addiction doesn't affect me anymore because I died and came back, but you aren't quite me. She built you, so maybe she was able to make a little change. But the addiction ends when the elf dies—sorry, Ran—so I was just wondering what would happen."

"Hmm," said Ranadar. "This is not a line of thinking I enjoy."

"Well," Talfi said, "how exactly are we going to stop your mother? Reason with her?"

"I was hoping, yes," said Ranadar. "She wants me back on the throne, either beside her or beneath her. She will have to listen to some of what I say."

"Uh-huh." Talfi chewed a thumbnail. "I don't think you know your mother as well as you think you do."

"How can I kill my own mother?" Ranadar tried to say, but it came out as a half wail.

"I know, Ran, and I'm sorry. But she killed *me*," Talfi said. "And all those Stane. And a bunch of Kin."

"Yes." Ranadar's face was pale. "But . . . could you kill your own mother?"

"I don't remember her," Talfi said truthfully. "It's not an easy thing, but it's a necessary thing, Ran."

"We can use reason," Ranadar said. "And we don't have to kill her. Danr and Aisa and Kalessa probably have the Bone Sword by now, and they will use it to free Pendra. Once that happens, my mother will lose nearly all her power and we will not need to kill her."

"Sure," Talfi said doubtfully. "I just think we need to keep our options open."

"Mother said she was at the Lone Mountain," Ranadar went on doggedly. "We need to get there before Danr and the others show up with the Bone Sword so we can run interference."

"How?" Talfi said.

"My arrival will help a great deal," Ranadar said seriously. "It will lull Mother into a sense of security and put her off her guard. If I take my position as crown prince, I can change the patrols and make it easier for our friends to get there. Or, if they are captured, I can stop them from being killed outright."

"Let's go, then." Talfi turned to Other Talfi. "But not you. You're staying behind."

"Do either of you know the way to the Lone Mountain?" Other Talfi countered.

Ranadar and Talfi exchanged looks. "Not from here," Ranadar admitted.

Other Talfi grinned. "Then it looks like I'm leading the way."

Chapter Seventeen

The mud monsters reached for Danr with cold, squashy hands. His roar echoed across the Garden and he backswung a heavy arm. His fist and forearm smashed through them with a squishing sound and most of them flopped to the Garden floor in pieces. They reminded Danr of halfformed golems, an army of faceless, vaguely human forms made of mud instead of clay. Aisa swung her sickle through several more with a yell of her own, neatly severing them at the waist. They toppled backward amid flailing limbs. Another wave lurched toward them both while the ones on the ground slurped and slithered about, melding their bodies back together again. Several paces behind Danr and Aisa stood Nu and Tan, looking withered and tired within their cloaks. Tan leaned heavily on her hoe and Nu's seed sack hung slack and empty from her clawed hands.

"More here!" Danr shouted. He grabbed one mud monster by the arm and used it as a club to smash some of the others. They fell apart as well, but joined the others in slithering back together. Some of the first group was already rising from the ground. Their muddy groans filled the Garden air. Two of them grabbed Danr's shins from the ground, rooting him in place like cold quicksand. The ground wasn't level, and it was hard to keep his balance.

"This is useless!" Aisa sliced three more in half, but more stepped forward to take their places. "They are endless."

Danr tried to pull his feet free, gave up, and bashed more mud monsters. Unfortunately, this time his right fist got stuck in one of them. He raised his arm, but two more mud monsters grabbed hold and dragged it back down. "What do we do?"

"Keep them busy! I have an idea." Aisa retreated and dashed back to the Gardeners. She snatched Tan's seed sack from the Fate's unresisting hands.

Danr lashed out with his left hand and flung more mud monsters away, but others were crawling up his legs. He was sinking in foul-smelling mud, even though he was standing in one place. So far he was buried up to his waist on the slanted ground. "Whatever you're going to do, make it fast!" He managed to pull his right hand free, but that only buried his left hand. Mud rose to his chest.

Aisa sprinted up to him and opened the sack. From it, she scattered seeds over the mud monsters—a dozen seeds, a hundred, a thousand. Tiny seeds, large seeds, even downy seeds that floated on the still air and stuck to the mud monsters' heads and shoulders. Maple tree seeds twirled away and drilled into the mud monsters' bodies. Pinecones pelted them, even as the mud came up to Danr's chin. He gasped for air.

"*Grow!*" Aisa said in a strange, deep voice Danr had never heard before.

The chilly mud covered Danr's mouth, and his heartbeat sang in his ears. Then it all paused. There was a whisper of sound, a breath of movement. The mud monsters and the pile of mud shuddered. Danr inhaled sharply, trying to draw breath through just his nose while the mud pressed hard against his chest. Tiny green leaves sprouted all over the mud, popping up in ones and pairs and trios. Stalks pushed up next, faster than any plant had a right to grow. In a second, a tangle of plants was crawling over the mud pile and the mud monsters. The monsters who could move tried to flee, but the plants weighed them down. Flowers burst in a riot of colors. Small trees put out long branches and dug into the mud with their roots. Every mud monster lurched, tripped, and finally dropped to the ground, pressed down by the new life. A few twitched and trembled, but eventually they went still.

Danr found himself buried in a patch of petunias. He heaved, but the earth was simply too heavy. After a moment's thought, he gathered his own power and took his human shape. He shrank, leaving a great deal of free space around himself. A hole opened up around his neck and head, allowing him to dig around. Aisa arrived, and with her help, he clawed his way out, leaving his ruined clothes behind.

"Whoof!" Naked, he collapsed to the muddy grass beneath the shady light, though he had to brace himself so he wouldn't roll away—the slant was fairly bad here. "Are you all right? Is the baby all right?"

"The baby is fine," Aisa said. "You must stop asking that question every time I sneeze or visit the privy or fight a dread monster."

"I'm the dad." Danr pushed muddy hair out of his eyes. "I get to ask as often as I like."

"Hmm." Aisa touched her belly in what was already becoming a habit, though even Danr knew it would be many weeks before anything showed. *Dad* and *Father* were still new words to Danr, and he liked saying them aloud to get used to them. He closed his right eye and looked again, just as he had yesterday. Huh. There was the baby, still healthy and perfectly fine, as Aisa had said. A boy—ha! But . . .

"You are looking again," Aisa accused.

"You said I could," Danr shot back, "any time I wanted to."

"Has anything changed?"

"No," he sighed. "I can't tell if he's going to be mortal or immortal or something else. I can't even tell if he'll be Stane or Kin or a shape mage or anything else."

"That is because his fate has not been decided yet." Nu hobbled over, using her hoe as a cane.

"He is but a seed," added Tan, retrieving her seed sack from Aisa. "He can have no plant here until he is born."

"So he has no fate or future?" Aisa finished, unconsciously.

"How could he?" said Tan. "I do not know where to plant him yet."

"So he could be . . . anything," Danr said. "Mortal or immortal. Stane or Kin. Shape mage or not."

"Well, yes," said Nu. "But that is true of all children. Even Fell and Belinna were formless to us until they emerged from Grick's womb."

Danr dropped back on his elbows as a great weight lifted from him. He hadn't realized until now just how frightened it had made him to look at Aisa's belly and see a formless nothing around their child. Hearing from the Gardeners that this was normal relieved him so quickly it made him light-headed.

"You are naked again, my Hamzu," Aisa said, "and covered with dirt. I cannot begin to tell you how attractive that makes you."

He grinned at her. "Is this monster stuff going to happen every time we come here?"

"It also happens when you are not here." Nu leaned on her hoe. "We are simply unable to fight."

"Unable to repair." Tan folded her seed sack.

"Barely able to work." Aisa retrieved her sickle. "It's getting worse and worse in here."

"And you're getting more powerful." Danr sat up. "Why is that?"

"She is not fully connected to the Garden yet," said Nu. "The corruption does not affect her as badly."

"But we can feel the Tree tipping," said Tan. "The Garden is sliding away. Can you not feel it?"

"The ground isn't level," Danr was forced to say. "I can feel it."

"Anyone can," Aisa said. "What do we do about it?"

"Find the Bone Sword," said Nu.

"Free Pendra," said Tan. "Time is running out. In a week, perhaps ten days, all will be lost."

This brought Danr's head around. "What? A week? We thought we had months, maybe even a year."

"Things have become worse," Nu murmured. "The elf queen is draining more power from Pendra than we knew. She creates unnatural Twists, reaches through iron in ways the Fae were not meant to do. And she continues to create the flesh golems. The imbalance of her power speeds the corruption of the world."

"We are seeing earthquakes," whispered Tan. "Soon, we will see much worse."

"Can't you help us?" Aisa said. "It would go faster."

"If we would, we could," said Tan sadly. "But we cannot fight simple mud, let alone raise a hand against the elven queen."

"The Tree tips," said Nu.

"Why does the Tree have to tip at all?" Danr burst out. "Every thousand years, Ashkame tips. It shakes up the world and creates wars and Sunderings and disasters that kill thousands of people. Why can't it just be anchored?"

Nu sighed. "It is the nature of being."

Tan shrugged. "It is how the universe works. Three Gardeners tend the Garden. Two pivot around a third, and therefore the Tree must always tip. So it is, and so it must be."

Danr shot a glance at Aisa. Now that he was going to have a child who would inherit this world, Danr found the idea of a constantly tipping Ashkame more and more repugnant. How could he leave a world of constant upheaval and strife to his son? Or his grandson? Or any of his descendants? Resolve filled him, and he put a dirty arm around Aisa. If he had to die one day, let it be trying to ensure that his children would have a better world than he did.

"What did the mud men and the new plants do to the

Garden?" Aisa asked, adroitly changing the subject. "We should look."

"Many new lives have entered the world," said Nu.

"A burst of births," agreed Tan.

"They balance out the deaths," said Aisa, leaning over to examine some of them.

"Hey!" Some distance away from the mud monster area, Danr knelt by a bright red spineflower, its prickly blossoms and sturdy scarlet stem standing defiantly amid a patch of fingerlike pickleweed and smooth cord grass. "These grow on the shore, don't they?"

"In the Garden, anything can grow anywhere," Aisa said, joining him.

"This spineflower seems . . . familiar. I can't say why." Danr reached down to brush it with his fingertips and a rush of impressions washed over him: a tall, half-troll girl wrestling with her human older brothers, the same half-troll girl grown to womanhood boarding a ship for the first time with a simultaneous sense of awe and homecoming, the woman getting into a fight with four sailors and knocking all of them flat, the woman weeping over the death of the first mate and being startled at receiving his position herself, the woman putting on a heavy felt hat against the sun and taking her ship's helm as captain herself. Startled, Danr snatched his hand away.

"This is Captain Greenstone!" he said. "The plants around her must be the crew of the *Slippery Fish*. Incredible! I haven't thought of her in months."

"Delightful woman," Aisa murmured. "Always with a soft spot for you."

"You aren't jealous, and don't pretend you are," Danr said, still lost in memory. "I did like her. The first other half-blood I ever met. I'm glad to see her plant is blooming. She must be doing well."

"I think we have had enough of the Garden for a single night," Aisa said. "The new plants will slow the corruption, at least a little."

"Ten days," said Nu. "That is the most you will have."

"Ten days," echoed Tan.

"Ten," said Aisa. "Come, Hamzu. Back to Xaron."

He raised his eyebrows. "Can you Twist us out now?"

"I can Twist us in and out of the Garden when we sleep, but not elsewhere," she said. "I cannot explain it now, but I can, and I can do it without help from the . . . Two."

"This is a fine thing," said Nu, sinking to the ground. "We have little power left."

"We are weak," agreed Tan, settling beside her.

"We will hurry," Danr said, earning him an odd look from Aisa. Before he could ask about it, she took his hand.

There was a *wrench* and salt water filled Danr's mouth and nose. He coughed and spluttered and flailed about, but there was only water beneath his feet. Vik! What had happened? Panic squirted through him. Trolls tended to sink more than swim. Then he remembered he was human. That wouldn't help him breathe. He tried get his bearings, but had no idea which way was up. Already his chest was growing tight.

A pair of arms wrapped around him from behind and hauled him to the surface. He broached and sucked in sweet air, then coughed out salt water. Frightened, he looked around. Blue ocean stretched in all directions under a cloudy sky. Aisa in her mermaid form was holding him up. Her fierce, tattooed face looked as serious as he felt.

"I am glad you took your human form," she said. "I doubt I could carry your birth shape for long."

"How did we get here?" Danr spluttered.

"I am unsure. I aimed for Xaron, where we entered the Garden. I cannot imagine how we came to be here. Or even where *here* is."

"Take us back to the Garden!" Danr said.

"I do not know how." Aisa looked around desperately. "When I am half-asleep at night, the Garden calls to me and I can find it. Now—"

A wave washed over them, plunging Danr underwater.

Aisa brought him back to the surface again. "You can't hold me up forever," Danr said. "Can you change into a whale or something?"

"I can." Aisa's long black hair trailed in the water behind her. "But I do not know what that will do to the baby."

A pang went through Danr, mingling with the salt in his mouth. "You took your mermaid shape."

She gasped. "I did, and without thinking. Was it a mistake?"

Another wave washed over them. This time Danr was ready for it and was able to hold his breath, but Aisa still had to pull him to the surface with firm strokes of her tail. Worry for the baby, however, made him heavy and he wondered if it would pull him back down again. What if something had gone wrong with him? What if he had changed into some kind of monster?

"Let me look," Danr said when he could breathe again. He closed his right eye. For a heart-stopping moment he saw nothing. Then he saw it—their son was still there, undamaged, and Danr still couldn't tell if he was mortal or immortal. "He's fine. He's perfectly fine."

Aisa let out a soft cry, and he knew she'd been just as worried as he'd been. She threw her arms around Danr and kissed him, which had the effect of sending them both beneath the waves. There was an explosion of golden light, and Danr found himself clinging to the back of something cool and slick—a great whale. Water rushed past his head and they broached the surface. Aisa blew a fine mist from the blowhole just in front of Danr, and he laughed. He didn't know whales, had no idea what kind she was, but her skin was a grayish blue and her body was a good thirty or forty feet long. Danr pressed himself to her back, glad the day was warm, for all that it was cloudy.

Warm. The water and the air were warm. That meant . . .

"We're in the northern part of the South Sea!" he called to her, not knowing for sure if she could hear. "We must be pretty close to land, too."

Aisa's massive tail flukes slapped the water behind him, though he couldn't tell if that was acknowledgment or disagreement. She swam carefully off with Danr trying to maintain a handhold on the ridge on her back.

After a fairly short time, Danr came to the conclusion that riding whale-back was far from a comfortable way to travel. It was slippery, so he was always fumbling for a handhold, which was tiring, and the wind turned even the warm air uncomfortably chilly. He was thirsty from the salt water, and he wished the sun would come out.

And they had to find the Bone Sword. A week, the Gardeners had said, or ten days at most. How in Vik's horrible name had they come down here, in the middle of the ocean, when they should be on a pair of wyrms, running to Alfhame to find the Bone Sword? Gwylph was poised to invade Balsia with her horde of flesh golems while the world crumbled around her, and the only people who could stop her were a half troll and a pregnant whale. He would have laughed at the absurdity of it if he weren't so worried. Aisa swam with strong strokes of her tail, though he had no idea where she was going. Perhaps she had none, either.

Danr became hungry as well as thirsty. His hands and arms ached from keeping his position on Aisa's back. At least in his human form, the daylight didn't bother him. How far away from land were they?

A terrible smell wafted past. It reminded Danr of rotting meat and festering sores. His eyes watered. He wondered if Aisa could smell it. Maybe something had died in the water and was floating on the surface. The smell faded but returned a moment later. Danr turned his head, trying to find a way to escape it, but it wouldn't leave him alone. It was like sliding through a cloud of awful insects that insisted on following him.

The smell abruptly vanished. A speck appeared on the horizon. The speck grew. A tiny mast climbed over the edge of the world and grew larger. White sails appeared like little clouds. Danr drummed excitedly on Aisa's back. "A ship! Do you see it?"

Aisa was already swimming toward it. Her speed increased, and he had to work harder to cling to her back. Wind sang in Danr's ears and blew his dark hair back. The ship rushed toward them now. When they were forty or fifty yards away, Danr managed to stand up and wave. One of the sailors waved back and tossed a rope ladder over the side. That was when Danr recognized the vessel.

"It's the *Slippery Fish*!" he shouted. "Aisa, it's Captain Greenstone's ship!"

Aisa slapped a fluke in acknowledgment, circled around, and swam up alongside it, bringing Danr under the ladder. Several sailors were peering over the gunwale now.

"You all right, mate?" one of them shouted.

"Vik's balls! That's a whale!" said another.

"We'll get you some clothes," called a third.

Danr remembered then that he was naked—his over-size clothes had peeled off him when he squirmed out from underground in the Garden. At least the ocean had washed the dirt off him. He grabbed the rope ladder, and Aisa sank beneath the surface, leaving him to scramble onto the rung. A moment later, Aisa burst above the surface, flinging the hair from her face. Her tattoos were gone, which meant she was human again. The sailors shouted in consternation and surprise.

Danr hauled himself up the ladder to board the ship, then turned to help Aisa aboard. Something to his surprise, none of the sailors made a single remark about a wet, naked woman heaving herself over the gunwale. Then he caught sight of the females among the crowd of sailors and remembered where he was. Of course they wouldn't say anything. Not with—

"You!" bellowed a familiar voice. "Vik's thundering ass cheeks, what are *you* doing here?" A big woman, as tall as Danr himself when he wore his birth shape, rumbled across the deck and hauled both of them into an embrace, one in each massive arm. Her jaw jutted forward, letting her lower fangs poke upward just a little, and her swarthy face was hidden under a wide felt hat from which peeked a lot of coarse, dark hair. She wore her habitual loose white blouse tucked into red trousers with a curved sword sheathed at her waist. No boots. Like Danr, she preferred to go barefoot. As did most half trolls.

Danr and Aisa had met Greenstone almost two years ago. She was one of the few female ship captains on Erda, and the only one to hire female sailors. Her ship had taken them to the Iron Sea and the Nine Isles on their search for the power of the shape. More than once she had saved their lives. At first Danr had been a little put off by her gruff manner and expansive personality, but later he had warmed to her and now counted her as a close friend. Privately, he occasionally wondered what kind of turn their friendship might have taken if he hadn't already fallen in love with Aisa.

"Captain Greenstone!" Danr said into her shoulder. He was grinning with relief and happiness, though no one could see it right now. "You have a talent for showing up just in time."

"And you and Aisa have a talent for showin' up naked in the most amazing places," she said, releasing them and turning to her first mate, a tall, wiry man with receding sun-bleached hair. "Harebones! Our friends need some clothes! And probably food and water, yeah?"

"Indeed, yes," said Aisa. "I do not believe I have ever been so glad to see you, Captain."

"I'd say the same about you two," Greenstone said, releasing them, "if I knew how you got out here and why the Vik you ended up on my ship. And why you're in human form again, Danr-boy. I thought you'd gone back to your trollish ways like the rest of us. And where's Talfi? If he's gone and gotten himself killed again, I'll beat his *regi* ass."

"It was the Garden!" Danr said in sudden realization.

Greenstone scratched her head beneath her heavy felt hat. "Garden?"

"I found your plant in the Garden just before Aisa and I left," Danr said, not sure whether to be excited or mystified or both. "It was a spineflower. I must have been still thinking about you and the crew, and that pulled us here, close to the ship."

Harebones showed up with a pair of cloaks, which he dropped over Aisa and then Danr. Danr pulled his more tightly about himself, but Aisa barely seemed to notice hers. The deck moved up and down beneath Danr's feet and over his head creaked the tall white sails.

"That would be . . . odd," said Aisa. "Only a Gardener or Death can Twist to and from the Garden."

"I didn't Twist," Danr protested, accepting a mug of water from one of the sailors and taking a long pull. "If I did anything, I just . . . pulled us."

"Hmm." Aisa took her own mug. "We will have to discuss it later. We have bigger problems."

"What's going on, then?" Greenstone demanded.

Danr and Aisa gave a quick sketch. Greenstone's eyes grew wide, then narrow, then wide again. "Ten days to find the Bone Sword," she repeated at the end.

"Where are we, exactly?" Aisa asked.

"About halfway between Flor and Briat," Greenstone replied. "We're heading to Briat right now."

"Can you change course? Take us to Balsia?" Danr said. "Or maybe even sneak us up the coast to where the Sand River meets the sea? We can get to the Lone Mountain from there."

Danr and Aisa exchanged frantic looks. "That won't leave much time. The Tree is tipping."

"Then we'll sail like Vik himself is coming for our tits and testicles." Greenstone raised her voice to a bellow. "Harebones!"

They sailed five, six, seven nervous days. Danr barely

slept, wondering what Kalessa and the orcs must be thinking, but there was no way to let them know. Aisa refused to enter the Garden for fear she would emerge only to find the *Slippery Fish* had moved away while she had not, stranding her in the middle of the ocean and unable to find the ship again, but she was plagued by visions of creatures rampaging through the Garden, and Danr smelled rot on the air almost continuously. He became certain the smell was connected to the Garden, and Aisa agreed.

On the morning of the eighth day, a great gout of water spouted into the air and a dozen forms vaulted over the edge of the gunwale. They landed gracefully on the rail. Everyone, including Greenstone, jumped back. Merfolk. Men and women both. Their spiky scarlet and cobalt blue facial tattoos were seeded with pearls, turning their faces into ferocious warrior masks. None of them wore clothing, and they carried wicked two-pronged spears or thin, curved swords. Their strong tails gleamed like living gems.

"Are they your family?" Danr breathed in Aisa's ear. "Maybe they can help."

"They are not here to help," Aisa breathed back. She looked as though she wanted to be anywhere else.

"The merfolk are always welcome aboard the *Slippery Fish*," said Greenstone, stepping forward. "I already paid the toll back in—"

"Aisa," hissed one of the women. "I am glad for this day. I have waited a long time."

Aisa let out a short breath and straightened her spine. "Imeld. It is good to see you."

Imeld. Danr had never met her, but the name sent a chill through his veins. Just before the Blood Storm, he and Aisa had rescued a mermaid named Ynara from slavery and returned her to her people. That was when Aisa had discovered she herself was half mermaid on her mother's side. In gratitude, Ynara's mother, Imeld, had welcomed Aisa into their home. Later, after Danr and Aisa's showdown with Grandfather Wyrm, Aisa had brought the power of the shape to the merfolk, including Ynara. The power had granted its shape-shifting magic to Imeld, but it had killed Ynara. Aisa had fled Imeld's wrath and had not visited the merfolk since, not even to see her own rediscovered family.

"Do you know what we do to people who kill merfolk?" Imeld said, sliding a finger along her sharp, thin blade with grim delight. "We slice their skins off, piece by piece, and drag them through a school of little sharks and baby barracuda. For you, Aisa, I have much worse in mind. You made a mistake when you tried to cross my ocean."

"Your ocean?" Aisa said. "You are not—"

"Queen?" Imeld finished. "But I am. You infected the elder members of our clan with the power of the shape and killed them. It left me queen. Or did you not think of that when you killed my Ynara?"

"I did not want to kill Ynara," Aisa said with a note of pleading in her voice that half broke Danr's heart. "On so many nights, the guilt has wakened me and stopped my breath. If I had known the power of the shape would do that, I would never have brought it to you. I would have killed myself first."

"We will help," said Imeld.

The other merfolk made a hissing sound. Their own weapons glinted in the sun, seeming to slice the light itself. The sailors reached for weapons of their own, but Danr was all too aware that all the merfolk had to do was dive overboard and start sawing.

"My lady," Danr said, stepping forward with his hands out, "we have a bigger matter here. The entire world is—"

Imeld threw her two-pronged spear. It *thunk*ed into the deck at Aisa's feet and stood quivering. "This is the only matter. Defend yourself, Aisa!"

She changed into a great eel and launched herself across the deck.

*   *   *

Aisa flung herself aside just in time to dodge the eel's snapping teeth. The borrowed cloak twisted around her legs. Imeld gathered her long coils with a great hiss. Sailors scattered in all directions. Danr stood on the deck looking stunned. Aisa had heard of shape-shifting duels in old stories but never dreamed she would take part in one. All the ones in the stories ended in the death of at least one of the participants.

Imeld lunged at Aisa again. Aisa drew on her power and snapped into the shape of a hummingbird, which zipped out of the cloak just ahead of Imeld's teeth. Imeld changed into an osprey and flapped after her. Aisa's tiny heart skittered within her feathered breast. She had to get away from the ship. If Imeld took on a large shape, she might sink it and kill everyone on board. The osprey screeched and picked up speed. So did Aisa, and the ship fell into the distance. Damp air penetrated Aisa's feathers. The hummingbird shape was fast, but it was not suited to the ocean. She skimmed over the wavy surface, trying to think, and in desperation popped into the form of a sea otter and plunged into the water.

A great splash came directly above her. Imeld had changed into a shark, and she dove straight at Aisa, showing rows of pointed teeth. Her flat black eyes reflected nothing but darkness. Aisa changed into a great sea turtle and pulled in her legs and head. Imeld bit at her, but her teeth did nothing more than scratch Aisa's shell. Imeld changed into a black-and-white killer whale large enough to bite Aisa in half and swallow her whole. Her great pink mouth opened wide. Aisa was growing tired after so many rapid shifts and she was not sure she could manage another change. Then she felt the line of magic leading from herself to Hamzu. He gave and she took. Power rushed through her, and she snapped into the first thing she could think of—another killer whale.

It was a poor choice. Imeld was already poised to bite her, and she bit hard, tearing a great piece of flesh from Aisa's side. The pain ripped through her, and Aisa screamed in an orca's voice.

And she remembered then Imeld's father, Aisa's own grandfather, speaking to her after Ynara died and Aisa fled Imeld's anger. *"If you ever need us,"* he'd told her, *"cry for us like the orca. Three times."*

Aisa cried again as loud as she could, and then a third time. She turned, leaving a trail of blood in the water, and rammed into Imeld, who backed away. Aisa rammed Imeld again, and Imeld screeched in pain, a sound that echoed back and forth across the sea. That was when Aisa noticed it. The sound echoed strangely, in a way she could not describe because she had never been an orca before. There was a dark spot, an empty spot, an odd silence in the middle of the return sound. Something big was coming toward them, and it was moving very, very fast.

"So this is how you want it to be?" Imeld said, and Aisa was surprised to hear speech. She did not know whether she was hearing orca speech and her mind was creating human words for it, or if Imeld was somehow speaking Kin words. It did not truly matter at this point.

"I do not," Aisa replied in the same way. "Please, Imeld! I do not wish to—"

Imeld changed again. Her body lengthened even farther. Her snout grew longer and filled with sharp, backward-facing teeth. She grew flippers and a long, heavy tail that swept from side to side. Aisa had never seen this creature before, but it was large enough to bite any whale in half. Blood continued to run from Aisa's side. She started to gather more power, intending to change into something small and quick.

"Either allow me to devour you," Imeld boomed in a thunderous voice, "or I will smash that tiny ship to flinders and devour everyone aboard."

Aisa froze. "You cannot mean this," she whispered.

"I will count to three, and then your friends will die," Imeld growled. "One . . ."

In the water behind Imeld rose a great form, easily three times bigger than Imeld herself. It was an emerald wyrm with horns on its head and crest, each as big as an oak tree. His jaws could encompass a herd of horses, and his body was so long it disappeared into the depths. Imeld was reflected in his great golden eyes. Aisa made a small sound.

"What is this, yes?" said the wyrm.

Imeld barked in alarm and whirled in the water. When she saw the great wyrm, her skin turned a pale green and a smell of urine tanged the water. Her form wavered and crumpled back into her own mermaid shape. She looked tiny and insignificant in front of the huge wyrm. Aisa realized her blowhole was leaking, and she clamped it shut.

"Do I see two Kin fighting a duel of shapes?" asked the wyrm in a slow, measured voice. "In this time and place, yes?"

Imeld tried to speak but seemed unable to form words, or even move. Aisa, who had forgotten the pain in her side, now felt it again. Swallowing hard, she reached into herself and took back her mermaid form. The pain vanished as the wound healed. Then Aisa hesitantly sipped a little more power from Hamzu, who was no doubt worried to death, and made herself grow and grow until she was four times taller than a normal mermaid. She was nowhere near as tall as she had been when she fought the harbormaster's giant golem, but she was tall enough to get the wyrm's attention.

"Grandfather Wyrm," Aisa said, forcing her voice to remain steady. "This is an unexpected pleasure. I hope you remember me."

Grandfather Wyrm moved his great golden gaze toward her, and even fourfold taller, Aisa felt small and vulnerable. She told herself she talked with Death and walked with the Fates, but it was difficult to remember such things when this wyrm turned his attention on her.

"Yes," he said. "Of course I remember, yes. Aisa and Danr and Talfi, who came to visit me and returned my wife's name to me and bargained the power of the shape from me, yes. Do you have more squid ink, Aisa?"

For a wild moment, Aisa considered trying to change into a giant squid and squirting some at him. "I do not, great one," she said with real regret. "But it is . . . odd to see you outside the Nine Isles and the Key."

"It is," said Grandfather Wyrm. "I have not left the Key in many weeks, yes."

"Your pardon, great and glorious one," Aisa said, "but it has been more than a year since I visited you and more than a hundred years since you have been sighted outside the Key."

"Truly?" A slightly puzzled look crossed Grandfather Wyrm's face. "I must have fallen asleep, yes. The elf queen's magic woke me." His great coils swept back and forth, creating currents that pushed against Aisa and nearly swept the still-startled Imeld away. "Can you not feel it? The elves infect the water. The fairies degrade the earth. The sprites poison the air. The Kin are under siege, so I have emerged from the Key to lend my aid, and what do I find? You Kin are using the power I gave you to squabble amongst yourselves while the world burns, yes."

Aisa found herself wanting to point at Imeld, the words *She started it* on her lips, but she stopped herself. "We are but foolish sparks next to the bonfire of your wisdom, O great and magnificent one, and beg your forgiveness."

"Granted, yes," said Grandfather Wyrm. "When the Tree tips, it is always we Kin who are crushed beneath it, and we must work together to stop it."

Imeld spoke now, and although her voice was thin and hesitant, Aisa had to admire her courage. "You . . . are Kin?"

Grandfather Wyrm looked hard at Imeld. "Of course.

And you are merfolk Kin, yes, and queen of the ocean, and yet you are trying to kill your own family. A Kin killing your kin."

"She brought the power of the shape that killed my daughter!" Imeld cried.

"That is a tragedy, yes," Grandfather Wyrm said. "It is painful and harsh. A thousand years ago, I watched a man give up his own son to be murdered for magic. It sundered the continent and killed countless Kin, including my dear wife, yes. This is what happens when Kin kill Kin. Tell me, child, will sending Aisa through Death's door make the world a better place? Will it make you a better queen?"

"It will be justice!" Imeld said.

"Justice does not always make the world better, yes," said Grandfather Wyrm. "It is a lesson leaders need to learn."

"Imeld!" A group of merfolk were swimming up to them, speedily but cautiously. At the forefront was an older merman Aisa recognized with gladness. His aging face and graying hair wavered in the water. It was Aisa's grandfather Bellog, and also Imeld's father. "Imeld! What does this mean?"

"Grandfather!" Aisa swam toward him and only barely remembering how big she was. She shrank to her normal size, and Grandfather Wyrm loomed behind her like a floating mountain. "I am happy you have come!"

"Aisa! Are you well?" Bellog embraced her with one arm. The other brandished a two-pronged spear. "We heard your call. And saw . . . the great one."

Another group of merfolk, the ones from the ship, swam down from the surface and also stopped in hesitation when they saw Grandfather Wyrm.

"Be careful what you say, Bellog," Imeld said dangerously. "Rebellion is rebellion."

"Imeld!" said Bellog, both hurt and mystified. "I lost my dear wife to the power of the shape! Ynara's death pains us all, but anger does not win us a thing."

Imeld's dark expression said she disagreed, but she shot Grandfather Wyrm an uneasy look and touched the tattoo on her face.

"Very well," she said. "The merfolk will not stop you, Aisa. But neither will we help. And should you enter the ocean again, you had best keep your wyrm with you."

Imeld and her entourage dove into the depths and vanished.

"My granddaughter." Bellog opened his arms for an embrace. "I am so sorry that—"

"There is no time for petty Kin with petty problems," Grandfather Wyrm interrupted. "Already there have been more earthquakes on the land, and there will be quakes under the ocean soon. And much has become worse. When the elf queen's magic woke me, I saw what she was doing, yes. She has devastated the orcs of Xaron, stolen a weapon of great power, and created an army out of living blood that is unharmed by iron. Without the orcs of Xaron and the iron of Balsia to keep her at bay, the only thing that keeps her in check is the fact that her son and heir lives in Balsia. But he is already fleeing to Alfhame, yes."

"Ranadar?" Aisa gasped. "Why is he going to Alfhame?"

"I do not know," said Grandfather Wyrm. "But we must hurry, yes. The elf queen will move on Balsia very soon, and when she unleashes the full power of her new army, the Tree will tip and all will die. Can you not smell the rot in the water and in the air? The stronger it becomes, the more the Tree is tipping, yes. Aisa, return to your ship, and whatever merfolk wish may follow. Quickly now."

Mystified, Aisa swam back to the ship with her grandfather and the other dozen merfolk in tow. She gathered momentum and leaped up high in the air as Imeld had done, trailing long hair behind her. Halfway up, she changed into an eagle and swooped over the deck. Hamzu, Captain Greenstone, and the sailors looked up with incredulous looks on their faces. With a high-pitched screech, Aisa dove back down to the deck and took her own form just as Bellog and the other merfolk vaulted out of the ocean to land on the gunwale. The sailors tensed. Hamzu dropped a cloak over Aisa's nakedness and pulled her into an embrace.

"You're all right!" he breathed in her ear. "I mean, I felt you take power, so I knew you must be alive, but then it stopped, and I didn't know for sure."

"I am well," Aisa said. "These merfolk are friends."

Greenstone said, "Is Imeld . . . ?"

"She lives," Aisa said. "But there is more."

With a great wash of water, Grandfather Wyrm rose from the ocean beside the ship. Seawater poured down his sides and foamed off his massive jaws. Now the sailors panicked. They rushed about the deck, grabbing at any weapon they could find but not sure how to use them.

"Calm!" Aisa called. "Calm now! He is also a friend."

"Grandfather Wyrm?" Hamzu strode to the edge and grabbed the rail. "What brings you here?"

"You *know* this . . . person?" Greenstone gasped. "Halza's tits! I'll never make fun of you again."

"There is little time to explain, yes," said Grandfather Wyrm. "Bring the sails down, Captain."

Greenstone looked flustered for the first time since Aisa had met her. "The sails? Why should be bring down the—"

"Now!" boomed Grandfather Wyrm.

"Harebones!" Greenstone bellowed. "Get those sails down!"

The sailors scurried about like ants beneath Grandfather Wyrm's stern gaze while the merfolk watched with interest. Aisa quickly explained to Hamzu and Greenstone what had happened beneath the water, and then it occurred to her that Danr had never met Bellog, so she dragged him over to the rail for introductions.

"So I am to be a great-grandfather now," Bellog said. "We Kin are mingling more and more blood these days, it seems."

"The Nine People are coming together," Hamzu said.

"Aisa thinks we used to be one people, but the power of the shape changed us until we forgot who we were."

"An interesting idea," mused Bellog. "Perhaps Imeld should listen to it."

"Hang on to something, yes," Grandfather Wyrm bellowed.

They all clutched a rope or a rail. Grandfather Wyrm swam around behind the *Slippery Fish* and disappeared beneath the gentle waves. A moment later, there was a bump, followed by a soft crunch, and the *Fish* jolted forward. Aisa would have fallen overboard if not for the rope she was clutching. The ship rushed forward, picking up speed and plowing up an impressive white trough behind. It went faster, faster, and faster still, outracing seabirds, the wind, even the sky itself. The sailors whooped at the wonder of it.

"He's pushing us!" Hamzu shouted. "The Nine! He's pushing us!"

"What was that crunching noise?" Greenstone asked, looking worriedly over the side and nearly losing her hat.

Aisa turned her face to the salt breeze as the ship sped toward the horizon.

Chapter Eighteen

The second bronze-headed arrow caught the rabbit's heart, and it was dead before it hit the ground. Talfi lowered his bow and gave Ranadar a look.

"Fing!" he said. "You still owe me a favor from the first time, you know."

Ranadar sighed from inside his hood. His own arrow was stuck in the ground half a pace away from the dead rabbit. "This was not a contest."

"It was to the rabbit." Talfi trotted over to retrieve the rabbit and both arrows. Already the sun was close to setting, and the mosquitoes were coming out. The forest of Alfhame lay close and heavy about them—tall, wide trees covered in moss at the base and scraggly undergrowth between. Direct sunlight was sporadic, and it occurred to Talfi that this place would suit Danr nicely. Thinking about that was better than thinking about the fact that he was heading straight into the arms of the elf queen. He couldn't die—so far—but his final days were linked to Ranadar's, and what would happen if Ranadar was killed? Would Talfi die, too, or would he live half of the days Ranadar was originally supposed to live? He didn't like thinking about that, either. Maybe he should have offered to clean the rabbit—it would have taken his mind off everything.

Back at the place they had designated as tonight's camp, Other Talfi was piling deadwood for a fire. No one in Alfhame chopped from a living tree, even—or perhaps especially—a prince of the Fae.

"Supper," Talfi said without preamble.

"Fire," said Other Talfi, setting to work with a scrap of flint and steel.

The earth rumbled beneath their feet. Fear jerked Talfi's heart into his throat. The chimney was cracking and dropping tons of rock on him again. He felt his bones shatter as birds took to the air in great clouds. Ranadar tackled Talfi and brought him to the ground, jerking him out of the past. Other Talfi dropped beside them. All around them the trees waved as if in a storm. The ground moved like a living thing. A few paces away, a tree crashed to the ground. Talfi heard a scream and realized it was his own. The fire went out.

The rumbling stopped. Silence fell like a heavy cloak. Talfi's breathing came hard and fast in his own ears. Slowly, he became aware of Ranadar's arm around his shoulders. He pushed himself upright, as did the others.

"What was that?" he asked unnecessarily.

"I am sure they will worsen," Ranadar replied. "At least none of us was hurt."

"Not yet," Other Talfi agreed. "Uh . . . I'll see to the fire."

"You *are* all right, *Talashka*?" Ranadar asked.

"He doesn't ask me," Other Talfi muttered in a barely audible voice from the fire pit.

"I'm fine. Just shaken." Talfi gave a little bark of laughter. "Ha! Shaken!"

"You are as bright and funny as ever," Ranadar said gravely. "And now I will clean the rabbit."

When the rabbit was spitted and sending the fine smell of roasting meat in all directions, Talfi drew a target on one of the trees and got out his bow. His hands were still shaking a little, and he used the practiced moves of archery to calm himself. He wasn't crushed beneath a pile of rubble. He was alive, here, with Ranadar.

On his way to see a queen who would happily see him dead.

Stop it, he admonished himself. *Breathe.*

The first arrow went wide. The second, however, hit the outer edge of the target. The third hit the exact center. Much better. He retrieved and sheathed the arrows.

"How long to the Lone Mountain from here?" Talfi shaded his eyes and peered into the forest as if he could tell by looking hard.

Other Talfi turned the meat. "That's the ninth time you've asked that today, and the answer is still three more days."

"Maybe not," Ranadar said.

Talfi whirled and Other Talfi looked up. A half circle of Talfis surrounded them, all staring with identical blue eyes, all wearing bloodred tunics. Talfi's stomach crawled with unexpected nausea. He thought he was getting used to seeing other versions of himself, but so many all at once put a cold, tight fist in his gut. Accompanying them was an elf in bronze armor with a sprite hovering behind her. The elf's armor was battered and pocked and worn, with sagging leather hinges and cracked buckles. The elf carried her helmet instead of wearing it. The chin strap was broken. Clearly, this wasn't someone who spent a great deal of time close the royal court, and the angry expression on her face made Talfi guess that the duty she was performing— patrolling the forests between Alfhame and Balsia—was far from choice. Wonderful. Their first meeting with an Alfhamer Fae, and she was likely to be in a bad mood. Her hair was so blond it was more silver than gold, her brown eyes were as hard as oak bark, and her broad build bespoke a hard life in the field instead of a leisurely one in Palana. Talfi had no idea how old she was—no Kin could judge the age of an elf.

"Er . . . hello." Talfi put the bow over his shoulder with a half wave. "We—"

"What are you doing out here?" demanded the elf. "No

other patrols have been commanded for this area. Vik! I should drag you back to Alfhame by your ankle tendons."

"Enjoyable as that sounds, perhaps you could just bring us to the queen, Sharyl. Before another earthquake hits." Ranadar took down his hood.

All the flesh golems gave identical gasps. Talfi kept his face carefully stoic. The sprite bobbed in midair, and the elf snapped to attention and bowed. Her armor creaked.

"My lord prince," said Sharyl. "I did not realize you had returned. Your lady mother has instructed any elf who finds you to escort you to her. Very kindly."

There was no mistaking the heavy tone in the word *kindly*.

"Excellent," said Ranadar, a little too brightly. "How far is it?"

"As the golem here said, it's three days. Less if we run," said Sharyl. "Assuming your time playing among the Kin has not made you soft. Your Highness."

"No softer than licking sheep testicles has made you, Lieutenant," Ranadar growled.

Sharyl's jaw tensed and her fingers flicked toward her sword. Ranadar stared coldly at her. Talfi tensed, and he could see Other Talfi looked nervous as well. Then Sharyl burst out laughing.

"Ranadar! You sap-sucker!" Sharyl caught Ranadar in a rough embrace and kissed him on both cheeks.

Ranadar laughed and pounded Sharyl's armored back. "Still poking pine needles up your ass, I see."

"I would say the same about you, except it is definitely not a needle," Sharyl said. "Halza's hellish head, what are you *doing*? You are the crown prince, but you dash about like a pouting *mal rishal* child. The queen is put out with you."

"Then take us to her," Ranadar said.

Sharyl spread her hands. "If I were you, I would keep running. But I have my orders." She gestured at Talfi and Other Talfi. "Are you bringing these toys along? They're supposed to be in Balsia."

Talfi wanted to feel relieved, but the insult was too great, made worse by the fact that Sharyl didn't even seem to realize it was an insult. He took a step toward her, but Other Talfi put a hand on his arm.

"You know what it's like in Alfhame," he murmured.

Talfi glanced at Sharyl and the sprite, and tightened his jaw. Right. At least he didn't have to worry about the elves addicting him by touch. But judging from the looks of adoration the flesh golems were giving Ranadar, they felt—or remembered feeling—the same way about the elf that Talfi did. Talfi felt a little cold inside at that. An entire army of men who thought they were in love with Ranadar. What were they supposed to do with that?

Did it matter how the golems felt? Were they really alive? Not long ago, Talfi would have instantly said they weren't. But the more time Talfi spent with Other Talfi, the more Talfi himself thought about the question, and the less sure Talfi became. Ranadar could touch their minds, but he couldn't touch the minds of clay golems—because they had no minds. Flesh golems seemed to think. Or they *thought* they could think. Was there a difference? The idea made Talfi's head hurt.

And then there was the question about how they all felt about Ranadar. How could you know if you were in love or not? Was there a difference between being in love and just thinking you were in love?

Talfi wasn't worried about one of them stealing Ranadar away. Not anymore. But the rancor he had felt earlier for Other Talfi was shifting more toward pity. It wasn't Other Talfi's fault he felt the way he did.

Except, and this was a big *except*, the flesh golems hadn't *earned* their love. They hadn't met Ranadar for the first time and felt that quickening thrill at how handsome he was. Their breath hadn't caught at the way his scarlet hair caught the light, and their hearts hadn't skipped at the sound of his voice. They hadn't felt the delicious mixture of fear and anticipation of sneaking through the palace to see him or shaken with excitement when Ranadar hesitantly leaned in to kiss him for the first time. They only remembered it.

It was a strange situation—the lack of memory caused Talfi pain, while the load of memories hurt the flesh golems. Perhaps there was a way to change all this, free the golems of the memories that chained them to Ranadar. And to Talfi.

"The . . . toys are coming with me, yes," Ranadar said. "And we must hurry."

"Perhaps we should Twist, then," Sharyl said. "I do not relish a days-long run any more than you do."

Before Ranadar could comment, Sharyl put out her hand, and the sprite landed on it. She whispered to the sprite, who changed color from sunshine gold to sky blue to sunset red and back to sunshine gold.

"Can you Twist that far?" Ranadar said doubtfully. "I do not remember you being able to—"

"Ved-Kal-Who-Skims-the-Emerald-Grasses-Beneath-Autumn-Leaves is alerting Her Highness to your presence, O my great prince," interrupted Sharyl. "She will open a Twist for us."

"Ran," whispered one of the flesh golems in a voice that sent tight tension down Talfi's back. "Ran, it's me."

"I know," said Ranadar quietly. "We cannot discuss this right now."

The look on the flesh golem's face was painful to watch. "But—"

"We will talk later," Ranadar said.

A soft shimmer grew in the air. Ved-Kal-Who-Skims-the-Emerald-Grasses-Beneath-Autumn-Leaves skimmed around the edge of it, drawing a circle of golden light to mark the boundary. "Time to go, we know," he said.

"First," Sharyl said, putting out her gauntleted hand, "I am afraid you will have to give up the weapons. Arrows and knives. You understand, I am sure."

"Do you think I have come to assassinate my own mother?" Ranadar asked archly.

"You know how it is," Sharyl said blandly. "Can we be civilized about it, or must I . . . insist?"

Silently, Talfi handed over his quiver and knife while Ranadar did the same. Sharyl was letting them keep the bows, Talfi assumed, because they were useless without the arrows. Sharyl handed Talfi's equipment to one of the guards. The Twist continued to shimmer.

"Quickly, now," said Sharyl. Her words were friendly, but her tone was hard. "It will not go well to keep the queen waiting any further."

Ranadar stepped through the Twist. Talfi's heart sped up a little. Twists still made him a little nervous, and this one had been spun by the queen of elves, who didn't like him. He forced himself to leap through. As the Twist took hold, he saw movement behind him. For an awful moment, he was everywhere and nowhere all at once, and then he snapped back together. He was standing on green grass. Nausea swept him, and he went retching to his knees. Beside him, Ranadar was standing straight and tall, unaffected—or managing not to show it. The shimmer shifted, and Other Talfi popped out of it in his ragged red cloak. He didn't seem affected by nausea, either, the bastard. Sharyl emerged last with a creak of armor. The Twist vanished.

Talfi pushed himself upright, the vomit still a sour taste in his mouth. Already his heart was pounding and his palms were sweaty. The Twist was the easy part. He managed a glance around.

The scene took some time to absorb. They were standing ankle-deep in dead leaves on the bank of a gleaming silvery river that flowed in from the north. The river smashed into the base of a great, sharp-edged mountain that rose like a razor to the sky. Lone Mountain. A thousand years ago, the Sundering had pushed up a single mountain here, split the river, and dried up the original bed. Talfi blinked up at the slope, a little unnerved at the idea that he was nearly twenty years older than this mountain.

The river torrent was doing its best to drill through the

slope, but the rock was too much for it, and the river grudgingly poured off to the east and west, forming the Silver
and Otra rivers. From somewhere in Talfi's head rose the
memory that the southern side of Lone Mountain still
sported a dry riverbed that went all the way down to the
South Sea and was called the Sand River.

Also on the bank of the river stood an enormous ash
tree. Actually, *enormous* didn't begin to describe the size.
It was easily five times taller than any tree Talfi had ever
seen, but also stooped and bent. It hung over the river like
a grim ancient giantess trailing a cloak of rotten leaves.
Heavy, arthritic branches twisted around one another. In
fact, the more Talfi looked at the tree, the more it looked
like a massive, ancient woman. A wrinkled, aging face
seemed frozen in the bark. Her bark-covered arms reached
outward in pain or supplication. Her bent and broken legs
sprawled among the roots beneath her, stretching toward
the river.

A rank smell of dying wood and decaying leaves hung
heavy on the air. The tree's shade loomed over everything,
blotting out nearly all the sunlight and creating a dark
space beneath, and she rumpled the earth in all directions.

Within the branches of the great tree hung small houses
and what looked like giant beehives, all connected by catwalks constructed of wood and vines. Elven army officers
in bronze armor tromped along the catwalks with swords
and spears, and more elves and fairies had set up camp
beneath the tree and along the bank of the river. Sprites
darted among the tree's branches, trailing light as they
went. The dank shadow of the tree loomed over all. The
Fae preferred to live in trees—the elves in houses, and the
fairies in the beehive structures—but Talfi couldn't imagine wanting to live in *this* tree.

The ground camp extended beyond the tree's shade.
Tents and thatched shelters made of elven ivy stood in
orderly rows that stretched all the way to the horizon.
Flocks of sprites skimmed overhead. Gaggles of fairies

scuttled about on errands. More armored elves saw to their weapons. And waiting among them all were the flesh golems. More and more flesh golems, all looking just like Talfi.

The main trunk of the tree swarmed with yet more fairies. They skittered up and down the bark like great spiders, their sail-like ears quivering and swiveling as they worked. Three of them were massaging a knot in the bark together. Even as Talfi watched, the knot bulged and grew larger and larger until it was the size of a cartwheel. The bark thinned like skin and finally split with a wet, peeling sound. Out spilled the smell of rotting meat and a great deal of greenish yellow fluid. The fairies reached into the hole and together pulled out a naked Talfi. His skin was stretched and smooth as the left half of Other Talfi's face had once been, and he had no hair. Talfi's stomach roiled with horror and he tasted bile again. The air itself weighed him down as the fairies dragged the dazed flesh golem to the river and flung him in with a splash. When he burst to the surface, some of his scars had already healed, and curly brown hair was growing atop his head. He waded ashore, where the fairies tossed him an old cloak and a ragged red tunic. Meanwhile, another trio of fairies massaged another spot of bark.

"Lovely, is it not?" said a familiar musical voice. Gwylph, queen of the Fae, stood only a few steps away, and when Talfi caught sight of her, he dropped to his knees in dread and awe. Her flawless, golden beauty was woven of sapphires and sunshine. Thrilling, gleaming light trailed her every graceful movement. She wore battle armor of gleaming bronze links guarded with more bronze on her gauntlets and greaves. Her soft, braided hair begged Talfi to stroke it, even as he called himself a blasphemer for wanting to put his filthy human hands on her. On her back she wore a quiver of arrows slung with a slender silvery bow. In her hand, she held a white sword. The pale, paper-thin blade winked translucent as an ivory shadow in the shaded light. Runes scrawled down the blade and met more runes inscribed on the heavy cross-guard. A ruby shone red as blood in the pommel.

Talfi's heart jerked. "The Bone Sword," he whispered in wonder. Gwylph must have stolen it from the trolls somehow. He felt even better. It was right and proper that Queen Gwylph should liberate the Bone Sword from lowborn Stane. No one else in the world could wield the Sword's power with more wisdom, more greatness, than she.

The Bone Sword quivered in the queen's hand, and Talfi felt a similar quiver in his left leg, a faint vibration that twisted his gut into a hard knot. For a moment, Gwylph looked less beautiful. Then the quiver halted, and her perfection rolled over him again.

"The tree is my own creation," Gwylph continued. "If I cannot be a Gardener, I will create my own garden."

Her voice was cold and icy, but it slid over Talfi like melted love. Other Talfi looked rapt as well. Ranadar touched the back of Talfi's neck and leaned down to breathe in his ear.

"Rise, *Talashka*," he whispered. "She has no power over you."

And with his breath, the glamour vanished. The love turned to chilly slush, and the twitch in his leg put a strange, coppery taste in his mouth. He looked at Gwylph and saw a middle-aged elven woman in creaky bronze armor. The armor needed polishing. Ranadar touched Other Talfi, whose face also cleared.

Sharyl stepped in front of Ranadar and Talfi with a stiff bow. "My queen," she said, "I have brought your son."

"Good work, Lieutenant," Gwylph said. "You may return to your patrol."

Sharyl said hesitantly, "Your Highness, may I request—"

Gwylph waved an absent hand, and Sharyl vanished into a Twist. From the ground came a small thump and a clatter. Gwylph looked down, and an expression of distaste crossed her face. "The Nine!"

Lying on the ground was Sharyl's right hand, still in its
armored gauntlet. Thin smoke rose from the cauterized
stump, and the smell of singed flesh hung in the air. A
fairy scampered over, snatched up the hand, and rushed
away with it. The tree that shaded everything shuddered,
and a few leaves drifted to the ground.

"Mother!" Ranadar said, aghast. "That was . . . you
should have—"

"She's just a *mal rishal* lieutenant, Ranadar," Gwylph
said absently. "If she were worth something, she would be
at court."

Now that the queen's glamour had vanished, the Bone
Sword at Gwylph's belt was calling to Talfi. He wanted to
touch it, run his hands down the blade, and feel his flesh
quiver while he did so. It was a hunger he couldn't describe,
and it overwhelmed the horror he would have felt at
Sharyl's mutilation.

Ranadar pursed his lips, then held out his arms.
"Mother!"

"My son!" Gwylph embraced him and genuine tears
slipped down her cheeks like little gems. Her armor
clinked, and the arrows in her quiver jumped about. "How
much I have missed you! Look at you." She took his chin
in her hands, then turned his head to examine it critically.
"Your hair! What has your body slave done to it? You must
have him whipped! I have found the flesh golems are a
wonder with a lash."

"It is fine, Mother," Ranadar said. "I have no body
slave."

Talfi couldn't pull his eyes from the Bone Sword at
Gwylph's waist. What would happen if he snatched it from
her belt and sprinted for the tree? It wasn't more than fifty
yards away. He ran his tongue around the inside of his
mouth and shot a sideways glance at the heavily armed
elves and fairies and sprites moving in troops and crowds
under the tree's shade, along the banks of the river, and in
the endless camp that stretched beyond. He wouldn't make

five feet. Sure, he'd come back to life, but Queen Gwylph would be on her guard. Did Gwylph even know the Bone Sword could release Pendra from the tree? She must. Why else would she have gone through the effort to steal it from Vesha?

Unless there was some other reason she wanted the Sword.

The sounds of the endless camp clattered and clanged behind them. Smells of smoke and cooking food drifted on the air. The fairies pulled three more Talfis from the tree with a wet sliding noise and threw them into the river.

"My poor prince." Queen Gwylph couldn't seem to keep her hands off Ranadar's face. She touched it or patted his hair with a maternal thrill on her face. It made Talfi a little ill. "How did you stand it? Filthy humans and their filthy iron. You must have been miserable! But you are home now. We will hold your coronation immediately!"

Ranadar cocked his head. "Coronation?"

"Of course. Now that your father is . . . no more, you will be king beside me. Or rather, beneath me." She grinned, a little too wide. "You will be such an asset, *Ranadka*, when we wake the flesh golems and crush Balsia. And we must invade Xaron again. The orcs should not be allowed to rally, and it is such fun to hear the wyrms pop on the end of a sword."

Talfi's gut tightened further, and Ranadar went pale. "Mother, you swore that you would never again invade Kin land if I came home. I am home. You must keep up your end."

"Oh, my son." She reached out to touch his cheek again. "Living among the Kin has addled your brain. I promised to do as you asked. You *asked* me to free Talfi and the other flesh golems. This I did. You only said you *wanted* me never to invade again. You never asked."

"No." Ranadar's voice was shaky. "Mother, I came home for you. You cannot—"

The elf queen seized Ranadar by the throat with one

gauntleted hand and lifted him bodily off the ground. He choked and his feet swung like a hanged man's. Ranadar clawed at his mother's arm, but he might as well have clawed at a stone. Talfi was so shocked he couldn't move. Gwylph's voice became deep and harsh. "Do not tell me what I cannot do, boy. You will sit on the throne while you obey my every command. You will rule the world while I rule Ashkame, or you will spend your days begging for Death to ram her knitting needles through your skull!"

A shout rang from under the tree. Other Talfi burst forward and, with a speed Talfi knew as his own, snatched the Bone Sword from the queen's belt. Surprise riveted her. She gave a tiny gasp as Other Talfi plunged the blade through her armor and into her chest.

A soft moment passed. Ranadar froze in his mother's grip. Gwylph looked down at the sword hilt sticking out of her chest. Her body quivered. With a small sound, she released Ranadar. He dropped panting to the ground. Talfi gaped, rooted to the spot. Other Talfi backed up a step with a wild look in his blue eyes.

"Never touch Ran!" he shouted. "Never!"

A number of other Fae had noticed what was happening, and they rushed toward their queen. With a tilt of her head, the queen seized the Bone Sword hilt and drew it carefully out of her chest. It made a quiet sound, like a leaf dragging across dead flesh. The wound left no blood behind. Talfi felt the world turn inside out.

"Vik!" he breathed.

"No," whispered Other Talfi, still standing before her.

"Mother!" Ranadar choked, one hand on his throat. "What have you done to yourself?"

The queen swept the blade in an ivory arc and sliced off Other Talfi's head. His head dropped to the ground and rolled away. There was little blood. Other Talfi's body collapsed to its knees just behind Ranadar, who scrambled out of the way.

Queen Gwylph swung the sword again before the body

could fall farther. She cleaved Other Talfi in two from neck to groin. Again and again the queen swung, and the Bone Sword slipped through pink flesh, yellow bone, and glistening organs like paper, reducing Other Talfi to a pile of inert flesh. The raw smell of it tinted the air.

The queen finished with a flourish. Talfi couldn't quite believe what he was seeing. A moment ago, Other Talfi had been walking and talking and alive—yes, alive! He had memories and he liked the color red and he helped dig Talfi out of the earthquake rubble. The queen had butchered him like a cow.

The other Fae arrived, but the queen waved them off with the Bone Sword. They retreated, but only a few yards.

"How could you?" Talfi said in a near whisper. He wanted to fling himself at the queen, but the Bone Sword and the other Fae kept him from it.

"That was so sweet," the queen cooed. "The flesh golem loved you, *Ranadka*. I made them better than I thought. Do all of them feel that way? Or just the ones you have pierced?"

Tears streamed down Talfi's face. "He was alive," he said, and even though he had never said the words before, he knew he believed them now. "He had a right to live, just like anyone else."

"That must be an awkward position for you to take," said the queen affably. "If you believe the flesh golems are alive, and if they all feel the same animal lust for my son that you do, then you must feel they all have the same right to his . . . love that you do. I would love to see bedtime."

"Mother." Ranadar coughed and pushed himself to his feet. "I have never heard you speak this way or act this way. Your body has changed. *You* have changed. How?"

She turned the full brunt of her smile on him, but although Talfi could see the glamour, it had no effect on him. It was like eating with his nose pinched shut—all texture and no taste. It didn't affect Ranadar, either.

"I am more myself than ever before, son," she said.

"The Bone Sword removed my heart and released my true self. So liberating! Like breathing for the first time. Like drinking seawater all my life and then tasting wine. I could show you."

"The Bone Sword should have killed you," Ranadar said.

She waved the pale blade in a hypnotic pattern. Shadows fell across the runes and etched them deep into the ivory. "The Bone Sword cannot kill me, darling," she countered. "Not when it saved me."

Ranadar rubbed his throat. "I do not understand, Mother."

"You were always simple, just like your father." Gwylph slid the Bone Sword back into her belt and pulled on her hauberk. The chain mail was cut where Other Talfi had sliced it with the Bone Sword, and the links parted just far enough to show Gwylph's sternum. The bloodless wound Other Talfi had dealt her was already vanishing, and beneath it was a longer scar, pink and shiny as a baby mouse.

"You see?" she said. "I felt the Sword's presence in the world the moment that hairy-twatted ogre Vesha created it, and I have been trying to lay hands on it ever since. A means eluded me until Pendra's power gave me a deeper understanding of the Twist, and I found the box Vesha gave that troll's boy. That was a good day. So much screaming. Like music."

Talfi barely heard. The Bone Sword was calling to him again. He wanted to touch it, run his fingers down the deliciously thin edge, even let it cut him just a little, to see what it felt like.

"The Bone Sword cannot kill me," the queen finished. "Nothing can. I have the power of a Gardener trapped in that tree, and I have become immortal. Soon, I will conquer this world and take my rightful place as a Fate. And you will help me."

An awful understanding crossed Ranadar's face. "You cut your own heart out and put it into the ash tree with

Pendra. It stops you from dying and connects you to Pendra so you can use her power," he said hoarsely. "Oh, Mother. I cannot help you. I do not think anyone can."

The queen made an upward gesture with one finger. Ranadar stiffened and his chin came up. His nostrils flared, and further words died in his throat. Gwylph drew the Bone Sword and casually sliced Ranadar's tunic open from throat to navel. She left a thin trail of blood behind. Talfi's heart nearly burst in his chest with fear and outrage. The queen set the point of the Bone Sword at his throat.

"I know what you are feeling," she said, a little too cheerfully. "You are angry and outraged and you are in love. A mother knows. When that troll's boy killed your father, I felt the same outrage. I wanted to kill every Stane in the world, and crush every Kin who had helped them. I wanted to listen to their screams beneath my toes. I railed against the Nine and the Three and Death herself, and I decided to do something about it. I understand your love and outrage, my son, because I feel the same."

"And what do you feel now?" Ranadar said through tight teeth. "Do you love me now?"

The queen gave a sad shake of her head. "I understand but do not sympathize. I understand you the way a butcher understands a cow. You are a disappointment, my weak little *Ranashka*. You father no children, not even bastards. Your magic is limp. You hide in the forest and pout over the death of a human toy. Worst of all, you betrayed me. How could I hold my head high as queen when my son followed his scrotum to live among Kin?"

Talfi watched the words fall on Ranadar like lumps of granite. He went limp beneath their terrible weight. Even in his precarious position, Talfi felt his pain and wanted desperately to go to him and comfort him even as he raged at the queen for saying such things to her own son.

"So what now, Mother?" Ranadar whispered. He was still upright, head held high by her magic.

"The Bone Sword," she said, and sighed beatifically.

"One clean cut, and all that foolish outrage and fear and love vanishes like a troll's courage. You cannot imagine the relief! I know it does not sound palatable to you now, but when it is over, you will thank me. We will cut your heart out and place it in the tree next to mine, my darling. Forever."

Sick nausea oozed out of Talfi's stomach and into his chest. It was hard to breathe. The possessive look Gwylph was giving her own son made Talfi's skin crawl with snakes and worms. The awful pile of meat that had been Other Talfi lay on the ground, gathering flies, adding to Talfi's nausea. He cast about for something to do but came up empty. The group of Fae was still watching from its vantage point a few paces away, and Talfi was still in the middle of an army. Things couldn't get worse.

"There will be no world to rule if you continue with this madness, Mother," Ranadar said in a shaky voice. "The Tree is tipping, and this time it will destroy the world. Please, Mother. If you remember anything about how you once felt for me, end it. Release Pendra, and I swear I will do anything you want."

"Would you?" For a long moment, she fixed him with hard emerald eyes; then she lowered him to the ground with a gesture. "Very well, then. Repudiate your love for the human boy."

Talfi's legs weakened. Ranadar's mouth fell open and his eyes automatically sought Talfi's. Talfi swallowed hard, unsure what the queen meant. Another Talfi went into the river with a splash.

"Repudiate," Ranadar said slowly.

"Yes." The queen leaned forward with soft glee. Her armor clanked. "Give him up, and I will release Pendra from that tree over there."

"No tricks?" Ranadar said. He licked his lips and looked about like an animal that had just realized it was trapped in a cage. Talfi's heart was pounding again. Ranadar said, "No semantics? You will follow the spirit and not the word?"

"I will." She drew the Bone Sword. "I swear on this blade."

"I . . ." Ranadar looked at Talfi again. Talfi's head spun. He stumbled toward Ranadar. One of the Fae moved to stop him, but the queen held up a hand. Ranadar caught Talfi around the shoulders.

"My *Talashka*," Ranadar said. His eyes were filling up.

"You have to do it," Talfi said hoarsely. "It'll save the world. We don't matter against all that."

"How can you be so cruel, Mother?" Ranadar said over Talfi's head. "Just free Pendra. Why torment me?"

"It is for your own good," Gwylph said.

Ranadar sighed heavily. Talfi felt Ranadar's arms around him, solid and strong. Inside, Talfi's heart was falling to pieces. He couldn't think of what it would be like.

"It will not hurt," Gwylph said, noting his distress. "Truly. That is how the repudiation will work."

"What do you mean?" Talfi demanded.

"Ranadar will not simply swear he no longer loves you," the queen said with a small smile. "That would hardly be enough, would it? Your love must be removed entirely."

"You can't remove love!" Talfi said.

"I can remove memory." The queen sheathed the Bone Sword. "It will take but a moment, spiderweb soft, and you will forget your disgusting love. You will remember everything else—every sloppy kiss, every sticky fumbling, every poke and prod—but you will not remember the love. That is my price."

Her words punched Talfi's heart with an obsidian fist. He couldn't breathe. He had no strength, no bones. Ranadar would truly remember Talfi as a toy, a thing to be discarded. It was worse than anything he had imagined.

"You can do that," Ranadar said in a horrified voice. "Make me forget I love him?"

"Of course not," the queen said, genuinely surprised. "You

are Fae and my son. I cannot tamper with your memory." She pointed at Talfi. "I speak of him."

"Me?" Talfi's mouth went dry. "How do you mean me?"

"I will remove that part of your memory. Are you not used to it, boy? Once you have forgotten your love, I will cut my son's heart out with the Bone Sword, and he will no longer love you at all."

"Why both of us?" Ranadar was white-lipped now.

"If either of you is allowed to harbor this foolish love, you will spend your days trying to rekindle it in the other," the queen said primly. "This will ensure that it ends."

Walls were closing in around Talfi. There was no way out. The rest of his life, his long, undying life, would be spent without any hint of love for Ranadar, not even the memory of it. "You're willing to give up being a Gardener for this?" he said, hating the plaintive note in his voice but unable to keep it out.

"I always was, child," she said.

"But you're still going to invade," Talfi said.

"I am. You cannot stop that. But I will free Pendra from her tree."

Ranadar grabbed Talfi's hand, and a jumble of emotions rocked him. Hatred for the queen. Despair for the upcoming loss. Fear for what his life was becoming. And through it all, a love, a *need* for Ranadar. He met Ranadar's eyes again and he saw hesitancy there. Ranadar was ready to refuse. He would let the Nine Worlds die rather than let Talfi go.

"My uppity elf," Talfi said, and his voice caught.

"Talashka," he replied softly. "There must be another—"

Talfi raised his voice. "Do it!"

"Truly?" The queen looked triumphant. "Once I take your memories, they vanish forever. Not even the Nine can rebuild them."

"I said do it," Talfi said, still clutching Ranadar's hand. It was like holding both their hearts. He could feel Ranadar's pulse beating with his own, and he never wanted to let go. He held on to the sensation, kept it close. She could not make him forget everything.

"Done!" The queen pressed her hand against Talfi's forehead and pulled it back. A ribbon of multicolored light followed her fingers. It coiled into her palm. The world shifted, took a hint of a tilt. Talfi leaned sideways, and only Ranadar's grip on his hand kept him upright. The queen drew the Bone Sword and swiped it through the coil of light. It shattered with a *pop* and vanished.

"It is done," said the queen. Talfi realized he was still holding Ranadar's hand. It was rough and dry in his. Strange to be holding the hand of an elf. He pulled away and wiped his palm against his trousers. Ranadar made a small sound and turned away, as if he had something in his eye, but Talfi didn't care. Why should he? Ranadar was just an elf.

Talfi's mind shifted. He remembered. He remembered slipping away with Ranadar from the palace at Palana, walking in moonlight, stealing kisses, listening to Ranadar sing. He remembered giving his life for Ranadar, and more than once. He remembered laughing over their archery contests. And he remembered countless times of moving his body against Ranadar's. His skin prickled and a small shudder worked its way over him. He had prostituted himself to an elf. Talfi felt sick.

"You have cut my heart out once already, Mother," Ranadar said quietly. "Are you ready to do it a second time, then?"

"In a moment," said the queen.

"You have to fulfill the bargain," Ranadar insisted. "You will free Pendra."

"Of course I will. But first—"

The queen snapped her fingers and a pair of flesh golems, both disfigured, dragged over a golden tub, intricately inlaid

with silver ash branches and ivy. Gwylph drew the Bone
Sword and pointed with it at the tree. Ranadar flinched.
Talfi watched warily. Now what?

"The fairies feed blood to Pendra, and she produces a
full flesh golem for us," Gwylph said. "But we are running
out of material."

Hard hands seized Talfi from behind. White-hot fear
ripped through him and he struggled, but the flesh golems
behind him were too strong. With hands exactly like his
own because they *were* his own, they hauled him over to
the tub and bent him backward over it. The bow on his
back pressed awkwardly into his skin. Gwylph's face came
into view above him. He looked up at the queen, into her
glassy emerald eyes, and saw nothing behind them. No
mortal sympathy, no love, no empathy. Her heart was long
gone. She waved the Bone Sword under his nose, and his
skin cried out for its touch.

"Mother, no!" Ranadar roared. He dashed toward them,
but the queen gestured again and Ranadar flew backward.
With a grunt, he plowed into the ground, sending up a
cloud of dead leaves.

The queen said to Talfi, "You like this sword, child. I
can see it." Her voice was silk. Water. A leaf on a cold
breeze. "Enjoy this, then."

The golems held Talfi's arms outstretched in fleshy
hands while the queen slashed open his chest with the
Bone Sword. He felt the blade whisper through skin, muscle, and bone, but the white-hot pain that sliced through
him also exhilarated him. It was delicious agony, delightful pain, happy anguish. He wanted more even as he
babbled at the queen to stop. Ranadar was screaming
somewhere in the distance, but Talfi barely heard. The
queen's grinning face loomed over him, filled his universe
with pleasurable pain.

"I will release Pendra," she said. "But first your flesh
and blood will create a hundred, a thousand, a million,
golems for me."

The Bone Sword dripped his blood, and the queen was careful to let it run into the tub. Talfi tried to respond, but he couldn't catch his breath under the glorious pain. Every sensation was sharp and unending—the warm blood running down his sides, the bruising grip of the golems at his wrists, the chill air running over his exposed lungs, the dead leaves rustling under his feet. This was going to be how every day went for the rest of his life. He hated the queen then, hated her for perverting the gift Death had given him, the gift he had died so many times to earn. His blood burned with the hatred. It ran like lava through him, gushed out his veins, and ran into the tub. The world dimmed. Talfi turned his head and saw one of the golems. For a moment, its—his—face reflected the same hatred Talfi felt, and with the insight that came just before death, Talfi understood. He and the golem didn't simply share blood. The golem's blood was Talfi's blood. The golem's flesh was Talfi's flesh.

"The First," said the golem.

Something inside Talfi shifted, like a drop of blood finally gathering enough weight to fall. Instead of trying to pull away from the flesh golem, Talfi reached toward him. But it was more than a reaching with mere hands. It was reaching with blood and with bone.

"I'm you," Talfi whispered, and died.

Chapter Nineteen

The *Slippery Fish* skimmed over the waves. Danr stood with Aisa at the bow with a wide, idiotic grin on his face. The speed was sensational. Glorious! He had thought riding a wyrm was the fastest thing in the world, but now they were outracing birds. Danr wanted to spread his arms and join them. Wind whipped through his ears, tugging at the thick felt hat tied under his chin. Speed or no speed, his half-troll shape still disliked the sun.

Beside him, Aisa looked more pensive. The breeze whipped at her skirts and loose blouse, teased at her hair, but she barely seemed to notice. Waves curled in white slices away from the prow, and she stared thoughtfully down at them.

Danr was about to ask what was on her mind when he felt it: a shift beneath his bare feet, as if the deck had become rippling sand for just a moment. Aisa's head came up.

"Did you feel that?" she asked in a distant voice.

"I did," he replied, worried now. "What was it?"

"*Why* did you feel it?" she added.

Here he had no answer, and so he was able to shrug. "Is that important?"

"Ashkame tips and the world is sliding," she said in the same distracted tone. "I can feel it more and more with every passing moment because of my connection with Nu and Tan. I do not understand why *you* feel it. Or why you continue to come to the Garden. Or why you join in with the Gardeners' triple conversations."

"I do?" Danr said. A pod of dolphins leaped in and out of the water just ahead of the ship, racing ahead of it, laughing in a strange language all their own.

"Too many times." Aisa looked into the distance, her eyes glassy. "Something odd is happening to you."

The ship slowed so fast that Danr was thrown off balance. He swayed. Aisa stumbled and would have fallen over if Danr hadn't caught her. Ahead lay the green, forested shore of Alfhame, and the ship coasted slowly toward it.

"Land ho?" said one of the sailors, and the others laughed nervously.

"Most fun I've had outside the bedroom," Greenstone boomed, striding up to them in a heavy felt hat of her own.

A wide cleft opened between the trees, a cleft the width of a good-sized river, though no water poured from it. Nothing grew in the cleft, either, though the ocean lapped at it like a silvery cat's tongue.

"Is that—?" Danr began.

"The Sand River," agreed Captain Greenstone. "Been dry for a thousand years."

Danr eyed it speculatively, hands on the gunwale. "How long to walk to the Lone Mountain from here?"

"Three days, maybe four," Greenstone said. "And that's if you don't get elves poking their heads up your arse."

Aisa put her hand atop Danr's. It was hot and dry. "The Tree tips tonight." Her voice changed. "After sunset." It changed again. "Midnight."

"Aisa, are you all right? What's wrong with you?"

"The Gardeners are fading," Aisa said dreamily. "Slipping. Sliding."

"Dying?" Danr's mouth was dry now. "What are we going to do, then? Maybe you could get there now. Change into a hawk and fly."

"And face the queen alone." Aisa's voice was a whisper of water across stone. "I do not have the power."

Danr looked about frantically, as if the answer might be written in the rigging. "Then what do we do?"

The ocean gushed. With a rush of seawater, Grandfather Wyrm's great head rose from the ocean beside the ship. The sailors made a uniform sound of dismay and backed away, even though the great wyrm had been pushing the ship for the past two hours.

"Did you feel the earth move, yes?" he boomed. "The second earthquake?"

The pieces fell together. That had been the strange sensation Danr and Aisa had felt. "I did," he called. "What did it mean?"

"The Tree tips, and the earth is sliding away, yes," said Grandfather Wyrm in his deep, measured voice. "We have little time to stop the Fae queen. But the earthquake will help us. First, you will need the sails. Second, your captain must be ready at the helm for some skillful maneuvering. Follow me!"

Grandfather Wyrm plunged toward the shore. To Danr's awe, he didn't stop when he reached it. Instead he slammed straight into the cleft. A wave of sand and dirt exploded to the left and right banks of the old riverbed. Grandfather Wyrm's massive body plowed up the cleft, creating a channel that filled with seawater in his wake.

"Follow," Aisa said, pointing.

"Harebones!" bellowed Greenstone. "Get the foresails up! Follow that wyrm!"

Danr gaped. "How is he doing that?"

"He uses Stane magic to change the shape of the earth." Aisa's breath came quick and her pink tongue ran over her lips. "The Tree tips, Hamzu, and boundaries blur. Water becomes earth becomes fire. All magic is the same. We are all the same, yes."

The *Fish* slid forward under creaking canvas. The end of Grandfather Wyrm's tail had already disappeared.

Seawater gushed into the channel, creating a current that helped move the ship forward. Greenstone had moved to the aft deck to take the helm herself. Danr ran back to join her, dragging the dazed Aisa with him. Worry chewed at him with cold teeth. She seemed between worlds, half in this one and half somewhere else. He didn't know how to help her, or if she even needed help. He was a truth-teller, but he didn't know what was going on. Danr looked at Aisa again. She was still clearly somewhere else. Was she dying like the other Gardeners? He had to find out.

There was only one way. But he had promised he would never look at her with his true eye again. Sworn.

Vik take it, he thought. *Forgive me, Aisa.* He closed his right eye to look at her.

Everything around him vanished. Rotting air filled his nose with its heavy stench, and he found himself ankle-deep in mud and shit. The sickly light of the Garden twisted his eye and pounded at his brain. In all directions sprawled a tangle of dying, rotting plants. In the center of it all stood Aisa. She had one foot in the muck and one foot on the deck of the ship. Within her nestled the tiny, shining light of their son. Behind her stood the shadowy, emaciated figures of Nu and Tan, barely visible inside their ragged cloaks. And looming over them, taller than a castle, was the golden form of Queen Gwylph. The elf queen was leaning against the wall of Ashkame's bark. With a start, Danr realized she had always been there. She had merely loomed so large that he never noticed her, the way a rabbit never noticed a mountain. Ashkame's power was draining into her, and the great tree was rotting through and through as a result. It was leaning, tilting, tipping, and this time it wouldn't simply upend itself as it had done a hundred other times. It would crash into oblivion.

"Aisa!" Danr called.

"Do you have the Bone Sword yet?" Death strode up to him, eyes blazing. "It shouldn't take this long, boy."

"Why don't you just kill her?" Danr gestured frantically at the giant Gwylph. "You're Death!"

"I told you, I can't touch her." Death pulled a knitting
needle from her hair and jabbed at Gywlph's golden shin.
It rebounded as if her skin were granite. "See?"

"Is Aisa all right?" Danr demanded.

"Course she isn't. The Garden is dying, and she's connected to it. You only have a couple hours. After that, I'll
get a rush of business and close up shop forever."

"This wasn't supposed to happen!" Danr cried. "It
wasn't supposed to be *me*! I'm just a farmer! I hoe rows
and plant seeds and pull weeds. Why am I doing this?"

Death gave him a strange look from within the darkness that continually overshadowed her face. "If it makes
you feel better, child, you're nothing special. Your seed
just ended up in the right row at the right time. Otherwise
someone else would be standing here bawling like a
wounded calf. The only difference is that if you keep
feeling sorry for yourself, we're all dead. Including me.
Now get!"

She jabbed him with a bony finger, and his right eye
popped open in surprise. He was standing next to the still-
dazed Aisa and Greenstone next to the helm of the *Fish*.
The *Fish* was just entering the new channel, and Greenstone
was staring intently ahead.

"Where'd you go, handsome?" she asked.

"The Garden," he said shortly. "The whole world is
dead in two hours if we don't get the Bone Sword."

Greenstone's fingers went white on the wheel. "I don't
know if we'll make it. Even with this current, the—"

For a moment, the *Fish* halted, then drifted backward a
little. Greenstone glanced over her shoulder. "Vik and
Halza humping on hardwood! Foresails down! All hands
brace!"

Sailors scuttled around the deck, repeating her order to
one another. Several secured loose equipment. The sails
collapsed like dying clouds.

"What is it? Why are we moving backward?" Danr spun, trying to understand what was going on. The water level in the channel, indeed in the entire ocean, seemed to be dropping.

"Now I know what that damn wyrm meant by a second earthquake," Greenstone muttered. "We're in for it now."

"For *what*?" Danr grabbed her shoulder.

"Tidal wave."

A wall of water skimmed over the horizon and rushed toward the shore. Danr's insides shrank to see it coming. This was a force of nature. It had no thoughts, no emotions. It didn't care what lay in its way or what happened to anyone or anything. There was no way to fight it or stop it. It would simply happen the way it happened. Danr grabbed the unresisting Aisa with one arm, wrapped the other around a set of ropes, and prayed aloud to the Nine.

"The Nine don't have shit to do with it, handsome," Greenstone said. "Gonna depend on how good a pilot I am. Just like that damn wyrm said."

The wave slammed into them. It created a chaotic wash big enough to engulf a city at the mouth of the channel and rushed inward. The roar was a thousand angry lions. The *Fish* bolted forward, bobbing like a toy in a torrent. The sailors shouted. Wood creaked. Danr's stomach dropped, then came up, then went back down again. Wind rushed past his ears. He clutched Aisa hard.

"Hang on, handsome!" Greenstone yelled. "Gonna be the ride of your Vik-sucking life!"

The *Fish* pinged from side to side along the newly carved channel, jerking and jolting and smashing as it went. With every crunch and crack, Greenstone bellowed in protest, as if she herself were hit. The saltwater river bellowed back, challenging her, but Greenstone kept her powerful hands on the spoked helm.

"Wyrm ahead!" shouted Danr.

They were indeed catching up with Grandfather Wyrm, who was still using his great body to plow the channel deep enough for the ship. But also ahead now Danr could see Lone Mountain rising out of the forest. Earth and sand spouted out on either side of Grandfather Wyrm, covering the trees as he rushed ahead while the *Fish* came roaring up behind.

"Go, Grandfather!" The shout tore itself from Danr's throat before he even thought. "Go! You can do it!"

He didn't know if Grandfather Wyrm heard him, but the wyrm seemed to speed up. The *Fish* careened ahead. It slammed into the left bank, recovered, and rushed on. The mountain loomed bigger. They were almost there. But Grandfather Wyrm was tiring. The *Fish* was catching up with him, and they had a good quarter mile to go. Moving so much earth was draining even his mighty reserves. Danr stared helplessly at him as the ship rushed closer. What—?

And then he remembered the day he had gotten his own power of the shape. Grandfather Wyrm had bitten off Danr's hand to force Danr to change shape. He flexed his regrown hand in sympathy of that moment. His blood. Giving his blood to someone else let that person share his power. And Aisa said Danr had a *lot* of power.

Danr closed his right eye. Grandfather Wyrm . . . changed. The wyrm was still there, but deep within it was a human, a man, the shape mage Grandfather Wyrm had been before the Sundering. Danr also saw a thin golden line running from his hand to Grandfather Wyrm. Exhaling hard, Danr thrust out his hand and *pushed*.

Power pulsed from his hand, zipped down the line, and infused Grandfather Wyrm's body. He paused a tiny moment and raised his head. Then he plowed forward again with renewed vigor. Sand and earth vaulted high into the air, and the *Fish* zipped along in its wake, pushed by the current and the remains of the tidal wave. Danr pushed more and more power, feeling the strength drain from his muscles. He went to his knees as Grandfather Wyrm boomed forward.

"Almost there!" Greenstone shouted. "A few more seconds!"

The last of Danr's strength left him. He brought his hand down. Ahead of them, Grandfather Wyrm reached the base of the mountain. With the last of Danr's energy, he bored around the western side and headed for the River Bal. Greenstone frantically spun the helm so the ship would follow.

"Captain!" A sailor scrambled up to the poop deck. "We're taking on a lot of water. Cracks in the hold."

"Get a full crew on the bilge pumps," she snapped. "Double time!"

"You're taking a beating," Danr panted.

"We all are, handsome," said Greenstone grimly.

The ship bumped and smacked its way around the mountain, slower now. Every jolt drew a grunt from Greenstone, as if the mountain were hitting her own bones. They hove fully around it and on the other side stood the biggest tree Danr had seen this side of Ashkame. It shaded the river that flowed west, and Danr also noted both the biggest Fae army the world had ever seen camped just beyond it.

Grandfather Wyrm had put on a final burst of burrowing. In moments, he would smash through the last piece of earth standing between the Sand River and the River Bal. When that happened, the water from the Bal would wash them backward. His eyes met Greenstone's, and he knew she had the same thought.

"Go!" she said. "I've got the ship."

"Aisa!" Danr shouted. "We have to get off!"

Aisa didn't respond. Danr was so tired now he was barely able to stay upright. Frantic, he grabbed Aisa's hand, the same hand that she had cut so she could take in Grandfather Wyrm's blood and become a shape mage. He felt the power inside her and without thinking, he drank from it. Energy surged through him, and he felt he could leap to the sun.

The move snapped Aisa out of her trance. "Hamzu! What—?"

"Come on!" Without waiting further, he hauled her to the rail and leaped overboard with her. They went under together in the murky salt water, but when they surfaced, Aisa had changed into a dolphin wrapped in a wet cloak. The tidal wave current had slowed now to nearly nothing.

Grandfather Wyrm broke through the earthen barrier to the Otra River. Water exploded in a mountainous fountain. Aisa chirped and sped for the southern shore, opposite the tree, with Danr clinging to her back. He only barely managed to save her cloak from floating away.

"Hold on!" he heard Greenstone bellow faintly from the ship above them.

Like opposing gladiators, the two rivers met. A snarl of waves and water thundered against Danr's ears, and a white wall roared toward them. The *Fish* creaked as Greenstone frantically brought it about. Danr's feet scraped bottom, and Aisa changed back into herself. They crawled onto the muddy shore just in time for the maelstrom to tear past them. It swept the *Fish* sideways back the way it had come. For the first time in a thousand years, fresh water coursed down the ancient riverbed.

With an earthshaking thud, Grandfather Wyrm flopped down onto the southern bank of the River Bal, opposite the Fae encampment and only a few yards downriver from where Aisa and Danr were sitting.

"Nice, yes," he murmured. His golden eyes closed in sleep. With him, Danr supposed, went all hope of any help.

Aisa pulled on her sopping cloak. "That was . . . a fine ride, my Hamzu. Now what do we do?"

Danr pointed to a company of elves standing in consternation on the far side of the river. A flock of sprites wheeled over their heads and dashed back to the great, ugly tree. "They can't cross the river yet, but they know we're here."

"I had hoped to arrive by stealth," Aisa said. "That hope is lost now. What do we do? We only have a few hours before all this"—she gestured—"falls apart."

As if to underscore her words, the earth shivered. Trees waved and the river splashed in wild whirlpools. The elves careened about, and several lost their balance. Grandfather Wyrm slept straight through it. Danr's stomach tightened with desperation. Everything was falling apart—literally. The world would end in moments. How would it happen? Would everything cease to be in a blink? Perhaps the world would fall to pieces and everyone would tumble into some endless void. Or maybe everything would dissolve into sludge and muck. Gwylph didn't seem to know or care, whatever it was. A blinding hatred overtook him. She was the center of all this. She caused all this pain and suffering to his friends, to his Aisa, and she didn't have the slightest care. All that mattered to her was power, a power she hadn't earned and didn't deserve to wield. She had no heart.

They had to do something. That was why they were here. But what? Why did evil always seem to have the power? Where was the help for their side? Where was—

"Do you require assistance?" said a familiar voice.

Danr and Aisa scrambled to their feet. From the rushing river in front of them rose two emerald wyrms. They slid ashore, curled around Danr and Aisa in a scaly fortress, and looked down at them, tongues flickering.

"Kalessa!" Aisa cried.

"My sister," Kalessa said with joy. Both wyrms spun about in a flash of golden light, and standing on the shore were two orcish women—Kalessa and her mother, Xanda. Danr clapped his hands with joy of his own.

"You can both change now!" he said, ignoring the fact that both of them were naked.

"More than that," said Xanda. "Come! Ride!"

The women spun themselves back into wyrms. Danr gingerly climbed atop Xanda while Aisa rode Kalessa. The wyrms plunged into the tumult, swimming with strong strokes around the mountain, away from the elves, to the other side. They emerged dripping from the water and kept going, widdershins, around the mountain through the forest, until they reached the banks of the Otra River, which flowed way to the east. Without hesitating, they plunged across that as well, and Danr realized that, thanks to the Sundering and now Grandfather Wyrm, the Lone Mountain was at the center of four converging rivers that divided the area into four sections. The elves were in the northwest section, and Kalessa and Xanda were taking them to the northeast section.

"Was that Grandfather Wyrm?" Kalessa asked as they came ashore. "He was quite . . . breathtaking."

"That was he," Aisa said. "I never expected to see him again, but I was glad to do so."

"A fine, fine wyrm," Kalessa said. "Pity he is asleep."

"He quite exhausted himself." Aisa climbed down. "How did you know to come here?"

"All of you?" Danr added, staring.

The forest on the riverbank bristled with orcs and wyrms. Hundreds and hundreds of them. They filled all the spaces between the trees and made the branches sway. When the closest saw Aisa and Danr, orc and wyrm alike rose in salute.

"We followed the smell of rotten magic!" Kalessa swirled back into her birth form.

"We?" Danr blinked at this. "All of you?"

In answer, Kalessa raised her hand and every orc, including Kalessa, changed into a wyrm. They raised their heads and roared to the sky. The sound thundered against Danr's bones and filled him with hope.

When the sound died away, Kalessa changed back one more time with an ease Danr envied. She didn't seem tired in the slightest. Aisa clapped her hands, and her eyes were bright with tears.

"Sister!" she breathed. "Words cannot express!"

"How did you do it?" Danr asked in wonder.

"It took a little blood and a lot of anger," Xanda the wyrm hissed. "And now the queen of orcs is ready for battle!"

"Queen," Danr said. "You're the queen!"

"The return of magic made us First Nest." Xanda raised her head in triumph. "I am queen, and Kalessa will rule after me! Victory to the Nests!"

Another roar of wyrms echoed off the mountainside. When it ended, the orcs changed back into their original shapes, drew their iron swords, and beat them against their shields while the wyrms, the ones that had been born such, hissed like a hundred thousand kettles.

"If the Fae did not know we were here before, they know now," Aisa observed.

An orc brought Kalessa and Xanda heavy cloaks and handed Kalessa a knife. She flipped it into the air and caught it on the way down. It changed into a heavy, wicked-looking iron sword.

"You left this behind, sister," Kalessa said. "Now that I have reclaimed it, I will use it to slice through a horde of Fae. They failed to notice us slipping through their lands in our new forms, so we can destroy them with cold iron."

"Perhaps, daughter," Xanda said. "Our forces have been increased thanks to the new magic you have brought us, but the Fae are numerous and experienced, they have the flesh golems, and their queen has the power of a Gardener to draw on. We will have to fight with great intelligence if we are to have any hope."

"If we lose, nothing will matter ever again," Aisa said.

"Maybe it won't matter if the orcs win or lose at all," Danr said.

"What are you thinking?" Kalessa said. "We need to move quickly—the Fae will attack us if we do not attack them."

"Nothing of this will mean a thing unless we can get the Bone Sword away from Queen Gwylph," Danr said. "Maybe the orcs can distract the Fae so Aisa and I can slip in there and get it away from her."

"If it involves killing as many Fae as possible, I am all for it," Xanda growled, and Danr remembered that the elves had only recently killed her husband—Kalessa's father. And they had iron weapons. The trouble was, even the brief glimpse he'd gotten of the Fae army told him they were outnumbered at least three to one, and that was before the flesh golems and Queen Gwylph's magic were factored in. Still, they had to try. Even now he could smell the rot on the air and feel the earth turning greasy beneath his toes.

"Let's do it, then," he said. "The Nine help us."

"I would rather have another army," said Aisa.

Chapter Twenty

Ranadar twisted within the ghostly grip of the sprites while Talfi's bloodless body slumped to the ground. The two flesh golems, one with a bad leg and the other with a scarred arm, let him go. Ranadar's heart dropped sickeningly in his chest, and he tried to reassure himself. Talfi would come back. Talfi always came back. He had even come back after the chimney had crushed him.

How much did it matter, though? Talfi no longer loved him. Ranadar's soul filled with lead. He had seen the total indifference in Talfi's eyes. Worse, he had seen dislike, even loathing. Everything they had done together—slipping away from his family, hunting for the flesh golems, outwitting each other at archery practice, teasing each other with their pet names—Talfi had done because he loved Ranadar. Now the memory of love was gone, but the memories of their actions were still there. Talfi had done all those things with someone he did not remember loving. In seconds, Talfi had become a stranger.

A piece of Ranadar's own self turned black and died. He wanted to flee back to the forests, become *mal rishal* again, let the cool green leaves close behind him so he would never see another living person. He never wanted to feel again. But he could not flee. Not when his mother had not completed her part of the bargain.

As if reading his mind—and perhaps she had—Mother turned to him next. "Do not worry, my son. I will release Pendra as I promised. At sunrise tomorrow, I will return to her station, and I will content myself with ruling the physical world."

Sunrise tomorrow. Very well, then. Talfi's motionless body lay on the ground, as it had so many times. He would return to life, yes, but not in any meaningful way to Ranadar. Worse, the flesh golems, thousands of them, walked the earth and every one of them professed the very love for Ranadar that Talfi had lost. Ranadar wanted to crouch on the ground with his arms wrapped around his head. It was too much. The world balanced on his back, crushing him beneath its weight. He wanted not to think, not to feel, not to exist.

"It is your turn now," Mother continued. She drew the awful Bone Sword and pointed it at his chest. "You have your side to finish. Become immortal with me. And you will see how unimportant your pet was."

Before, these words would have filled him with dread and horror. Now they gave him hope and relief. No more sorrow, no more pain, no more worries. He would truly become the uppity elf Talfi always accused him of being. Wordlessly, he spread his arms. Two elves from the Fae who had assembled earlier took them and held him firmly in place. The two flesh golems watched from their vantage point next to the tub of Talfi's blood. Ranadar wondered how they felt about all this, though it did not matter much. In a moment it would all be over.

With a triumphant smile, Gwylph raised the Bone Sword.

And the enormity of what he was doing crashed over him. He was giving up his heart, his life, everything he had. How foolish! He had lived more than a hundred years in the forest as *mal rishal*, and eventually he had found purpose and meaning again. Even a *mal rishal* elf had hope. He would not give that up.

"No!" he said. "I refuse!"

Mother paused. "Refuse? You made a bargain."

"I am breaking it." Ranadar tried to pull himself free, but the other elves held him fast. "You will not take my heart."

"Your heart is dead on the ground behind you, Ranadar," she said. "I am just finishing up."

She raised the pale blade again. Ranadar fought, but the elves were stronger than he was. The Bone Sword descended. No! He would not let this happen! Anger and fear focused behind Ranadar's eyes and he let it loose with a great shout.

Power flashed from his head. The two elves dropped to the ground. Queen Gwylph staggered backward, pain written across her face.

"Ranadar!" she panted. "What did you do?"

All the anger that had been building for the past several weeks raged through him. The power thundered in his mind. He slashed with it at Gwylph, felt it connect in her mind, and she staggered back another step.

"That *hurt*," she said, and put a hand to her nose. It came away smeared with blood. "How are you—?"

With one more yell, Ranadar slammed his mind into Queen Gwylph. He poured every bit of rage into it. He smashed into his mother's mind, and the leaves around her erupted in a maelstrom. The other Fae nearby collapsed, unconscious. The queen gave a terrible scream, and Ranadar felt her mind flicker. He kept up the pressure, pushed hard. He could win this. He could—

Pain crashed through his own mind. He dropped to his knees with a scream of his own. Sky and leaves wobbled. Clanking footsteps. His mother stood over him.

"Where did you learn to do that?" she asked. When Ranadar did not answer, she said, "I suppose it does not matter. Hold still, now."

With the point of the Bone Sword, she pushed open the

front of his tunic, the one she had already sliced open. Ranadar was too tired to stop her. She pressed the sword's tip to his chest, and it broke the skin over his breastbone.

The earth shook like a dog emerging from a bath. The golden tub of blood trembled, and the flesh golems went down. Talfi's body shivered. The queen Fae stumbled, and the blade skittered about in her grip, slicing a shallow cut across Ranadar's chest. A few arrows spilled from her quiver. The sprites and the other Fae in the tree and the camp were startled as well. Ranadar, already on his knees, managed to keep his balance. The ground rippled like the surface of a liquid. Mother went down to one knee and dropped the Bone Sword. Ranadar reflexively dove for it, pretending that Talfi's lifeless corpse was not jittering next to a tub of his blood and two confused golems that looked like him.

"No!" Mother cried, but the shuddering ground kept her off balance.

Ranadar reached for the bloody hilt. The slippery feel of the ivory brought bile to his throat. But the queen flung out a hand.

"Not yet!" she cried.

The sword moved toward her and slid out of Ranadar's grasp. With a shout, he snapped his hand in her direction. A spray of blood caught Mother full in the face. She screeched in horror and swiped at her eyes. It was long enough for Ranadar to get hold of the Bone Sword again.

The earthquake ended. But before Ranadar could regain his footing, the river exploded. Water thundered in all directions and the earth shook again. Everyone including the queen turned to stare. A wyrm so big it insulted the word *giant* plowed around the mountain and broke into the Silver River. Grandfather Wyrm. Ranadar had heard of him from Talfi, and there was no mistaking him. Ranadar clutched the Bone Sword tight in his scarlet hands. Ideas flicked through his head. The first, and this one came with elation, was that if Grandfather Wyrm was here, Danr and

Aisa must have something to do with it. His second thought was that Grandfather Wyrm had come to battle the Fae, but this hope was dashed when the great wyrm flopped motionless onto the far bank. His third thought was that Grandfather Wyrm must have caused the earthquake. Or had he?

A ship hove into view, then spun wildly in the current. Was that...? It was! The *Slippery Fish*! Danr and Aisa definitely, then!

Mother recovered herself quickly. Already a hundred sprites were rushing to the riverbank to see what was going on. She shouted something to one of the flesh golems, but Ranadar failed to catch it. The golem blinked uncertainly with Talfi's eyes in a way that wrenched Ranadar's heart, and he had to remind himself that this was not Talfi. Talfi still lay dead at Ranadar's feet. Mother straightened herself and held out her hand.

"Give it to me," she said. "If I must take it from you, it will go badly."

Ranadar crouched over Talfi's cooling corpse like a wild thing. His ivy green eyes were hard, his red hair a mess, and he could not decide if he wanted to do as his mother said or not. He wanted to slice her in half, but the sword wouldn't hurt her. No weapon would. How was that fair or right?

"Now," the queen said imperiously. "Shall I count to three?"

With a yell that was half howl, Ranadar spun and swung the sword. It cleaved the golden tub in two. The gathered blood gushed over the rotting leaves and drained away. Some of it ran across Talfi's skin. The flesh golems stood by, impassive. Or perhaps confused. Ranadar could not tell.

"You won't have his blood," he said. "I will keep it from you."

The queen sighed. "He will return, strong, with more blood in him." She brought a fist down, and an invisible force slammed Ranadar to the ground. The Bone Sword fell from his hand. "You will become strong, too. Once I slice out your heart and put it in the tree next to him, you will forget your foolish fixation for this human boy and rule as a strong king."

Mother picked up the Bone Sword and raised the blade over him. Ranadar tried to roll away, but the power of her mind held him in place beside Talfi's unmoving corpse. Ranadar felt his own pulse beating at his throat and realized this would be the last time he felt such a thing.

"My queen!" An elf ran up to her, a sprite trailing after him. "The orcs! The orcs have an army!"

This brought Mother's head around. "An army?"

"At least a thousand of them. On the far side of the Otra River."

She spun. Perhaps fifty yards away and across the river, orcs and wyrms were visible among the trees on the opposite bank, just as the elf had said.

"We are not in a highly defensible position, my lady," said the elf. "The area around the encampment has been cleared, leaving us more exposed. They are in the forest, and difficult to attack with arrows. And they have . . . iron."

"But they cannot stay there forever," Mother pointed out. "And we outnumber them three to one, and that is before we count the flesh golems. Ready a force of golems and elves to cross the river on my command and have the fairies set our defenses on this side! Then alert the rest of the troops. I want those orcs crushed into dust! And get me a report from the sprites about where that giant wyrm came from and what happened to the river. Move!"

The elf spoke to the sprite, which sped away. The elf followed.

"You will lose, Mother," Ranadar gasped from the ground.

"Do not be foolish," she retorted. "Even with iron, a force such as theirs has no hope. The flesh golems alone will overwhelm them."

As she spoke, the sprites rushed down from the tree and spread throughout the encampment, shouting their strange rhymes as they went. The flesh golems left off what they were doing and marched down to the riverbank where the orcs were waiting beneath the trees. A disciplined regimen of bronze-armored elves joined them.

"Why has he not wakened yet?" Mother asked, pointing at Talfi with the Bone Sword in exasperation. She gestured at one of the flesh golems, the one with the bad leg. "You. Bring the corpse along and follow. I do not want him out of my sight." She sheathed the sword and turned to Ranadar. "Come along, son. See how Mummy leads the troops to war."

She strode toward the river, her emerald eyes blazing. Ranadar hesitated, but the three sprites spat painful sparks at him, forcing him forward. The flesh golem slung Talfi's body over his shoulder and followed behind. Across the river, the orcs crashed their curved swords against the iron guards on their wicker shields. Ranadar winced and put his hands over his ears. Mother barely seemed to notice. A sprite flew up to her and bobbled near her head. Mother listened to it.

"Grandfather Wyrm?" she said. "He is just a legend."

The sprite spoke again, and this time Mother's face creased with anger. "The half troll and his slut cannot possibly be—"

The sprite spoke further. Mother made an effort and regained control. "Very well. Warn the troops and scouts to watch for them. Anyone who brings me their heads will be rewarded."

Gladness flicked through Ranadar's chest. Aisa and Danr were here. Somewhere. He had no idea what they might be able to do, but the news gave him a golden ray of hope.

They reached the riverbank, which was shaded by the massive branches of the twisted, terrible tree. Ranadar looked at it, almost able to feel the power pulsing inside it. Pendra and his mother's heart were buried deep inside it. The Bone Sword would free both. But he had no way to get it. He might be able to snatch it from her belt again, but her magic was far stronger than his, and she would only take it back.

The regiment of elves and flesh golems stood impassively a few paces back from the shore, out of range of the short bows favored by the orcs. Orcs moved in and out of the trees on the river's far bank, as did the great wyrms. It made the forest look like a living, writhing thing. Ranadar scanned the forest, looking for any sign of Danr or Aisa or even Kalessa. He did not know if she was here or not, but if the other orcs were, he doubted she was far behind. To Ranadar's left, beyond both armies, rose Lone Mountain. The new river encircled it. The water here was calm enough, but closer to the mountain, it boiled and roiled with the aftermath of Grandfather Wyrm's efforts.

An orc woman wearing nothing but a cloak emerged from the forest. She brandished no sword, but her manner was imperious and proud.

"Queen Gwylph!" the orc woman boomed above the sound of the water. "I am Queen Xanda of the First Nest of Xaron. For your crimes against my people, for your crimes against this world, I call for your death! Surrender yourself now, and we will spare your people."

Ranadar caught his breath. Xanda. Kalessa's mother.

Gwylph chortled and raised her own voice. "We destroyed so many orcs that the wife of a third-rate chieftain now calls herself queen! You have no fight, no power, no magic. Run home, little orcs, and lick your wounds with your forked tongues!"

Xanda raised her fist and screamed a battle cry. A horde of wyrms and naked orcs streamed from the forest and charged into the river. Xanda herself came with them.

"Idiots," Gwylph snorted. "Notice, *Ranashka*, the most basic rule of strategy—never let the enemy catch you in water. They even took their armor off for us." She raised her voice. "Elves—arrows! Golems—attack!"

The golems charged toward the water while the elves

raised their bows. But then the incredible happened. The orcs changed shape. Their bodies lengthened and thickened, and in no time the golems were facing a legion of giant wyrms, each half again the height of a man.

"What?" Mother gasped. Ranadar backed up a step, himself caught off guard.

The new wyrms eeled across the river with sinuous ease and knocked the golems aside. The golems were armed with only their fists and their great strength, and neither did much against an opponent the golems were unable to grasp. Their hands and fists slid off the wyrms' emerald scales. The wyrms whipped their heads around, snapping at the golems and flinging them about like rag dolls. The air shook with roars and hisses.

The elves loosed their arrows. Mother unslung her bow and joined them. A hail of arrows rained down on wyrms and golems alike. The weapons did not bother the golems, most of whom did not even bother to pull the arrows out of bloodless wounds, but a few pierced the wyrms. The wounds were mostly shallow. Several of the wyrms rushed at the regiment of elves, who drew swords. On the other side of the river, another group of Xaron soldiers, these in the woven leather armor favored by the orcs, leaped aboard normal wyrms, which swam across in the confusion.

Bronze clashed against scales as the elves fought the great wyrms. Hisses of anger and pain slashed the air. One wyrm tossed an elven soldier high in the air, caught him on the way down, and swallowed him whole. An elven warrior sliced a wyrm open from throat to gullet, spilling warm guts across the carpet of dead leaves. Still, the elves were being beaten back closer to the tree.

The other orcs were reaching the shore now. Their swords were of iron, and would wreak greater havoc. Ranadar was an elf, but he found himself glad of this, and he kept his eyes carefully averted from the elven troops in case he saw someone he knew. Sharyl had lost a hand, but she was nowhere near the battle.

"Next rule of strategy," Mother said, "deal with the unexpected."

She put her bow over her back again, drew the Bone Sword, and charged into the battle with a yell of her own. The Bone Sword whirled. It sliced a wyrm in half, leaving it writhing and lashing on the leaves. Without a pause, Gwylph turned and ran an orc through the eye. It stiffened and died. A wyrm tried to bite her, but Mother brought the sword up and bisected the wyrm from chin to forehead. Dark blood splashed in all directions. Another wyrm fell, and another, and three more orcs. Queen Gwylph was a whirlwind, a force of nature spreading destruction all around her. And more regiments of Fae were running at them. Sprites, crackling with electricity, swarmed the sky. Hordes of fairies with their sharp little swords streamed down from the tree to leap and skitter into the fight. Elven centurions in gleaming bronze armor marched toward the battle.

Ranadar cast about for something to do. The orcs were vastly outnumbered and going to lose. Bronze clashed against iron. Screams and hisses and cries of pain and anger echoed under the tree's sky-shading canopy. It was like watching a battle in twilight, though it was late afternoon.

A pair of wyrms swam up the river and emerged, dripping, on the riverbank. Riding each was a pair of familiar figures that sent a stab of joy through Ranadar. "Aisa! Danr!" He tried to run toward them, but the three sprites guarding him shocked him into immobility again. Talfi's body lay motionless on the ground between the two flesh golems and Ranadar kept a nervous eye on him as well.

The sprite guards saw Danr and Aisa and, remembering the queen's edict, flashed toward them, chittering in wicked excitement. The flesh golems started forward, then hesitated. One of them, the one with the bad leg, looked at Ranadar.

"Do you love me?" Ranadar said in wild desperation.

"I do," whispered the golem.

"So do I," murmured the other.

Every word pierced Ranadar's heart, but he forced himself to continue. "If you truly love me, do not move. Do not hurt my friend."

The flesh golems stayed.

The sprites attacked. Aisa drew an iron knife that flashed into a great sword. It extended forward and skewered the sprite, which turned into a black ball of mush and slid off the end. One of the wyrms snapped the other sprite out of midair and swallowed it whole, and Danr grabbed the third one in one meaty hand. Before it could do anything else, he squeezed.

The sprite changed shape. It became Talfi, and his hands clutched at Danr's forearm. Danr's eyes widened.

"It's an illusion!" Ranadar shouted.

"I know," Danr said, and squeezed. The sprite changed into Aisa, who fought and tore, but still Danr squeezed. And then the sprite became a baby with a long jaw and dark hair. Danr gasped and let go. The sprite flew into the air, toward the canopy of leaves above them.

"Damn it!" Ranadar snatched Aisa's sword from her startled grip. The iron burned his hand like fire, and a headache slammed his skull. The sword flicked into a knife when it left Aisa, and Ranadar threw it. The blade spun end over end and barely nicked the sprite, but it was enough. The sprite fell back to the ground and Danr dropped from his wyrm to crush it with one foot.

One of the wyrms shifted shape. It squirmed into a naked orc woman—Kalessa! Where had she learned to do that? But the pain in Ranadar's head drove further thought away. Kalessa snatched up the knife from the dead leaves. The battle raged on. Mother seemed unstoppable. Already hundreds of orcs and wyrms lay dead amid the heavy smell of orcish blood.

"Are you all right?" Aisa asked. "Ranadar! Can you hear me?"

He held up his hand. A burn scored palm and fingers. "I will be fine eventually. Where did you come from?"

"Explanations later," Kalessa said. "Is Talfi—?"

"Dead again," Ranadar said, dropping to one knee beside him. The flesh golems remained motionless. "I do not know why he is not coming back."

"The elves are winning," Kalessa said. "I should go help."

"It's the Bone Sword," Danr said. "We have to get the Bone Sword!"

"We cannot," Aisa said. "Not in the middle of all that."

The earth moved again. Everyone lost their balance. The fighting paused while Fae, golem, and orc alike flailed about. The tree trembled, and leaves fell like rotting green snowflakes. And across the river, a landslide of rock and earth split away from the mountainside cascaded into the river, revealing a gaping cave wide enough for a dozen horses to ride side by side and tall enough for three trees to stand atop one another. At the entrance of the cave stood an army of Stane—trolls, dwarfs, and even giants, all armed with picks, crowbars, and wicked-looking swords. Standing at the forefront was Queen Vesha.

"Gwylph, you Nine-damned bitch!" boomed Vesha in a voice. "Get your head out of your own twat and give me back my Bone Sword!"

"How in Halza's nine hells did she get here?" Ranadar breathed.

"She dug," Danr said. "Just as she promised."

The entire battlefield had fallen silent. Everyone turned to look at Gwylph. The queen, covered in gore, stormed to the riverbed while the Fae paused in confusion. Should they continue fighting or was the queen calling for parlay? The orcs and wyrms took advantage of the moment to retreat downstream.

"Vesha!" Gwylph called. "You have no stake in this. Crawl back under your rock! You and your beastly Stane cannot even enter the battlefield while the sun shines."

A trio of trollwives emerged from the blackness behind Vesha, who crossed her arms. "Have you forgotten the old magic you stole from us, Gwylph? It returned to us when Danr reforged the Iron Axe."

The trollwives raised their massive arms. From the cave oozed a great silent shadow. But this shadow did not fall across the ground. It slid up to the sky and spread like ink spilled into water. The sun darkened and twilight dropped over the battlefield.

"The old magics," Danr said in awe. He took off his heavy felt hat. "Grandmother Bund mentioned them before she died. The Stane can walk in daylight."

"Return the Bone Sword," Vesha called across the new twilight.

Gwylph raised the Bone Sword mockingly above her head. "Come take it."

There was a flicker of light and in an instant, Vesha was standing next to Gwylph. Before Gwylph could even react, the troll queen balled up a fist and smashed the top of Gwylph's head. Gwylph dropped like a stone. Vesha snatched up the Bone Sword before it even touched the ground. Ranadar wanted to feel bad but found he did not.

"She forgot that trollwives can Twist," Aisa said in satisfaction. "A mistake she can only make once."

"Isn't Vesha . . . ?" Danr began.

"Cursed," Aisa said grimly. "Yes."

The dead leaves near Vesha's feet swirled in a lazy circle as if stirred by an invisible hand. A heavy feeling stole through the air, the feeling of lightning licking a cloud. The sprites all froze and then fled in a thousand directions, squealing as they went. The cloud of leaves grew larger. Queen Vesha backed toward Danr and Aisa, the Bone Sword at the ready and a grim look on her heavy face. Leaves exploded upward and settled into the form of a woman. Her black dress was nearly invisible in the twilight, and her red shawl showed up like a splash of blood. Darkness overhung her face, but Ranadar cringed at the feeling of rage and hunger that surrounded her. This was a hunger that squeezed stars dry and drank their light. This was a rage that split planets in half and devoured the lava within. This was a power that had existed from the moment a few cells had learned to live and would continue to exist until the final bit of life was exterminated forever. The Nine feared it, the Fates respected it. And Vesha had angered it.

"Time's up, girl," growled Death.

Chapter Twenty-one

S tane poured down the mountainside. Dwàrfs scuttled on stumpy legs. Tall trolls stomped behind them, and last of all came the giants. The orcs at the river shouted and beat their shields with their head-splitting iron again. They had clearly decided that any enemy of the Fae was a friend. But Danr barely noticed any of it. His attention was rooted on Queen Vesha and Death. So was everyone else's. As one, the Fae backed away in terror. To such a long-lived race, death—or Death—held a particular terror, and no one wanted to get her attention.

"You cannot kill me, girl," Death said. "I am what does the killing."

"But I do know your secret," Vesha said. "This sword of still-living bone can *stop* you. You cannot take the life that overcomes Death."

"Immortality is a heavy burden, child," Death said.

"I am happy to take it from you."

Danr gasped. "Aunt Vesha wants immortality, too?"

"Perhaps she and Gwylph are not so different after all," Aisa murmured.

Quick as a lightning stroke, Vesha cut her palm with the Bone Sword and made a gesture with her bleeding hand. Dark blood flew into the air and hung there. A shadow,

pulled from the others, rose to join it like sand mingling
with rainwater. Vesha gestured again with the Bone Sword,
and blood and shadow settled down to the carpet of leaves
beneath the leaning tree in a ring.

At that moment, an elf noticed Queen Vesha and
charged at her, his bronze sword held high. He reached the
boundary of the circle. A silent wave of darkness rose and
engulfed him. The elf had time for one small scream. Then
he was gone.

"We will not be disturbed," Vesha said. "Only those
with the proper blood can cross the boundary. You will
lose, lady."

"I've devoured worlds," Death said to Vesha. Her voice
was frozen lead. "I've listened to threats from gods, and
moments later ushered them through my door. I will reach
down your throat and drag you into oblivion by the entrails.
You, mortal girl, *laid hands on me*, and now you will learn
what that means."

Death drew her knitting needles from her hair. In her
hands, they lengthened and thickened into whipcord rapiers. She raised one rapier above her head and used the
other as a guard. "Accept your pain."

Vesha charged. She brought the Bone Sword down,
attempting to cleave Death's head in two. Death crossed
her rapiers and caught the sword at the juncture. Thunder
boomed and green lightning leaped from the spot where
metal met bone. The stroke caught a retreating elf in the
back and he dropped stone dead to the ground. The fight
was eye-twisting to watch. Vesha was more than a head
taller than Danr, and Death barely came up to Danr's
chin, but there on the dark battlefield beneath the rotting
tree, the two women seemed to be the same size, though
whether this was because Death grew or Vesha shrank,
Danr couldn't tell.

Meanwhile, the Stane rushed toward the riverbank. The
earth trembled again, but this time it was from the

footsteps of giants. The orcs rushed to join them. The Fae recovered. Generals shouted orders to the sprites, who rushed to deliver them. The Fae army swiftly reorganized itself into disciplined regiments that turned toward the advancing Stane, pushing the golems ahead of them.

Danr didn't have time to worry about this. Death lashed out with a foot beneath the cross and caught Vesha in the stomach. She staggered backward, closer to where Danr stood. In fact, she was only five or six paces away. She stabbed at Vesha's sternum with both rapiers. Vesha eeled sideways with a grace Danr didn't expect from someone of her bulk and brought her arm down on the rapiers, intending to sweep them away or wrench them out of Death's grip. Flesh sizzled instead and Vesha cried out. Danr gasped. Vesha backed away again.

"Mustn't touch," Death said with a grin in her voice. She lunged again.

The Stane and orcs met the Fae at the riverbank. The clash of metal exploded on the air. Sprites rushed at the giants, flinging bolts of electricity at their eyes. The giants swung great clubs that plowed up enemies and earth indiscriminately. Elven arrows rained down on orcish wyrms and blinded them. Orcs took terrible wounds, then changed into wyrms to heal themselves and bit their attackers in half. Danr caught sight of his brother, Torth, swinging his great club and roaring orders of his own, and his heart swelled with familial pride. Then the battle closed between them and Danr couldn't see him. The fairies darted in and out, slicing hamstrings and gutting the wounded. The Stane trollwives shaped shadows and flung them at the enemy, which the Fae dispelled with bursts of light and countered with mind-altering illusions, which the Stane, in turn, destroyed with a touch of iron. For a moment the sides looked evenly matched. But the Fae army was bigger and better trained, and the Stane were tired from the long journey. Even with iron weapons, the Stane and orcs were fighting a losing battle. Xanda stood atop her wyrm shouting commands and swiping at fairies in the center of it all, and Danr could see Kalessa wanted to join her.

"Go, sister!" Aisa said. "You will do more good there than here."

Kalessa raised her sword high and bolted into the battle with an ear-splitting yell.

"What good *can* we do?" Danr said. "We need that sword!"

Vesha feinted to Death's left, then spun in a circle and swept at her right. Death blocked with both rapiers, but only barely, and the Bone Sword nicked her shoulder. A second boom of thunder cracked beneath the tree, and the green lightning stabbed at the sky. The terrible stench of sulfur permeated the air. Danr watched, entranced and horrified. It was watching gods battle.

Death pushed the Bone Sword away with her rapiers and Danr thought he heard a tiny sound, one easily overwhelmed by all the other noise of the battlefield. He closed his right eye and looked at the Bone Sword. A thin line ran up the blade. The Bone Sword had cracked. A chill ran down Danr's back. His eye saw how the crack would soon spread, weakening the sword until it shattered in Vesha's hands.

Death fought on, uncaring in her rage. She lashed and jabbed at Vesha, who parried and blocked with the Bone Sword. She also made thrusts and jabs of her own, and more than one scored hits. Death actually seemed to be tiring.

"Die, loathsome beast!" Death screamed, but not as loudly as before. "Die, like all the others!"

Through his true eye, Danr saw to his surprise that Vesha could actually win the fight. Vesha's expertise and the Bone Sword's powerful magic were working against Death, despite her threats. Death's main weapon was her rage, and Vesha was refusing to let it affect her. Except Danr also saw something else. He clutched Aisa's hand.

"If Vesha wins, the sword will break," he told her.

"And the world will end," Aisa finished. "The Nine! We have to stop her!"

"How?" asked Ranadar. "We cannot enter the circle."

The battle of the Stane, Kin, and Fae raged on in the background. Danr's entire world focused to the cut and parry of troll and Death near the elf queen's unconscious form. He felt it then. A sickening jolt and a brief sensation of falling. The entire world flickered and vanished. For a dreadful moment, Danr had no body. He panicked, but he had nothing to panic with. He couldn't see, couldn't breathe, couldn't—

And then he was back beneath the terrible tree. It seemed to moan softly above him. He turned to Aisa, eyes wide.

"Did you—?" he began.

"Was that—?" she said.

No one else seemed to notice. The battles raged. Kalessa swept the heads off two fairies and ducked beneath an elven sword. A giant stumbled beneath an onslaught of Fae arrows, caught his heel, and crashed to the ground, where he lay without moving. Two wyrms squirmed and writhed, partially disemboweled. Death backed up a step and Vesha jabbed at her with the cracking Bone Sword.

"The world is ending," Danr said. "It's almost over."

Blood sang through Danr's body. It hadn't hit him until this moment that Aunt Vesha would soon die. Either she would lose the battle with Death and be taken, or the Bone Sword would break and she would die with everyone else in the world.

"What do we do to stop them?"

"We cannot get past her blood," cried Aisa.

Her blood. The words burned through Danr like bits of lava and he knew then what to do. It was the blood. His aunt's blood.

Resolve overtook the unhappiness. Death always took someone, didn't she? He glanced at Aisa, his dear, kind, sarcastic Aisa. She was carrying their son. No matter what, she would have that.

He ran toward the fight between Death and the queen.

"Hamzu!" Aisa shouted. "No!"

He felt more than heard her change shape behind him, but he ignored her. He ignored the battle, ignored Talfi's death, ignored everything except the way the Bone Sword, forged from the living flesh of his best friend, cracked against the rapiers of Death.

Danr flung himself at the boundary of blood and shadow. He crossed it, and there was a flicker, a tiny moment of ice when he wasn't sure if he had been right, and then he was inside the circle. He and Vesha shared the same blood, and her circle wouldn't harm him.

Death and Vesha continued their fight, oblivious of his presence. Death was losing, but the Bone Sword was badly damaged now. One or two more hits, and it would break. Vesha drew back the Bone Sword. The ruby on the pommel gleamed. Death raised her needle rapiers. The entire world slowed. Danr vaulted forward. He would take the stroke himself. Vesha would lose the Bone Sword, Death would take her, the battle would end, and someone else—Aisa, perhaps—could use the Bone Sword to free Pendra from her wooden prison. Air rushed past Danr's ears.

And then he was slammed to the ground. The world jolted forward. A mountain lion leaped over him and vaulted between Vesha and Death. Vesha's stroke with the Bone Sword missed Death's rapiers and slashed the lion deeply. Blood spouted in all directions. The lion dropped to the ground with a sickening thud.

Danr's heart stopped. He tried to scream, but all that came out was a choke. His mind refused to take it in. He looked back over his shoulder, expecting to see Aisa with the others outside the circle of blood and shadow, but Ranadar stood there alone with Talfi's corpse and a shocked look on his face. The lion was Aisa, and she was dead.

Danr crawled to her, kneeling between Death and the queen of trolls. He pushed at her, ran his hands over her. But she didn't move. Her body was slack and heavy. Blood matted her fur, and her eyes were half-shut. Panic swept him. *No, no, no!* She wasn't dead. She was wounded. She could change shape and heal herself. There was life in there, he knew it! He slammed his right eye shut and looked at her with his true eye.

Darkness swept over her body. There was no soul inside. Both Aisa and their son were gone.

Grief like nothing he had known before tore at him with blackened claws. He pounded the leaf-covered ground beside her body. It wasn't true. It couldn't be. His eyes grew hot and his throat closed. There was no world without Aisa. She had brought life and love and reason to live to him. She was breath and sweetness and salt and everything he needed to survive another sunrise. Now she was gone. The uncaring, awful battle raged on between the golems, the orcs, the Stane, and the Fae, but Danr could not notice.

In a helpless rage, Danr rounded on Vesha. Death hung back, though she kept her rapiers ready. "What have you done?" he roared. "What did you do?"

"I don't understand," Vesha said. "It's a lion. But it shouldn't have crossed the circle without the right—"

"Aisa was carrying my child!" Danr bellowed. *"She carried my blood!"*

Vesha paled. "Aisa? I didn't mean . . . I wouldn't have . . ."

"She saw you die during the blood storm, dear," said Death, who knew these things. "I don't think she was able to go through that again, so she gave herself up before you could."

Vesha worked her long jaw. "This was to be between you and me," she said to Death.

"You brought an army to this fight and expected it to be

between you and me alone?" Death sighed. "The short-sightedness of mortals never ceases to amaze. You can't win this, Vesha. You knew that the moment you put the chain around my neck. You were hoping to put it off a few more years, but all you did was hand me one of your dearest friends."

Vesha hesitated a long moment. Danr knelt next to Aisa's motionless body, feeling the heat leave it. He felt as if his own life was draining away.

At last, Vesha dropped the Bone Sword. It tumbled to the ground and lay there among dead ash leaves. "Just . . . remember I gave it up, would you?"

"I always remember," Death said. Her rapiers shrank. She slid them back into her hair and, without further fanfare, touched Vesha on the shoulder. The troll queen vanished.

"Wait!" Danr flung himself at Death's feet. "You have to—"

"I can't change anything, dear," Death interrupted sadly. "Greater powers than you have asked, and I gave them the same answer. Your love's fate was decided the moment she chose to cross that circle. It's best not to linger on it."

And Death was gone, too.

A dry, dusty sound followed. The circle of blood and shadow crumbled into nothing. The Bone Sword, sleek and pale and stained with blood, lay near Aisa's motionless body. He had come all this way, fought shape mages and Fae, to find that very object, and now he couldn't summon the strength to pick it up. Danr touched Aisa's fur, wishing she would at least change back into herself when she died. But shape magic didn't work that way; indeed, it didn't. Aisa was even being denied the dignity of going to the funeral pyre as a human being. The Nine were crueler than Danr had ever imagined.

"Ha!" Gwylph rolled to her feet and crossed the boundary of the circle. Without Vesha's magic, it failed to keep her out. Danr realized with a start that she must have come to quite some time ago and was only waiting. She reached for the Bone Sword.

"No!" Danr made himself lunge for her. Gwylph's fingers touched the grip just as Danr slammed into her. They rolled across the ground, spilling Gwylph's arrows as they went. Her armor ground into Danr's skin. He punched, but she caught his fist and shoved it aside. Vik, she was strong! It was like fighting an oak tree.

"Filthy Stane!" she shrieked. "Get your hands off me!"

Ranadar chose that moment to bolt forward. He crossed the boundary as well and snatched up the Bone Sword. Without looking back, he sprinted toward the tree with the Bone Sword held high over his head. Aisa's scarlet blood stained the edge.

"Ranadar!" Gwylph thrust her hand against Danr's chest. Something punched him with such force that he flew backward and landed hard several feet away. The wind burst from his chest and he gasped for air. The dreadful sounds of battle echoed all around him. Wounded Stane, elves, orcs, and wyrms lay on the ground in the trollwives' twilight. Dead giants made mountains of flesh at the riverbank. The Fae were winning, but barely.

"Ranadar, stop!" Gwylph had snatched up her bow and was aiming an arrow at her son's back. He was only a few paces from the trunk of the tree now, running like a deer. Danr tried to push himself upright, but he couldn't catch his breath. "Do not move!"

Ranadar ignored her. He reached the tree where Pendra was imprisoned and drew back the Bone Sword, exposing his side to Gwylph.

Gwylph whispered a word and fired. Time slowed again and Danr's blood thundered in his ears. The arrow flew in a slow, aching arc toward Ranadar. The Bone Sword descended toward the bark of the tree.

The arrow pierced Ranadar's side with a meaty thunk. It stuck there, quivering as if in joy at finding its target.

Ranadar stiffened. He turned. Scarlet blood poured from the wound in his ribs. Danr touched his side with a fist in numb disbelief. Ranadar looked at his mother.

"You really do hate me," he managed.

The Bone Sword dropped from his nerveless fingers to the roots of the tree. Ranadar fell beside it.

Talfi wandered, everywhere and nowhere. This was like Twisting, but without the fear and potential for pain. His own blood and flesh called him, drew him in a hundred directions all at once. He walked a street in Balsia, where yet another earthquake had struck and the citizens wandered in both shock and fear. He limped through the Rookery, his face hidden under a ragged hood. He marched through the forest behind a grim-faced Lieutenant Sharyl. He punched wyrms and battled orcs and was crushed under the foot of a giant. His arms were chopped off, his heads rolled across bloody leaves, his legs broke. All these things, these incredible, impossible things, happened at once. He was a puzzle with thousands of pieces scattered across the world, and each bit thought it was the whole. But even though the big picture was broken and scattered, it still existed. Talfi saw the full picture now, though seeing everything made it difficult to concentrate on any one thing. He had thousands of hands and eyes, ten times that many fingers. Some of him froze and refused to move. Some of him continued with whatever task it had been given—fighting, hiding, walking.

Talfi backed up from himself, his whole self, and looked down.

"Well," he whispered, and all the golems all across the continent paused in what they were doing to say the same thing. Thirteen golems were cut to pieces in the battle, but they felt no pain, and neither did they die.

Each piece contained memories. He touched them, and his past came rushing back at him. This part of him remembered nursing at his mother's breast. That part knew what it was to take tottering first steps. Another part recalled laughing on his father's shoulders. Talfi touched every part of his past—sneaking a sour apple from a neighboring orchard, staring at the dark-haired boy who lived across the street, finding a dead owl with his sister and touching its soft feathers, discovering the shivering wonder of the hardness in his groin on a crisp fall morning, eating oatmeal with salt and butter while his parents argued in the next room, practicing his letters on a sand table while splinters dug into his backside—all the parts rushed back at him like a flock of birds fluttering back to their accustomed perches.

How had he ever forgotten any of it? It was walking down a familiar street and knowing every door, every window, every face and name. It was turning a key in an old lock and feeling it turn with the usual ease. It was smelling simple cheese, bread, milk, boiled eggs, wine, and potato soup in the kitchen.

It was coming home.

And there was more. Each piece from his other selves contained memories of Ranadar. Memories of *loving* him. It was a shared love among all his selves, and together it was more powerful than any of the parts. Love itself and love's memory were no different, and the second restored the first. Talfi's heart and soul swelled with both and he wanted to find Ranadar, tell him, let him know it would be all right, share in the relief that spilled across his face.

A sigh rippled through all the golems. All but one. One piece of Talfi—a big piece of him—lay motionless between two other parts of him, and this bothered him. It shouldn't be so. He focused in more deeply, entered the motionless piece, and inhaled. He opened his eyes and sat up.

It was dark. Twilight. How much time had passed? He was expecting Ranadar nearby, but the elf was nowhere to be seen. Neither was the elf queen. This was going to be a hell of a thing to explain. He tried to get to his feet, but the feeling of being in so many places at once washed over him, and he staggered dizzily. Automatically, he reached out for something to balance with, and the two parts of him, the two flesh golems, steadied him, which was also like standing on his own. They weren't mere flesh golems. They were Talfi's own arms and legs and eyes and ears. They were *him*. Vik, this was hard to get used to.

The Fae were winning the war. The other Talfis were—Talfi himself was—helping them. He pulled back, and the Talfis stopped fighting. He thought about it again, and those that could walk left the battlefield. They walked and hopped and crawled toward him. Surprise and confusion broke out through the fighting.

But now Talfi noticed the scene beneath the tree. Gwylph was aiming an arrow. Talfi followed the line of fire and saw Ranadar with the Bone Sword under the tree just past Danr and a dead lion. What?

The arrow flicked across the intervening space and punched into Ranadar's body.

Everything stopped for Talfi. He couldn't understand what he was seeing. A spasm worse than any Twist wrenched every cell in his body. This couldn't be. It was some hallucination. Ranadar said something—Talfi and his other selves couldn't hear it—and then he dropped the Bone Sword and crumpled to the ground.

Talfi didn't remember getting to his feet. He didn't remember screaming. He didn't remember leaping over the dead lion. He only remembered holding the warm, bloody body of the one person who had meant anything in his life, who had given up everything he had ever known just to be with him.

Who had simply loved him. Talfi stroked his sunset red hair, and waves of memory washed over him—fingertips in the dark, thrilling laughter on a balcony, the frightening clink of coins, angry words across a blanket, confused footsteps in a forest. Tears rained from his eyes.

"He had to die," called the elf queen, bow still in her hand. "It was sad, but inevitable. You humans are so weak. When one of you dies, you become utterly helpless."

The Bone Sword flipped upward by itself to fly toward

her. Talfi lunged for it, but he was tangled in Ranadar's body and he missed.

"The rest of you will die now," the queen said in the twilight. She dropped the bow and put out her hand to catch the blade. "None of you can—"

The Bone Sword smacked into the hand of one of the other Talfis. Talfi cocked his head, and the other Talfi swung. The Bone Sword sliced off the queen's left arm. There was no blood, but she screamed anyway. Yet another Talfi clapped a hand over her mouth. A third grabbed her bodily from behind. A fourth grabbed her ankles. Gwylph kicked and struggled. Her body glowed with golden light, and Talfi's other selves were flung backward, but yet more of them, dozens of them, hundreds of them, piled on top of her. She screamed and howled like a mad beast, but there were too many.

"The Nine!" Danr gasped by the dead lion.

Talfi's other self tossed Talfi the Bone Sword. He snatched it out of the air. When the heft touched his palm, his entire body quivered. Only the crushing sorrow kept him from crowing with delight. He leaped to his feet while the elf queen fought and spat under her burden of flesh.

"No!" she howled. "This is my kingdom! This is my world!"

"You didn't mention your son," Talfi said hoarsely. He slashed the tree with the Bone Sword.

Chapter Twenty-two

An explosion of white light and dreadful sound thundered across the river and crashed against the Lone Mountain. Talfi and everyone else flew backward and landed hard, flattened by the terrible force. Ranadar's limp body landed nearby. Blood continued to leak from the awful wound. The Bone Sword shattered into a thousand pieces. Everywhere across the battlefield, Talfi's other selves bowled over. Many painlessly broke bones.

The twilight vanished as the trollwives lost their concentration. The surviving dwarfs, trolls, and giants, already blinded by the explosion, shrieked in agony as the evening sunlight burst across the battlefield. Howling their pain, they ran, limped, and crawled back toward the cave. The earth shuddered beneath their heavy footsteps. The Fae were too dazed to do anything but stagger.

The tree was gone. Even the leaves on the ground had disappeared. Where it had all been was a crater several yards wide, surrounded by flattened grass, stunned Fae, fleeing Stane, and staggering Talfis.

Danr and the lion were utterly gone. Vanished.

Talfi didn't have time to think about this. Gwylph was already righting herself. She was missing a gauntlet and her hair was blown wild. "No," she groaned, and her voice came to Talfi from one of the nearby other Talfis.

From the crater rose the figure of a woman. Her features were both ancient and ageless. On her back she wore a cloak that looked woven of autumn leaves, and in her hand she bore a battered silver sickle. Scarlet blood streamed from her wrists. Power radiated from her in great waves, and Talfi found it hard to keep his feet in her presence.

"Pendra," Talfi whispered.

Still hovering over the crater, Pendra turned toward Gwylph. Her expression was as flat and cold as a stone in a glacier above her sickle. The curved blade spat blue sparks, and the very air curled away from it. Terror overtook Gwylph's face, and Talfi almost felt sorry for her. Almost.

"Death did not come for you," Pendra said in a hungry voice, "because I have."

Gwylph suddenly straightened, missing arm and all. "You do not dare."

Pendra slashed the air with the sickle. The front of Gwylph's mail shirt sprang open with a metallic tear and the linen shirt beneath it was slashed as if by an invisible knife, but the skin beneath remained unscathed.

"That can't be!" Talfi said.

"Not even fate can stop me." Gwylph raised her remaining fist in triumph. "I am still immortal and I will rule this world!" Her voice, amplified by elven magic, spread across the battlefield. "Rise, my troops! Destroy the orcs. Grind the Stane to dust!"

Spurred by the queen's words, the Fae army roused itself. Commanders shouted orders. Elves and fairies scrounged for their swords. Sprites rose drunkenly back into the air. The orcs and wyrms, now vastly outnumbered because of the forced retreat of the Stane, tried to rally as well. Kalessa bellowed orders. Xanda exhorted her troops to pull together. But the orcs were tired and their morale was dropping.

A groan rose from the edge of the crater. It was Ranadar. Talfi spun like a startled cat. Ranadar blinked and touched the arrow in his side, as if he didn't understand what was happening. Then he pulled the arrow out with a small scream. Blood leaked from the wound. Talfi felt the world sliding out from underneath him. Ranadar wasn't dead. Only wounded. Talfi's heart leaped into his throat.

"Ran!" Talfi pulled off his shirt and shoved it against the bloody wound to stanch the flow. "You're alive! I thought I'd lost you."

Still dazed, Ranadar reached up to touch Talfi's face. His fingertips rasped against Talfi's unshaven cheek. "You . . ."

The emotions of a thousand Talfis flooded him at the touch, and every flesh golem in the world wept with joy. "I remember, Ran. She couldn't stop it. I remember!"

And Ranadar was kissing him and the flesh golems shouted their ecstasy across the battlefield.

Pendra broke in. "The queen's heart was in the tree, but I cannot touch it. Perhaps you can put it back where it belongs."

Talfi peered over the crater's edge. He found a simple wooden box the size of a human head just within reach and pulled it to himself. Queen Gwylph paled. "Leave that!" she shouted, running toward them. "Leave it!"

Ranadar, his hands shaking, snatched the box from Talfi and opened it while Pendra smiled above him within her cloak of leaves. Inside the box lay a red, pulsing elven heart. It was only just smaller than a human one. Ranadar plucked it from the box and held it up. Gwylph halted a dozen paces away.

"My son," she said softly, all love and honey. "You know I would never—"

"Hurt me?" Ranadar clutched the bloody shirt to his side and staggered to his feet. Talfi helped him. On the battlefield, the Fae were destroying the orcs and wyrms and felling the fleeing Stane with arrows while the flesh golems watched. "I know. Even after you shot me, Mother, I still hoped . . ." He swallowed. "You are not yourself. But you will be."

"I will not take that back," Gwylph said. "And you will not force me. You do not have the power. You are weak, and soft, and—"

Ranadar pointed the heart at her and squeezed. Gwylph went to her knees with a cry. "I have more power than you know, Mother."

Ranadar gestured with the heart again, and Gwylph fell backward. Ranadar stumbled toward her, and Talfi knew what he intended. He looked at Pendra, who continued to hover over the crater. Blood streamed from her wrists, and a tiny part of him wondered desperately where Danr and Aisa had gone to.

"He can restore her heart." Pendra was fading away. "All he must do is touch it to the original scar."

"Will she love him again?" Talfi asked.

"Only those who loved before can love again," Pendra murmured, and vanished.

Ranadar stood over his mother, one hand clutching her heart, the other clutching the bloody shirt pressed to his side. Gwylph was struggling to rise, but Ranadar's grip on her heart prevented her. The gap in her mail shirt showed the scar on her chest.

"You will be yourself again, Mother." Ranadar moved the heart toward her chest. "And all this will end."

Talfi took the bow from his back, the one Sharyl had failed to take from him. He cast about for ammunition, and his eye fell on the bloody arrow the queen had shot at Ranadar. With shaky fingers, he nocked it to the bow and aimed.

But should he? Once Ranadar gave her heart back, the queen might be restored to her old self.

A self that cared about her son, but didn't *want* to. Had wanted to be rid of caring so much that she had stolen the Bone Sword and started a war just so she could cut her own heart out. Her original self was just as heartless as her current self. Only those who loved before could love again.

Talfi drew back the bowstring. Gwylph struggled on the ground, and Ranadar pressed the heart toward her breast. Talfi fired.

The arrow missed. It skidded across the ground. Ranadar looked up at Talfi with a startled look on his face. "*Talashka!* What—?"

Damn it! "Ran, don't," Talfi begged, limping toward him. "She'll only—"

Ranadar set his mouth and pressed the heart toward Gwylph's chest. There was a rush of air. Three arrows flicked in from nowhere and pierced the queen's heart.

A tiny moment passed. The queen looked at the pierced heart in horror. Then she looked at Ranadar. She gave a small gasp. Beyond them, three other Talfis lowered their bows.

"Fing!" one of them said.

Ranadar dropped the bloodless heart in shock. It fell, arrows and all, onto his mother's chest. Gwylph stiffened, arched her back with a scream that rent the air, and then exhaled. Her body stilled, and the queen of the Fae died.

Across the fields and the woods and the riverbank, every flesh golem faltered, stumbled, and collapsed. Talfi felt them all fade from his mind, but their memories, their thoughts remained with him, implanting themselves in him like birds coming home to roost. It was *knowing* and *seeing* and *remembering*. It was memory. It was self. It was *him*.

"Mother!" Ranadar cried. "Mother!"

Talfi went to him and knelt at his side. Gwylph's green eyes were wide and sightless. "Ran, come away now. Call it the third favor."

"You did this," Ranadar choked. "It was you."

"Yes," Talfi replied quietly. "It had to be done. She was heartless, even before she lost her heart."

Ranadar set his mouth again, and for a sick moment,

Talfi was afraid he would turn away. But Ranadar only touched Talfi's shoulder and nodded. "Third favor was that you did for me what I could not do for myself."

Cries and screams rose from the field again. The war was still raging. The orcs and wyrms were being beaten back toward the river, and the mountainside was littered with dead Stane.

"The battle!" Talfi said. "We have to stop it! Can you take command? With your mother dead, you're king!"

Ranadar shook his head. "They will not listen. We can only—"

The water in the river stirred and foamed yet again. From it marched another army, a massive one. Talfi's mouth fell open. Thousands of soldiers poured dripping from the river. They wore shirts of scales that gleamed like diamonds and carried double-pronged pikes and razor-edged swords. Talfi made out that they were changing shape as they came. They started out in the river with tails that formed into legs as they came into shallower water. Some of the soldiers carried conch shells, which they blew in a booming call that rattled the remaining trees and echoed against the mountainside. Riding high in the middle of them on a giant crab came a woman in armor of her own.

"It's the merfolk!" Talfi cried.

"I am Imeld of the merfolk!" the queen shouted. "The Kin have come at last to defend their own!"

The merfolk soldiers charged into the battle. The Fae, caught off guard by this, retreated briefly and tried to regather, but it was difficult. The merfolk were fresh troops and relentless in their tactics. The orcs and wyrms used the breathing space to regroup themselves and come in beside the other Kin. Kalessa and Xanda climbed onto the crab's back, and Imeld welcomed them.

"Four queens," Talfi said. "We have a war of four queens. Queen of the trolls, queen of the Fae, queen of the orcs, and queen of the merfolk."

"Even if one is dead," Ranadar said sadly.

The sound of the conch shells roused Grandfather Wyrm, asleep farther up the riverbank. He woke fully and rumbled up the bank to see what was going on.

"Ah!" His hiss rebounded from one end of the battle-field to the other. "This is much better, yes. Kin united once again. And they are defending the Stane, yes. It has been a long time since I have enjoyed a good fight."

He also plunged into the melee, his mountainous body wreaking havoc everywhere he went. Entire regiments of Fae were crushed beneath his coils. Whole troops disappeared down his great gullet. That decided it. The Fae retreated and fled.

Ranadar sank to the ground next to his mother's body. Talfi crouched next to him. "We'll get you someone to help with that wound," he said.

"Just stay," Ranadar replied. His face was pale. "Please, *Talashka*. I will be all right for the moment, and could not bear to be alone right now. Besides, someone might think me a wounded enemy to be put down."

Sudden exhaustion weakened Talfi's legs. He sat then and put an arm around Ranadar's shoulder. All around them, the long process of cleaning up the battle began. Soldiers and officers looked for the dead and wounded. The sun was setting now, allowing the Stane to reemerge from the mountain in the fading light to retrieve their own dead and wounded. Trolls and giants roared their pain. Grieving orcs beat their shields over the bodies of fallen comrades. The merfolk, who had taken few casualties, strode swiftly about, helping with injuries and comforting the dying. Flies buzzed and settled on the face of the elf queen. Talfi positioned himself between Ranadar and his mother's body. It was a very strange sort of place to hold Ranadar's hand and talk.

"The flesh golems died when your mother did," Talfi said. "I felt them go. But . . . they're still here." He tapped his head. "I remember now."

Ranadar looked at him. "How much do you remember?"

"Everything." Talfi ran his thumb over Ranadar's smooth forefinger, noting the way the skin fit over the joints and slipped around his flat fingernail. People expected elves to have long, slender hands, but Ranadar's were more like squares. "I remember how all the other Talfis—and Other Talfi—loved you. They did love you, because they were me. *Are* me. They're still here. Even Other Talfi. We're all one. We just didn't know it."

"We are all one," Ranadar repeated. "Yes. Look at this battlefield, and how many died." He winced again. "Every time the Nine Races come together, it is for war. We must not do this again, *Talashka*. It must stop with us. With me."

"What do you mean?" Talfi asked.

"I need to stay in Alfhame," Ranadar said. "I must take her crown and change this. We will reach out to Balsia to give it help from the earthquake—labor if Karsten will accept it, treasure if he will not. And we will open talks with the Stane and the orcs. We must unite. And I will need your help."

"Mine?"

"You are . . ." Ranadar winced again. "You are human, but you are long-lived, like the Fae. You can help bridge the gap between Kin and Fae as an emissary. I will rule, and you must help as a diplomat between Alfhame and the Kin. It will not be easy, but we have to start."

At that moment, Kalessa darted over to them. Her eyes were shining. "Glorious battle!" she said. "Already we will live forever! No one will ever forget this!"

"Indeed not," Ranadar agreed.

"Why did the merfolk come?" Talfi said. "I thought they were angry with Aisa."

"Imeld was," Kalessa said. "But she changed her mind after Grandfather Wyrm spoke with her. Or that is what she tells me. It takes strength to admit when you are wrong, and I commended her for that."

"You will make a fine queen, Kalessa," Ranadar said. "I want to be the first to congratulate you and your queen mother on your win today, and I hope our people can reconcile and forge an alliance in the future."

"Why are you talking like a ruler?" Kalessa seemed to truly see him for the first time. "You are injured! I will fetch a healer. The merfolk are very skilled."

A rumble shuddered the air. Everyone turned their eyes toward the source of the sound. "What now?" Talfi groaned.

Some distance away, Grandfather Wyrm was shuddering. He quivered and shivered and shook. The orcs and wyrms that surrounded him hurried away in consternation as his shape . . . changed. He shrank and twisted and dwindled away. There was a final *whump* of inrushing air that blasted Talfi's hair. In Grandfather Wyrm's place stood a tall man, naked, with a craggy face and muscles sculpted like a statue's. His skin had the faintest hint of green to it, and his night black hair hung nearly to his waist.

"The Nine," Kalessa murmured.

"*That's* what Grandfather Wyrm looks like as a human?" Talfi said.

"What were you expecting?" Ranadar said.

"I don't know. Something more . . . grandfathery." Talfi sniffed. "Wow."

"You," Kalessa said, "already have a mate. The Nine, Ten, and Eleven! He is coming this way! Where is Aisa? And Danr? I do not see them."

The abrupt change in subject caught Talfi off guard. He thought back. So much had happened so quickly. The last he or any of the golems had seen, Danr had been standing over a dead lion near the giant tree. Had Aisa changed into a lion? She couldn't be dead. Not now. Not after all this. He needed a few minutes to recover, a few minutes of normalcy to gather his wits.

"I'm . . . not sure where they are," he temporized. "I lost track during the fighting, and then Pendra came and everything happened so fast."

Grandfather Wyrm strode up, still naked but obviously

unbothered by the fact. Talfi found it hard to find a place to look, so he settled on staring at the man's eyes. They were a deep, compelling green, greener than Ranadar's. He didn't look older than thirty-five, and every muscle moved like oiled butter under his skin. Several orcs followed him, both fascinated and uncertain.

"Good evening, yes," he said in the voice Talfi knew so well. "I recognize you, young Talfi, though I suppose by the time one reaches our age, a few years difference in age makes little matter, yes."

Talfi remembered that Grandfather Wyrm had been a mortal man on the day of the Sundering, when Talfi had been seventeen. Talfi might look half Grandfather Wyrm's age, but they were essentially the same age.

"It is good to come out from under the ocean after all this time, yes," Grandfather Wyrm continued. "And it is good to see the Kin and the other races coming together. Perhaps this will help things along."

He knelt and removed Talfi's bloody shirt from Ranadar's wound. Ranadar gasped. A golden light flared under Grandfather Wyrm's palm. When he pulled it away, the wound was gone.

"Simple shape magic that has been forgotten," Grandfather Wyrm said. "Perhaps it is time to remember it, yes."

"Thank you, Great One," Ranadar said in obvious relief, and Talfi felt the absence of the pain himself.

"And who is this powerful woman?" Grandfather Wyrm asked, rising to take Kalessa's hand. "Such power and grace and beauty on the battlefield, I have never seen, yes."

"Kalessa, daughter of Xanda, heir to the First Nest," Kalessa said. "And the orc who wonders where her sister and good friend have gone to. We must find them."

"Aisa's dead, isn't she?" Talfi said. The grief he had been holding back hit him then. His mouth filled with sand, and tears pricked the backs of his eyes. "She changed into a lion to save Danr, and she . . . died. But where did she go? Where did Danr go?"

"Dead?" Kalessa rounded on him. "No! My sister walks with gods! She cannot be dead. She *will* not be dead! I will not believe it until I have seen her body. And where is Danr? He would never abandon us."

"That's true." Talfi wiped at his eyes. "But where did they go?"

Chapter Twenty-three

T he Garden stretched away in all directions but behind, where rose the tall, solid trunk of Ashkame. The rotting smell was gone, replaced by the pleasant smell of herbs and flowers and fresh green leaves. Everywhere Danr looked, the plants were healing. They stood straighter, reached up higher. The rot was gone. Even the tilted ground had straightened, allowing him to stand upright.

But he didn't want to stand. Sorrow and pain forced him to the newly solid earth. He knelt next to Aisa's lioness body, stroking her cold fur and the stiffening muscles beneath. The tree had exploded, filling his eyes with painful white light, and when his vision had cleared, he and Aisa—her body—were here in the Garden. Danr didn't know or care how it happened, no, he didn't. All that mattered was that he would never hear Aisa's voice, never touch her skin, never see her face.

And what about their son? He was dead, too, before he had even lived. Every thought and dream Danr had enjoyed about raising a boy—gone in an instant. The loss was too great. He would never move, never live, never exist again. He buried his face in her unmoving side and wept.

A gentle hand touched his shoulder. He looked up and found himself surrounded by the Gardeners. Nu wore her spring green cloak and carried a bulging bag of seeds. Tan's cloak was sleek and summer brown, and the sturdy hoe over her shoulder looked sharp and ready. Pendra, however, was sickly and fading. Her sickle was pitted and rusty. Danr could see the plants right through her. Blood trailed from her wrists, watering the ground beneath.

"The Tree has tipped," said Nu.

"Tilted," said Tan.

"Turned over," whispered Pendra, and her voice was nothing but a leaf on the breeze. "It is finished."

Black anger filled Danr now. "You let Aisa die!" he raged. "She was supposed to save you. She was supposed to keep the Tree from tipping ever again! She was supposed to have our child!" His throat was so heavy he could barely speak. "And now she's dead."

"It is how things were," said Nu.

"How things are," said Tan.

"How they must be," finished Pendra. "There is no other way, dear, dear Danr."

"I don't understand." Danr pushed salt water off his face with the back of one hand. "She's dead, and now you don't have anyone to replace you. And I don't have anyone at all."

"Now, Danr," said a new voice, "you should know better than that."

From around Ashkame's trunk emerged Death, her black dress unruffled, her scarlet shawl about her shoulders, her gray hair held firmly in place with her knitting needles, her face in shadow. She was leading Aisa by the hand.

Danr's heart stopped. It couldn't be. His mind rushed in tiny circles like a trapped mouse. Slowly, achingly, he got to his feet. He wanted to believe it, but he had been pulled in so many different directions he wasn't sure he could allow himself. Aisa left Death behind and came toward him.

"My Hamzu," she whispered. "Oh, it is you. I thought I had lost you forever."

He crushed her to him then, and she was solid in his arms. No scent of the lion about her. Her dark hair was soft under his fingers and he felt her breath on his shoulder. His knees shook with the intensity of it.

"My Aisa," he said thickly. "How?"

"If she was to become a Gardener," Death said, "she had to die first. She was fated, as I said. It just happened a little faster than we would have liked." Death chuckled. "I had to pop down and stop her from going through my door, but we're all right now."

"What about our son?" Danr asked, not sure whether he was talking to Aisa or Death.

"He is well, Hamzu." Aisa touched her stomach. "I am well. When I . . . shed my body to come here, I made sure to bring him with me. How could I let him go?"

"That one will shake the world," said Nu.

"Level mountains," added Tan.

"Metaphorically speaking," finished Pendra weakly.

"And Aunt Vesha?" Danr asked.

"On the other side of my door, where she must be," Death said. "I know you loved her, Danr, but she made her choice, and so it must be."

"That doesn't make it any less sad," Danr said.

Death shrugged and turned to Aisa. "It is time now, my sister. Your mortal life has ended. Are you ready to take your place among the Gardeners?"

Aisa straightened. Danr felt the tension in her, and she stepped away from his arms. Suddenly, Danr didn't want this. He had just gotten her back, and now he was going to lose her again. Perhaps not right away, but soon enough. There was no way for them to stay together as long as he was mortal. And in a thousand years, the Tree would tip once again, and all this would start over again with someone else.

"I am ready," Aisa said.

The Garden and its soft, enticing light spread before him. This place was peaceful and fine. All his life, Danr had wanted nothing more than to find someplace to farm in peace with Aisa at his side—and now their son. Such peace would never happen now.

Or would it?

Danr inhaled appreciatively. He *felt* the garden. He had come here more than once on his own. He had culled the plants, used them to find their way to Captain Greenstone in the mortal world. He had spoken to Nu by himself and finished sentences. What if . . . ?

No. There were always three Gardeners. Two pivot around a third.

Three . . . and one. There was always the one that changed the balance, wasn't there? Tikk who had tricked his way into the gods. Death, who trucked with the Fates.

As Aisa stepped forward, Pendra glided weakly toward her and reached out her bleeding hands. Danr closed his right eye, and his true eye saw that Pendra had almost nothing left. Just a spark of power she would give to Aisa, who would then take the sickle and her place. Aisa took a deep breath, then glanced over her shoulder.

Three . . . and one.

His true eye told him that she was thinking the same thing. Pendra reached for Aisa's hand, and Aisa took it. At the last moment, Danr lunged forward and grabbed Pendra's other hand and took Aisa's free one.

The spark thundered into him, into both of them, into all three of them: Danr, Aisa, their son. *Three . . . and one.*

Danr inhaled an entire universe. Wonder exploded through him. Clouds of gas whirled around a center and blazed into life. Countless trillions of planets spun lazily around these warm, life-giving stars, and on those planets, tiny beings turned their faces to the light. Awed, Danr touched all of them at once. He *was* all of them. When one died, the death sent tremors through all the others, and when a new one was born, the entire cosmos shouted with delight. Danr touched everything, and everything touched him. Every atom, every particle, every speck streamed through him and through Aisa. He felt her there, too. And also Nu and Tan.

Danr backed away, saw systems instead of stars, galaxies instead of systems, a universe instead of galaxies, and that was when he saw Ashkame, drilling down and growing up through the Nine Realms. The leaves were planets, the branches were stars, and the trunk was galaxies. Ashkame twisted the eye, making itself everywhere and nowhere all at once. Scattered about the branches, trunk, and roots were the Nine Gods. Olar, Grick, and Rolk looked down from the branches. Urko, Bosha, and the twins Fell and Belinna scratched around the trunk. Vik, Halza, and Kalina looked up from the roots. Tikk scuttled around where he pleased. Below the bottom was Nu with her bag of seeds. Above the top was Tan, with her hoe. In the center, becoming a pivot, was Aisa with a new silver sickle. The Tree was already trying to tip, just a bit, an atom's width, the amount that would take a thousand years to send the great Tree falling over and revolving once around the center, wiping stars and shaking planets. But now Danr stood next to Aisa, simultaneously seeing himself and being himself. The Tree tried to tip that tiny bit, but nothing could pivot with two centers. Four in a line became firm. The Tree would never tip again.

Galaxies, systems, and worlds rushed past Danr and he was standing in the Garden again, even though he was also elsewhere. Aisa stood next to him, along with Nu, Tan, and Death. Pendra was gone.

"So now we have four," Death observed. "How delicious."

"We wondered," said Nu.

"We considered," said Tan.

"We won't," interrupted Danr, "need to talk this way."

"New Gardeners always say that." Nu slung her seed bag over her shoulder. "But after five or six hundred years, it happens. You start talking that way, and another two hundred later, you *think* that way."

"I won't," said Danr.

"They all say that," agreed Tan.

"I did," said Nu.

"Oh dear," murmured Aisa.

"I must be getting back to my door," put in Death. "My knitting won't ravel itself. I look forward to trading barbs with you, Aisa."

"We will see," said Aisa.

"And you, Danr," said Death. "Now that you're going to be around for a while, I can tell you something."

He looked at her warily. "What's that?"

"Do you remember that day we first met, all the way back when you were a sixteen-year-old boy, still squalling like a baby troll brought into daylight?"

"I'll never forget it," he said. "You told me not to kneel."

"I also said if you were very brave, you could kiss my cheek." She tapped it. "And you did. Danr, my dear, I have met so many people that not even Nu and Tan here can count them. I made the same offer to any number of them, and do you know how many took me up on it?"

"No," Danr said truthfully.

"None," Death sniffed. "Not one of them dared give Auntie Death a kiss. You were the first. Right then you became my favorite. Right then."

"Oh," said Danr, not sure what to think of that.

"A dubious distinction," said Aisa.

"Now, *that* is why I'm glad you got the position instead of Gwylph, Aisa," said Death. "Stuffy as a used handkerchief, that one. You, on the other hand, will be *fun*."

"Gwylph!" Danr said. "The battle! Talfi! Ranadar! Kalessa! We need to find out what happened to them!"

But even as he formed the thoughts and the words, knowledge flooded his mind. He stretched out his hands and found the Garden plants. Ranadar—a twisting ivy that reached far from its roots to twine around the sturdy, ageless bristlecone pine that was Talfi. Kalessa—a fierce and thorny thistle that was leaning toward an odd and long piece of wormwood. They were all alive and well. He sighed with relief.

"They have separated," Aisa said. "How much time has passed since we left?"

"That is one problem with interacting with mortals," said Tan. "Their lives are so short, and they move so quickly. It's why we stay so busy."

"So occupied," said Nu.

"Can't we see them?" Danr said plaintively.

"You don't need anyone's permission," Death said. "Do whatever you like." And she was gone.

"But don't be long," said Nu, belying Death's words. "We have gardening to do."

"Much," agreed Tan.

Twisting was so simple Danr couldn't imagine why he'd been unable to do it before. He and Aisa slid with ease between the roots and branches of Ashkame until they landed directly in front of a group of orcish tents in Xaron. Kalessa, her mother, Xanda, and a craggy-faced man Danr didn't recognize were looking out over a pitted area of ground. Danr thought a moment and the knowledge he needed came to him. The pitted area was a new breeding ground for wyrms, and the man was Grandfather Wyrm in his human form. That last caught Danr truly by surprise.

"Sister!" Aisa shouted, and ran to Kalessa. With a startled yell, Kalessa embraced Aisa and then Danr. A great deal of chatter followed, with Kalessa rocked back on her heels.

"So," she said, "my blood sister is one of the Fates. And pregnant! The universe literally trembles."

"But what has happened to you?" Aisa asked. "How long has it been?"

"You do not know?" Kalessa countered. "That seems odd for a . . . goddess."

"We're still learning our way around," Danr said.

"Everyone calls it the War of the Four Queens," Kalessa said. "That was four months ago. Can you not see that it is autumn? The grass is turning brown. The orcs are trying to recover. So many died in the war that we have combined Nests so we have six instead of eight, but in time I am sure we will increase our numbers."

"Grandfather Wyrm is teaching us much about shape magic and how to raise better wyrms," Xanda put in. "He and my daughter have become quite close. Is that not delightful news?"

"Mother," Kalessa warned.

"Since you are in charge of such things, Lady Aisa," Xanda continued, ignoring her, "perhaps you could arrange for something to happen? Kalessa and Grandfather Wyrm would make a fine royal match."

"Hmm," said Aisa.

"Do not dare!" Kalessa said.

"Wouldn't dream of it," Danr laughed, putting up his hands. Then he leaned in with mischievous confidentially. "But I will tell you, Lady Xanda, that their plants already grow very close in the Garden."

Xanda clapped her hands. "I knew it! I knew she would find—"

"Mother!" Kalessa warned again.

"We will return," Aisa said, "but we want to see what has happened to Ranadar and Talfi."

"Encountering any number of difficulties, I am sure," Kalessa said.

They found Ranadar and Talfi in a council that was arguing in the shade of an oak tree at sunset. Ranadar sat on the ground at the head of the group. A silver crown shone in his deep red hair. Talfi, richly dressed in scarlet embroidered with gold, sat next to him. Two elves, one of whom had only one hand, were there as well, along with three humans who, upon closer inspection, turned out to be two humans and a shape-shifted mermaid. Sprites hovered overhead, and fairies scuttled in a circle around them. And bundled up in a heavy cloak against even the weak, fading sun was the great heavy form of a troll. With a start, Danr recognized him.

"Torth!" Danr said as he and Aisa stepped out of the Twist. "Vik's balls, what are you doing in Alfhame?"

The shouting that had been going up around the circle instantly died. It was followed by a mad fumble for weapons—which no one had—and a general chaotic uproar. Danr held up his hands.

"Silence!" he bellowed.

The grass beneath the tree flattened for twenty feet in all directions, and the surrounding trees of the Alfhame forest trembled. Everyone froze.

"I did not know we could do that," Aisa murmured. "We must experiment further."

"We aren't here to hurt anyone," Danr said. "Please. We just came by to see our friends."

"Danr! Aisa!" Ranadar finally gasped out. He bolted to his feet and ran to embrace both of them. Talfi, also shouting their names, joined him. Danr hauled both of them and Aisa off their feet with a great laugh. He had thought he would never laugh with his friends again, and it felt astounding.

"Brother," said Torth. "Where did you come from?"

Danr embraced him as well. "I could ask you the same question."

"I am forging a new alliance with the Kin and even the Stane." Ranadar looked pointedly at one of the elves and the sprites who bobbed overhead. "The world has changed and we need to change with it."

"Your hold on the throne is touchy, Your Highness," said the two-handed elf. "Not everyone will follow your—"

"He is the son of the former king and queen," interrupted the one-handed elf. "If he wants to ally with even the Stane, we will do so!"

"*Even* the Stane?" retorted Torth.

"Thank you for your support, Lady Sharyl," said Ranadar. "We recognize it will not be easy to—"

"Not easy?" interrupted the other elf. "Impossible! The filthy Stane cannot be trusted to—"

"Who is filthy?" Torth snapped. "You invited me here to talk about terms, not insult me. My father, Kech, is king under the mountain, and you flimsy Fae will remember that."

"We were not so flimsy at the War of the Four Queens," retorted the elf. "You Stane ran like cowards for your stinking cave."

Danr slammed his fist down in the center of the circle. The *boom* silenced the circle. Danr drew himself up. "Look at who I am. Mortals," he added for effect.

Everyone, including Ranadar and Talfi, looked at him. Danr let out a breath of power from the Garden. Green light, pure and powerful, gushed up to the sky and down to the center of the world. It poured through him and out of him. The circle of people dropped to their knees.

"I Am Power," Danr boomed. "I Am Life. I Am Fate. And You Will—"

"Hamzu," Aisa interrupted.

Danr looked around. Everyone had stopped moving. Even the column of light he was standing in had frozen. Only Aisa seemed unaffected. Confused, he stepped out of the light and crossed to her.

"What did you do?" he asked.

"I think it is a form of Twisting," she said. "I will show you later. But for now, I do not think we are supposed to do such things."

"What do you mean?"

"I mean that we are . . . well, we are gods. And we are not supposed to tell people what to do."

"Why not?" Danr folded his arms. "We're fate. That's what we're *supposed* to do."

Aisa shook her head. "We tend the Garden, but in the end, it grows the way it wants. If we tell everyone what to do all the time, no one will do anything but what we say. Life will grow stale. The Tree will wither and die."

"But—"

"The Gardeners didn't force *us* to do anything," Aisa

pointed out. "We chose. Always. And they must choose as well."

Danr started to object, then stopped himself. He remembered how he'd felt when Death called on him to go places he didn't want to go, pushed him into fighting monsters he didn't want to fight. Was this any different?

"All right," he said. "We'll try something else."

"Go," she said.

He stepped back into the column of light, and time moved again. The light blazed and the people cowered. He gave himself a fraction of a moment to think about how incredible it was, going from the half-blood son of a thrall to . . . a god. But only a fraction of a moment. He had already learned that moments were different for mortals.

Danr clapped his hands and the light vanished. In a more reasonable tone, he said, "I would never tell you what to do. You are mortals and must choose your own way. But I've seen the long row, and it would be . . . pleasing to me if you would choose a certain way. The Nine Races used to be one people, you know. There's no reason they can't be again. Maybe you could . . . choose to think about that."

He held out a hand to Aisa, who joined him in the circle, and he winked at Talfi, who was grinning widely at him. The Twist opened before them. Just before they stepped through, Aisa said, "And if you were thinking of making life difficult for Ranadar because he loves Talfi, think again. Love is never a bad choice."

They stepped through the Twist and appeared in the Garden once again.

"What was that last bit for?" Danr asked.

"Just another form of peace." Aisa straightened her dress. "Our first acts as gods. I think it went rather well."

He touched her belly with a gentle hand and kissed her. "Will this be our second?"

"And our third," she replied with a smile. When they separated, she was holding a sickle. "Hmm. It would seem the Garden awaits." She cocked her head. "So far, among the Fates, we have seeds, a hoe, and a sickle. What will your tool be, my husband?"

It was the first time she had called him that, and it took him a little aback. "We haven't officially been married."

She laughed, a light, free sound that carried from one end of the Garden to the other and lifted spirits all across the Nine Worlds. "There is no higher authority in the universe than ourselves, my strong one. But still, you are correct. So." She took his hand in hers. "Danr, my Hamzu, the strong one, from the day I met you, I knew you were special. My heart felt safe and loved when I was with you, even if I could not immediately admit it to myself. And when I could at last admit it to myself"—her voice broke—"I knew there was no one else I could ever trust with my life and my love. You are my strength. You are my life. You are my world. I take your hand in marriage."

Danr felt himself fill like a bowl with water and gold. "Aisa, words aren't my way. I never know how to show what's in my heart. I can only say that I have always loved you. Before I knew your face, I knew what was in your heart, and I loved you. I cannot imagine life without you, and"—now his voice grew thick—"and you know that even now I have to tell the truth. I love you forever, and I take your hand in marriage."

"So be it," said Nu and Tan together, and Danr knew that they had always been there, while Death smiled in the background. Danr wrapped his arms around Aisa for a long, welcome kiss, the first one of many over thousands of years.

"Well." Aisa dabbed at her eyes with her free hand and waved her sickle with the other. "With that taken care of, I believe we have work to do. You have not chosen a tool. My husband."

He held up his hand. "I think this will do just fine."

Together they turned toward the Garden.

ABOUT THE AUTHOR

Steven Harper McClary Piziks was born with a name no one can reliably remember or pronounce, so he usually writes under the pen name Steven Harper. He sold a short story on his first try way back in 1990. Since then, he's written twenty-odd novels, including the Clockwork Empire steampunk series.

When not writing, Steven teaches English in southeast Michigan. He also plays the folk harp, wrestles with his kids, and embarrasses his youngest son in public.

CONNECT ONLINE

stevenpiziks.com
twitter.com/stevenpiziks

Also Available from

Steven Harper

IRON AXE

The Books of Blood and Iron

In this brand-new series, a hopeless outcast must answer
Death's call and embark on an epic adventure....

Although Danr's mother was human, his father was
one of the hated Stane, a troll from the mountains.
Now Danr has nothing to look forward to but a life
of disapproval and mistrust, answering to "Trollboy"
and condemned to hard labor on a farm.

Until, without warning, strange creatures come down
from the mountains to attack the village. And Death
herself calls upon Danr to set things right....

Available wherever books are sold or at
penguin.com

R0211